BOAR WAR

A NOVEL OF PORCINE TERROR

R. GUALTIERI

COPYRIGHT © 2024 RICK GUALTIERI

No part of this book may be reproduced or transmitted in any form or by any means, electronic or mechanical, including photocopying, recording, or any information storage and retrieval system, without prior written permission of the author. In addition, no part of this book may be used for machine learning or to train artificial intelligence, language models, or similar technologies without the prior written permission of the author. Your support of authors' rights is greatly appreciated.

All characters in this novel are fictitious. Any resemblance to actual persons, living or dead, is purely coincidental. The use of any real company and/or product names is for literary effect only. All other trademarks and copyrights are the property of their respective owners.

Cover by Miblart

Published by Freewill Press

DEDICATION

For Michelle MacKinnon – beloved mother, wife, grandmother, and one hell of a fighter. She may be gone, but will never be forgotten.

ACKNOWLEDGMENTS

Throwing out a special shout-out of thanks to my awesome patron crew: Sean, Condor, Benoit, Rachel, Mark, Derek, Eric, Leendert, Stephanie, Vinny, James, Randal, Jennifer, MRB, Sandra, Stephen, Jeffrey, James G., Angela, Pete, Michael, Simon, Nick, Caprice, Hasteur, David, Vikki, Nicole, Lee, Tina, AJ, Patrick, Shari, David, Michael L, and Kenny.

You guys make this dream possible.

PROLOGUE
1957

In conclusion, funding for this project has been terminated, so you are hereby ordered to destroy any and all files that have not already been remanded to Washington, including any duplicates that have been made.

The facility itself is slated to be decommissioned, as such it is to be cleared of any remaining equipment and/or laboratory samples.

As for the subjects, they are no longer considered viable. They are to be euthanized and their bodies cremated. All remains are to be buried. Please see to the completion of this task post haste.

-Major Carl Bell
USAC
Piedmont Creek Facility Commander

Merle Hoskins let out a loud belch as he read the letter again. Then he crumpled it up in disgust and threw it into the wire wastebasket that sat next to his old beat up desk in the basement closet that his superiors dared to call an office. He picked up the half empty bottle of Jim Beam sitting upon it and took a long pull.

The fuckers! Not only had they fired his ass, but they expected him to clean the goddamned place out before locking the doors for the last time. Sure, they hadn't exactly worded it that way, but as groundskeeper of the facility – and a civilian no less – that was more or less what it had come down to.

"The army takes care of its own," he muttered. "To hell with the rest of us."

With the closing of the complex, he was left unemployed and with nowhere to go. Sure, there was his sister Bernice, but he'd sooner live on the street than accept any charity from that bitch and her stuck-up tightwad of a husband.

"Didn't even get a letter of merit from Major Asshole," he slurred, taking another generous belt of whiskey. Merle sniffed the air then wrinkled his nose. It smelled like shit, just like always. Sadly, the one sense the liquor never seemed to dull was his sense of smell.

He picked himself off the chair and, with bottle in hand, walked out the door and up the stairs. He still couldn't believe it. He'd gotten nothing out of the deal except his final paycheck, and now they expected him to kill the entire sounder before burning the bodies.

"Gonna be a hell of a barbecue," he said with a humorless laugh, opening the door leading outside. The holding pens were only a few dozen yards away and he could already hear the occupants' eager snuffling as he approached.

He stepped to the fence and leaned over, watching the creatures mill about with their typical aimless stupidity.

No, that wasn't quite right. Hadn't one of those useless scientists always been blabbing on about how smart the damned things were? Hell, he'd even claimed they could outsmart a dog most days of the week.

"Heh. Not smart enough to stay off a sandwich platter," he muttered, idly picking the seat of his pants. That was, of course, complete bullshit, not to mention the entire reason the project was being shut down in the first place.

There was no doubt they'd gotten the size part right. Merle didn't know the specifics – hell, despite his high and mighty title of Facilities Supervisor, he was little more than a glorified garbage man. But whatever was in those injections the government scientists had been pumping into these swine had done its job. The goddamned things were twice the size of any pig he'd ever seen.

Too bad they don't taste half as good.

Though declared fully edible by the research team, not even *Cookie* Gimlin, the base's mess hall chef, had been able to make a palatable meal out of them.

Merle chuckled at the memory. They'd flown some bigwigs in from Washington for a celebratory feast after declaring the herd to be viable breeding stock. He had hunted his fair share of rabbit and squirrel, but even the gamiest of bush meat was far better than what Cookie had served that night. He'd seen more than one muckety muck unceremoniously spit out their first bite. Major Bell had tried to rally their support, telling them it wasn't so bad, that it was merely an acquired taste. But the scuttlebutt around the base was that he'd paid dearly for it - spending the next day sequestered in the officers' latrine.

Merle let out another laugh before upending the bottle. He swallowed the remainder of the whiskey, enjoying the comfortable burn as it went down his throat.

"They should've added some seasoning to all them vitamins they pumped into ya," Merle said aloud. "A little salt, a little pepper. Hell, maybe some of my memaw's special chili rub," he added with a grimace, watching the nearest of the group dip its oversized head into the empty slop trough.

He wouldn't be refilling it again. There wasn't any need to. He'd be damned if he was gonna break his back feeding the damned things one last time, only to have to break it again burying them.

"They sure as shit ain't paying me enough for this."

He stood there watching the so-called *failed experiments* for a little while longer before making up his mind.

"The hell with this," he said to the oversized beasts. "What gives them the right anyway? You didn't ask for any of this. Hell, it ain't none of your fault you all taste like crap."

He smiled as he threw the now empty bottle, listening to it shatter against the side of the empty research building. His eyes then turned to the woods beyond it. The damned things were probably gonna die anyway. Winter was only a few months off. He'd still be earning that final paycheck, just without busting his ass in the process.

Stepping to the pen's reinforced gate, he pulled the ring of keys from his pocket and quickly located the right one. With a snap, the heavy lock sprang open. He removed it from the catch and unceremoniously tossed it over his shoulder, knowing it wouldn't be needed again.

He unlatched the bolt and gave the heavy gate a shove, pushing it open.

The creatures inside glanced idly in the direction where freedom awaited, but otherwise didn't seem to care much.

They'll figure it out eventually, Merle mused as he turned and walked away, certain in the knowledge that he had another bottle waiting for him in his bunk.

1

1974

"SOOIE! SOOIE!" Bert Cooper shouted again, cupping his hands together over his mouth and raising the pitch of his voice. "Come on, ya goddamned pigs!"

He was in a foul mood. His no good nephew had disappeared again, leaving Bert to tend to the chores he'd assigned the boy. He'd been hoping to finish repairing the southern fence before the temperature climbed too high. Hammering posts in the sweltering heat of the noontime sun wasn't his idea of fun. But now he was stuck pouring the slop for the hundred strong drove he kept.

It wasn't that he couldn't handle the task. He'd been running the farm for years, the largest in Cooper's Bluff – named after his great grandfather. Sure, there was the occasional seasonal hire, but mostly it was just him and his wife Linda. Neither was a stranger to hard work. All the same, Bert believed that a deal was a deal. When his nephew Martin had come into town hat-in-hand needing a place to stay, that was what they'd agreed on – a few chores in exchange for a dry roof over their heads.

He's probably off with that girlfriend of his, Bert mused, continuing to shovel slop. He knew how randy a young man in his prime could be. After all, he'd been one himself not too long ago. Regardless, he had to wonder what his nephew saw in the girl. Martin wasn't a bad looking kid and he wasn't stupid either. Had a bit of a silver tongue too, the kind that could talk bees out of their honey.

His girl Charlene, on the other hand, was none of the above. Speaking with her for a few seconds was enough to realize you weren't exactly conversing with one of the great intellects of the twentieth century. As far as looks went, well, guilty as it made him feel to even think it, he just didn't see the appeal. Bert knew he wasn't exactly the greatest catch on the planet but even so, back when he'd been Martin's age he would've been as likely to date her as he would one of his sows.

Not that he was about to voice that opinion within earshot of his nephew, or Lin for that matter.

It simply didn't make sense to him. Having grown up in Cooper's Bluff, he knew the local pickings tended to be slim. Heck, Linda was originally from Pennsylvania, a little Podunk town by the name of High Moon. Meeting her had been nothing but dumb luck on Bert's part, a case of being at the right place at the right time. But Martin had been living down in Nashville. A young man like him should've had his pick of the litter in a city that size.

"That's why it's called love," Linda had told him one day not long after Martin and Charlene had arrived. "It's not supposed to make sense."

It sure as hell didn't, especially since his nephew hadn't seemed to exude much love for anyone except himself.

Bert stood up straight, cracked his back, and then wiped the sweat from his brow. It had been a hot dry summer so far and today was aiming to be a bad one.

Standing there musing about the mysteries of his nephew's love life wasn't going to make the temperature get any cooler. Regardless, Martin was definitely going to get a piece of his mind when he saw him again. Though he wasn't about to put his nephew out on the street, he had no intention of letting him off easy. His home was a working farm, not a flophouse.

Sadly, it looked like all that work was going to fall on his shoulders this morning. Not only was his nephew nowhere to be found, it was just his luck that Linda was out, too. She'd taken their truck over to Piedmont Creek to keep her friend Patty company. The woman was all out of sorts because her husband Elmer had up and left her. Linda, being a good friend, had gone over to help take her mind off things.

"Good on him," Bert muttered to himself, shoveling the last of the slop. "Hard to blame a man for leaving that shrew when he saw the chance." Though he knew he was alone, he looked up and glanced around anyway, certain Linda would've scolded his ears off if she heard him talking like that.

He chuckled to himself at his fearful reaction. There he was, a grown man with his shit supposedly in order. He'd inherited the family farm and had done a decent job keeping it profitable. Hell, the only debt he owed were the payments left on his Dodge Challenger V8 hard top – one of the few luxuries he'd allowed himself to indulge in over the years.

He smiled as he thought of his *baby*, remembering the first time he'd taken Lin for a ride in it. After turning onto Champ Lane, a long stretch of dirt road that ran past the McCallister place, he'd opened it up, letting the engine roar. Though his wife had been horrified at first, she'd eventually gotten into it – whooping like an excited teenager. The night had ended with them parked down near the bog at the southern edge of town and, well, there they'd taken a ride of a whole other variety.

Alas, Lin was usually far too reserved to let her wild side out like that, especially now that they had company staying with them.

Speaking of which, the Dodge was yet another source of consternation as far as his fool nephew was concerned – constantly pestering Bert to borrow the keys even as he seemed intent to skip out on his chores.

Fat chance of that ever happening.

Bert finished feeding the drove. Then seeing them happy as, well, pigs in shit, he went to go fetch his tools. He briefly considered a shower, noticing he smelled pretty damned ripe, but decided that would have to wait. There was no point in getting clean, only to wind up filthy again from the rest of the day's work. As he gathered what he needed, he tried to hold onto the vain hope that maybe Martin would come moseying back in time to lend a hand, as highly unlikely as that seemed.

He'd first noticed the damage the previous day. He and Lin kept a few dairy cows and he'd gone out to check on them following breakfast. Instead, he'd discovered a wide break in the fence and one of them missing. It wasn't the first time this had happened, so he'd rounded up the rest with the help of Milo, his aging collie, and brought them back to the barn – glad that all three hadn't wandered off when given the chance.

So far Gertie, the missing cow in question, hadn't returned yet, but he wasn't overly worried. She was likely happily grazing her fool head off somewhere. Eventually she'd either wander back home or one of his neighbors would spot her and let him know. It wasn't as if it hadn't happened before.

Now, with Milo fast asleep on the porch – *even the damned dog is ditching me today* – he headed out to survey the damage more closely and then fix what he could.

It wasn't a long walk, but Bert was sweating hard by the time he got there. The sun had reached its zenith and was baring down on him relentlessly. Not helping was the faint stench of diesel fuel and asphalt that seemed to perpetually hang in the air these days.

For the past seven months, construction crews had been tearing down trees and flattening the land at the southeastern end of town. Some bigwigs from the east coast had purchased about three-hundred acres of marshland and were hellbent on draining it to make way for a new housing development.

Not only were they stinking up the place with all their machinery, but they'd created a nightmare of detours and closed roads for anyone trying to get in or out of Cooper's Bluff.

The scuttlebutt around town was that the rich sons of bitches were convinced that people would soon be heading west by the bushelful. With the price of gas on the rise and the east coast being crowded with so-called undesirables, they intended to be at the forefront of this new age gold rush.

"They're gonna be at the forefront all right," Bert's friend Scooter McNeil had told him. "The forefront of the bread line after they lose their goddamned shirts."

Bert considered his friend's words as he neared the break in the fence. He was probably right. It was hard to envision a small town like Cooper's Bluff becoming anything more than it was – a quiet township full of quiet people who mostly knew one another.

That was all a worry for another time, though. Reaching the breach in the fence, he realized the damage was more extensive than what he'd taken note of during his quick inspection the day before.

Guess Gertie must've really wanted out.

That thought was cemented by the myriad hoofprints covering the ground.

Putting down his toolbox, Bert got to work. So intent was he on his task, that he failed to realized that most of the damaged posts were leaning inward – as if something had broken in, not out.

2

"Are you sure you'll be okay here by yourself?"

"Of course, Linda. You don't need to worry a lick about me."

"I just don't want you to be alone right now. That snake in the grass. I still can't believe he walked out on you like that."

"Oh I can," Patty Gantry said. "But don't you worry. I'm sure Elmer's wicked ways will catch up to him. The Lord shall smite the wicked. I have faith in that. Now go on. Get yourself back home."

"Well, if you're sure you'll be fine."

"I will, dear. And thank you for the pie."

"Enjoy it. It's the least I can do for you."

"I'll be sure to."

Linda Cooper began walking toward the pickup parked at the end of the driveway. She stopped and turned back, but Patty gave her a reassuring wave - making sure to keep a friendly smiled plastered upon her face.

When at last the vehicle disappeared from sight, Patty let out a disgusted sigh and went back inside. The Cooper woman was nice enough, but she practically reeked of her husband's touch. Though she wouldn't have dared speak of such things in Patty's presence, Linda talked fondly enough of her husband that she was sure those two were up to no end of wickedness.

She weaved her way through the small house she called home. It was cozy, well kept, and now entirely hers. She could at long last work on her knitting or poetry without having to worry about Elmer pawing at her every time she turned around. The man had been an insatiable animal. He was gone, though, now, thank goodness – gone and not coming back.

Though she hadn't cared as to where he'd been headed, he'd told her before leaving that he was setting off for a commune of free thinkers located in Oregon.

More like a commune of whores.

Patty's mother had explained it all to her very clearly during her formative years. Fornication was for marriage and marriage alone, and even then it was a disgusting act only to be performed for the purpose of procreation. Anything else was a sin in the eyes of God.

"But Preacher Machelin said a woman's place was to serve her husband," Patty had naively pointed out one day, to which her mother had set her straight on matters.

"The word of God has always been perverted through the mouths of men, my dear Patricia," her mother had said. "That's why most of them, whether they be preachers or laymen, are going straight to Hell. You see, God created man, but the Devil spoiled the mix. Every single one of them carries between his legs the same serpent that ruined Eve in the Garden. You can tell because, just like Lucifer himself, it can control their mind and drive them to wickedness."

Patty had learned that lesson first hand.

A former soldier, Elmer had seemed so worldly when they'd met. She thought they'd connected on a deeper basis and had convinced herself that he was one of the good ones.

She'd willingly given her virginity to him on their wedding night, despite closing her eyes and praying that it would end quickly. It had, but then, after she'd cleaned herself and was preparing for sleep, he'd wanted to do it again.

So began a never ending cycle. The man was constantly trying to climb atop her, even during the times of the month when she wasn't fertile - always telling her she should learn to enjoy it. After a couple years, with no children forthcoming, she'd finally had enough.

Patty had given him an ultimatum. They could live together, but in separate rooms like brother and sister. If not, he could pack his bags and leave.

In the end, he'd chosen the latter and she was glad for it. Every time she thought of the things he wanted to do to her, she would drop to her knees and pray to the Virgin Mother. Lord only knew what other evils he had in his wicked mind that even he was too ashamed to speak of.

The night after he'd left had been the first peaceful sleep she'd gotten in a long time, free from wondering whether he'd slide up against her – his *serpent* pressing insistently against her backside.

The only problem now was the constant stream of neighbors and busybodies stopping by to offer their condolences on the *great injustice* which had been done to her.

Patty didn't need their pity, though. In reality she was the one who pitied them.

She grabbed the pie Linda had left on her countertop and stepped out the back door.

Linda really was a sweet woman and Patty desperately hoped that one day she'd realize the mistake she was making in whoring herself out to her husband's carnal desires. But until that day came she wouldn't accept anything from the woman's unclean hands. Heck, she wouldn't even tolerate it being in her home.

She stomped to the edge of her backyard, opened the gate, and walked toward the tree line. Those who fornicated for the pleasure of the flesh were little more than rutting animals in her opinion, thus whatever they made was not fit for the righteous.

Maybe the squirrels will enjoy it, she thought, rearing back her arm and letting loose – sending the pie, plate and all, flying into the nearby bushes.

Patty had been expecting nothing more than the sound of the pie hitting the ground, thus she let out a yelp of surprise as a loud grunt emerged from where she'd tossed the treat. There came a squeal of annoyance from the dense brush, followed by a snuffling noise as if something were eagerly sniffing along the ground.

Feeling foolish at having been scared by a stupid pig, Patty stepped forward.

It was probably from the McNeil farm down the road. Wouldn't be the first time one of their swine had gotten out.

Judging by how the bushes ahead of her began to sway,

it was a big one too, maybe one of their prize slaughtering hogs.

Serves that idjit Scooter McNeil right. She let out a sniff and continued onward. It might be rooting around in the back-brush now, but if she didn't chase it off it would only be a matter of time before it was in her garden uprooting her petunias.

Parting the branches she cried, "Get out of here! Go..."

The words died in Patty's mouth as she spied the creature's thickly muscled back, covered in course brown hair and rising nearly to the same height as her.

It lifted its heavy head from the pie it had been devouring and turned her way. A set of malevolent brown eyes glared back at her as it let out a snort of annoyance.

Patty screamed and began to back away. She made it about ten feet before the bushes appeared almost to explode as the beast's bulk forced its way through. Linda continued to backpedal right up until her rump hit the picket fence surrounding her backyard. Before she could correct her course toward the gate, though, a two foot long tusk ripped through her midsection, spilling her intestines to the forest floor.

The boar pulled its head back and she sank to the ground, clutching at her ruined stomach.

Patty Gantry had just enough time to consider the disturbingly phallic shape of the boney appendage that had done her in – *the serpent takes many forms* – before fifteen hundred pounds of angry beast descended upon her.

For the next minute, the woods rang out with her cries, only to be replaced by the sound of frantic snuffling as the creature once more began to gorge itself.

3

"Where's the rest of my bread, bitch?"

"That's all there is, Martin. None of the fish are biting today."

Silence greeted her reply as the man stood there looking at her expectantly.

"Sorry," Charlene said, eyes downcast. "I mean that's all there is, *Koolaid*."

Martin "Koolaid" Belanger shook his head in disgust. He couldn't believe how far he'd fallen. Just a few months ago, he'd been at the top of his game living in Nashville – or so it had seemed. Now, he was stuck in this backwater town, living at his uncle's shitty farm, and with only one of his *flavors* left ... the ugliest one at that.

Just a few years earlier, he'd been shiftless – fresh out of high school and with no idea what to do with his life, other than knowing he had zero intention of becoming another nine-to-fiver at the local factory. He'd put it off for as long as he could, telling his parents he was looking for other opportunities, all while spending his days smoking weed and hitting on chicks. Soon enough, though, his folks had grown wise to his bullshit.

But then lightning had struck.

He'd gone out with some friends to see a double feature of *Shaft* and *Super Fly*. To his buddies they were badass movies full of all sorts of crazy shit, but it had been more than that to Martin. It had been like one of those revelations the preachers used to screech about in Sunday school.

Where once he was blind, now he could see – and what he saw looked fine as fuck.

He finally knew where his path was destined to lead. He was meant to be in the big game, selling drugs and pimping out whores. Right then and there he'd vowed to earn his fortune, enough to drive a big old Cadillac Eldorado just like in *Super Fly*. Hell, it barely seemed like work at all. He'd already been earning some side cash selling lids to his friends, and there was no doubt he was a smooth talker with the ladies. It had been a match made in heaven.

Within a week, he'd packed up his belongings, grabbed what money he could – including some that wasn't his to take – and set out for the biggest city in the state: Nashville.

For a while, his dream had been exactly that. He'd adopted the name Koolaid, bought himself some fly threads, and set to work.

Soon enough, he had a growing stable of bitches. Then came the money – enough to afford the charmed life he knew he deserved. At the height of his *empire*, he'd commanded the services of four *flavors* for customers to sample. Darla and Cherry had been the lookers. They weren't quite as hot as they thought they were, but each was more than able to command good money from the Johns they reeled in. There was Shonda, too. She might've been a butter face, but that bitch had an ass that just wouldn't quit. Bend her over a table and you'd think you'd died and gone to heaven.

Then there was Charlene.

Goddamn if she wasn't the worst prostitute in Nashville, but Martin was wise beyond his years. He'd seen her potential. When he'd first met her, she'd been drunk off her meaty ass – giving blowjobs for a quarter behind some dive bar. Seeing her there, though, he'd had an epiphany. Bunnies like Darla might've been the dream, but they were pricey lays. The oil crisis was getting worse and people were losing their jobs left and right. Even her steady clients were cutting back – a situation that wasn't so hot for Martin's bottom line.

With Charlene, however, he found a solution to that problem. Feast or famine, men were men. Even in the worst of times, they were up for sticking their dicks into whatever hole was available.

Charlene became that hole.

Charging rates that even a welfare case could dig, she was a steady earner. While his other flavors were always dealing with assholes trying to haggle over price, Charlene was flat on her back bringing home the bacon.

Then it had all changed. Both his flash and his cash had attracted the wrong kind of attention. A couple of the more seasoned *managers* working his part of town decided to move in on his territory. Cherry was the first to be seduced away – always a sucker for a silver tongue, that one. Sadly, Darla and Shonda soon followed. Martin, overestimating his clout, had finally confronted his chief rival, a man who went by the unimaginative name of Big Daddy.

It was a mistake on his part.

Their *discussion* had ended with Martin hightailing it out of town, fearing for his life. He had only the clothes on his back and the loyalty of the one girl who'd stayed with him – mostly because none of the other pimps wanted her skanky ass.

Unwilling to return home a failure he'd instead ended up in Cooper's Bluff, knowing his Uncle Bert wouldn't turn him away.

Now, as he considered the nothingness his life had become, he began to wonder if maybe he should've just toughed it out and taken his medicine back in Nashville.

"What the fuck, Lene?" he asked accusingly. "You losing your touch or is country life making you lazy?"

The one bright spot to having Charlene's dumb ass following him everywhere like a lost puppy had been learning about the construction work going on at the edge of town. Some bigwigs were trying to develop this jerkwater town, hoping to entice those fleeing big cities in the wake of the shitty economy.

Martin didn't care about any of that, but construction sites meant workers – men stuck on a job away from their wives and girlfriends. Such men tended to get lonely, and Charlene was just the girl to fit both their needs and budget.

At first, it seemed to be going well. Sure, Martin was stuck shoveling pig shit during the day, but at least his pockets were starting to fill up again. The only downside had seemed to be a few of the well-meaning local yokels, sticking their nose in his business to warn him that his *girlfriend* might be straying. AKA a bunch of dumb hicks with nothing better to do than gossip.

Now, though, it seemed as if Martin's fortunes were once again turning sour.

"I'm doing exactly what you told me to do, Koolaid,"

Charlene complained, flashing her cleavage in the way-too-tight mini dress she'd stuffed herself into. "I show up, make sure I get noticed, and then get to work. It just ain't happening today."

"Why the fuck not?"

"I don't know."

"Is there some other whore trying to muscle into our territory, because if so..."

"No. Or at least nobody I've seen." She appeared to think it over for a moment or two. "Maybe it has something to do with those missing men. Every John I've seen today has been too busy talking about them to want some tail. I think they're spooked."

"Too spooked for some ass?" he asked doubtfully before raising an eyebrow. "Wait, what missing men?"

"The ones who went missing."

Martin counted to ten, trying to suppress the urge to slap the shit out of Charlene right there on the street. Not only had she been his ugliest flavor, she was easily the dumbest too. Still, he didn't need the attention. His uncle was probably going to be up his ass for missing his damned chores as it was. Martin didn't look forward to the extra work he'd have to do to make up for it. He wasn't able to afford his own place yet, which meant he'd be pulling even more pig shit duty.

Fuck that. If such was his fate, then Charlene was going to help for a change. But that was a worry for later.

He looked her directly in the eye and said, "I want you to stop talking all that static and try to focus for a minute, baby. What were they saying about those missing men?"

She smiled back, seemingly pleased by the attention. "I think they said something about the foreman."

"The foreman?"

"That's right. They said he and a few of the guys went

out into the woods. I think it was some shit to do with trees." She let out an annoying titter. "Maybe they were looking for some knotholes to grease."

I'll grease your *knothole*. "So what? Did they get lost or something?"

"I don't know," she replied wide-eyed, "but they never came back, and there was this one dude talking all this crazy shit. Said they found the foreman's shirt all torn up like something had been at him."

Martin rolled his eyes. He'd spent enough summers in the Bluff as a kid to know the area. There were bobcats in the woods as well as the occasional black bear, but nothing that would go after a fully grown man. More than likely the dumb fucks had gotten lost out in the marsh, maybe even hit a patch of quicksand. As for their crew, they might act big and tough, but with their boss missing they were all busy spreading rumors like a gaggle of bored housewives.

"So the Johns are too spooked, eh?" he muttered.

"That's what I said."

Once more Martin felt the urge to crack her one in the mouth. She was getting uppity now that they were out of the city. Knowing her, she'd started to believe the bullshit story he'd spread about them being a couple. He'd need to straighten her out on that one sooner rather than later.

For now, though, business was his top priority.

He looked her in the eye and said, "Hear me out, baby. Scared men need comfort too, and you're gonna be the one to give it to them."

"How, Koolaid?"

"Listen up. It's time we had us a sale. Half price to take their minds off their worries for a while. That's a bargain not even a man scared out of his wits can refuse."

4

Byron Hoffsteader was not a happy man. They were already behind schedule on the Cooper's Bluff development and costs were only going to continue rising. Now, Reg Murphy, the project's foreman, had apparently gone missing.

Missing … uh huh, and I was born yesterday.

He could see it clearly in his mind – the man lounged against a tree, drunk out of his skull and having a good laugh at having gotten a few days off.

Not on my watch, you Irish bastard.

He'd been burned more than enough over the years by lazy assholes. So as a result, the second anyone called out sick or tried slacking off in any way, Byron immediately jumped to the conclusion that they were up to no good. More often than not he was right.

Never mind that Reggie had worked for him for five years and had a spotless record. He'd never even heard of the man taking so much as a drink during his lunch hour, much less on the job. Nevertheless, it was Byron's experience that most men wouldn't fail to disappoint if given the opportunity.

Even worse, the son of a bitch had taken Grant Nickson, his chief surveyor, with him, as well as some ditch digger – Byron was damned if he could remember the man's name. Either way you looked at it he was down three warm bodies, two of whom were key members of the crew. If they thought he was going to tolerate their excuses when they showed up again, they had another think coming. They'd be lucky if he only docked their pay. After all, there were plenty of good men looking for work these days.

Far worse than their absence was the work stoppage, putting their schedule in further jeopardy. From what he'd been told, the local hillbillies they'd hired were too busy gossiping like schoolgirls to actually do their damned jobs. Oh how Byron hated them and their lazy asses.

He had worked for years at his old man's firm back in New York before striking out on his own. He'd been fortunate to realize early on that the well-to-do were always looking for new getaways – places to vacation that had all the comforts of city-living but none of the people. He'd amassed a small fortune by being smart enough to scout out those spots before anyone else even thought to build there.

Most recently, his instincts had told him that Cooper's Bluff held that kind of potential. Columbus and Cincinnati were a puddle-jump away to the North, while to the south there was nothing but pristine wetlands. It was the perfect locale for anyone looking to get away from it all but still be close enough to civilization to easily enjoy its trappings should the need arise.

For the bulk of his work force on these projects, he always hired locals whenever he could. Creating new jobs never failed to endear him to the small-fry politicians when it came to zoning laws. Sure, it was all temporary. Afterwards, once the work was done, the yokels could go fuck themselves. By then he'd already be onto his next project.

This godforsaken place, though, seemed determined to give him an ulcer before he was through with it. First there were the goddamned marshes. His men would be driving the heavy equipment over what seemed like solid ground only to then find themselves stuck – sunk down to their axles in mud.

Then there was the petty vandalism. On at least three occasions, reports had hit his desk of their vehicles being damaged overnight. The first couple had been minor, but then one of their pickups had been found lying on its side with the passenger door crushed.

With his insurance company now climbing up his ass, Byron had suspected either local moonshiners protecting their stills or hippie dipshits on some half-assed crusade to save the Earth.

Whatever the case, he'd instructed his people to hire a night watchman – only for the man to quit two days later, claiming to be spooked by strange sounds in the night. They were still trying to find a replacement, no thanks to the stupid hick spreading the word at the local watering hole as if he were telling goddamned ghost stories to scared children.

Now Reg was AWOL too, the latest in a string of bullshit he had to deal with. With him gone and things in disarray it meant Byron would probably have to step in and take charge. He knew the job well enough, having worked with construction crews since he was fourteen. It was more that he shouldn't have to do it.

Byron had moved on from that shit. These days he

favored crisp suits and polished belt buckles over digging grime from beneath his fingernails for half the night. Unfortunately, he was rapidly being backed into a corner. If they didn't make their proposed deadline, things would slow to a crawl over the winter – playing hell with his revenue stream. If so, he'd probably lose even more having to regrease the local selectmen come spring, as the greedy bastards seemed to have a short memory when it came to zoning permits.

Sadly, time was of the essence. Besides, for all his bluster about firing the missing men, he doubted there was anyone local who could think their way out of a paper bag much less replace Reg in the short run.

Knowing he was the only man qualified to take charge, Byron stood up with a sigh. He removed his sports jacket and then rolled up the sleeves of his striped dress shirt. Once done, he grabbed his briefcase along with the hastily packed suitcase he'd brought with him this morning.

He stepped from his office and turned to the secretary seated outside, a young Hispanic woman with the kind of curves that could make a man forget she couldn't brew a decent cup of coffee to save her life.

"Hold my calls and tell Jose to bring the car around. I'll be out of the office for a few days." When she hesitated a moment too long for his liking, he barked, "Ándale! Time is money!"

5

"Mmm, something smells good," Bert said, enjoying the fragrant scent of simmering stew as he wrapped his arms around his wife's waist.

She leaned into him, for a moment anyway, before slapping his hands away. "Yes, and it sure as heck isn't you, Bert Cooper. I swear, if I didn't know better I'd say you've been wallowing in the pigpen."

"Trust me, I'm well aware. It was a long day, hot as hell too. Thought I was gonna melt in the back field." He stepped to the fridge, pulled out a cold Budweiser, and popped the tab. "When did you get in?"

"A little after three. Patty sends her regards by the way."

"I highly doubt that. We both know that if looks could kill she would've skewered me through the heart years ago." He took a sip of his beer. "Although, maybe I shouldn't complain. If old Elmer ever shows his face around here again, she'll almost certainly aim for his balls instead."

"She's not like that."

"Oh really?"

Linda opened her mouth, probably to protest, but instead let out a laugh. "Okay fine, maybe she is like that a little. But you should still be nice. She's going through some stuff. Oh, and watch your language, mister. I don't need either of our guests overhearing you and thinking less of us."

"I'll worry more about their opinions when they start paying rent. That reminds me, have you seen either of them since you got home?"

"Can't say that I have." She inclined her head. "Why? I thought Martin was supposed to be helping you out today."

"So did I, but he was a no show. Can't tell you how much me and my aching back enjoyed doing both our chores today."

Linda shook her head. "I'll have a word with him when he gets in. But don't be too cross. He and Charlene are young..."

"And stupid."

"Yes, that too, Bert. But you know darned well how couples their age can be. They probably found a secluded spot and..."

"Screwed like rabbits while I was out sweltering under the sun?"

She pursed her lips. "I was going to say lost track of the time."

Bert couldn't help but smile at how she tried to be all prim and proper with her wording, even when it was just the two of them alone. At least it gave him something to think about other than Martin and Charlene off doing the horizontal mambo. That was a mental picture he really didn't need bouncing around in his noggin. "Talk to him all you want, but he owes me some chores and I aim to collect. We're not running a flophouse here, Lin. I know he's your brother's son, but..."

"But what?" She fixed him with her gaze. "You'll throw them out onto the street if they don't shape up?"

"No," he backpedaled, not wanting a fight. "I'm just saying a few chores in exchange for room and board isn't a bad deal these days. And it's not just him. There's Charlene, too. The girl needs to do something with herself rather than sit around like a doe-eyed..."

"A doe-eyed what?"

He shook his head. "What I'm trying to say is, we're doing all right for ourselves and I'm happy to share that with family. But I also don't want either of us, especially you, being taken advantage of."

Linda put her hands on her hips but then she stepped forward and gave him a peck on the cheek, albeit not without wrinkling her nose. "The only one here who gets to take advantage of me is you. Although not if you don't go wash up first. I'll tolerate a lot from my man, but smelling like a pile of cow flop is where I draw the line."

"Yes, ma'am," he replied with a grin, admiring her as she turned back toward the stove.

After seven years of marriage she was still able to cause his heart to skip a beat. Linda wore her auburn hair a bit shorter these days, but she was still every bit the knockout. Life on the farm could be rough, but you wouldn't know it from looking at her. Her hands had a few more calluses these days and her face was a bit more weathered, but the curves of her body were still more than able to get him to stand at full attention.

More importantly, she was a good soul, the type of woman who smoothed out his rough edges perfectly.

He knew deep down that whatever proverbial line in

the sand he might draw with regards to their nephew, he could never say no to her.

Rather than continue down that path, though, he decided it was best to change the topic. "Speaking of cow flop, you didn't happen to notice if Gertie was out in the yard, did ya?"

"Can't say that I have," she replied over her shoulder. "Why, did she wander off again?"

He nodded even though she couldn't see him. "Yeah. The fool cow busted through the fence yesterday. The rest are accounted for, but I haven't seen hide nor hair of her."

"I hope the poor thing's not stuck in a bog somewhere. I'll tell you what. Dinner should be ready within the hour. Afterward, if you want, we can go out looking for her."

"I appreciate that, hun, but it's gonna be another hot one out there tonight. Why don't you stay home and keep cool. I'll give Scooter a call and see if he's up for taking a look around with me."

She turned and raised an amused eyebrow. "Oh, so you'd rather spend time with Scooter than your wife?"

"No offense, but if it involves dragging a dumb cow out of a dirty bog then yes."

"Fair enough. Then I guess I won't harass you about getting cleaned up, at least not until later. But I swear, if you climb into bed without taking a shower first, I'm liable to shoot you for a stranger."

"Well then, I'd hate to be shot before I get a chance to..."

He trailed off from what he'd been about to say as the front door opened, revealing their nephew and his girlfriend – him looking bored, her looking considerably more disheveled.

It was an instant for him to realize that opportunity hadn't knocked so much as barged right in.

"What's cooking?" Martin asked, taking a sniff of the air as if nothing were amiss.

"Dinner," Bert said with a grin. "Why don't you go grab a plate ... and a flashlight while you're at it."

"What for?"

"Because you and me have a date tonight."

"A date? As in together?"

"Oh, it's not just us. There's a lovely little lady named Gertie who requires our attention." He threw a wink Charlene's way. "Don't worry. No need to get jealous. Trust me when I say he's *really* not her type."

6

The night was hot, humid, and miserable just as Bert had predicted. Making it even worse, though, was the thick ground fog rising up past his knees – a result of the balmy air meeting the relative coolness of the damp bog.

Though this was familiar territory to him during the day, right then it reminded Bert more of those old wolfman movies he used to enjoy as a kid. He had to admit it would've been creepy as all hell had he been out there alone.

Fortunately, he wasn't. His earlier threat to bring Martin along hadn't been an idle one – despite the kid's protests to the contrary.

Mind you, Bert wasn't an idiot. He'd suspected that his nephew would almost certainly be useless as tits on a bull as they looked for the wayward cow. It had been a prophetic bit of insight as, in truth, Martin was turning out to be good at only one thing that night – complaining. If anything, he was more trouble than he was worth.

Too bad for him, Bert was still sore about being ditched earlier and wasn't about to let him off the hook so easily.

On the bright side, his longtime friend Scooter had been free as well, and more than happy to lend his services to the search.

Too bad it had all been in vain, at least so far. If Gertie was anywhere nearby, she was keeping real quiet about it. In fact, so was everything else. Maybe it was the fog playing tricks with his senses, but he couldn't remember it ever being this damned quiet out there after dark. Usually there was at least the incessant chirp of frogs and crickets to remind one they weren't the last living thing on Earth.

Though he wouldn't have admitted it out loud, Bert was secretly glad that Scooter had shown up with flashlight in hand and his shotgun strapped to his back. Though he doubted they'd need it, the silence was unnerving to the point of having him on edge.

"It's way too hot for this shit. We should go home."

Or the silence would've been unnerving if not for Martin's constant bitching and moaning.

"Fine, we'll head in," Bert told him.

"Now you're finally making sense."

"*After* we find Gertie."

"Come on, man! I'm sweating my balls off here," his nephew whined, seemingly far more concerned with his family jewels than doing his part to find the damned cow they were looking for.

"What a coincidence," Bert replied. "Mine were doing the exact same thing this afternoon – while I was busy doing *your* chores."

"I already apologized for that. Geez, do you want it in writing? I told you, Charlene had some stuff to do in town and she wanted me to keep her company."

"What kind of stuff?"

"You know, just stuff."

"Uh huh. Well, while I can appreciate any man who stands by his woman's side while she does *stuff*, excuses don't keep the pig pen clean."

"That it don't," Scooter interjected, "but standing here arguing about it ain't gonna help find your cow neither."

Despite Harold "Scooter" McNeil being Bert's senior by ten years, they'd been close friends for as long as he could remember. Scooter's blunt no-nonsense attitude and willingness to always lend a hand had ensured it. It didn't hurt that they both owned their respective family farms, giving them plenty of common ground to talk about at the end of a long day.

"Fair point, Scoot."

Martin shook his head in disgust. "I don't see how we're gonna find anything out here in this shit. It's like walking through pea soup."

"I'd agree, if we were out here looking for a few escaped hens," Scooter drawled as they made their way further into the bog – their flashlight beams doing little to cut through either the gloom or the thick vegetation. "But a big ole Holstein like Gertie is gonna be a bit harder to miss. Trust me on this, Marty."

"Koolaid."

"Scuse me?"

"I said call me Koolaid."

"This ought to be good," Bert muttered to himself.

"You mean like the drink?" Scooter asked, sounding confused.

"*Oh yeah*!" Martin cried, doing a poor imitation of the commercials. "It's like I keep telling Uncle Bert here…"

"And I keep telling *you*," Bert interrupted, "there ain't no way in hell I'm calling you that. You sound like a goddamned fool."

"You're just too old to understand."

"Thirty-six isn't old."

"It is from where I'm standing."

"I'm with your uncle," Scooter said. "You'll end up locked in the looney bin if you keep saying crazy shit like that."

"It's not crazy, old timer. It's my street name."

"That so? Well, considering we're not on a street right now, you'll forgive me if I stick to Martin instead of Hawaiian Punch."

"Whatever, gramps. Let's just get this over with. I'm dying out here."

Scooter let out a laugh as they continued onward, the beams from their flashlights reflecting off the fog and making the shadows almost seem alive. "This ain't nothing. If you wanted to see a real scorcher, you should have been here back in fifty-seven. Hottest July on record and the months that followed weren't much better. Hell, we had an Indian summer that lasted well into January. I swear, folks could've worn their skivvies on Christmas day just like it was the Fourth of July."

"I remember that," Bert replied. "Seemed like most of the town was in a perpetually foul mood for a good chunk of it."

"The heat played a role, no doubt, but that was only part of the reason folks had their knickers in a bunch."

"Oh?"

"You were just a kid, Bert, so you probably don't remember too well. That's the year the army shut down the base next door in Piedmont Creek. No warning or anything. They just padlocked the doors and moved on. Lots of folks lost their jobs because of it."

"I know that place," Martin said, sweeping his flashlight haphazardly around at a pace that would have made it near impossible to spot an elephant much less a cow. "Kids used to say it was haunted."

"Boys will say anything is haunted if'n they think it'll make a girl weak in the knees," Scooter scoffed. "Nah. The only spirits out there are whatever they forgot to take when they packed up the mess hall. Truth is, was more just a research building and a couple of barracks than a full base. The army built them by the dozens right after the war. Back then, the government was willing to fund just about anything the military asked for, no matter how crazy."

Martin shook his head. "Anything to keep the war pigs fat and happy."

"Feh. You can take that hippie talk and shove it up your ass, boy. Besides which, it wasn't like that. We're talking science here. It wasn't just about seeing how big of a bomb they could build."

"Really?"

"Yep. Didn't witness any of it firsthand, mind you, being I was mostly busy working the farm, but scuttlebutt around town was they were experimenting on livestock."

"What kind of experiments?"

"The kind that were none of my business I suppose. Either way I'm guessing it didn't amount to much. Whatever they were doing must've failed because like I said, they closed up shop and left town. End of story."

"That's it?" Martin asked, shining his flashlight at the older man. "That's all there is?"

"Get that goddamned light out of my face before I shove it sideways up your ass." Scooter raised a hand to shield his eyes until the younger man did as he was told. "Better. And what do you mean *that's it*? What else would there be?"

"I don't know. Didn't anyone ever like get curious about what was going on there?"

"Wasn't much to get curious about. Like I said, they cleaned the place out. As for those who worked there, they kept their mouths shut just as they were told to. Loose lips sink ships."

Bert nodded. "It may surprise you to hear this coming from a big city like Nashville, but folks around here know how to mind their own beeswax."

Martin inclined his head. "So this place is still sitting out there abandoned?"

"Yep, just like Scooter said."

"Cool to know."

Bert raised an eyebrow. Something about his nephew's tone was telling him this wasn't mere interest on the boy's part. However, before he could question him, Martin cried out.

"Shit!" he bellowed before falling to one knee, the fog swallowing nearly half his body in his semi-prone position.

"Are you okay?" Bert asked as he and Scooter raced to his side.

"I'm fine," Martin griped. "Just slipped in the damned mud."

"Shit is right," Scooter said, bending down and focusing his light on the ground at Martin's feet. "A whole lot of it."

Martin looked at the sizeable pile of excrement the older man was pointing at, disgust coloring his face. "You've gotta be kidding me!"

He stepped away, trying to wipe his shoes off on the grass as Bert moved in for a closer look.

"What do you think?" Scooter asked. "Definitely big enough to be Gertie's."

Bert nodded. "No doubt on that, assuming it's actually cow flop."

"That size, what else can it be?"

"Aside from a big pile of shit with two sneaker prints right in the middle of it?"

Both men let out a hearty laugh, to which Martin groused, "Oh yeah, real funny! That's it, I'm done. I'm heading back."

"Not so fast, Kemosabe," Bert replied. "Nobody's heading home just yet, not when we're finally on the right trail."

7

Harold McNeil, Scooter to his friends, put his hands behind his back and stretched while standing next to his 1965 Ford pickup – not that it helped his aching muscles much.

It was just after midnight and he was both tired and sweaty after combing the woods near the Cooper farm. That boded ill for the work day to come. After all, it wasn't as if he could just stay in bed like some sort of layabout.

That said, his family would understand if he asked them to do a bit more than their share. When a friend came to you in need, you helped them. That was how he'd been raised, and how he and Irma had raised their sons. James was long gone, having left home to pursue a career in sales, but Michael was still with them. The boy was only thirteen but he had a strong back. A few extra chores wouldn't break him.

Though he hadn't minded giving Bert a hand, in the end their search for his lost cow had been for naught. The trail had run cold not long after they'd found that pile of flop. The only good thing about it had been watching

Martin dirty his shoes in shit and then throw a fit afterward.

That one's a slacker, no doubt about it. Harold could spot them a mile off. He'd been half-tempted to pull Bert aside and tell him to kick that boy to the curb until he learned some proper respect. However, Martin was Bert's family and you didn't do that to kin – something Harold had also been raised to believe.

Even if they deserved it.

Imagine that, a grown man insisting he should be called Kool-Aid. And yet people still smoke that damned reefer as if it's not poisoning their minds.

Sadly, watching the fool boy step in crap had been the high point of the evening. Afterward they'd found nothing but diddly squat. Whatever direction that cow had wandered off in, it hadn't been the way they'd gone.

In the end, he'd probably been wrong to assume it was cow dung at all. It had made sense at the time, considering how much there was, but then they'd come across a section of ground that was all torn up.

It was a sure sign of boars hunting for roots and grubs – a lot of them from the look of it. Thankfully they hadn't run into any before heading in. Feral pigs could be nasty fuckers when they set their minds to it, and he'd been the only one of their number who'd shown up armed.

That part had been a no brainer as far as Harold was concerned. He didn't venture into the woods at night without proper protection, not even onto land he was familiar with. Others figured he was just being mindful of bobcats or other critters, and he was happy to let them believe that. It was easier than folks thinking he'd lost his mind.

It was a lesson he'd learned years back – one he didn't

talk about, not to Bert or even his own family. Some things a man needed to keep to himself.

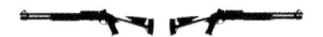

Harold had been on a hunting trip in Kentucky, one of the few vacations he'd allowed himself over the years. On what had turned out to be their last morning there, he'd let his eldest sleep in while he'd gone ahead to their blind. As the sun began to crest the horizon, he'd spotted something through the scope of his rifle.

It was no deer.

Hell, he wasn't sure what it had been, save that it was hairy, walking on two legs, and the sight of it was enough to send him racing back toward camp. Within the hour they were packed up and on the road, with James probably not quite believing the lie he'd been told about his father simply being homesick. Thankfully, the boy had been wise enough not to question it.

Harold had never seen anything like it again and he hoped never to, especially in the woods near his home. Nevertheless, ever since that day he kept his trusty Mossberg twelve gauge close by whenever the sun was low and he knew he needed to be outdoors for a while yet.

Harold slung the gun strap over his shoulder as he prepared to head inside. At least he didn't have to worry about tiptoeing through his own house like a thief in the night. Both Irma and Michael slept like the dead.

It was the sort of sleep earned by a day of good honest labor, the sort he was looking forward to ... in a few minutes anyway.

Though he was worn out, he decided to grab a smoke before heading inside. It was finally starting to cool down a bit and the mugginess of earlier was giving way to a clear night sky above. It wasn't likely to be nearly this pleasant once the sun was up again, so he figured he might as well try and take a little enjoyment from it.

He pulled the pack of Winstons from his pocket and dug one out. Irma didn't like him smoking indoors anyway – arguing the smell got into the furniture. He secretly thought she was full of it, but it wasn't a hill he was prepared to die on. Easier to light up outside than to risk World War Three breaking out in his parlor.

Harold walked around to the passenger side of his truck, where he grabbed his old Zippo lighter from the glove compartment before shutting the door – the slam of metal against metal sounding extra loud in the night air. He cocked his head, noting it was every bit as quiet on the farm as it had been while out searching for that cow. Though he hadn't wanted to admit it in front of Bert or that shithead nephew of his, it had gone a ways toward unnerving him.

The idea that the outdoors were peaceful and quiet was a load of hooey, no doubt concocted by those who lived in the city and wanted desperately to believe the grass was greener elsewhere. Harold had lived in Piedmont Creek for most of his life, though, save for a brief stint as an Air Force mechanic. He knew the outdoors were anything but quiet. There was always something chirping, squawking, or otherwise causing a racket.

It was when things got quiet that you needed to worry, because it meant a threat was nearby – giving everything reason to shut their pie holes until it had passed.

That held true out in the wilderness but in truth living on a farm wasn't much different. No matter the hour, there was always something causing a stir. Whether it was the barn cats getting into a tussle, owls hooting their heads off, or coyotes yipping in the distance, there was always something to be heard.

But not now. Sure, the critters that should be asleep probably were, but it was downright eerie how still everything else was. He could've heard a pin drop.

All at once, his breathing sounded disturbingly loud to his ears, telling him he was likely making himself the target that everything else was hoping not to be.

He found his hand inching slowly toward his gun as he contemplated making a bolt for the relative safety of his house. Then the silence was broken by a heavy snort coming from the direction of the pig pen on the far side of the yard.

Harold let out a breath he wasn't even aware he'd been holding as he turned that way. Unlike the Cooper farm, he didn't raise pigs for wholesale. Instead Irma kept a small drift of Hampshires. Besides providing the family with meat for the winter, she also entered them at the yearly county fair. He wasn't ashamed to admit she'd claimed a blue ribbon three years in a row for her prize hogs.

As his eyes settled in that direction, though, his relief turned to confusion as he realized something was off. In the meager light shining down from the stars he saw something moving in the pen. It was too dark to make out other than it was obviously far larger than any of the swine they kept there. That's when he noticed the breach in the fence. One of the sides of the pen had been caved in – as if something had plowed through it from the outside.

"Son of a bitch," Harold muttered, heading that way.

His first thought was that it must be a bear. A hungry bruin wouldn't hesitate to try its luck with a solo pig, but a full pen's worth was something else entirely. A black bear would have to be either starving or desperate to be that ambitious.

As he slipped the shotgun from his shoulder, he took note of the large humped back visible above the fence slats. There was one other distinct possibility – Gertie. Why Bert's missing cow would be compelled to break into his pig pen wasn't obvious, but they could be damned stupid animals when they wanted to be – stupid and stubborn. When they got a mind to do something, they just did it.

That would also explain why the pigs weren't raising absolute hell.

The broken fence was a pain in the ass, but fences could be mended. And he was sure Bert would lend a hand once he learned who the culprit was. The Coopers were good people that way. It was just a damned shame God hadn't seen fit to grace them with children, although Harold was tactful enough to not say such things in front of Linda.

Such thoughts could wait, though. First he needed to secure Gertie, lest she wander off again. Then he could give Bert a ring in the morning to let him know. Was too late to bother him now.

There came a faint crunching sound from the pen as he approached, like something was being chewed on, but he didn't pay it much mind. The dumb cow had probably found an errant corn cob mixed in with the pig slop.

"All right, Gertie," Harold said as he reached the side of the fence nearest him. "Fun time's over. Time to get your ass into the…"

A snorting scream rent the night, drowning out his words as whatever was in the pen reared its head and charged him.

Harold cried out as the creature slammed into the

fence, cracking the boards in the process. He tried to simultaneously backpedal and raise his gun, but instead ended up toppling over onto his backside in the dirt.

Before he could right himself again, the thing changed direction and took off. It raced out from the same spot where it had broken in and ran off into the night. He could feel the thud of its heavy footfalls vibrating through the ground beneath him as it disappeared from sight.

Harold scrambled back to his feet, shotgun in hand, only vaguely aware that he'd pissed himself at some point in the last minute.

Thank goodness the fence on this side had held, otherwise he'd have certainly been trampled or worse.

He stepped back to the pen and leaned against one of the posts, his heart racing a mile a minute as he looked around trying to make sure that thing, whatever it had been, was actually gone.

Harold stood there for several long minutes, gun at the ready, before he was finally able to accept that he was alone again – alone except for the pigs in the...

His eyes opened wide as he turned his attention back toward the pen, realizing in one horrified instant why Irma's hogs hadn't been raising a ruckus despite the intruder in their midst.

They'd been torn to pieces, each and every one of them, as surely as if they'd been run over with a thresher. Bone, gristle, and intestines were strewn about, trampled into the mud covering the ground. He was suddenly thankful for the darkness because it almost certainly obscured the worst of it.

Something like this was more the work of an angry grizzly than any black bear he'd ever seen. Only problem was they weren't native to the area. Besides which, Harold had only gotten a glimpse of the creature as it raced away, but it had been enough for him to be certain that it was no bear.

He wasn't sure what the hell it had been, save he would've bet every last cent he owned that it hadn't been a lost cow either.

8

"Yes! Right there. Don't stop!"

"You like that, baby? That make you howl like a wolf?"

Whatever satisfaction Sandra Gilbert might've gotten was immediately ruined as her boyfriend Aldrick Kent lifted his head from her neck and bellowed, "Aww-wooooo!" into the night air.

He probably thought it was cute, like he was Wolfman Jack. To her, though, it was corny as all hell, a real mood killer – especially when she'd been so close.

Sadly, any chance of getting back into the groove was rendered moot as he stiffened atop her and she felt his release.

"For heaven's sake, Rick!" she cried, pushing him off. "You were supposed to pull out."

"Sorry, babe," he replied, breathing hard next to her. "You just bring out the beast in me."

"Yeah, well, I'd prefer you keep your *little beasts* to yourself."

He rolled over onto his back atop the blanket they'd laid out beneath the stars. "Don't worry about it. You know that if anything happens I'd do the right thing, don't you?"

She glared at him, but inwardly smiled. Sandra was on the pill and taking it like clockwork, but he didn't need to know that. After a year and a half of sneaking off into the woods for rolls in the hay, she was ready for more from their relationship.

She'd been slowly dropping hints to Aldrick about wanting to be made an honest woman. Sadly, he was either too thick to take the hint or was purposefully playing dumb.

She wasn't about to let him off the hook that easily, though. He was too good a catch, a top-notch insurance salesman with Sentry out of their Piedmont Creek branch. She, on the other hand, worked as a waitress down at Kelly's Diner. It paid the bills but was a thankless job, usually resulting in her having to tolerate a lot of hands brushing against her behind if she hoped to earn a nice tip.

She was tired of it and looking for an out. Unfortunately, the opportunities for a single woman in this part of the country weren't exactly limitless. Women's lib was great and all, but apparently only if you were in a big city on one of the coasts.

Sandra wasn't in love with Aldrick, but she liked him well enough. He was smart and funny if a bit weird at times, although he definitely considered himself a much better lover than he actually was. But that was most men in her opinion. Besides, unlike some of the other jerks she'd dated since moving out on her own, he was mostly a good guy. Being a housewife while he brought home the bacon was an endearing thought, even if it meant dealing with him howling like a weirdo every time he shot his load.

She'd been hoping to find a ring on her finger soon. If not, she might be forced to resort to *desperate* measures.

Aldrick had confided in her that he was embarrassed to buy rubbers at the pharmacy, as if the cashier ringing him up cared one way or the other. Though she wasn't quite yet ready for kids, she had toyed with the idea of fibbing a bit and telling him she was late – just to see if it might light a fire beneath his bum.

She hated herself a bit for thinking that way, but lately the girls at work had been teasing her – saying stuff like there was no reason for him to buy the cow so long as she was giving up the milk for free.

After a while stuff like that tended to sink in.

She grimaced at the thought as Aldrick lit up two cigarettes, passing one to her as they lay naked beneath the stars.

They were in a small clearing right next to Berryman Lake, a favorite fishing spot for the locals, at least during the day. Come nightfall, though, the small lot next to the boat launch was often frequented by young lovers seeking a quiet spot to fool around, as well as cops making the occasional sweep of the area to chase them out.

That was all on the far side of the lake, however. Out there in their *secret* spot, a quarter mile hike from the road down an old foot path, it was far more secluded.

She knew the way by heart, having used this particular clearing since her high school days. Usually there was a cool breeze blowing off the lake, perfect for keeping the mosquitos at bay while engaged in some vigorous love making.

That wasn't the case tonight, though. The heat wave

that was currently pummeling the area seemed intent on sticking around for a while.

Speaking of sticking…

Aldrick reached down and adjusted himself. "Ugh, my balls are stuck to my leg."

"Well, whose fault is that?" she chided. "We could've just as easily done the deed in a nice air conditioned hotel room, but you're the one who wanted to come out here tonight."

"Come on, Sandy. You don't get a view like this holed up in some two-bit motel and you know it."

She sat up, turning his way and putting a little jiggle into it. "Are you saying this view isn't enough to keep you interested?"

He took another drag from his cigarette before leering at her. "Hell yeah I'm interested. Want me to show you how much?"

While she wasn't averse to another lay, she was pretty certain he wasn't ready yet. He might talk a big game, but it usually took him a lot longer to coax his worm out of its hole for a second go.

Thankfully, she had a way to bide the time. "No way, mister. You're all hot and sweaty."

"So are you."

"I know, which is why I'm taking a dip in the lake first."

"Ugh. Aren't you afraid of leeches and stuff?"

She put her cigarette out in the dirt and stood up. "Not really. Besides, leeches aren't the only things that can suck a man dry. Play your cards right and maybe I'll show you what I mean when I get back."

"That a promise?"

She shrugged as she stepped away. "We'll see how nice

you are to me when I get back. Just make sure you're ready by then."

"Yes, ma'am!"

The clearing was about twenty yards from the shore separated by a thick wall of bushes, so it made no sense for Sandra to get dressed only to immediately get undressed again. Being it was dark and she was naked as the day she was born, though, she took it slow – stepping gingerly through the vegetation and being mindful to not scrape the hell out of herself.

Earlier, there had been a layer of mist rolling across the water, giving it an eerie look – unsurprising considering the current heat wave – but now it was mostly gone, having cooled off a bit over the past few hours. Sandra looked across the lake, seeing nothing but darkness. That wasn't much of a surprise. She doubted anyone would be out this late. It was almost the wee hours of the morning. Fortunately for her, she was working the night shift at the diner. There would be plenty of time for another screw before heading home to catch some shuteye.

Aldrick could wait, though. It was her turn now.

She waded into the water – unseasonably warm, yet still much cooler than the surrounding air. After giving herself a moment or two to acclimate she plunged in all the way, enjoying the feel of the sweat being washed off her body.

Sandra's intent had been to cool herself off a bit while also getting a bit of alone time to finish the job Aldrick had started. There was no point in risking hurting his ego, not when she was so close to reeling him in.

Now that she was in the water, she was half-tempted

to take a swim to the middle of the lake and back instead. However, it was nearly pitch black out there. She didn't relish swimming out, only to get disoriented and end up accidentally returning to a completely different part of the shore line. Though she was certain they were the only people around for miles, hiking back to Aldrick through the dark woods while naked as a jaybird wasn't something she…

There came a heavy splash from somewhere off to her right, almost causing her to jump out of her skin.

"Rick?" she squeaked, her voice barely audible.

She wasn't entirely sure why she was whispering. It wasn't like there was anyone else around to hear her. For some reason, though, all the hairs on the back of her neck were standing up. All at once, every instinct in her body was screaming that she should stay quiet and not give away her location.

Whatever had made that sound must've been large, as the ripples from the disturbance reached her and continued to fan out.

Her first thought was it must be Aldrick. But that made no sense. He absolutely hated swimming in any water that wasn't absolutely crystal clear. Heck, she could barely get him to join her in the pool over at the Lesterfield Y two towns over. Even at his horniest she wouldn't have expected him to dive in and join her.

She turned in that direction to see if she could tell what it was. Sadly, even with the stars shining down from above, it was too dark for her to make out anything.

There came another splash, followed by more ripples in the water. Whatever was in there with her was moving.

A fish maybe? Every rural town west of Maryland had stories of big catfish in their local waterways. Cooper's Bluff was no different. Every summer someone would boast about how this was the year they'd catch Old Grinder, the legendary gamefish supposedly haunting these waters. Yet she'd never once heard of anyone landing anything bigger than a largemouth bass from the surrounding lakes.

Another sound broke the silence, a huff of breath or maybe a snort coming from near the shore.

An animal then. The problem was not knowing what kind? From the size it was likely a deer. If so then no problem. They could swim and it's not like she could blame one for wanting to cool off after the sort of day it had...

"OH GOD, SOMEONE HELP ME! SANDY, PLEASE..."

The scream shattered the night air before falling quiet again, instantly sending a chill down Sandra's spine that had nothing to do with the temperature of the water.

It was Aldrick, and it had sounded like he was terrified out of his mind.

Whatever was in the water with her was quickly forgotten as she began to wade back in the direction she'd come. Missing, however, was the quiet of earlier, as she could hear a ruckus of bushes rustling and branches breaking from back where they'd set up their little love camp.

A small voice in the back of Sandra's mind told her to turn around. She was a strong swimmer. Reaching the opposite shore would be no problem. From there she could...

Could what? she asked herself. The only thing she was liable to do was end up getting arrested for streaking.

Instead she turned back, forcing herself to think rationally. Yes, it was possible something had happened to Aldrick, but wasn't it equally likely that he was just playing a prank on her?

That sort of thing would be just up his alley with that weird sense of humor of his.

The more she thought of it, the more likely it seemed. He'd known she'd opted for a midnight swim, but rather than let her take her time, he'd decided to scare her – hoping she'd come running into his arms so he could *comfort* her ... with his penis no doubt.

He probably thought it was hilarious, throwing stones into the water to make her think there was a damned sea monster out there with her, all while knowing he was practically invisible to her on the shore.

"This isn't funny, Rick!"

There came no response, save the snap of more branches.

"That's it, mister," she muttered, heading back toward the shore. "When I get there I'm putting my clothes on. The only rocks you're getting off are whatever you can skip across the lake."

Angry with him for being a jerk, she stepped onto dry land, nearly slipping on the rocks before catching her balance. She kept her eyes peeled for him as she made her way back – expecting him to jump out and try to scare her. No way was she going to give him the satisfaction of hearing her scream while she...

That thought along with all others scattered to the wind as Sandra walked back into the clearing where they'd recently made love. She may as well have stepped into a completely different world, though.

There was no sign of Aldrick. Not only that, but the blanket they'd put down had been torn to shreds. She could just barely make out deep indentations in the remnants of the fabric, as if something heavy had trampled it first.

Worse, the pile of clothes they'd left after getting

undressed had been scattered. If this was indeed some sort of sick joke on Aldrick's part, it had gone way too far.

"That's it," she stammered, her resolve starting to break. "Come out now or ... or we're through."

There, she'd said it. It was a bluff, but one she hoped he wouldn't call, assuming he was okay and not in actual danger. If she was wrong, though, and something had happened to him while she'd been...

A response finally reached her ears, not in the form of his voice but from a heavy snort off to the side. She turned that way just as another answered from the opposite end of the clearing.

There was no way he could've circled her so quickly, not unless he'd managed to teleport like they did in that *Star Trek* show he liked to talk about.

But that either meant they weren't as alone out there as she'd thought or...

A bellowing roar sounded from close by, echoing through the trees. It was answered by others, equally close and every bit as terrifying.

All the strength went out of Sandra's legs and she collapsed to the ground, horrified out of her mind – yet still trying to rationalize that this had to be some sort of prank on Aldrick's part.

She clung to that delusion right up to the point when several massive shapes burst from the surrounding bushes and bore down on her – trampling the life from her body before she even had a chance to finish screaming.

9

"Why do I have to keep my eyes closed, Koolaid?"

"Because it's a surprise," Martin replied from somewhere up front, "and because I said so. Now get your ass moving, bitch. Time is money when you're the top flavor in town."

"Awe, that's so sweet of you to say, honey-bun," Charlene replied, gingerly stepping forward as directed.

"That's me, the sweetest drink in the fridge, baby. Now hurry your ass up and don't trip over your own two feet. No damaging my merchandise."

Eyes still closed, Charlene took a step and then proceeded to trip over something anyway, a divot in the pavement from the feel of it. Trying her best to keep her eyes shut, lest she disappoint Martin, she pitched forward – at least until she was stopped by his strong arms saving her from a painful tumble.

"Aww, you're my hero," she said, grinning from ear to ear.

"I'm gonna be the foot up your ass if you keep fucking

around." He steadied her back on her feet then turned her to the right a little bit. "Now open your eyes and take a look. Ta-da!"

She did as told, only to find herself staring at a large boarded up structure set behind a locked chain link fence covered in warning signs – all of them clearly legible in the glow of the rising sun. "It's ... a building."

"Fuck yeah it is," he replied proudly.

"An old grey building."

"All the better. Nobody will suspect a thing."

"Suspect a thing about what, Koolaid?"

"Ain't it obvious?"

He stood there looking at her expectantly, as if the answer should've immediately popped into her head. For the life of her, though, she had no idea what he was talking about.

Far as she could tell it was just a dumb old building.

However, she forced herself to focus, desperately hoping not to disappoint him. Because the truth was she'd been in love with Martin Belanger since the moment he'd taken her under his wing.

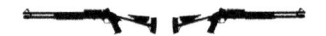

Prior to meeting Martin, Myrtle Cranford's life had been an absolute shambles. She'd dropped out of school at a young age. Her father was a hopeless drunk, unable to hold down a job, so she'd been forced to do what she could to keep a roof over their heads. It had been no good, though. As she got older, her father's drunken rants had grown ever more angry, as if he blamed her for his problems. Finally, she'd had enough and, at the encouragement of her friends, ran away from home.

Things hadn't improved much from there. With few

skills to her name other than wiping whiskey-scented puke off the floor and cabinets, she'd turned to selling her body. Myrtle wasn't like those other girls in the business, though, with their long legs, thick eyelashes, and tits to the moon. She was a plain Jane at best, lacking the self-esteem to think she could ever do better for herself.

Then she met Koolaid. At that point, he'd already had two flavors working for him, Shonda and Cherry, both of them glamorous whores, the kind you expected to find in a classy city like Nashville. So she was surprised beyond belief when he'd invited her to join his stable of bitches. From that moment on, it was as if she'd been born anew.

Fitting then, that the first thing he'd done was to have her change her name.

"Nobody wants to fuck a bitch named Myrtle," he'd said. "That's like cornholing your own grandma."

That had been the end of Myrtle Cranford and the beginning of the glamorous lady of the night named Charlene.

It kept getting better from there. Overnight, she'd gone from wearing thrift store threads to fine dresses, as if she was Cinderella herself. She began servicing more clients – but in motel rooms with actual beds instead of back alleys and park benches. No longer did she have to worry about rats sniffing her ass while some John finished in her.

It was like a dream come true.

Then there was Martin himself. Yeah, he yelled a lot, but that was to be expected. After all, he was a smart entrepreneur trying to manage his business. The truth was, though, yelling aside, he treated her far better than any man she'd known up until that point.

And then came the moment that had truly cemented her feelings for him. Following a confrontation with Big

Daddy, he'd asked her to come with him as he hurried to leave the city.

Well, okay, it wasn't an ask so much as him hustling her onto a bus, but still. He could have packed up and split without saying a word to her.

He hadn't, though, and now there she was, in a new town with him, starting fresh and doing her best to make him proud.

Finally, after several long moments in which it hopefully became obvious she had no idea what he was talking about, Martin rolled his eyes and said, "You're looking at the site of the new Koolaid Chalet! Ain't it great?"

"Chalet? Isn't that like some kind of fancy wine?"

He shook his head. "I swear to God, Lene, some days you make my head hurt."

"I have some aspirin in my bag if you..."

"Trust me, that ain't gonna solve my headache. But maybe this will." He turned once more toward the abandoned building. "We're going to use this dump as our new love motel. Johns check in, but their cash doesn't check out."

Martin stepped toward the gate, unslinging the bag hanging off his shoulder and pulling a pair of bolt cutters from it. He then proceeded to snip the lock holding the rusty old gate shut.

"I don't think that's legal, Koolaid," Charlene pointed out.

"Of course it ain't legal. Neither is sucking dicks for a dollar. But if you're gonna break one law, might as well break them all."

"I suppose."

"Think about it real hard, baby. There's only two choices around here for any man looking for a quick lay. You got that fleabag motel over on Millers Crossing and the Howard Johnson's down near the highway off-ramp. And both have the same two problems."

"No vacancy?"

Martin buried his face in his hand for a moment, rubbing his eyes. "And this is why I do the heavy lifting. No, you dumb broad. They're both in a small town full of shit-kickers who can't keep their mouths shut. More importantly, both cost moolah. That's bread that's going in someone's pocket other than mine."

Charlene nodded, finally beginning to understand what he was talking about. "So you want us to get into the motel business?"

"Not quite. What we're gonna do is break in and fix it up a bit. Grab some hay bales from Uncle Bert's barn, maybe an old mattress from the dump, shit like that. Nothing fancy. It ain't gonna be free, but it'll be cheap enough for the tightwads. Think about it. An extra ten bucks buys them a quiet place to make the beast with two backs, all without having some nosy busybody seeing them come and go. That's pure profit in my pocket, baby."

Charlene clapped her hands together with glee. *He really is a genius.* "I think it's brilliant, Martin! Um, I mean Koolaid."

"You're damned straight it is. And it's all ours. Or at least it will be as soon as we jimmy the lock."

He started toward it but she hesitated for a moment before falling in line. "Wait. Won't the owners notice if we start fixing it up?"

He had an answer for her, though, once again proving his smarts. "Nope. You're looking at the former home of the Piedmont Creek Army Research Facility. God, what a fucking mouthful. Like, couldn't they have come up with something better?"

"You mean the government owns it? I don't know, Koolaid."

"Relax. Your Koolaid man knows what he's doing. This place has been shuttered for going on twenty years now. I sincerely doubt *the man* is suddenly going to give a shit just because we're borrowing it for a bit."

"If you're sure."

"Of course I'm sure."

"Then ... I think it's great."

"Glad to hear it, because after we find a way in I need you to start cleaning shit while I head back. It's bound to be a fucking mess after all this time."

"You're leaving me here?"

"Got no choice, babe. I have to go help Uncle Bert shovel pig slop before he crawls up my ass about it."

"But, you want me to go in there ... alone?"

"You won't be alone," he replied. "Hell, I'm sure there's plenty of spooks in there just waiting for a fine young piece to shake her ass the right way."

Her eyes opened wide at the thought of it being haunted. "Koolaid!"

"Oh for Christ's sake, relax. I was kidding. Nobody's been in there for twenty years, save maybe kids looking to get high or laid – and those fuckers are gonna have to find a new spot for both because the Koolaid Chalet is getting ready to open for business. Now run back to the truck and grab a broom. We've got work to do."

10

Bert hadn't known what to expect when he got to Scooter's place, but what he found waiting for him was far worse than he could have ever guessed.

Scooter had given him a frantic call in the early hours of the morning, just after Bert had awoken, to tell him what had happened the night before. His friend had sounded both harried and exhausted over the phone, so Bert had wasted no time hopping in the Dodge to head over and see what all the fuss was about – albeit not before waking Martin up and giving him a list of chores he expected to be completed before day's end.

The drive over had given him a chance to digest what he'd been told, leading him to the conclusion that Gertie was the only logical answer. The old gal had likely made her way to the McNeil place, looking for fresh hay and a place to sleep before getting spooked and running off again. Scooter's mind had probably been playing tricks on him, tired as he'd been, making him think he'd seen something he hadn't.

Now, standing there looking at the carnage within Irma McNeil's pig pen, he was forced to reconsider. Gertie was a big girl, twelve-hundred pounds if she weighed an ounce. There was no doubt she could've caused the damage to the wooden fencing had she been in a mind to. But why would she? She was normally as sweet-tempered as Milo and twice as docile.

Then there was what had happened to the pigs inside. No way had a simple dairy cow been responsible for this bloodbath. Bert would've bet every red cent he owned on that.

"How's Irma holding up?" he asked his friend as they stood there surveying the scene of the slaughter.

"She's beside herself but she'll be okay," Scooter said. "She's a tough one. Understands that life sometimes kicks you in the balls and there ain't much you can do about it save brace for the next hit."

"Ain't that the truth. What about Mikey?"

"In town, picking up some supplies his mom ordered. Told him there was a bear in the area so to make sure to keep his bike to the main roads. No shortcuts, otherwise I'd tan his hide."

"Sure that was a good idea?"

"He's not alone. Met one of his friends at the end of the drive. They'll be okay."

"Still, if there's a bear around..."

"That's just what I told him. But weren't no bear did this."

"Come on, Scoot, what else could it have been?"

"I don't know. You tell me."

Bert looked once more at the pig pen turned slaughterhouse. The animals inside had been literally torn apart. There wasn't much else in these woods that could've done that. A mountain lion maybe but they weren't native to the area. And why would a lion have killed the entire herd instead of simply dragging one off to eat? No. That didn't make sense. "Wild dogs maybe?"

Scooter shook his head. "I caught a glimpse of it. Was only the one and it weren't no dog either. Far too big. Made a Saint Bernard look like one of them Toy Poodles. I swear to God, the damned thing must've been the size of a grizzly."

Before Bert could say anything, Scooter held up a hand. "No, I ain't saying that's the case either. Come with me and look at this."

His friend led him to a patch of mud about thirty feet from the pen. He knelt and pointed at something there. The ground had been pretty well disturbed by something large passing through, but Bert was able to make out a few fairly clear tracks nonetheless. He stared at them, trying to make sense of what his subconscious was telling him versus what he knew to be true.

"Tell me those aren't swine prints," Scooter said.

Bert shook his head, opened his mouth, but then second-guessed what he wanted to say. "They're way too big. The ground around the prints must've settled. Gotta be an elk or..."

"You saying some elk had a serious mad-on for my pigs?"

"A bull maybe?" He glanced back at the destroyed pen. "Would have to be a real ornery son of a bitch, though."

Scooter shrugged. "Anybody we know missing one?"

"Not that I've heard."

"Me neither."

Bert looked at the prints once again then shook his head. "Well, you tell me what sounds more realistic, an angry bull or a boar the size of a Buick?"

"When you put it that way..." Scooter put his hand

beneath his chin and nodded. "That still leaves something big and mean out there. And me with a pen full of slaughtered swine that need to be buried before every coyote in the county converges on this place like one of them all-you-can-eat buffets."

"Then I suggest we grab a couple of shovels and get to work."

"I appreciate it, Bert."

"What are friends for?" he replied as the two men turned and headed back to begin the grisly work ahead of them.

Byron Hoffsteader was a man on a mission. He knew he needed to go down to the sheriff's department to file a report on his missing men, but was also more than aware of how these things worked in small towns. He almost certainly stood to lose half the morning telling the desk sergeant the same damned thing over and over, as if he were some kind of suspect. In the meantime, that would be more lost work he'd have to contend with.

So, expecting the worst, he'd set out early and dragged a member of the survey team along with him, a man named Ted … Something-or-other. There was a patch of land that needed to be cleared today and he aimed to make sure his men didn't have any excuses to slack off.

The plan was to kill two birds with one stone. He would try to convince the local constabulary to form a search party – preferably at taxpayer expense – to look for his missing men as well as assuage the fears of the work crew. Before that could happen, though, he intended to give Ted crystal clear instructions, the kind that even a moron could follow, as to what needed to be done.

They drove past the existing construction site – a complex of luxury townhouses in various stages of development. At the nearest end, the foundations had been laid and work on the frames was well underway. As they continued onward, though, it was like time went in reverse – the finished work became less advanced until, at the far end, it was just a cleared lot peppered with large mounds of dirt. Beyond that point lay dense forest – for now anyway. By tomorrow it would be another slab of barren land waiting for the team to start excavating.

But first he needed to examine the markers that had already been put down to make sure nothing had been disturbed – either by the wildlife or any asshole hippies seeking to make his life more difficult than it already was.

Afterward, he could deal with his missing foreman.

It was plain as the nose on his face that Reg Murphy's disappearance was at worst a stupid accident. Why the men refused to understand that and instead chose to act like scared school girls he couldn't begin to understand.

No. That was a lie and he knew it. Byron had read Aldous Huxley's *Brave New World* years back. The book had struck a chord deep inside him – the idea that a future society could engineer people to fill specific needs. Those of greater intelligence were meant to lead, while the ditch diggers were destined to dig ditches. Byron understood it was an allegory for the human condition, if a particularly apt one. He personally identified with the Alphas from the story, seeing himself as one, meaning he was better prepared to accept rational logic. His work crew, on the other hand, were all Gammas. They simply lacked the capacity to see what he could. So it was up to him to make them understand, even if it meant threatening to dock their pay.

They had to be kept in line. It was for their own good.

More importantly, it was good for his bottom line, which ultimately was what he cared about.

"Park here," he commanded the other man, refusing to acknowledge him by his first name. After all, the last thing one wanted was to become familiar with the Gammas of the world, lest they fall under the delusion they were equals.

Nope. Best to keep folks in their proper place. Besides which, a little fear could go a long way. That was more Machiavelli than *Brave New World*, but that was fine as far as Byron was concerned.

They got out of the truck and Ted grabbed his equipment from the bed. Byron knew he was mostly there to supervise the other man, but had a feeling the margin of error would be greatly reduced by his presence alone.

"There's the first marker," Ted said, pointing toward the tree line. "Let's start with that and..."

"No," Byron interrupted. "We'll head in and start at the far end, work our way out."

"But that'll put the sun in our eyes."

"So? There's these things called sunglasses. Or has that innovation not made it to these parts yet?"

The pecking order thus established, Byron led the way. He wasn't particularly comfortable in the woods, but wasn't about to show it in front of a subordinate.

Though he strode confidently, he silently counted his steps. The last thing he wanted was to overshoot a marker and have to be corrected. Ted Something-or-other needed to know he was dealing with a man who wasn't easily duped. Nothing else was...

Byron stopped as the breeze shifted, bringing with it the most godawful stench imaginable.

"What the hell?" Ted cried from a few steps behind him.

Fighting the urge to retch, Byron considered things. He knew that stagnant water from the nearby bog could stink to high hell, especially on a hot day. But the sun was just barely up. Besides, that tended to be more like a ripe fart that stuck around long past its welcome. This reek was different. It was the odor of rotting flesh. It was the stench of death.

Knowing he already had a full day ahead of him, but curious nevertheless, he turned in the direction where it seemed to be thickest. "Come on."

"Are you sure, Mr...?"

"Did I stutter? Let's move. Ándale!"

They didn't have to go far. No more than a couple dozen paces later a swarm of flies took flight as they approached something upon the ground. Whatever it was, it was big. It was also dead as fuck, torn to pieces with rotting guts and offal strewn about. No wonder it was stinking up the place.

"What in the Sam Hill?"

Ted caught up to him a moment later, his hand over his mouth – no doubt futilely trying to block the worst of it.

The few pieces of skin that remained on the corpse were discolored with dried blood, making it impossible to tell what color it had been. But then Byron spied the beast's heavy head – its empty eye sockets staring sightlessly back at him.

"Is that a cow?"

"I ... I think so, sir."

"What the hell happened to it?"

"I don't know, but it looks like something's been at it."

"No shit, Sherlock. Probably a lot of somethings." Byron nodded, more to himself than anything as an image of the animal's probable fate began to form in his mind.

"Look at the way those bones are broken," Ted said. "Whatever did this must've..."

"Nonsense. Probably broke its leg in a ditch and died, nothing more. I bet every scavenger in these godforsaken woods has been out here to get a piece."

"You're probably right, sir. Still, we should let the sheriff know. Maybe one of the farms reported a missing..."

"You'll do no such thing," Byron snapped. "What you're going to do is go to the truck, grab a shovel from the back, then come back here and bury this goddamned thing. I'm meeting with the sheriff later on. I'll tell him about this. In the meantime, there's work to be done and I'll be damned if I'm going to lose a single hour of daylight because some shit-kicker was too stupid to close his barn doors. Now get moving. Time is money."

11

Deputy Sheriff Wilbur McCoy couldn't remember a time when he had liked his job less than that particular summer.

Under normal circumstances, he would have told anyone who listened that he loved what he did. He was on a first name basis with almost everyone in town, got his coffee for free down at Kelly's, and was being groomed to take the top spot in three years when Sheriff Heller planned to retire.

Crime, real crime anyway, was almost a non-event in the shared municipality his office served. Usually the worst they had to deal with was petty vandalism by the local teens. Other than that, his job mostly entailed writing parking tickets and letting the local booze hounds sleep it off in the drunk tank.

Best of all was that his job commanded respect, something that had been in short supply for him and his crew back in high school. They hadn't been jocks and he sure as heck wasn't an A-plus student, but now he had a career he enjoyed. The fact that nobody gave him any lip when he showed up on the scene was just icing on the cake.

Or at least that *had* been the case. Now it seemed he had twin devils chasing his heels. First was the blasted heat wave that had been hammering the area relentlessly. Wells were running dry and farm animals were dying left and right, so of course people were coming to him with their problems, as if he could simply perform a rain dance and fix all their woes.

Then there was that new construction going on at the southern tip of the Bluff. It was providing men with much needed jobs which in turn was helping the local economy, but it brought its fair share of headaches too.

For starters, it didn't help that the town aldermen were up his ass about zoning crap, because god-forbid their palms go five minutes without being greased. More importantly, weekend rabble-rousing had been on an upswing and now there were even rumblings about prostitution – as if their cozy little neck of the woods was turning into goddamned New York City.

On top of it all, there were rumors of some out-of-town workers having gotten lost in the marshlands. To date, nobody had stepped forward to file an official report on it, but that was apparently about to change judging by the blowhard sitting across the desk from him.

Wilbur looked at the sheet of paper still set in the typewriter before him. "So let's go over this again, Mr. Hoffsteader. You're the owner of…"

"Hoffsteader Contruction LTD," the man said proudly, as if he thought it should be displayed in giant neon lights. "We own the contract for the townhouse development on the south side of town, next to where the new shopping center will…"

"I'm aware of it," Wilbur interrupted. "And you say

that three of your men, Reginald Murphy, Grant Nickson, and Pablo Ramirez respectively, haven't been seen since they left to go on a routine survey check ... have I got this right, six days ago?"

"That's correct to the best of my knowledge, at least on those first two. You have to understand I didn't know the third man personally, Sergeant. All I can go by is the name listed in our staff ledger."

"It's Deputy."

"Sorry, *Deputy*."

Wilbur didn't like the way the man emphasized his title, as if it were a dirty word, but decided to mind his tongue. He was there to take his report, not judge him as the asshole he obviously was. "And yet you waited until now to come forward with this. Why?"

"I figured they'd turn up. It seemed a reasonable assumption."

"How do you figure?"

"It's happened before, part of the cost of doing business. Give a man a chance to goof off on company time and he will." He leaned in and lowered his voice to a conspiratorial whisper. "Especially when they're Irish. You know how they can be."

Wilbur narrowed his eyes. His grandfather had been a proud Irishman. The tough old bastard had never slacked a day in his life. Had anyone tried to tell him otherwise, especially a suited shit-heel like this clown, he'd have knocked their damned teeth out.

Pleasant as that little fantasy was, Wilbur had a job to do, and sometimes performing the duties of said job involved dealing with self-important pricks.

Six days. The asshole waited six days. In the big city that was probably nothing. Out in the woods, though, and especially the bogs neighboring Cooper's Bluff, that was far from promising. If someone were to up and disappear into that sort of country for nearly a week with no supplies, it wasn't even remotely reasonable, despite Hoffsteader's proclamations, to assume they'd simply walk back out – right as rain and with no idea what all the hullaballoo was about.

Though miracles did indeed happen, there was a far greater chance they'd end up sending what was left of those men to the coroner instead of the hospital.

If anything, Wilbur was tempted to talk to Sheriff Heller when he got in, to see if there was a way to charge this jackass with criminal negligence. Chances were, though, that Hoffsteader spent his cash the way a lot of blowhards like him did – on cheap suits, expensive women, and even pricier lawyers.

Instead, he continued his line of questioning. "And who did you say first noticed them missing?"

"I didn't. My secretary received a call from one of our heavy machine operators. His name escapes me, but I can ask her if you want. I've personally only been here since yesterday, to ensure the work continues of course."

Of course. "And the area where the men were last seen?"

"That would be the southwestern grid of the complex, the section they're clearing today."

"Wait. Did you say today?"

"Yes," Hoffsteader replied before quickly adding, "but there's nothing there. I was just out that way this morning with one of the survey team."

"You went out there with one of your crew *before* coming to see me?"

"I'm a busy man, Sergeant. My firm stands to lose thousands from any delay as I'm sure you can understand. But again, I assure you nothing was amiss."

"And you're absolutely certain of this?"

Hoffsteader paused for just a moment before shaking his head, something that didn't escape Wilbur's notice.

"Uh huh, and I take it you're trained in these matters?"

"Excuse me?" Hoffsteader replied.

"You say there was nothing out there. So I assume that means you know how to look for tracks or other signs that someone's been in the area. Signs that would be of importance to any investigation into the whereabouts of these missing men."

"I'm not sure I follow."

"Clues, Mr. Hoffsteader. We're talking potentially important information with regards to this case that your people are even now trampling all over as they proceed to clear the area."

"Now see here, Sergeant," the other man said, getting huffy, "I'll have you know…"

Thankfully, for Hoffsteader's sake anyway, before he could say something he might regret, the front door opened and in stepped two men Wilbur knew and respected – far more than the stuffed shirt he'd been speaking to anyway.

"Scooter, Bert," he said as way of greeting. "What brings you two into town? I don't suppose this is a social call."

"Fraid not, Wilbur." Bert replied. "There was an incident this morning, one you should probably know about."

"Oh?"

Scooter nodded. "Something's been at Irma's pigs. Something big. Tore up the whole damned drift."

That caught Wilbur's attention, distracting him just as he was about to order Hoffsteader to cease work until such time as either he or the Sheriff could get out there and take a look around.

Great. Just what he needed, yet another problem to add to the growing list. It wasn't likely to be something easily dismissible either. Both Bert and Scooter were known to be level-headed, so either they were finally cracking from the heat or something was genuinely up.

Neither the Sheriff nor Ellie were in yet and Hendricks was out on a call, which left no one else to take their statements. So for now he gestured the two men toward the station's *waiting room* – a haphazard collection of folding chairs. "Take a seat, fellas. I'll be with you both in a sec, just as soon as I'm finished with..."

"Hold on," Hoffsteader interrupted. "Did you say something killed your pigs?"

Scooter nodded. "Yep. Knocked down the side of the pen to get at them and then slaughtered the whole bunch."

"Really? Any idea what did it?"

"Hell if I know. Something mean and hungry I'd reckon."

Wilbur didn't consider himself to be a world-class detective but he'd picked up certain instincts on the job. He couldn't help but notice how Hoffsteader had perked up at the mention of Scooter's pigs – far more so than he'd done while talking about his missing men. "Anything you'd like to add to your report, Mr. Hoffsteader?"

"Who me?" he asked, suddenly wide-eyed. "No. Why would there be?"

"I don't know. Figured I'd ask is all. The more information I have, the better I can help you."

"It's nothing," the man backpedaled. "Just interested is all. One animal lover to another. So ... is there anything else you need from me?"

Wilbur raised an eyebrow. He would've bet good money the man was full of shit up to his eyeballs. Something about what Scooter had been saying had riled him up. But why?

For the life of him, he couldn't see the connection – unless the bloated fool was implying that his men had gone feral over the course of a few days and had decided to take it out on some pigs rather than ring the doorbell and ask for help. Wilbur had seen men do some crazy things, especially when the weather got hot like it had been, but that seemed a stretch even for him.

Guess the heat's finally getting to me too.

"That'll be all for now, Mr. Hoffsteader," he finally said. "Sit tight. We'll be in touch if we need to discuss this matter further."

12

Fourteen year old Jack Heller had stars in his eyes as he kept watch in the raised hunting blind on his family's property – his well-used .30-30 Winchester in his hands.

He'd gone over to the McNeil place this morning to meet his friend Mike so they could ride into town together. Instead, Mike's father had walked his son to the end of their drive. As Jack had sat there on his Schwinn listening, Mr. McNeil told them both of how a bear had gotten to his hogs the night before. He'd finished by warning them to stay together and be careful.

Their trip to town and back had been uneventful, but Jack's mind had been stuck in overdrive ever since. After all, he could relate.

Two years prior, a bobcat had gotten into their coop and torn their chickens to shreds. That was the year his father Alan Heller, the county sheriff, had taught him how to hunt in the woods that bordered their property. Not long after, he'd bought Jack the rifle he now held – tasking his son with keeping his eyes open for any signs that predators were sniffing about.

It was a duty that Jack had taken seriously, not wishing to disappoint his father.

Since that day, he'd bagged his fair share of foxes, a couple coyotes, and even a bobcat or two – presenting each to his parents as if he'd just returned from safari.

So, upon hearing there might be a bear in the area, one that had developed a taste for livestock no less, his ears had perked up. If he could take out such a beast, not only would he earn his parents' praise but Mike's dad might even see fit to throwing a reward his way.

That would be the icing on the cake, especially since he'd started noticing girls in the last year or so, Sandy Claverman in particular. With a little spending cash in his pocket, he envisioned himself being bold enough to ask her to a matinee.

Going to the movies with Mike was a blast, but thoughts of Sandy made him weak in the knees. Heck, maybe she'd even give him a hand job while they were out together. He wasn't entirely sure what that was, but he'd overheard some of the high school jocks talking about it. Getting one was supposedly a true sign that a girl really liked you.

He could see it in his head plain as day – dragging the dead bruin home and presenting it to his father. "*Got me a bear, Pa. Now I could use a hand job.*"

Jack smiled, thinking how sweet that would be. It was just like the TV said – *the thrill of victory*.

But first he needed to stop daydreaming and pay attention. He'd baited his trap and was patiently waiting, but that wouldn't mean much if he got caught with his head in the clouds.

The blind, built by him and his father, was situated

out in their back lot. Just ahead, the tree line formed a deep concave indent, effectively creating a sort of false clearing surrounded by trees on three sides – one that offered him a near perfect view inside.

He'd strung up some deer entrails from a tree branch hanging over the interior – raising them far enough off the ground so that any predator, even a large one, would have to take their time reaching it, ensuring he could line up an easy kill shot.

It was a strategy that had paid off before. An easy meal was a hard thing to pass up for a hungry beast.

There wasn't much of a breeze to speak of, but the heat of the afternoon was helping ensure the meat's odor was strong and ripe – not the sort of thing he appreciated having to smell but it was almost certainly ringing the dinner bell for any nearby predators.

"Come on, you son of a bitch," he whispered, before turning to make sure nobody was around to hear him.

That was stupid of course. His mother was in the house preparing dinner and his dad was at work. Nonetheless, some habits were hard to break. His folks were mostly good people, but they had their lines in the sand. Cussing and lying were two of them. It wouldn't matter if he shot and killed a hundred bears, the wrong word would still end with him being whupped with the stock of his own rifle.

As his father put it, he had to deal with enough foul-mouthed *idjits* at work during the day. He had no interest in hearing that sort of thing at home too.

Jack didn't think any less of them for this. For the most part they were cool. Besides, he knew he had it good, unlike, say, Billy Higgins whose father spent more nights in the drunk tank than home in his own bed. All the same, it was sometimes a breath of fresh air to be outside their earshot and able to cut loose.

Some situations just couldn't be properly expressed by a simple, "darn it all." Hunting a bear for instance. That was a *fuck yeah* moment if ever there was one.

Likewise with the weather. There was no doubt the last couple of weeks had been beyond just hot. It had been *fucking hot as balls*.

Speaking of which, Jack took a break from his vigil to wipe the sweat from his brow and take a sip from the lukewarm bottle of Orange Crush at his side. It was uncomfortably hot inside the blind, making it tempting to strip down to his skivvies.

He wasn't about to, though. Noticing girls had come with a downside – discovering his own self-consciousness. Gone were the days when he'd blissfully walk around the house in front of his mom with nothing but his underwear on. He was now growing hair in strange places and his pecker would sometimes stick out like a...

Jack perked up at a sound coming from the direction of the woods, instantly dismissing those thoughts. He narrowed his eyes, resting the stock of the rifle against his shoulder as he peered down the sight.

He could see branches and bushes swaying as something made its way forward. Then he caught a glimpse of brown fur. It was here. His trap had worked!

Resisting the impulse to simply open fire, he waited. He still couldn't see much, obscured by foliage as the creature was, but he could tell it was big – a real whopper.

Forget a reward by Mike's dad. This was the sort of kill that could land him a picture on the front page of the Piedmont Gazette.

The beast stayed just out of sight for what seemed like

a maddeningly long time, enough for Jack's mind to start working.

Brown fur?

No wonder the damned thing was so large. This wasn't merely some black bear who'd wandered into the neighborhood. It was a grizzly. Had to be. Jack had never heard of one in those parts, but that didn't mean they weren't there.

All at once his rifle felt very small in his hands. He'd learned about grizzlies in school. They were one of the top carnivores in North America, renowned for their size, strength, and aggression. He took his eye off the target long enough to consider the blind around him. It was a simple wooden box, raised maybe three feet off the ground on two-by-fours.

If he wasn't able to fell this thing on his first shot and it managed to charge him, he doubted the thin walls would stop it for long.

What then?

Jack briefly considered hunkering down and hiding. Let the bear have its meal and be off. But then what would he tell his father? He could say he took the shot and missed, but his dad was an experienced cop. He'd smell the lie a mile away and probably tan Jack's hide for it. Worse, he would be disappointed – likely thinking he'd raised a coward.

No fucking way, Jack thought.

Yeah, it was definitely a word for moments like this.

He forced himself to remain steady as the animal began to move again. His rifle had never failed him. He needed to trust in it and himself.

He also needed to be ready to fire again and quickly, just in case.

Jack didn't wish to disappoint his father, but that didn't mean he was going to be stupid about it.

He let out a breath as the bushes parted and the beast finally showed itself.

That's no bear. It's just ... a stupid pig.

Jack almost laughed despite himself. He'd gotten himself all worked up over nothing more than a wild boar sniffing around the...

That thought ground to a halt as he realized the ridiculousness of it. Boar or not, it was massive – far larger than any pig he'd ever seen. Even as he watched it, he found himself thinking this had to be one of those mirages they'd learned about in science class. No way could this thing be real.

However, there was no doubting what was right there in front of him. The meat he'd left hanging was strung up at about chest level, making it roughly four feet off the ground. Yet the beast barely had to raise its head to poke at it. At the top of its humped back, it was easily his father's height if not taller. Two vicious tusks rose from either side of its broad head – one as long as his forearm, the other short and jagged as if it had been broken off in a fight.

That was almost enough to unhinge his mind right there. What on Earth could possibly pick a fight with such a creature?

The boar snuffled as it nosed the meat, no doubt showing interest. Though they didn't raise pigs, he'd been around them enough to know they ate pretty much anything they could get. And this thing, it had to have a monster of an appetite.

Appetite. Mike's dad had told them that a bear had gotten to his pigs but was it possible he'd been wrong?

That served to remind him of why he was out there in

the first place. A bear was a heck of a prize to take down, but this ungodly beast...

Not only was its sheer size bound to gain him some notoriety, but his mother would surely appreciate filling their freezer with meat once this thing was properly butchered.

He took aim, trying to line up a shot while silently hoping the beast's hide wasn't thick enough to keep a bullet from penetrating its heart.

It's skull might be, though, he realized as it shifted position, denying him a clean kill shot. He could try to put one through its eye but with it snuffling about the chances of a miss were too high. He needed it to move, just a little.

The hell with it. He opened his mouth and called out, "SOOIE!"

It was a pig call he'd heard Mike and others use. In truth, it probably meant nothing to the animal he was looking at but that didn't matter. He just needed to catch its attention enough for it to...

The beast lifted its head, turned its malevolent eyes his way, and let out a series of grunts. Finally, it shifted its body, giving Jack the angle he'd been hoping for. He tightened his finger on the trigger just as there came an answering grunt from ... off to his right.

What the hell?

He fired in the same instant he realized what this meant, throwing off his aim. The boar jerked as the bullet struck it's back, throwing out a squealing scream that was immediately answered from the same direction as a moment before.

Jack turned just in time to see the narrow window on the blind's side fill with the sight of something massive bearing down on him.

In the next second the entire structure was knocked off its perch and Jack was sent tumbling with it, trying his best to curl into a ball as the wooden blind came apart around him.

Moments later, he found himself face down in the mud, chunks of plywood atop him. Long seconds passed as he waited to die, certain he would be trampled or worse, but then all became quiet once again.

Jack pushed the boards off him and sat up, desperately looking for his gun in the debris, but he needn't have bothered. The clearing was once again empty. There was no sign of either beast.

The only indicator that anything was out of sorts were the destroyed pieces of the hunting blind all around him and the empty rope that was no longer holding any bait.

Jack was, of course, miraculously still there too – left to sit alone bewildered, frightened, and with no idea how he was going to explain this to his parents.

13

"Think Wilbur believed us?" Bert asked, lifting his glass and taking a sip.

After spending half the day beneath the hot sun burying what was left of Scooter's pigs and then having given a statement to the police, the cold beer was like ambrosia going down his throat.

He knew dinner would be on the table soon but figured he and Scooter had earned a pint down at the Dammed Beaver Pub.

Silly name aside, it was a relatively new bar in town – far nicer than Morty's Tavern, the local dive that had been a staple in Cooper's Bluff ever since right after the war.

"Even if he didn't, Sheriff Heller is good people," Scooter replied, taking a drink from his own glass. "The question is what are they gonna do about it?"

"I'd say the bigger question is *when*," Bert replied. "From the sound of things, a couple of workers are missing from that construction on the south side. I'm guessing the Sheriff is gonna give that one priority and get a search party organized."

"A fair bet. Hell, with any luck they'll find Gertie too while they're at it."

Bert nodded. "Can't say I would mind that."

Scooter turned toward him. "Planning on volunteering if Alan gives you a call?"

"I don't know. Maybe."

"Don't bullshit a bullshitter, Bert. I know the type of man you are. So I imagine you'll be out there doing your part, which I can't say is a bad thing. I just want you to promise me one thing. You'll keep your eyes peeled."

Bert moved to answer, but Scooter held up a hand.

"I don't mean for those missing fellas. That goes without saying. I'm talking about whatever got at Irma's pigs. It's still out there somewhere."

Bert considered this for a moment. "You don't think whatever got to your hogs went after those men too, do you?"

"I don't think nothing of the sort. I'm just saying to be careful."

Silence descended between the two for several long minutes, until Bert said, "Aw, hell. Maybe we'll all get lucky and it'll turn out those men just took off on account of their boss being an unpleasant son of a bitch."

Scooter let out a chuckle. "Good to see it weren't just me who noticed."

"Are you kidding? I thought ole Wilbur was about ready to shoot him like a stranger."

"Yup. If you ask me, there'd be less strife in this world if more folks got the ass-full of buckshot they deserved."

Bert let out a laugh and then clinked his glass against his friend's. "Ain't that the God's honest truth. Speaking of which, we should probably start heading back. It's getting dark and I want to make sure Martin did what he was supposed to today."

"We taking bets on that?"

"Nope."

"Just do me a favor then."

"I already said I'd be careful, Scoot."

"Not that. I just mean maybe don't let your nephew get mixed up with any search party that gets going. No offense to your kin, but that boy couldn't find his head if it was jammed up his ass."

Pig shit. Everything smells like pig shit!

Martin wiped his feet on the welcome mat and opened the door, feeling like ten miles of bad road and probably smelling twice as bad.

As if in testament to this, Milo lifted his head from where he'd been sleeping in the foyer, took one sniff of Martin, then let out a chuffing snort before trotting off into the living room.

Fuck you too, mutt.

Outside of his ill-fated encounter with Big Daddy, Martin couldn't remember a less pleasant day. His uncle had apparently taken it personally when he'd blown him off last time. As far as chores went, today's had been the equivalent of being bent over a chair and cornholed with a traffic cone. And the worst part was he knew he didn't have any choice but to get it all done. He and Charlene were living there rent free after all. It was the only situation amenable to his current finances, one he couldn't afford to mess up – at least not yet.

It wasn't like he could offset it much either by having Charlene help out around the house. For starters, she was busy setting up the Koolaid Chalet, a task that would likely keep her busy for some time to come. That old government building was a mess, having sat mostly vacant these past twenty years.

At least the bitch had better be busy.

As for the rest, sad to say but Charlene was mostly terrible at just about anything his aunt and uncle might find useful. She couldn't cook to save her life and Martin would've trusted the damned cows to milk themselves before letting her near them. About the only thing she could do was clean, but Aunt Lin didn't seem to need any help on that front considering she somehow kept the house spotless all on her own.

There were very few floors that Martin would have ever considered running his tongue over willingly, but he was willing to bet those in his aunt's home were about as safe to lick as any.

It was quite the feat, especially when one considered how much of the work on Bert's goddamned farm revolved around pig shit.

A part of him wanted to come as clean as the floors and tell them both of his plans to make some fast cash, maybe even offer to cut them in on it so long as they cut him some slack with the chores, but he knew that was a pipe dream. Bert wasn't a bad guy, but he was most definitely a square. The dude was like the Farmer's Almanac given life. There was that phrase *salt of the earth*. Well, if so, his uncle was the saltiest motherfucker on the planet. He doubted the man so much as jaywalked if he could help it.

Soon, Koolaid, soon. Just bide your time and then you can tell them all to take a long walk off a short pier.

That's what he kept telling himself. The sooner that Lene could get that army base cleaned up, the sooner she could be on her back doing what she did best – earning him some greenbacks. Once it was all up and running then he could focus his efforts on finding some new flavors to fill his stable with. That one might require a bit of work, though. The pickings were slim in Cooper's Bluff and neighboring Piedmont Creek. Shit, on average the local ladyfolk almost made the livestock seem preferable.

His Aunt Lin was probably the only looker in town, at least as far as older broads went. But hey, some dudes were into that. Hell, if he'd had her back in Nashville, he'd be driving a Caddy by now. Too bad he had about as much chance of talking her into the trade as he did of growing horns and udders.

Then there was the problem of Cooper's Bluff being a small town. The people all knew each other and as a result they talked – boy did they talk.

He and Charlene had the benefit of being outsiders and mostly uninterested in starting up conversations with the local shit-kickers. What he needed was more of the same, which meant reaching out past the county line and finding girls from elsewhere. Martin wasn't too worried about his sales pitch. There were plenty of chicks who loved to slobber a knob for free. All he had to do was identify them. Then, once he pointed out they could be making some bread from the deal, it was a comparably easy sell.

He still had some fly threads packed away in his room. The real problem was his wheels. Rolling up in his Uncle's pickup would make him look like some dumb hayseed who didn't know his dick from a corncob. If he were to approach a group of smokin' honeys in his uncle's Dodge, on the other hand, they'd see him in a whole different light. That was a car that demanded respect, especially with a young stud like himself behind the wheel. He would look like a man who knew how to bring home the bacon.

And that's what being Koolaid was all about.

The issue there was Bert treated the damned car as if it were his own child – probably better in fact because the car didn't have to shovel pig crap on a regular basis. Borrowing it had been a no-go from the start. As for simply taking it, well, Martin was willing to risk driving the pickup without asking – nobody seemed to give a shit about that – but he had a feeling being in Dutch with his uncle over the Challenger would shine a spotlight on him that he preferred not be there.

He considered this. His best bet might be to find an old junker - something cheap that still looked decent. Maybe he could offer one of the mechanics down at Leroy's Garage a deal – a discount on Charlene's services in exchange for a bit of elbow grease.

Yeah, he thought, grinning. *That could work*. Hell, that was how he did his best business – wheeling and dealing. That was the place where the *Koolaid Man* packed the most *punch*. "Oh yeah!"

"Bert, is that you?" his aunt asked from the kitchen.

Crap! "No, Auntie Lin. It's me."

"Oh, Martin. You're just in time to help set the table."

Of course I am.

"Is Charlene with you?"

"Charlene?" *Shit*! He'd been hoping to sneak in, scrub the muck off, then sneak out again to pick her up – preferably without anyone being the wiser.

Fuck it. It was only a few miles from the army base back to the farm and she had legs. It's not like a little exercise would kill her. "Um, no, Aunt Lin. She ... um ... got a gig cleaning houses. So, she'll probably be a little late."

"A job cleaning homes?" his aunt asked, stepping from the kitchen. "Oh that's wonderful news."

It will be, he thought, *soon as she gets that dump cleaned out so the good times can finally roll.*

Charlene wasn't sure what to do next. She'd spent the day cleaning as Koolaid had instructed – sweeping, dusting, and trying her best to organize things so that the place didn't look like a bomb had gone off in it.

In truth, the work had reminded her of living with her father. However, every time the darkness of her memories threatened to overwhelm her, she stopped to remind herself that was the past. Near the end, there had been no pleasing her father, but that was then. She fully intended to make Koolaid proud of her.

Unfortunately, it was getting late, meaning it had gotten too dark out to see what she was doing in the already dim confines of the building. With no light to see by, she was more liable to trip and break her neck than accomplish anything useful.

The building itself had already been kind of spooky during the day. Now it felt more like a haunted house, although she knew that was just her imagination playing tricks on her. No ghouls or ghosts had made their presence known as she'd worked. In fact, she'd encountered nothing more threatening than a couple of mice that had scampered away as soon as they saw her. The place was simply old and empty.

Well, not entirely empty. There were still desks, tables, and chairs strewn about, as well as some equipment she couldn't readily identify.

In one such desk she'd found a stack of papers – some

of which had official looking markings on them. They couldn't have been that important, though, as a quick glance seemed to indicate they were mostly about pigs. Tempting as it had been to stop and examine them in greater detail, she'd put them aside knowing full well what Koolaid would say.

"This ain't no library, bitch," she'd told herself, imitating his voice.

She found talking to herself like that kind of comforting – almost as if her sweetie had been right there cleaning alongside her.

Koolaid wasn't there, however. He'd had chores of his own to see to. His Uncle Bert could be a stick in the mud that way. The man simply didn't see how brilliant his nephew was. No, all he saw were his smelly pigs.

Maybe he should look at those moldy old papers then.

Speaking of the farm, Koolaid hadn't made any mention as to when he'd be back to pick her up – assuming he was coming back at all. She wasn't sure if she was supposed to wait for him or start walking back herself.

With the last of the daylight rapidly fading, it would soon be as gloomy outside as it was in the building. Not relishing a walk back to the farm in the dark, she'd waited for a bit.

After a while, though, when there was no sign of any cars heading toward the abandoned lot, she began to feel foolish.

"What are you standing around for, you dumb broad?" she finally said in his voice. "You got legs. Use them!"

"You're right, Koolaid," she told herself. "You always are."

Telling herself that there was nothing more to be scared of than there had been inside the building, Charlene opened the gate to the chain link fence and prepared for the long walk home.

Taking a few tentative steps, she realized it wasn't all that bad. It was a warm night, but not as hot as it had been during the day. Besides which, the stars were out.

What was the worst that could possibly happen?

14

"I was wrong, Koolaid. It's a whole lot scarier out here than it was back at the chalet."

"Of course you were wrong, ho. That's why I do the thinking for both of us."

"You're right, Koolaid. I'll listen to you next time. I promise."

"I highly doubt that," Charlene replied to herself, mimicking Koolaid's voice as best she could. "You just never seem to learn, girl."

Talking to herself had helped pass the time while cleaning up the abandoned base. Out there on the old country road, however, with no light to guide her way save the stars in the sky, it was the only thing keeping her from outright panicking.

For perhaps the first time, she truly realized the difference between nighttime in the city and out there in the sticks. Walking the streets of Nashville after sundown could be a perilous endeavor, no doubt about it. There was no shortage of drunks, punks, and lechers to be found, many of which were happy to harass a girl out by herself.

Scary as that could be, at least it was never completely dark. There were streetlights, neon signs, and more – all of them ensuring she could usually spot an obvious threat from a safe distance.

Right at that moment, though, some maniac could literally be five feet in front of her and she wouldn't know it until she bumped into him. The trees and tall grass on either side of the narrow road only served to make it worse, making her feel boxed in. It was like walking through a train tunnel, one in which spooks and boogeymen could be waiting at every turn.

Then there were the sounds. Back in Nashville, there was always the rumble of a car engine or the sound of raucous laughter – something to remind her that other people were never far away. Walking back to the farm, however, she might as well have been the last person on Earth. The chirp of crickets had followed her most of the way so far, not particularly comforting as Charlene wasn't a fan of bugs. But that wasn't the worst of it. In the distance could be heard all sorts of cries – howls, barks, and some she couldn't begin to identify. Every so often she'd hear a twig snap from somewhere nearby – which would cause her to hasten her steps as she silently hoped that it was just a bunny or maybe a deer. But not a mean deer, more like a cute *Bambi* sort of deer.

"That's just a stupid kiddie movie," Koolaid's voice reprimanded her.

"I know, Koolaid, but I always liked it. Except for that part with Bambi's mom. That was way too sad."

"Yeah, well, going to the movies costs bread, the type your lazy ass should be busy earning for me."

"I'm trying my best, Koolaid. I really am."

The little snippets of conversation would've likely sounded supremely odd to any eavesdroppers, but they kept her from bolting like a rabbit whenever her anxiety began to spike. She knew if she ran, it would likely result in nothing more than falling in a ditch and breaking her leg, leaving her helpless against whatever might be out there.

Charlene wasn't entirely sure what sorts of nasties lurked in the woods around Cooper's Bluff but there had to be plenty. Back in Nashville there had been stories about travelers getting lost out on the open road – the sort of thing the working girls would tell each other on slow nights when the Johns weren't biting.

Cherry had liked to tell them about an escaped psycho who'd broken out of prison only to replace one of his hands with a rusty meat hook. Then there was Irene, a whore who'd worked for Big Daddy. She claimed to have a cousin who'd gotten attacked by a lion that had been set loose by its former circus owners.

Charlene had thought it all good fun at the time, but suddenly neither tale seemed all that humorous. What if both were true, and there was not only an escaped lion stalking her right now but a hook-armed psycho as well?

"That's some crazy-ass shit even for you, Lene," Koolaid's voice told her, but this time it seemed to lack its former conviction.

"I-I hope so, Koolaid. I..."

She was interrupted by a low, deep rumble that seemed to reverberate through the trees – distant but still powerful.

Was that thunder?

She looked up and found the sky wasn't nearly as clear as it had been earlier, although she could still see the stars. There hadn't been so much as a light drizzle since she and Martin had arrived in town, so of course it would be just her luck to be stuck out there on the road when the weather finally changed.

Still, it had sounded far off. Probably nothing she needed to worry about anytime soon. Besides which, it couldn't be that much further to the farm. It felt like she'd been walking for hours, not that she had any way to tell. What she wouldn't have given right then to own one of those fancy watches with the radium dials.

Why isn't there any freaking traffic? Even a single car passing her by would've been a comfort, something to tell her she wasn't all alone. She knew there were people living in this stupid town. Heck, a few had even paid to diddle her. What, did they all go to bed the second the sun was down?

Or ... maybe they're smart enough to stay indoors because of the things in the woods.

"Now you're just being stupid."

She'd meant for the voice to be Koolaid's, but it had come out as her own instead. Either way, she hoped she was right.

Almost as if fate decided to answer her, from somewhere off to the left, well into the tree line, there suddenly came the sharp crack of branches snapping.

In an instant, everything else fell deathly quiet.

Where before there had been the constant chirp of insects, now there was just the frantic beating of her heart along with her footsteps, each one sounding like a gunshot in the oppressive silence.

That's it. Next time I'm wearing sneakers.

That was perhaps what worried her most of all. It was going to take some time to get the base up to Koolaid's high standards. That meant there would be more days spent cleaning and more nights where she'd have to pass through this damnable darkness to get back home. She'd already planned on pilfering some candles from the farm, to give her more light in the dark base. Now she wondered if maybe she should see if they had a flashlight that wouldn't be missed as well. Maybe a kitchen knife too, just to be safe.

She knew Bert had a gun rack but, tempting as it sounded, that might be pushing her luck.

"You'd shoot your own damned foot off anyway," Koolaid's voice said.

He was probably right. Her father had owned an old .38 Special, which she had stolen when she'd run away from home. But that had always been an empty threat to get assholes to back off, nothing more. Not once had she ever loaded it, much less had to use it for real.

Heck, she wouldn't have even known what sort of bullets to load it with.

Right at that moment, though, she would've risked it, especially as the silence was broken by what sounded like heavy grunting coming from that same section of woods to her left.

Oh God!

What was a missing toe or two compared to protecting herself from whatever was out there?

This time even Koolaid didn't speak up against it.

Back in Nashville, she'd had a regular named Zeb – a real porker of a man who owned a gas station just outside the Gulch. Whenever he'd fuck her, he would make a similar sound, grunting so hard that she feared he was about to have a stroke.

She was fairly certain, however, that Zeb wasn't out there in the dark with some whore – even if the deep squeal that followed was vaguely reminiscent of how he sounded whenever he'd shoot his load.

Charlene opened her mouth, meaning to ask who was

there. All that came out, though, was a protracted breath of air as her vocal cords refused to form the words.

She began to walk again, faster this time, telling herself it was nothing but a Bambi deer out there looking for its mom. Sadly, the ponderous crunch of twigs and dry grass told her that if *Bambi* was indeed out there, he'd gotten considerably larger since the end of the movie.

There came another rumble, probably more thunder, but she ignored it – freezing in place and locking her eyes on the spot where the sounds were coming from. She didn't want to know what was out there, but at the same time *needed* to know. The thought of being ambushed from behind – never seeing her attacker as she was torn to shreds – was somehow worse than facing this beast head on, whatever it was.

So she stood there, waiting for the end and praying that it would be quick.

"I'm sorry, Koolaid," she muttered. "I know you're gonna be disappointed in me, but..."

The rest was lost to a shrill scream that escaped her lips as the road abruptly lit up. She turned to find a pair of luminous eyeballs bearing down upon her, ones belonging to a beast of truly nightmare proportions.

It let out a screech that seemed to come straight from the gates of Hell itself as it closed in for the kill.

15

"Charlene?" Bert called from the open window of his pickup, breathing hard from the near heart attack he'd given himself after slamming on the brakes to bring the truck to a screeching halt in time.

She slowly looked up toward him, a mix of confusion and terror etched upon her face.

"What the hell are you doing in the middle of the road? Damn it, girl, I almost ran you over."

"Friend of yours?" Scooter asked from the passenger seat.

"Martin's girlfriend."

"Is that so? She do this often, wander the roads like a deer in the headlights?"

"Not that I've noticed."

Outside, Charlene continued to stare at them wide-eyed, until at last she seemed to realize who they were. "I... Uncle Bert?"

"In the flesh," he replied. "Well, don't just stand there. Get in. We'll give you a lift."

That got her moving as she practically bolted to the passenger side door.

"You might want to scoot over, Scoot."

"Gladly," he replied, making room for her on the wide bench seat.

Charlene climbed into the truck, looking like she was scared half to death. She slammed the door behind her, rolled up the window, and then pushed down the lock.

"Not sure you want to be doing that," Bert remarked. "The AC system in this heap ain't what it used to be."

"You okay, girl?" Scooter asked. "You look like you've seen a ghost."

"There-there's something out there," she stammered, pointing past him. "In the bushes."

"The bushes?" Bert turned that way, but of course it was too dark to see anything.

"Something big."

His curiosity piqued, Bert reached past his friend to the glove compartment and pulled out the flashlight he kept in there.

"Now's not the time to do anything foolish," Scooter warned, suddenly sounding nearly as tense as Charlene.

"It could be Gertie, Scoot."

"Could be, but probably ain't."

"I need to check. Relax, this'll only take a minute."

Bert cut the engine and stepped from the driver's side door. He then turned on the flashlight only for it to flicker weakly. *Guess it's time for new batteries.* He slapped it on the side a few times until the beam grew more steady, then aimed it toward the tree line on that side of the road.

He might as well have had his eyes shut for all the good it did. The vegetation was simply too thick to cut through with a cheap flashlight that was on the verge of dying.

"Gertie?" he called out, listening for a response.

The night air, however, was deathly quiet, not unlike how it had been when they'd searched the bog.

Or maybe not that quiet, as there came the faint rumble of thunder. It was pretty far off, though. *Probably just from heat lightning*. A pity since Lord knows they could've done with a good thunderstorm right about then, so long as it brought some rain.

"Bert."

He ignored his friend's call, stepping closer to that side of the road and doing his best to listen. *There*! He was certain he heard the sound of something moving around just past the tree line. It seemed maybe Charlene wasn't imagining things after all.

"Gertie, that you, girl? Come on. Got a nice bale of hay waiting back home for you. How's that sound?" Though he felt a bit foolish trying to negotiate with a cow, he was hoping the sound of his voice would draw her out.

This wasn't the first time she'd wandered off. Considering it had been a few days now, she was probably longing for a return to familiar pastures.

That seemed more likely as the sound of movement caught his ear. Something was definitely headed their way – something large judging from the sway of the brush ahead of him.

Bert aimed his flashlight in that direction, catching twin reflections of dull red for a brief moment.

"Come on, girl. Time to go home."

He once again caught sight of a reddish reflection from the flashlight – a set of eyes staring back at him. Then he nearly jumped out of his skin as the truck's horn began to blare like a siren in the night.

Bert turned back to find Scooter leaning hard on the wheel.

"What are you doing?" he cried, although he doubted he was heard over the commotion.

He spun toward the trees again, but whatever had been out there seemed to be gone now – likely scared off by the racket.

Great! Just great.

Finally, Scooter laid off the horn.

"What the hell, man?" Bert cried. "You scared her off."

"I scared off something, that's for sure, but it weren't Gertie," Scooter replied, his face appearing gaunt and ghoulish in the glow of the dashboard.

"The hell it wasn't..."

"That wasn't no cow, Bert. Color was all wrong."

"Color? Did you see something I didn't? Because all I saw was..."

"Its eyes," Scooter interrupted. "Think about it. Shine a flashlight a cow's way and they'll light up blue or green, same way a deer's will. Tell me, did you see any green out there other than those trees?"

Bert considered this in silence.

"I'll say it again. That was no cow."

Bert wasn't sure what to think. He'd never seen his friend this riled up before. Whatever had gotten to his pigs must've truly spooked him badly. That, or Charlene's state of near hysteria was somehow contagious.

Either way, it didn't seem like there was any further reason to dick around in the woods with nothing but a half-dead flashlight to see by.

He tried to convince himself that was all the truth there was to it as he climbed back into the driver's seat – barely even aware as he too rolled up the window and locked the door once it was closed.

16

Distant thunder rumbled – coming from a far off weather system that many in Cooper's Bluff heard with hopeful ears, praying that it signaled an end to the heatwave that had been relentlessly baking their crops and livestock.

It wasn't to be, at least not that night, but it served as a turning point in the drought which had hammered the hapless town for weeks on end. Once again clouds could be seen in the sky and for some that was enough.

A storm was indeed coming.

Not yet, but soon.

Deep in the woods, where much of the former wetlands had become nothing more than thick, unpleasant smelling mud, the thunder served only to agitate the beasts within – igniting a fuse that had been smoldering for some time.

The surrounding environment had once supported the herd, allowing them to exist mostly unnoticed by the local populace. But now both their numbers and sheer size had become too great a burden for the afflicted woodlands.

Food was becoming increasingly scarce as nearly everything – plants, animals, and the water supply – had been affected by the merciless heat.

It was an unfortunate confluence of events for the beasts – the third generation removed from the animals that had been let go by the well-meaning but short-sighted caretaker of the former Piedmont Creek Facility.

As he'd predicted, the majority of the pigs released that fateful day hadn't survived the winter. However, a small handful had made it through, thanks in no small part to that year's relatively mild temperatures. Those survivors in turn began to breed with the local boar population.

Through either chance, luck, or the whims of unhinged science, their offspring hadn't differed much from normal feral pigs in terms of size or behavior. The changes to their genome, inherited from the original Piedmont Creek subjects, were mostly recessive in that first generation.

Indeed the only witnesses who noticed anything odd about them were a handful of local hunters in search of bushmeat. They discovered that the taste of the butchered pork from some of their kills was surprisingly unpalatable, no matter how they cooked it. Rather than suspecting the ominous truth, however, the unpleasant flavor was mostly chalked up to external factors – disease, diet, or something in the environment.

All these men knew for certain was that the wild pigs in the woods surrounding Cooper's Bluff tasted terrible. As a result, they simply hunted elsewhere, allowing the mutant pigs to continue breeding unchecked.

The next generation were the first to start showing changes – displaying a marked increase in both muscle mass and accompanying appetite. They began to outpace their natural predators in terms of both size and ferocity.

Many of the creatures that hunted them for food found themselves preyed upon instead, a turn of events nature had never intended.

Fortunately for the nearby human populace, these were fertile years for the wetlands. Though far more ravenous than that first generation had ever been, the herd was able to find plenty of food to subsist on.

As for any that were spotted by hunters or hikers during that time, their increased size was mostly dismissed as tall tales told by drunk patrons at the local watering hole.

There would be no way of easily dismissing the current generation, though, at least not for anyone lucky enough to have survived an encounter with them – of which there were few. Whatever changes had been wrought to their ancestors within the labs of Piedmont Creek were now dominant. The largest among their number were nearly fifteen feet from snout to tail – some with tusks as big as a man's arm. Without question, they were now the apex predator of the woods they called home.

Once fully grown they were constantly on the lookout for food, their metabolisms on overdrive as their genetically altered cells demanded a never-ending intake of sustenance. As the heatwave had settled over Cooper's Bluff and the surrounding area, that search for nourishment became more and more desperate, until some eventually turned their hungry stomachs in a new direction.

Their noses told them that the farms and homesteads close to the woods were full of food – livestock, pets, and the two-legged things that had once hunted their forebears.

These boars, much like their normal brethren, weren't picky eaters. It didn't matter to them whether their diet consisted of grubs, plants, or warm flesh, so long as their endless hunger was temporarily sated.

As the boldest among the herd began to stalk this new prey, the rest slowly started to take notice – their instincts warring with their need to eat. Though the people of Cooper's Bluff weren't aware of this, up to that point the only thing saving them from a potential bloodbath were the pigs' natural wariness of mankind – a shared remembrance among their species.

An empty stomach was a difficult thing to ignore, though. As the drought continued to wreak havoc among the pigs' normal food sources, desperation took hold. Faced with starvation, aggression replaced caution.

For a time they continued to prowl the woods, looking for anyone or anything foolish enough to stray from the safety of their home or den. But with each passing day their hunger grew, until the monstrous feral hogs that haunted Cooper's Bluff became much like the thunder rumbling in the sky – a storm threatening to lash out at the unprepared town with unbridled fury.

17

"Holy shit! You don't say. Uh huh. Yeah. I got you. And you're sure about this? No, I'm not questioning you, Kev, it's just that I don't want to get anyone's hopes up for nothing. You understand, don'cha? Good. Well, thanks for the news, buddy. Talk to you soon."

Deputy Wilbur McCoy hung up the phone, still not believing his ears. It was about goddamned time they got some good news. Not a moment too soon either, being that the sheriff had been in a foul mood all morning. Something had crawled up the man's ass and died there, leaving him mumbling to himself and snapping at folks for the slightest reason.

The whole office was already walking on eggshells on account of the general bad mood currently gripping the town. Hell, he couldn't even enjoy his cup of joe down at Kelly's this morning without having to listen to Seamus bitch about being short-staffed because one of his girls failed to show.

"So file a missing persons report," he'd joked as he'd left a tip at the counter and walked out.

Anyway, maybe this would finally give people something to smile about, his boss first and foremost.

He got up and walked over to Alan's office, the door open as usual to let in what little air circulated through the small police station.

Wilbur gave a quick rap on the door frame to get his attention. "You up for some good news?"

"Maybe," Sheriff Alan Heller replied, looking up from the stack of forms on his desk, his square jaw seemingly set in a permanent scowl this morning. "But just to warn you, if you're here to brag about hitting it big at the track last weekend, you can save it."

Wilbur forced a laugh. "Nothing that good, I'm afraid."

"Well, out with it then. I ain't getting any younger here."

"You remember my buddy Kev? The one who works way up in Wichita."

"You talking about the weatherman?"

"Meteorologist, but yeah that's the one. Anyway, I was just on the horn with him. He called to give us a heads up. Said there's a storm headed this way."

"This some kind of joke?" Alan growled.

"No, sir. He was dead serious. Sounds like a big one, too. Said it's been slamming the Midwest like a steamroller, wind and lightning knocking out power left and right."

"What about rain?"

"Falling by the bucketload."

"When?" the sheriff asked, his face an unreadable mask.

"Two days give or take."

"Give or take?"

"Well, yeah. We ain't talking exact science here, but he said it's definitely coming."

Alan let out a grunt. "Okay, then I suppose you and Cassius should get to work pulling the barriers out of storage. Make sure they're ready to go. Call the depo too, see how they're doing on sandbags. You know how the south side tends to flood when it gets bad."

Wilbur shook his head. "You did hear what I said, right? We're finally getting some goddamned rain." Alan glowered at him, to which he quickly backpedaled. "Sorry. But I'm telling you rain's on the way."

Wilbur liked his boss, but the man's near puritanical rules when it came to language were sometimes hard to swallow. He swore it was like working for his own memaw. There were days when he half expected Alan to threaten to wash his mouth out with soap.

"I heard you," he said. "Guess that means we should get a move on looking for those missing men. I don't know about you, but I sure as heck don't want to be out on the bog while it's filling up like a rancid bathtub."

Wilbur was about to nod and go back to his desk, but he decided to pry instead. "Everything okay?"

"Why do you ask?" the older man replied.

"No reason. Just you've had a burr up your backside ever since you got in this morning. I understand the heat. It's eating at all of us, but seems to me like you got more on your mind."

Alan looked up from his desk, the scowl deepening on his face for a moment or two before he finally let out a breath. "Sorry. Didn't sleep well last night. It's Jack."

"He all right?"

"Yup. Right as ... rain. Well, maybe not his bottom. Had to tan his hide good last night. Marianne and me, you know we try to raise him right, and for the most part he's a good kid. Smart, resourceful, knows how to take care of himself. But I can't abide us being told lies right to our faces, and he knows it. So what does he do? He goes and does it anyway."

"Oh?"

Wilbur knew Jack, as everyone in the office did. Seemed like a decent kid. Liked to pal around with the McNeil boy. Mostly kept his nose clean, save for the occasional bit of mischief all teen boys got up to now and then.

"Yeah. I got that blind on my property. You know the one, right?"

"The one little Jackie uses to keep the coyotes away from your chickens?"

"That's it. Save for the fact Jack ain't so little anymore. But anyway, that's neither here nor there. I got home last night, tired as a dog. Didn't want to do nothing but eat my supper, watch Mary Tyler Moore with the missus, and then go to bed. But you know what I found instead?"

"Do tell."

The blind in pieces and Jack's rifle, the one I bought him, with a big old dent in the stock. So of course I asked him what in tarnation happened and he goes off on some cockamamie story about monsters in the woods."

"That right?" Wilbur replied with a chuckle. "Monsters."

"Yup. Can you believe it? And after the way Marianne and I raised him. Well, I gave him a chance to take it back. I know how boys can be with their tales, but he stuck with it. Kept insisting that something had knocked over the blind with him inside. Even tried to get me to come out back and look for footprints with him, as if I were born yesterday."

"Ah the imagination of youth."

"I hear you on that, but I ain't one of his schoolyard friends. When I ask for the truth, I expect to hear it and when I don't... Well, let's just say he's putting in extra chores today. Probably a good thing since I don't imagine he'll be sitting all too comfortably for a while. I swear, Wilbur. I don't know what it is with kids today."

"If you ask me, he got off easy. If I'd given my old man any lip like that, I'd have been picking my teeth off the floor. I wouldn't sweat it either way, Sheriff. Your boy ain't the first to spin a yarn, won't be the last. It's like a right of passage for kids to tick off their parents every which way they can. Heck, it's a wonder any of us made it to adulthood."

Alan nodded. "I suppose you're right. The fact that the human race has made it this far ain't nothing short of a miracle."

"Now you're talking."

"All-righty then. How about I make you a deal? I'll quit chewing everyone's head off if you and Ellie start calling around – see if we can pull together enough men for a search party to go find those missing workers. If their boss is as big a blowhard as you said he is, then we'd best get on this before that storm of yours decides to bite us in our behinds."

18

It was amazing to Bert how the light of day could bring with it a complete change of attitude – making the *demons* of the night before seem like nothing but smoke and mirrors.

There hadn't been much use discussing things over dinner after he'd finally gotten home. He could tell Charlene was still spooked out of her mind. All she'd wanted to do was take a hot bath and go to bed. Hell, even he couldn't deny that his eyes kept turning toward the window as he ate, wondering what might be lurking out there in the darkness beyond.

Now, with the breakfast table cleared and the sun already high in the somewhat cloudy sky, he felt foolish for allowing himself such thoughts. He'd lived in Cooper's Bluff all his life and had spent more than his fair share of time exploring it at night. While he knew to respect nature, he'd never seen anything that had given him cause to have the heebie-jeebies like that.

Had it just been Charlene, he doubted it would've affected him much. The girl was ... well, easily excitable.

But seeing Scooter in such a state as well had pushed him over the edge. His fear had proven highly contagious. Speaking of Scooter, he'd need to have a word with his friend at some point. He knew the death of his wife's pigs was having an effect on him, but he hadn't expected it to unnerve his buddy as much as it had. Surely, there was a rational explanation behind it – probably nothing more than a rogue bear in the area, despite Scoot's proclamations to the contrary.

For now, he wanted to make sure there were no repeats of last night. Charlene had gotten lucky, but not because of anything lurking in the woods. There were plenty of drivers about who wouldn't have had the sense to hit the brakes in time with her wandering down the middle of the road like she'd been.

"What in tarnation were you doing out there, girl?" he finally asked once he had a moment to confront his two boarders. He threw his nephew some side-eye. "And why did you let her walk home alone in the dark?"

"Don't be mad at Kool ... Martin," Charlene replied. She was still a little doe-eyed this morning, but seemed far more in control of her faculties. "My new ... job let me go early, so I figured I'd walk home. It was nice out and I thought I had plenty of time to make it back before it got dark."

Bert was pleasantly surprised to hear that. "You got a job? Congratulations. Doing what, if you don't mind me asking?"

"Hotel management," Charlene blurted, still wide-eyed.

"House cleaning," Martin replied simultaneously.

Bert glanced between the two of them. "Okay, so which is it?"

Martin narrowed his eyes Charlene's way for a

moment before saying, "A bit of both. She's cleaning rooms at a new boarding house that's opening up over at the Creek. But the lady in charge says she has a good shot of moving up to the front desk one day."

Charlene was quick to nod. "That's exactly it. Just like he said."

If Bert had a bullshit meter, it would've been buried in the red right at that moment. Something was up with these two. All the same, they were adults and he wasn't in the mood to play detective. Whatever their game was, he'd find out eventually. For now, he just wanted to make sure Charlene was safe.

"Fine, whatever. Next time, just give us a call first even if you have to use a payphone. Heck, you can reverse the charges. That's too long a walk along an empty stretch of road. Cooper's Bluff is a good place full of good people but even so, bad things can happen to a girl alone out there like that. Accidents, wild animals, that sort of thing. You hear me?"

She was once again quick to nod.

He then turned Martin's way. "And when she does call, I expect you to do your part."

"With what?" he replied. "No offense, man, but I'm currently a bit short on wheels."

"Use the truck."

"You had the truck yesterday, and you told me that under no circumstances am I to borrow..."

"Fine," Bert snapped, letting out a sigh. "If it happens again and I'm not around you can use the Dodge." Martin's eyes immediately lit up, to which he was quick to add, "To her job and back, that's it. Nothing else. I'll be checking the odometer to make sure. And I swear, if I find so much as a single scratch on the paint I'm going to..."

"You got it," Martin interrupted. "I promise to treat her as if she were my own child."

"Do better than that. Treat her like she's *my* child."

Bert was about to say more, intending to put the fear of God into his nephew good and proper, but just then the phone rang.

He turned to pick it up, unsurprised to hear Wilbur McCoy's voice at the other end. He'd been expecting it, after all.

"Hey, Wilbur," he said into the receiver, waving his nephew and Charlene off. "Yep, figured you'd be calling. Of course you can count on me. Just tell me when and where. Uh huh. Anyone else?" He glanced back at where Martin was walking away, remembering Scooter's warning from the night before. "Nope, it'll be just me. Everyone else is already out for the day. All right. See you then."

"What do you mean, you expect me to be there?" Byron spat into the receiver. "This is your town, your jurisdiction. I did my civic duty, I reported it. Now it's your turn to do the job my taxes pay for. What? You can't be serious. This is outrageous. I'll call my attorney, I'll... Fine. But I expect results. Time is money, and far as I'm concerned you've wasted too much of both."

He hung up the phone red-faced.

Not long after giving his statement the day before, he'd gotten a call from one Sheriff Heller – a fitting name for a man whose jurisdiction was an utter hell-*hole*. He'd insisted that Byron pull his men from the southern grid and cease all work there until they could properly search the area.

Infuriating as that was, now he was looking at yet

another delay as that had been the sheriff once again. The shit-kicker was finally getting off his ass and forming a search party. The issue was, he wanted Byron to be part of it – to be on hand to consult with should the sheriff or his deputies have any questions while they conducted their search.

Byron was outraged at the prospect. Not only was he being forced to eat yet another day from his schedule, but now they were expecting free help on his part to do their job.

It was ironic in a sense. Under other circumstances, he'd have sent his foreman to stand in for him – as he would likely have a far better idea of the area and details than Byron would. However, being that his foreman was among the missing, that meant he had no choice in the matter, especially as he didn't trust the rest of his current crew not to fuck it up – probably on purpose too in the hope of causing more delays.

Well, if the sheriff insisted he be there, then he would, but it wouldn't be as a silent observer. He intended to see to it that this search was conducted methodically and efficiently. Then, once they were through with the parcel of land his company was trying to develop, he'd give the man a piece of his mind. If the sheriff then wanted to search the rest of this godforsaken town that would be his business. He could do so until he was blue in the face, but Byron would make sure the work continued on his end.

He owed it to his investors, after all. They were the true victims here, but nobody seemed to care a lick about their worries.

It was unamerican as far as he was concerned, but there was nothing to be done about it. Arguing would only mean more wasted money and in the end it would all be for nothing. He knew men like the sheriff. They were stubborn sons of bitches, happy to dig in and hide behind bureaucracy until they got their way.

No. Better to rip this bandage off. Then hopefully come tomorrow he could start moving this project forward again.

It was a solid plan. One more day wouldn't make a difference. If they found Reg in the process, all the better. But if not, that was okay too. Byron had done his duty. His conscience was clear as far as this matter was concerned.

19

"Whoooo! Listen to that motor purr, baby!"

Martin pressed on the gas, bringing the Challenger up to eighty and causing the engine to practically roar, making it sound almost like a living thing.

He hadn't felt this alive since his heyday back in Nashville at the top of his flavor empire. The best part was he didn't have to beg, borrow, or steal to achieve it. All it had taken was his uncle's overdeveloped sense of chivalry for the keys to this V8 monster to land in his hands.

Martin had originally felt somewhat bad about what happened the night before. Not so much that he'd made Charlene walk home. It's not like she didn't need the exercise. But when Uncle Bert had pulled up to the house with her in the passenger seat of his truck, she'd seemed genuinely scared.

At first, he'd wondered if maybe Bert wasn't the straight shooter everyone took him for. Out there at night, alone in his truck with Charlene, maybe he'd tried to sample the goods and gotten aggressive about it. Aunt Lin was a looker, sure, but men could be strange animals at times. A guy could have the Venus de Milo waiting at home, yet still feel the need to occasionally stuff his dick into a termite-infested knothole instead. It was just the way things worked.

But no. Something had spooked Charlene and it hadn't been Bert. She'd insisted on it, not that he'd gotten much out of her as she'd babbled on about things in the woods, but that was women for you. Sometimes they just didn't make a lot of sense.

She'd probably just frightened herself hearing an owl hoot, or something equally benign. What mattered was today was a new day, and that day had brought with it opportunity.

Not only had Bert agreed to let him use the V8 to drive Lene to *work*, but his uncle had then gotten called away by the cops. Some sort of search was going on at the southern end of the Bluff. Martin didn't care who or what it was for, just that he hadn't been asked to be part of it.

Bert had taken off in his truck soon after, bringing Aunt Lin with him so he could drop her off somewhere along the way – a friend's place it sounded like.

That had left him and Charlene free to load the Challenger's trunk with a few supplies from around the house, hopefully to make the clean-up down at the army base go a bit faster. After that, they'd hit the road with a vengeance.

The road leading to the base ran straight and true through a wooded part of the bog. He could understand how this stretch could be scary at night, but right then he was far more concerned with their sweet ride.

"You digging this shit or what?" he cried.

Next to him in the passenger's seat, Charlene let out a

whoop of joy as the wind from the open windows whipped her hair. "This is great, Koolaid!"

"What did you say?"

"I said this is great!"

He turned and smirked. "Come on. Is that the best you've got? Show some fucking excitement already."

"You want some excitement, Koolaid?"

"Hell yeah! Don't just talk about it, baby. Do it!"

She smiled at him then whipped her shirt off – holding it out the window like a flag on a windy day.

Martin let out a cackle as he forced the car ever faster. "That's right! Show me them big ole titties!"

"I could show you more if you want."

He felt a stir within his pants at the suggestion. Normally, he wasn't all that interested in what Charlene had to offer, especially not considering all the work that still needed to be done. It was no different than back when he was dealing weed. In such a business as his, one needed to be careful not to become their own best customer.

He was in too fine of a mood to waste a perfectly good hardon, though. Something about being behind a fly set of wheels really got his own motor humming.

Besides, the day was still young. There'd be plenty of time to get some cleaning done. For now, he had a knob in need of polishing.

Martin took a quick look around. Far as the eye could see, the road was empty. It would likely remain that way too with folks heading to the south side to help out with the search.

Fuck it!

He slammed on the brake, enjoying the squeal of burning rubber as the car screeched to a halt on the side of the road.

Boar War

"What'cha thinking, Koolaid?" Charlene asked, her face flushed from the excitement of the drive.

Martin was already unbuckling his pants. "I'm thinking you need to get your ass into the backseat pronto, so we can properly christen this love boat. You with me, baby?"

"Am I with you?" She leaned forward, her eyes gleaming with desire. "Say it, Koolaid! You know the words."

He grinned. "Oh yeah!"

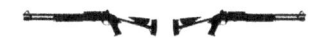

Charlene had already worked up a pretty good sweat by the time she and Martin got to the base, but that was okay, just a warmup for the cleaning that was still ahead.

She was glad his uncle had given his okay to take the keys to the Dodge. It made her feel so much better to know she wouldn't have to walk back to the farm after dark again. Of course, not nearly as good as she felt after getting a good lay from her honey bear.

Whenever she was with a John she always tried to put on a good act, but that's all it was. As far as she was concerned it was merely a business transaction. She took far more joy in watching Martin count his earnings at the end of a long day. But whenever they were together, which wasn't nearly enough for her liking, man oh man was it something special.

Her only regret as they'd finished up in the Challenger was that her legs were cramped and there hadn't been more time. That last one was understandable, though. Martin was no cuddler. He was a business man with important things to do, and her job was to support him and make sure he wasn't disappointed.

Although, judging by the way he'd screamed, "Oh yeah," right at the end, she was feeling pretty good on that front.

They parked just within the chain link fence and walked into the base together. Now that it was daylight and he was by her side, she felt a bit foolish about the night before. Thankfully, he seemed to understand – or at least he'd been too enamored by the drive over to yell at her. Either way, Martin appeared to be in a fine mood as they stepped inside the soon-to-be chalet.

While he surveyed the progress she'd made the day before, she began to unload the box they'd brought, full of stuff *borrowed* from the farm – candles, matches, a flashlight, spare batteries, and a sizable pile of dust rags.

Charlene glanced over to make sure Martin wasn't looking before checking on the box's final item, kept hidden beneath the rags – a carving knife she'd swiped from the kitchen.

It was stupid of her to take it, but there was no doubt in her mind that having it there would make her feel better. All in all, it was a good compromise between nothing at all and trying to steal one of Bert's rifles.

"Not too shabby, Lene," Martin called from the other room. "A couple more days and we should be able to start scouting the dump for used mattresses."

"That's great, Koolaid!" she replied, covering the knife back up.

"Hell yeah it is. I can practically feel my wallet growing heavy with greenbacks. This is without a doubt one of my best ideas yet."

"All your ideas are great, Koolaid," she replied.

"You know it, baby. The Koolaid man's got all the... Huh. What's this?"

"What's what?"

Martin reappeared in the doorway, a stack of papers in hand. "These."

"Oh. Those are just some old papers I found in one of the cabinets. The lock must've busted when I was moving it, cause they just came spilling out."

"Okay, so why are they still here?" he asked. "We're opening a love motel not a lending library."

"I know. I just put them aside for now."

He shrugged, leafing through them. "Goddamn, what is this shit anyway? Those jackboot fuckers leaving nuclear secrets behind or something?"

"I think they're about pigs."

"Pigs eh?" he asked, eyebrow raised. "Well what do you know. Guess that old bastard was right about the livestock."

"What?"

"Nothing, baby. So, you were looking through these?"

"It was only a quick peek, Koolaid, that's all," she quickly added. "But, anyway, if you think it's a good idea that is, maybe we can show them to your uncle, being he's a farmer and all."

"So ... you think we should give these to Bert?"

"Sure, why not?"

"Just because they're about pigs?"

"Yep."

"Even though they have *Piedmont Creek Facility* stamped at the very top, clear as day?"

She shrugged. "Yeah. Is that a problem?"

He took a moment to rub his eyes. "Only if we don't want him finding out about the Koolaid Chalet ... which we don't. Seriously, Lene, you got rocks in your head? If Bert sees this, he's gonna know where they came from, and then he's going to ask what the fuck we were doing here."

"Oh. I didn't think..."

"You can stop right there." He held up a hand but then, rather than yell, he took a deep breath instead. "It's okay. No harm done." He stepped over to the corner and set the papers down atop the chairs stacked there. "I'll tell you what. You find any more shit like this, just stick them atop this trash pile here. Then, when you're finished, you can take it outside and burn it."

"You got it, Koolaid."

"All right, good. Anyway, it's about time for me to split. We both got a lot of work to do today, so best get cracking."

"You heading back to the farm?" she asked.

"Are you kidding? And waste a chance to use those sweet wheels out there to add a few new flavors to my mix?"

"But didn't your uncle say he was going to check the odometer?"

"So what if he did, baby? That's what reverse gear is for. Trust me, he'll be none the wiser."

She started setting up the candles as he turned and strolled out the door. A few minutes later, there came the roar of the V8 and a squeal of tires as Martin pulled away, once more leaving her alone in the former government facility.

Nevertheless, Charlene felt pretty good as she got to work. She was better prepared this morning and had a spring in her step thanks to some good loving. And hey, if Martin was successful in his flavor quest, she might even get some help in fixing up the chalet.

True, the partially overcast sky outside meant it was gloomier than expected within the old base, nevertheless as far as she was concerned the day ahead was looking fairly bright indeed.

20

Lin Cooper kissed her husband and told him to be careful as he dropped her off.

She felt a bit guilty for the ruse as she watched him drive away, but was satisfied that it was for his own good. Bert was a decent man who always tried to do the right thing, but on occasion he needed to be reminded that he'd done his part, especially in cases where it was neither his circus nor his monkeys.

Lin fully supported her husband joining Sheriff Heller's search party, having made no effort to try and talk him out of it. After all, if she were the one lost in the woods, she'd hope that someone like Bert would be out there looking for her.

She'd tried to convince him to take Martin along but he'd seemed oddly reluctant on that point. That was a pity because she knew their nephew would almost certainly be eager to call it a day by the time the sun was going down. Mind you, Lin didn't think he was lazy. Such thoughts were unfair to the lad. If anything, he seemed to have boundless energy when his heart was in it. But she highly doubted this would be one of those situations.

The problem was, she knew her husband. If left to his own devices, Bert would be the first man out there searching for those missing people but also the last to leave. That was just the way he was built. Admirable of a trait as it was, he'd also end up neglecting his own well-being in the process. He was already giving up a full day of work to help out. If he pushed himself too far, he'd end up exhausted tomorrow as well.

Bert was a wonderful husband as well as a good friend, but there was no getting around him being stubborn as a mule. Tired or not, he'd insist on going out and getting the work done, running himself down even further.

Lin remembered a few years back when he'd been laid up for over a week with a bad case of pneumonia – brought on because he simply refused to acknowledge he had limits.

She wasn't about to let him do that to himself again, not if she could help it.

Instead, she'd purposely asked him to drop her off at Patty's first. It was a long walk home and, despite the clouds gathering in the sky, it was likely going to be another hot one out. Despite her being perfectly capable of making the trip on her own, she knew he wouldn't want her to. As a result, he'd diligently let her know that he'd pick her up at a reasonable hour. She didn't doubt it either. Bert could be a lot of things, but he seldom forgot a promise.

She felt comfortable knowing he'd have plenty of time to give a helping hand, yet also have a reason to call it a day before he ran himself ragged.

As for her timing, that had simply been coincidence. She'd tried calling Patty a few times over the last day or so, only to receive no answer. Her friend was a regular church goer but otherwise tended to be a homebody. It was possible she was simply keeping herself busy, maybe had even jumped back into the dating pool, although Lin didn't think that last one likely.

She suppressed a chuckle as she walked up the driveway. If anyone would be happy to die a spinster, it was probably Patty. To say her beliefs were a bit … *archaic* for nineteen-seventy-four was putting it kindly.

Lin herself had no such hangups. She was a firm believer in women's lib as well as a secret admirer of the free love movement. At the very least, she tried to make sure her and Bert's love life was both active and regular, although that had become strained as of late on account of their *guests*. In truth, she was beginning to miss having the house all to themselves. Keeping their loving limited to the bedroom was beginning to get a bit stifling.

Martin was family, though, and one didn't turn their back on family in need.

She pushed those thoughts from her head as she stepped onto the front porch. Sex was the absolute last thing Patty ever wanted to discuss. Lin had learned that lesson on more than one occasion, watching her friend's jaw tighten in disapproval whenever she'd dared let slip mention of her own happy marriage. The reality was, Elmer had been a jackass walking out on Patty like he had, but a small part of her hadn't been surprised to hear it.

Not that she would've ever admitted that out loud.

Lin knocked on the door. As she waited, she took a moment to look around – noting with some concern that the petunias ringing the azalea bushes in the front yard were all wilted. That definitely wasn't normal. Despite the drought, Patty had worked hard to keep the plants in her yard full and healthy.

Maybe she's sick.

That would certainly account for the state of her lawn. Although, being too ill to garden was one thing, but if Patty was too unwell to even answer the phone then Lin had been right to stop by and check on her.

She knocked again, this time more insistently, but there came no sound from inside. Finally, she tried the doorknob, finding it unlocked.

That wasn't particularly surprising. Crime in their neighboring towns was mostly relegated to teenaged pranks and the occasional bar brawl. Nevertheless, she announced herself as she slowly opened the front door.

"Patty, it's me. You home, dear?"

In response, the neat little household remained deathly quiet.

Unlocked or not, Lin didn't like the idea of trespassing in someone else's home. True, if Patty was actually sick then it would be justified. But if not, she'd simply show herself out and then speak nothing further of it.

"Patty? You there?"

She stepped inside, closing the screen door behind her. No point in trespassing *and* letting all the bugs in. The home appeared well kept as it had always been, albeit it was currently stuck in a bit of a transitional state, same as when last she'd visited. Unsurprisingly, Patty had already begun the process of erasing any trace of Elmer's influence in the cozy home.

His favorite chair, for instance, which had sat across from their tiny black and white TV, was conspicuously missing – Patty having wasted no time having it hauled to the junkyard.

They weren't exactly what she'd call the best of friends, but Lin knew the woman well enough to know she could be obsessive about projects once she got started. Two summers ago, she'd decided to wallpaper the main floor. Lin distinctly remembered having to listen to Elmer complain about being forced out of his own living room because his wife refused to take a break until she was finished. As a result, the sameness of the room stood out. It had only been a few days, but it appeared that Patty hadn't made a single lick of progress since then.

Not a good sign.

More resolved than ever, Linda began to check the various rooms – announcing herself at each doorway before entering.

All of them proved similarly empty, even the master bedroom. Nothing appeared to have been disturbed in the slightest. The bed was made, the counters clean, and there were no dishes in the sink.

In fact, the only sign that anything was amiss were a few potted plants hanging in the windows, all of them starting to wilt like the flowers outside.

If anything, it looked like Patty had simply walked out and not been back.

She supposed it was possible the poor woman was staying with kin. Lord knows she probably needed a few days to get her head on straight. But then why hadn't she asked Lin to stop by and take care of her plants?

Once again she chuckled, this time at her own arrogance in assuming.

It wasn't like she was Patty's only friend in town. Maybe she'd asked someone else and they'd simply forgotten to pop by. Either way, it was no big deal. It wasn't as if any pets had been left to starve.

Satisfied that no one was there, Lin prepared to leave – resolved to make the walk home. After all, Bert had just dropped her off. He wouldn't be back for some time and there wasn't any way to reach him out in the woods.

No matter. She wasn't nearly as fragile as he seemed to sometimes think. Besides, with the sky clouding up it might not actually be that bad. Not to mention there was always a chance someone she knew would see her and offer to drive her the rest of the way. Regardless, with any luck she'd be back home before the morning was through.

Linda looked around for something to write on, figuring she should leave a note on the front door – to let Patty know she'd dropped by, as well as informing Bert of her whereabouts when he came to pick her up.

She stepped into the kitchen, knowing Patty kept a to-do list on the refrigerator. It was one of those tearaway notebook fridge magnets. Surely she wouldn't miss a page.

That's when Linda realized the back door was ajar. That was strange. It was one thing for the front door to be unlocked, but to leave the back open? That was just asking for trouble. All Patty needed was one racoon to get curious and the entire place would end up ransacked.

Rather than simply close it, though, she stepped out into the backyard on the off chance that her friend was out there and simply hadn't heard her.

Lin took a look around, seeing nothing out of the ordinary – save more wilted flowers – when the breeze shifted ever so slightly, bringing with it a godawful stench.

She'd been working the farm long enough to instantly recognize the smell of death. Her first thought as she turned toward the picket fence separating Patty's yard from the woods beyond was that an animal must've died close by.

That thought scattered quickly, however, as she spied something amiss near the gate. A few of the normally stark white fence posts were stained brown. A bunch had been knocked askew, as if something heavy had rammed into them.

Patty and Elmer hadn't kept any animals, so there was no need to worry that one might've escaped. Nevertheless, she decided to investigate.

As she headed that way, a cloud of flies took flight from just beyond where the fence lay, buzzing annoyedly in the air around her head. Linda waved them away and took a deep breath, remaining undaunted. Life on the farm had hardened the once-shy school girl from High Moon, Pennsylvania.

She reached the break in the fence, fully expecting to find nothing more threatening than a deer carcass. Instead, she beheld a scene of utter carnage – rent flesh, broken bones, and, most damning, torn clothing.

Linda covered her mouth with her hand, her thoughts at first turning to those men who'd been lost in the woods. But then, just a few feet away, she caught sight of a dead eye staring back at her from a partially severed head. Just enough flesh remained on the ravaged skull for her to recognize Patty's features – her mouth open in a twisted grimace, suggesting the last emotion of her life had been one of outright horror and utmost pain.

That was what finally drove Lin over the edge. Though no sound would ever escape Patty's lips again, Linda managed to scream quite enough for the both of them.

21

"One of those missing fellas owe you money, Bert?"

"Huh?" Bert turned to find Wilbur McCoy heading his way.

The deputy grinned and then gestured to the rifle slung across Bert's back.

"Oh this? Just being extra cautious after what happened to Scooter's pigs. Besides, I figure there's always the risk of us stirring up a bobcat den while we're beating the bush."

"Fair enough. Just make sure you don't shoot anyone in the foot by mistake." Wilbur stepped in and then lowered his voice as he pointed toward the man currently yelling at Sheriff Heller. "Although if you *accidentally* hit that guy in the ass, I can guarantee I saw nothing."

Bert glanced over. If his memory served correctly, that was the guy in charge of the nearby construction. He'd been at the sheriff's office the other day when they'd arrived, making a bigger stink than was probably warranted.

Boar War

"No promises, Wilbur," he replied, causing both men to laugh.

The deputy wandered off a few minutes later, no doubt to get things organized. Bert saw he wasn't the only man who'd come armed outside of the sheriff and his deputies. That was good. Made him feel less self-conscious about it. He normally wouldn't have brought much more than a canteen, a few sandwiches, and maybe a flashlight for when it got dark, but Scooter's words had haunted him as he'd prepared to set out. In the end, he figured the gun was just something else to carry – even if he was unlikely to need it.

Same with his flashlight. He'd promised to pick Lin up from Patty's place before it got dark. He had a feeling that was purposeful on her part, a way to make sure he wasn't stuck out in the bog until the wee hours of the morning. If so, he was happy she had his back – knowing damned well how easy it could be to lose time once things got started. Bert had been part of enough search parties over the years to know from experience how long they could take.

Although this one might prove the exception to the rule.

He wasn't privy to Sheriff Heller's thoughts on the matter, but considering the time that had elapsed between the disappearance of those men and their boss reporting it, he doubted this would be a multi-day effort. By now the trail was long cold. Chances are he was just dotting the I's and crossing the T's on this one.

Regardless, taking a look around, he saw a good sized crowd had gathered to help out – most of whom he knew. There was Scott Debkins and his brother Jake. Nick Claverman was there with his two bloodhounds Apollo and Armstrong. Seamus Kelly too, having probably closed down his diner for the day to help out. Even Gary Higgins had seemingly dried himself out long enough to join them.

That was the thing he loved most about the people of Cooper's Bluff. They wouldn't hesitate to help if they could.

Heck, even Scooter had wanted to be there but Bert had talked him out of it. The events of the past few days had been hard on him and he'd sounded tired when Bert had phoned him. Best for him to take this one off. Nobody would think less of him for it.

He'd expected to maybe see a few of the construction crew there as well, but as he'd passed the site on the way to the meetup spot he'd seen them already hard at work for the day. Guess their boss had different priorities than the townsfolk when it came to these things.

It didn't make him think very highly of the man. Sure, he was there, but considering the way he seemed to lay into the sheriff at every opportunity, Bert doubted it was of his own volition. He'd just best mind himself. The sheriff might've had to take his crap for political reasons. It was part of his job after all. But he doubted anyone else present would hesitate to lay the man out if he said the wrong word to them. Would be well worth a night spent in jail.

Finally, Wilbur and the other town deputy – Luthor Hendricks – began rounding folks up to get them organized.

There were enough volunteers to split them into three teams. That was enough to allow them to cover a pretty wide stretch of land as they combed each grid the sheriff had laid out for them.

Sheriff Heller took charge of the centermost team which included Nick and his hounds but also that loudmouth, Hoffsteader if Bert's memory served him right.

Luthor was leading Team B, which was taking the westernmost spur. As for Bert, he was assigned to Wilbur's group – which would be searching the eastern grid.

The morning was already hot and humid, but at least the sun was partly hidden behind sporadic cloud cover. It was likely the best any of them could hope for on what was sure to be a long day.

But at least, or so Bert comforted himself, he didn't have to deal with that Hoffsteader guy. Small victories and all.

Two hours into the search and there wasn't much progress to speak of. The teams had gotten started by covering ground that had been marked by the construction crew's survey team. The area itself had apparently already been looked over by Hoffsteader's people, but Sheriff Heller wanted to be thorough – likely trusting the man's word about as far as he could throw him.

Because of the work that had been going on, there were plenty of tracks and other false alarms that kept setting off Nick's hounds – none of it fruitful. In truth, Bert had figured these first couple of hours would be a waste of time due to all of that but it still needed to be done.

The last thing any of them wanted was to be sloppy and miss a clue.

Then Wilbur's radio had gone off, causing him to step away for a few minutes.

When he came back, he'd told the team to take five before asking Bert if they could speak in private.

"What's the good word, Wilbur?" Bert asked, after following him for maybe ten yards.

"Ain't one. Let's just say when it rains it pours."

"Not following."

"I just got off the horn with Alan. Seems Ellie back at the station's been losing her mind trying to hail him and just finally got through. Anyway, she got a call a while ago. Something's happened back in town."

"What?"

"I'm not at liberty to say, but it requires immediate attention."

"We calling this off?"

"That's part of the problem. Alan doesn't want to, not unless it's absolutely necessary. Thing is, he was gonna head back and deal with this himself, but that Hoffsteader guy just about crawled up his ass when he suggested it. Threatened to make a stink at the next town hall. So he asked me to head back in instead."

"Oh?" Bert replied, having a feeling where this was headed.

"Yeah. I hope you don't mind me asking this, but I need you to take over until I get back." He pulled out a map and then unclipped the radio at his side before holding both out.

"Listen, Wilbur, I appreciate you asking, but I gotta be straight with you. Lin's expecting me to pick her up before end of day and..."

"This shouldn't take that long. I'll be back before then. Come on, Bert, help me out here. All the men know and respect you. Sides which, I know I can count on you not to dick around."

"What about Cal over there?" Bert asked, hooking a thumb. "You guys work with him and his crew all the time."

"Cal Summers is a good man, not saying he ain't, but

if I put him in charge he'll be calling for a smoke break every ten minutes. You know it too."

"I suppose..."

"So what do you say, man? Help a brother out? I'd appreciate it. All you gotta do is keep the men moving and check in with the sheriff should anything come up."

Bert sighed. He'd been part of enough searches to know the drill. He knew he probably should've declined, but also that he wasn't going to. After a moment he replied, "Fine. But I'm telling you, if your butt isn't back here by sundown Lin's gonna be madder than a wet cat. And if that's the case, I'm pointing her your way."

"Well, we wouldn't want that now." Wilbur nodded before throwing him a grin and handing the radio over. He went over a few things, like which channel to use, then finally said, "All right, that's about it then. I'd best be on my way before the Sheriff calls again. I appreciate it, buddy."

"Yeah. Just be careful heading in."

"Ain't no problem," Wilbur replied, turning away. "It's a straight shoot north and then I'm outta this mess. Don't worry about me none. I'll be just fine."

22

Wilbur felt bad about not telling Bert the truth, that his wife Lin had called and reported a *situation* at the old Gantry place.

A *situation. Hah!* That was putting it mildly. Alan obviously hadn't wanted to say too much in front of the men, but his wording over the radio had heavily implied that some serious shit had transpired.

Problem was, there was already shit going on and they didn't have nearly the manpower to properly handle two such emergencies at once. Even a small city would no doubt be better equipped for such things, but *situations* tended to be few and far between in their little shared township. And two at once, well, that was pretty much unheard of in Wilbur's experience.

From the brief description he'd been given, it sounded as if Lin was fine, maybe a little hysterical but nothing more. He knew Bert, though. The man was devoted to his wife. Even mentioning her name would've likely caused him to hustle his ass out of the woods to be by her side.

Wilbur hadn't been lying about needing him to take

over their search team. Truth was, he didn't trust any of the other members to do so competently. If Bert left too, it would mean the existing teams divvying up their resources again, likely entailing having to start from scratch.

Bert could always chew him out later if he felt the need, but for now Wilbur thought it best for him to head out alone and take stock of things. It would also give him a chance to talk to Lin without her husband hovering over her like a protective mama bear.

"I swear, when it rains it pours," he told himself as he trudged back toward where he'd left his squad car.

He glanced up at the sky, visible through the wilted treetops above. *Maybe sooner rather than later on that one.*

That was at least one bright spot. A touch of rain would do everyone good. Speaking of which, once he got the scoop on what had gone down at the Gantry's, it would free him up to give Cassius a hand with the storm prep. The old timer had retired his badge a few years back but still helped out at the station as a handyman. Too bad he was no longer deputized to handle cases, otherwise Ellie would have certainly sent him instead.

Wilbur's ears perked up as he continued walking. Sound carried far in the woods. In this case, it was heavy machinery. Somewhere up ahead, off in the distance, Hoffsteader had his crew hard at work on the new construction.

Cheap bastard. The son of a bitch had men missing. He knew full well that their chances of finding them would improve significantly with extra manpower, but had instead shown where his true priorities lay.

Wilbur didn't wish ill on the work itself, as plenty of locals had picked up gainful employment as part of the deal. All the same, he wouldn't shed a single tear if the company in charge went bust when all was said and done.

You couldn't reason with guys like Hoffsteader. All you could do was hope they got hit where it hurt most, in their wallets. That was the only way to show those...

Crack.

Wilbur inclined his head at the sound of movement from somewhere close by. His first thought was that one of the other searchers had called it off early. Wouldn't have surprised him. There were always a few who'd use any excuse to knock off – staying just long enough to claim they'd done their civic duty.

Normally, Wilbur didn't have much use for lollygaggers, but even he had to admit he wouldn't have minded some company for the rest of the walk back. Aside from the hum of distant machinery and the crackle of dead grass beneath his feet, the woods had been awfully quiet for most of his trek. Usually they were alive with all sorts of sounds, but not today – probably on account of the blasted heatwave. Even the damned frogs couldn't work up the energy to croak their fool heads off.

There came the crunch of more dried foliage – this time closer, from off to his right. Something was nearby, walking through the brush.

"Who's there?" Wilbur called. "Might as well come out and join me."

There was no response. That was the thing with the lollygaggers. They didn't like to admit when they'd been caught.

"Come on now. I ain't got no time for games."

This time there came a heavy grunt from the thick brush – a sound that hadn't come from any human lips, not unless they were in serious distress.

Fuck! Talk about shitty luck. It was an animal of some sort, a big one from the sound of it. And if it was this close, then it likely meant it had been stalking him.

Wilbur immediately thought back to Scooter's report from the other day, how he'd been going on about something tearing his wife's pigs to shreds. He hadn't thought old Scoot a liar per se, but the man was obviously upset. And when folks were upset they tended to exaggerate.

Now, though, he had to consider the alternative. Wouldn't something big enough to tackle a whole pen of swine also consider a lone man out in the woods to be potential prey as well?

Better safe than sorry.

Wilbur backed away slowly, keeping his eyes on the bushes ahead as he drew the S&W 19 holstered at his side. It was a solid weapon with a serious punch, meaning he wasn't too worried. So long as he kept his cool, it would be okay.

"Go on now!" he cried, hoping to scare it off. "Get out of here!"

With any luck it would get the hint. Either way, he made a note to radio Alan once he got back to his cruiser, so he could warn the others to keep their eyes peeled for any...

A deep snort came in return – making Wilbur wonder whether someone's horse had simply gotten loose.

However, that idea quickly scattered to the wind as the beast pushed through the thick foliage, trampling the surrounding bushes with ease.

Jesus!

It was a fucking pig, but larger than any Wilbur had ever seen or heard of – so big that he stood there dumbfounded for a second, wondering if he'd lost his damned mind.

It was only for a second, though. He'd had run-ins with feral hogs before. Though they usually minded their own business, they could be mean fuckers once a burr got up their ass.

And this one was staring at him in a way that heavily suggested its ass was currently elbow deep with said burrs.

He would've much sooner had a rifle or shotgun in his hands against the rhinoceros-sized creature, but beggars couldn't be choosers. Wilbur raised his gun and fired in the same instant the boar charged.

The roar of the handgun was followed by a squeal of rage from the hog as the bullet slammed home into its thick hide.

Too high for a kill, he realized, not that he was entirely certain his weapon was up to a task like this. Either way, there was no time to line up another shot as he was forced to dive out of the way lest he be trampled.

He hit the dirt as the boar thundered past, feeling its passage in the very ground beneath him.

Goddamned thing's gotta weigh over half a ton!

The beast skidded to a halt, gouging a heavy chunk of dirt from the forest floor as it once again let loose with an angry snort.

Wilbur quickly fired again, striking the beast in its haunches this time.

The pig stumbled but didn't fall. Sadly for him, it didn't run off either. It spun with an ungodly squeal, catching Wilbur's outstretched arm with a tusk as thick as a baseball bat.

The gun flew from his grasp as the bones in his wrist shattered, causing him to let loose with a scream of his own.

His weapon gone and his arm broken, blind panic began to set in. Wilbur desperately looked around for where his pistol had fallen, knowing that any effort to run would be futile.

He'd already put two rounds into this hog. It was injured and angry. No way was it backing off now and he knew it.

There! Spying his gun on the ground, Wilbur frantically clawed for it with his good hand, but it fumbled from his grasp just as the beast charged again. Realizing he had no choice now but to retreat, he began to scramble away from the monster, at least until his rump backed up against the thick trunk of a tree, halting his progress.

Before he could even consider whether to go left or right, the massive hog barreled into him like a runaway locomotive – shattering his ribcage like cheap glass and rupturing the organs within.

The entire tree shook from the sheer force of the impact, but by then Wilbur McCoy was far too dead to either notice or care.

23

Bert stopped in his tracks as a sharp *crack* of sound caught his attention.

"Hold up," he told the others, although he needn't have bothered. Most of the men on his team had apparently heard it too, with maybe the exception of Gary Higgins who'd been complaining about the weather.

"Was that gunfire?" Seamus Kelly asked?

"Pretty sure it was," Bert replied, holding up his hand to hopefully give them all the hint to shut up so he could listen.

Sound could carry far in the woods, so it wasn't hard to imagine the other teams stopping to do the same. The problem was that same sound could also be easily distorted, making it difficult to tell which direction it had come from.

A minute or so passed in eerie silence – the woods so still that it was painfully obvious when Cal Summers ripped one loose, a long mournful toot that spoke of an ill-digested breakfast.

Before anyone could comment on the man's irritable

bowels, though, there came the sound of another gunshot. This time there was no mistaking the direction. It had come from somewhere behind them – back in the direction Wilbur had gone.

In the next second that concern was given voice as something akin to a high-pitched squeal or scream carried through the woods to their ears. It sounded like someone had stepped on a bobcat's tail with cleated shoes.

"What in Sam Hill was that?" Cal asked.

Bert had no answer as he unclipped the radio from his belt and lifted it to his lips. All he could say for certain was it sure as hell had sounded far more potent than even Cal's farts.

Byron was already in a foul mood by that point. Not only had he started the day annoyed to high hell that they'd even requested his presence, but then the sheriff had dared to give him grief for not bringing more of his men along for this search – as if he was paying his workers to diddle themselves in the woods.

Things had gone downhill from there. For starters, the progress had been maddeningly slow. Had he been calling the shots, they'd have been over these woods twice by now and already called it a day – regardless of whether they'd found anything or not.

Instead, it seemed like every five minutes there was some excuse for the group to stop. First, there'd been a call from the sheriff's office – the woman who answered the phones there caterwauling about an emergency. They'd been forced to stand around with their thumbs up their asses while the sheriff stepped away to deal with it – ultimately resulting in him sending one of his own back to town.

If anyone had asked, Byron would've ventured that had probably been planned from the start – nothing but a ploy to waste even more of his valuable time. Nobody had of course. In fact, the men on their team had mostly given him a wide berth from the get-go. Unlike the sheriff, they seemed to understand when they were among their betters.

Not that such a thing would stop them from slacking off if the sheriff allowed it. He knew how these people operated. Most were one step removed from being on welfare – happy to collect a check on the taxpayer's dime while men like him worked for a living.

And now they'd been told to stop once again. Just as it seemed they were finally going to make some progress, there'd come a distant sound like that of a car backfiring, causing Sheriff Heller to once more bring the whole goddamned thing to a halt.

The sheriff was busy telling Nick Something-or-other to keep his mutts quiet when the sound rang out again. He gave the others an order to stay put, then stepped away to yap into his radio.

That's it! Byron had seen enough of this crap. Rather than wait around with the common rabble as instructed, he followed after the sheriff, intent on giving the man a piece of his mind.

He caught up to him maybe a dozen yards away, midconversation.

"Yeah, I'm sure, Luthor. It's probably nothing, but I'm not risking it just in case it isn't. Bring your team back here. You too, Bert. We'll consolidate our resources and then figure out who stays and who..." The sheriff trailed off and turned, no doubt at the sound of Byron approaching. "Can I help you, Mr. Hoffsteader?"

"Yes. You can start by actually leading these men and doing your duty. Daylight is a burning, as I believe the saying goes."

Heller let out a condescending sigh before addressing the radio again. "Sorry about that. Just get everyone back here pronto. We'll figure it out from there. Over." He then turned Byron's way again, the hostility in his eyes all too evident. "You may not believe this, Mr. Hoffsteader, but I *am* doing my duty."

"If that's the case, Sheriff, then why are we standing here?"

Heller raised an eyebrow. "Pray tell, what exactly do you think that was we heard just a few moments ago?"

"I wouldn't care to speculate," Byron replied. "After all, this is your jurisdiction."

"Those were gunshots, Mr. Hoffsteader."

"So? Someone's out hunting. These are big woods. I don't see why any of that is our concern."

"Hunting ... back the way we came from, the same direction I sent my deputy in? And where, I might remind you, your company's construction site is."

"I'm not sure what you're implying."

"I'm not implying anything. That's not how I or my men work. My aim is to figure out exactly what happened that resulted in the discharge of said weapon. However, I can't do that from here on account of Deputy McCoy handing his radio to one of the other volunteers helping to search for *your* men. So I'm recalling the other teams to this location, so we..."

"You're calling it off?!"

"Simmer down. I didn't say that. You've no doubt noticed some of the men came out armed today, correct?"

Byron let out a noncommittal grunt, a bead of sweat dripping down his forehead as he found himself wondering whether that was a thinly veiled threat.

"Now, that's not exactly uncommon in these parts," Heller continued. "These men understand the woods around the Bluff. They know they can be ... unpredictable."

"Your point?"

"I'm getting to that. Their foresight is a good thing for our cause here. I'm going to recruit a small group of those same men to go back with me so we can properly investigate. Now, it's probably nothing to be worried about. Deputy McCoy is..."

"If it's nothing then..."

The sheriff held up a hand, silencing Byron like he was one of the rubes. "As I was saying, Deputy McCoy is a competent officer and a good man. It's probably nothing, but we need to be certain of that. If there's something wrong out there, I'd be derelict in my duties to ignore it. However, I'll be leaving Deputy Hendricks behind to continue leading the search. Nothing's changed on that end, but I need to consolidate our resources and be smart about this until we know for certain."

Byron seethed at the man's arrogance, as if this hick thought he was stupid enough to believe such obvious bunk. "Unacceptable."

"Excuse me?"

"You heard me, Sheriff. That's simply unacceptable. Listen here. I've poured a great deal of money into the local economy. Too much for my needs to be cast aside for some bullshit snipe hunt."

The sheriff's eyes narrowed dangerously. "I'd ask you to mind your tone, Mr. Hoffsteader. You may be able to speak your mind in whatever way you like with the town selectmen, but that doesn't fly in my book. I won't have you throwing your weight around here especially where it concerns the safety of one of our own. You'd best remember that."

Byron felt himself sweating more profusely and it had nothing to do with the temperature. All the same, he refused to be talked down to. "Is that a threat?"

"Not at all, sir. I'm merely stating the facts. I'm taking a group of men to investigate what happened. You can either stay here or come with us. That's your call. But if you get in my way, I won't hesitate to cuff you for obstruction of justice."

"You can't possibly..."

"*If* it all turns out to be nothing," he interrupted, "then you're probably right. There won't be much I can do. But if something did happen to my deputy then I can promise you I won't rest until you're rotting inside a jail cell for a long time to come. Are we clear here, *Mr. Hoffsteader*?"

Byron backed up a step, his face so red with anger that for a moment he didn't know how to respond. His heart hammered in his chest at the aggressive hubris on display. In truth he wanted nothing more than to put this man in his place.

He wasn't stupid, though. Out there in the woods, the sheriff had every advantage. If he decided to arrest Byron, it would be his word against Heller's – with the locals probably happy to back the sheriff up no matter what lies he told. And if he decided to do worse than that, well, Byron was on his own with no backup.

Maybe I should have brought a few of my people after all.

Hell, the sheriff was probably itching to be given a reason. Byron understood how these slack-jawed hillbillies operated. For them, violence was always an option.

No, he told himself. He needed to cool down, bite his tongue. He could be patient ... at least until they were back in town where Byron was in his element. Once there, he'd talk to the town council. They understood their place on the food chain and they'd make sure the sheriff understood his.

After several long seconds, Byron took a deep breath and nodded to show his compliance. That seemed to satisfy the man, for now anyway.

Nevertheless, as Byron took another step back his heart continued to pound, so hard he was certain he could feel it beneath the soles of his feet.

Wait...

There actually was a vibration coming from the ground below him, a frantic cadence as if something heavy was...

Nearby, the dogs started to bray like mad, the racket making it hard to think.

"What in tarnation?" Heller cried, turning in the same instant something massive exploded out from the brush behind them, scattering both men like tenpins.

Byron landed hard on the cracked dirt, the wind knocked out of his lungs as something impossibly large loomed over him.

The nightmarish beast let out a squeal of rage, suddenly making Byron's worries regarding the sheriff, his company, and all the money he stood to lose, almost seem minor in comparison.

24

Scooter's warning had been playing in Bert's thoughts ever since he'd set out that morning. However, whereas before it had been a vague whisper reminding him to be cautious, it was rapidly turning into a screaming howl inside his mind as he heard the godawful ruckus from up ahead.

He and his team had been headed back toward Sheriff Heller's group as instructed when the silence of the woods had been instantly shattered by loud barks and snarls from somewhere nearby.

There was no doubt that it was Apollo and Armstrong, Nick Claverman's hounds. His first thought was they'd caught a scent, a strong one judging by their reaction.

If so, then it might not matter if a few of them headed back to check on Wilbur.

Whatever small comfort that idea brought didn't last for long as the braying hounds were soon joined by a screeching squeal that echoed through the woods, like a thousand nails on a chalkboard.

It was the same cry that had caught his and Cal's

attention just minutes earlier, save it was a lot louder, meaning it was likely much closer. He'd been able to rationalize it earlier, knowing how sound could get distorted, but now he had no such luxury. It was like the Devil himself had broken out of Hell and was now loose in the woods with them. A chill of fear crept up Bert's spine, making him glad he'd heeded Scooter's advice and come armed.

Speaking of his rifle, it was still slung across his back as they drew ever closer to whatever was going on ahead. He quickly rectified that situation – chambering a round and readying himself in case he had to use it.

Tempting as it was to open fire in the direction the strange cry had come from, he quickly reminded himself they weren't alone.

"Keep your eyes peeled and don't go off half-cocked," Bert called out, hoping he was heard above the racket.

With his and Luthor's team both converging on Alan's, all while something unexplained was going on, it wasn't hard to imagine an accident happening. The last thing he needed was to panic and start firing wildly into the brush.

If they were going to make it out of this without any injuries, then cooler heads would need to...

There came the sharp crack of wood from maybe two dozen yards ahead, driving that thought straight into the ground. Bert spied a small sapling as it toppled over. Then, barely a moment later, something barreled through the brush – thankfully headed away from where he and the others stood in shocked silence.

Holy shit!

Whatever it was, it had been partially hidden by the foliage, but there had been no doubt whatsoever that it was absolutely massive.

Bert couldn't be sure what he'd just seen. He'd only

Boar War

gotten a momentary glimpse as it tore through the woods, seemingly headed toward where Nick's dogs were still barking their heads off. The first thought that sprang to his head, though, was nothing short of crazy.

He was reminded of being back in grade school. He'd once written a paper for science class about extinct Ice-Age animals like mammoths and woolly rhinos. It was the image of the latter which stuck in his head for some reason.

But that was absurd.

What would an Ice-Age relic be doing alive in this day and age? More importantly, why would it be in Cooper's Bluff during a heat wave no less?

Regardless, whatever he'd just glimpsed was frighteningly large. Judging by the way the others had all stopped alongside him, he wasn't alone in that assessment.

"What in hell was that?" Gary Higgins gasped, just barely audible over the continued braying of the dogs.

"A grizzly," another of the men responded. "Had to be."

Rather than waste time on answers he didn't have, Bert turned toward Seamus, the only other man on their team who'd come armed – sporting an old forty-five strapped to his side. "Seamus, up here with me. The rest of you, stay behind us."

To Seamus's credit, he didn't hesitate, quickly checking his gun before stepping forward.

Cal Summers, on the other hand, seemed a bit more reluctant.

"You can't possibly be serious about following that thing, Bert. I mean, did you fucking see it?"

"Do I look blind to you?" he snapped. "Of course I saw it. That's why we've got to move. Those are our friends up ahead in case you forgot. You can leave them hanging out to dry if you want, but I'm not gonna sit around with my thumb up my ass while that thing is barreling their way."

His words belied the terror threatening to eat away at his resolve. It was an alien feeling to him, one he didn't like at all. Bert knew these woods, had hunted them many times before. Never once had he been afraid like he was now, not even that one time he'd accidentally surprised a black bear with her cubs. This was no black bear, though. Despite what had been said, he was pretty sure it wasn't a grizzly either, not the way it had been moving. But it sure as hell had been big enough.

Knowing that if he hesitated any longer Cal's words would start to make way too much sense, he turned and started moving again. Fortunately, the creature's trail was easy enough to follow. It had plowed through the thicket like a goddamned freight train.

He'd gone no more than maybe thirty feet, though, when another sound caught his ears.

"Help me!" a voice cried. "I'm ... I'm hurt! Someone please help me!"

It was coming from the direction the beast had appeared. Bert didn't immediately recognize who it belonged to. Nevertheless, he knew he couldn't ignore it.

He turned around, finding about half the men had followed in his footsteps – the rest still huddled back where they'd been.

"I need some volunteers to go check on whoever that is," he called, hoping that spurred them on even if they were too frightened to help him out. "See who's hurt and do what you can to help them."

When they still hesitated, he turned to Seamus. "I need you to go with them."

"You sure?" the burly diner owner asked.

Bert wasn't, but he nodded anyway. "Yeah. You know what you're doing and I don't want anyone out there right now without some cover. Just keep your eyes peeled. You see anything out of sorts, you empty all six into it."

"Shit, you don't need to tell me that," Seamus replied with a nod before turning toward the others. "Come on, you slack-jawed fuckers, let's go!"

Bert didn't stick around to see how many joined him. Seamus had a rep as a tough but fair boss, not to mention he cooked a mean meatloaf. More importantly, he'd done two tours in Vietnam as an army medic.

Satisfied that whoever was out there calling for help was in the best possible hands, Bert continued onward, focusing once again on the braying from up ahead – now more intense than ever.

Seconds later, there came the roar of a gunshot. It was followed by another angry squeal, then the sound of more men shouting. Within seconds, though, many of those shouts turned into cries of pain.

Bert started running, being mindful of his rifle as he pushed through the dried brush as quickly as humanly possible.

There!

He spotted a break in the trees, beyond which movement could be clearly made out.

The cries of the men up ahead grew more frantic, some of them turning to screams of terror. In turn, the dogs went absolutely ballistic, their barks becoming deep snarls as they seemingly faced off against whatever was there. Sadly, one abruptly became a high-pitched yelp before cutting off entirely.

What in hell is going on?!

Bert pushed through one last stand of bushes, skidding

to a halt as his mind tried to take in the scene of carnage before him.

At least two men lay on the ground dead. Jake Debkins had been gutted like a fish, his entrails hanging from a deep gash in his stomach and his discarded weapon on the ground alongside him. Another had been trampled so badly that Bert couldn't immediately tell who it was.

The rest of the search party was in disarray, having no doubt been scattered by the beast's initial charge. Some were barely able to crawl, obviously badly wounded, but those who could move were all desperately trying to get away from the monstrosity standing in the center of it all.

The creature was currently preoccupied, snuffling through the broken remains of one of Nick's dogs. The hound's bloody offal was probably the only reason the others were still alive, as the unholy abomination dug through it with an intensity that was as hard to believe as its size.

It was a wild boar, no doubt about it, but it was the pig's sheer bulk that kept Bert frozen in place. He'd seen some big hogs before. Hell, some of his own drove weighed north of three-hundred pounds, but even his largest sow was barely a kitten next to this thing.

The boar was not only larger than any pig Bert had ever seen, but any he'd ever heard of – possessing a body the size of a car and tusks like sabers.

The continued sound of barking caught his ear, forcing his attention away from the mammoth hog. Across the way he saw Nick Claverman visible through the trees. His feet were planted and his eyes wide with terror as he held onto his remaining dog's leash, doing everything he could to keep the angry hound at bay.

Bert couldn't blame him one bit. Rushing out to help the others while that thing was around was a death sentence, but at least he could keep his other dog from meeting the same fate its brother had.

There was no sign of Alan, either among the survivors or the fallen – making Bert wonder if he'd been the one they'd heard calling for help earlier. Either way, he couldn't worry about that right then. He needed to do what he could to ensure those still alive remained that way, and that meant putting this monster down for good.

He raised the rifle to his shoulder and took aim.

"Kill it!" Nick cried.

Tempting as it was to simply open fire, Bert knew acting rashly would likely do little more than get people hurt, himself included. The hog was already bleeding from multiple spots, likely the gunfire he'd heard earlier – making him hope to God that Wilbur had managed to climb a tree before this thing had gotten to him.

Regardless, Bert knew he needed to line up a solid kill shot because otherwise...

The creature shifted position, leaving him with nothing but its rump to stare at. It turned its attention toward one of the men trying to crawl away from it – Larry Powers who bartended down at Morty's.

Damn it all!

Despite the dog still snarling its head off only a few yards away, the hog had apparently decided Larry was the easier meal. It let out a snort and took a step in his direction.

That decided it. Shot or no shot, he couldn't stand by and let another man be gored to death by this thing.

"Yaw, pig!" Bert cried out, trying to get its attention. "Yaw!"

The boar's ears perked up and it let out a grunt, turning toward him much quicker than he would've anticipated a creature of its size capable of moving.

Bert was certain his heart skipped a beat as the monstrosity looked his way, its malevolent brown eyes locking onto him.

Take the shot, he ordered himself.

All at once, the rifle felt way too small in his hands as the hog lowered its head and charged. On the upside, there was almost no chance of missing the titanic beast as it closed in.

Bert squeezed the trigger, feeling the jerk of the gun against his shoulder as thunder roared from the barrel.

He saw the beast stumble as the bullet struck home high upon its thick forehead, giving him hope – but only for a moment.

Shit!

Instead of falling over, it let out a roar of anger as it righted itself and then...

The pig's squeals became a high pitched scream as another gunshot rang out, followed by a third. It jerked hard to the left as two sprays of blood erupted from its heavy flank.

Bert turned and saw Luthor Hendricks step into the clearing, gun drawn and barrel smoking, along with two similarly armed members of his search team.

Proper greetings could wait, however, as Bert chambered another round and took aim again along with the newcomers.

Within the next second, multiple gunshots rang out from the clearing, sounding from a distance much like the thunder that had been heard the night before.

25

"Help me up. I want to see it."

"No offense, Alan, but we need to get you to a doctor."

"All in good time, Bert. Now are you gonna help me or do I need to crawl over there myself?"

Bert shook his head but didn't say anything. There was no point to be had in arguing. All that would do was waste more time. The nearest hospital was three towns over in Kettelbury. They'd already contacted Ellie about what had happened so she could reach out to them, but there was only so far an ambulance could make it in these woods without bottoming out. They still needed to trek most of the distance back on foot.

Seamus had splinted the sheriff's leg as best he could with what he had to work with. They'd gotten lucky that it had been a clean break. Aside from that, Alan mostly seemed okay but Bert knew looks could be deceiving when it came to injuries.

The sheriff had been unconscious when they'd found him, having taken a pretty good hit from that thing. It turned out that Hoffsteader fella had been the one crying for help – sitting there blubbering like a baby despite there not being a scratch on him. In the end, though, they'd both been found so at least some good had come of the man's cowardice.

All the same, Alan was obviously in pain but Bert could understand him wanting to know that the creature was really dead. Some things you needed to see with your own eyes to accept. Nothing else would do.

Alas, any sense of triumph they might've felt at killing the boar was muted due to the carnage it had managed to inflict in such a small time.

Two men from Alan's search party were dead, with half a dozen injured – a few badly so. Wilbur was still missing, although Luthor had taken the initiative and already sent a group back to look for him.

Though Bert tried to be hopeful on that front, he didn't care to speculate as to what they might find. If Wilbur had run into that thing and hadn't managed to find cover in time...

Bert shook his head, horrified at all that had happened in the past hour. And that was only what they were aware of.

Who was to say what chaos the creature had caused in the days leading up to this? Bert didn't consider himself much of a betting man, but he'd had been willing to wager that, at the very least, the monster boar was the one responsible for killing Scooter's pigs. As for the men they'd been out looking for, nobody had said anything yet, but he had a feeling most of the other searchers were drawing the same conclusion that he was.

"Dear Lord have mercy," Alan said as Bert helped him into the clearing. Sadly, the only mercy to be had was that the bodies of the dead men had been covered – Luthor's doing after he'd taken charge of the situation. Driving home that this was indeed no time to celebrate was Scott Debkins – sitting alone next to his brother's body, his face unreadable.

Everyone was mostly giving him a wide berth while they kept busy. But maybe that was for the best. There was still too much work to be done. Grieving for those they'd lost would have to wait at least a little while.

Seamus was off tending to the other injured, while another group was hard at work fashioning litters so that the wounded could be safely brought back to town.

Despite all this, a few still milled around the beast's corpse, staring at it with a mix of fear and morbid fascination.

Bert could understand both sentiments. Once again, he was forced to think back to that paper he'd written about extinct mammals. Surely, this had to be some kind of throwback, some Ice-Age monster that had managed to remain hidden until now.

What other explanation could there be?

"So, we gonna talk about the elephant in the room or not?" Alan finally asked, his teeth gritted and sweat beading upon his brow.

"It's not quite an elephant," Bert muttered, "but close. Too damned close."

One of the men from Luthor's team, Ned Kirkwood, turned from where he'd been using his arms to try and measure the dead boar. "Ya ain't wrong on that one, Bert. This here son of a whore... Sorry, Sheriff. I meant this son of a gun's gotta be thirteen feet long if it's an inch. Maybe longer. That's gotta be a state record."

"You'll forgive me if I'm not too worried about the record books, Ned," Alan replied.

"Maybe you should be," another voice cried out.

They turned to find Byron Hoffsteader approaching. He'd still been cowering while Seamus had worked on the sheriff, but had apparently regained his composure at some point.

"What can I do for you, Mr. Hoffsteader?" Alan asked with barely concealed contempt.

"I think the better question is what can this marvelous creature do for us?"

"Do for us?" Bert replied. "Pretty sure this hog has done enough."

"I'm not talking about that," Hoffsteader said, glancing Bert's way before turning back toward the sheriff. "Think about what it could mean if we were to bring it back to town with us."

"Mean?"

"The attention, the press. Why, I bet we'd be on every news station in the state, maybe even nationwide."

Alan narrowed his eyes from where he continued to lean on Bert. "Let me see if I have this right. You want us to drag this thing back with us and string it up? For what purpose? So it can stink up the whole town?"

"A minor inconvenience compared to the attention it could bring." Hoffsteader held up his hands, as if miming a news headline. "Think about it. Come see *Pig Kong*, the eighth wonder of the world. We could turn Cooper's Bluff from an out of the way burg into a tourist Mecca."

Bert didn't say anything, but he could sense Alan stiffening in response.

"There's two good men lying dead over there, Mr. Hoffsteader, both of them lifelong citizens of this *out of the way burg...*"

"I understand that, Sheriff, but I'm sure their families would..."

"Not to mention I have a missing deputy out there

somewhere as well. And you're here to tell me you want to, what, sell tickets to see this blasted thing? I'll remind you, three of your own men are missing in these same woods. And while I don't care to officially speculate as to their fate, I'd say that thing right there is a pretty good candidate as to what happened to them."

"So you're saying the loss of life should be for nothing, is that it?"

"Not at all," Sheriff Heller replied, his tone low and dangerous, telling Bert he was doing all he could to hold his temper. "But I will be tarred and feathered before I stand by and let someone earn a dollar off those deaths."

"But..."

"We leave the pig."

"Be reasonable, Sheriff."

"I *am* being reasonable, Mr. Hoffsteader. If you want to see unreasonable, please continue testing me on this. Am I clear?"

Hoffsteader hesitated for a moment before narrowing his eyes. "Crystal."

"Same goes for all of you," Alan cried, raising his voice. "Consider this a crime scene as of right now. What that means is I'd best not hear that anyone tried grabbing any souvenirs on the way out."

There came no protest in response, not that Bert expected any. Most of the men present were hard working, honest folk. And the few that weren't knew enough not to press their luck where Alan was concerned. Hoffsteader was a whole other story, but the sheriff wasn't finished yet.

"Luthor, I need you to secure the scene best you can. Pick three good men to wait with you." He glanced sidelong at Bert for some reason, before turning back toward his deputy. "I'll have Ellie send the coroner and some fresh hands out here soon as they're able. Once that's finished, bury the *goddamned* thing as deep as you can."

Bert knew Alan wasn't one to use invectives. He'd probably done so to ensure he had everyone's attention. If so, it had succeeded.

When nobody moved to disagree, he then turned Bert's way again.

"*Now* we can get going. I don't know about you, but my leg is aching like the devil took a bite out of it."

26

Byron didn't consider himself a patient man by any means. No, patience was for fools who weren't willing to make the big decisions.

Whole fortunes had been lost on account of meek assholes waiting for the right moment.

Life was way too short for that kind of nonsense.

It was likewise too short to suffer fools, but sometimes concessions needed to be made. There was no doubt in his mind that Sheriff Heller was one such fool but Byron wasn't so stupid as to cross him, at least not in a situation where he held every advantage.

Despite wanting to do nothing more than cut the man down to size and remind him of his place in the grand scheme of things, Byron held his tongue. Though he typically despised those who advocated playing the long game, he understood that some circumstances warranted it. This was one such time.

With the excitement over, he was able to collect himself and take a proper read of the situation. Everyone there had their dander up over what had happened. There would be no talking sense to any of them regarding the opportunity that oversized pig represented – at least not yet.

It was painfully obvious that the more he fought for it, the more they'd push back – perhaps violently so. Byron wasn't a stupid man. He knew the score. There were at least two men dead in this forest. Would anyone back in town question a third, especially once the sheriff swore everyone there to silence?

Byron didn't think it would come to that, but he knew how these hillbillies operated. Far as he was concerned, they understood only two things: fucking and fighting. As the only outsider present, neither was a risk he was willing to take.

So instead, he got to work with the others, letting them all think he was complying with the sheriff's wishes – even going so far as to help care for the wounded. All the while, he made careful note of the area around them – committing every possible detail to memory.

He had every intention of finding this spot again, sooner rather than later.

The dead hog was massive, larger and far heavier than the remains of that stupid cow he and his surveyor had discovered the other day. Unless the sheriff was planning on sending a small army of men to take care of it, it was doubtful they'd be able to move the corpse far for burial.

All Byron had to do was wait them out and then recruit enough of his own people to do what needed to be done.

Yeah, the sheriff would likely be angry with him, but who cared? By then, he would have convinced the town's leadership that he had their best interest at heart. After all, who could argue against more money in their coffers?

Then, afterward, he'd set to work putting Cooper's Bluff on the map, whether the locals wanted it or not.

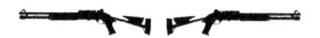

Miles to the north, Charlene let out a screech at the sight of the disgusting beast facing her.

The rat stood on its hind legs, sniffing the air as if debating whether she was a threat or not. Then, with a quick squeak, it scurried through her legs before disappearing into the darkness beyond.

She'd been about to start work on another room in the old base – a former office from the look of things – when she'd noticed a narrow door in the far corner. Curious, she'd opened it up, only for the vile thing to scamper out from inside, nearly frightening the life from her.

For a moment, she considered pulling the kitchen knife out and giving chase, before realizing it was probably both pointless and stupid. *Koolaid* was quick to agree with that assessment.

"Seriously, bitch?" she asked in his voice. "You gonna let a little rat scare you? Like you ain't had bigger in that whore mouth of yours."

"You're right, Koolaid. I'm sorry."

As his voice silently encouraged her to get on with it, she aimed the flashlight beam into the tiny space – hoping she didn't see any more sets of beady eyes peering back. Instead, she let out another whoop, this time one of joy.

From the look of things, this had been a janitor closet. Better yet, it was the proverbial motherlode. Inside were buckets, mops, boxes of soap powder, and more – pretty much everything she could've hoped for to make the job of cleaning that much easier.

If only she'd found this the day before, she could have gotten twice as much done.

I wonder. Charlene stepped inside the cramped space to where an old slop sink rested. She turned the spigot on, not expecting much. However, there came a wheezing rattle from the pipes. Seconds later, murky brownish water the color of rust began to pour out – a trickle at first, but gradually gaining strength. She let it run until it finally started to clear up a bit.

It was a lucky break of the highest order as far as she was concerned. She doubted any of it was fit to drink, but it was more than good enough for scrubbing the floors and any surfaces that needed polishing. That's what mattered.

Charlene reached for one of the pails, intent on getting started, but then she hesitated. A more thorough search of this place would've uncovered this room a lot sooner. Who was to say what other surprises the old base had in store for her? Heck, maybe there was even one of those fancy motorized floor buffers waiting somewhere. She wasn't sure why an old army base would need one of those, but it sure would be fine nevertheless.

She could only imagine the look on Koolaid's face if he returned to find the floors shining like polished glass.

Most of her work from the day before had been confined to the first two rooms they'd found – about as far as the light from outside had penetrated. That wasn't going to be enough, though, especially if Koolaid was successful in recruiting some new flavors.

"If?" she asked in his voice.

"Sorry. I meant *when* you bring back all those fly bitches."

That important detail out of the way, Charlene took a moment to consider things. She was much better equipped today for some light exploration. At the very least there was little chance of getting lost in the dark now. As for coming across any more rats…

She turned to the far corner of the closet, grabbing hold of the heavy handled push broom that was leaning there. It was the perfect deterrent against any rodents who might be so bold as to stand in her way.

"Don't worry, Koolaid, I'm not slacking off or anything," she explained, stepping from the closet – now duly armed for a bit of exploring. "I'm just going to take a quick look around, see what else is here. It'll just take a few minutes. That's all."

"Best be quick about it," Koolaid's voice warned. "This shit-hole ain't gonna clean itself. Okay, so what are you waiting for? Get moving, bitch!"

"You got it, Koolaid."

Her marching orders received. Charlene once again flipped on the flashlight, letting the beam play out before her as she turned toward a door leading further in – determined to do whatever it took to make this once-abandoned army base into the love motel of her man's dreams.

27

"Excuse me, miss. I ... I feel kind of nervous asking this, but if you wouldn't mind, could I maybe trouble you for an autograph?"

The young woman looked up from the pile of shoeboxes she'd been stacking. "Excuse me?"

"Your autograph," Martin repeated, feigning skittishness. "You're an actress, right?"

"No, I'm not," she replied cocking her head. "I think you might have me confused with someone else."

Martin shook his head, his eyes opened wide in what was hopefully a semblance of disbelief. "You're kidding me."

The woman let out a giggle. "I'm being serious. No fooling."

"I could've sworn that was you in this movie I saw just last week. Christ, I can't believe it wasn't. What was that actress's name?" He snapped his fingers a few times. "Cybill something."

"Cybill Shepherd?"

"Yeah, that's the one. Holy shit, you look just like her." He shook his head, once again feigning shyness. "But I bet you hear that all the time."

The woman, Laura according to her nametag, let out another laugh and smiled at him. Even as he prepared to butter her up some more, Martin was already thinking ahead.

Laura? Hmm. Sounds like I'm about to pork my fat cousin. Probably enough of that going on in the Bluff already. How about Lana? Maybe. Wait, I've got it. Lily! "Oh man, I really can't believe it. I swear, you could be her twin. That blonde hair, those baby blues." Now it was time to test the waters and see what shot he had at adding a Lily to his collection of flavors. "Please don't take any offense at this, but it blows my mind seeing a fine piece such as yourself working a dead end job like this."

Her reaction would tell him whether he had a chance or if it was time to take this show back on the road.

She blushed at his words, giving him the once over now that she'd apparently realized he wasn't just there to ask about their selection of loafers. "Okay fine. Just between you and me, this place seriously blows. Oh, and my boss, we're talking total creep here. But it pays the bills, so what can you do?"

"Bummer. Doesn't seem fair to me, especially the way some of the other chicks here seem to enjoy talking behind other people's backs."

She raised an eyebrow. "What do you mean?"

Time for a little fishing expedition. "Nothing. I was just up front browsing and the girls working the register were gossiping, that's all. I didn't mean to eavesdrop but they were talking some real nasty shit."

"Like what?"

Internally, Martin let out a wide grin, although he did his best to keep it contrite for his audience of one. "I really don't know if I should say anything..."

"Come on. Don't leave me hanging here."

"Okay, fine. I don't know if they were calling you out or someone else, but one of them was talking about how some blonde bitch, her words not mine, didn't know how to treat a fella right."

Laura's eyes narrowed. "Was it Jeanine?"

Martin pretended to think about it for a moment before replying, "Yeah, I think she's the one."

"Well, let me just tell you, that cunt's just jealous because she couldn't keep a man if he was tied up in her basement. Got a rearend like a dump truck *and* she stuffs her bra too."

Martin held up his hands. "I wouldn't know nothing about that."

"And just for the record, I do so know how to treat a man."

"If you say so."

Laura stood up and glared at him, although Martin could tell it was an act. "You calling me a liar?"

"Not at all, queen," he said. "I'm just saying I have no way of knowing either way."

"Is that a fact?" She took a quick look around, then gestured for him to follow. "Come with me."

"Where are we going?"

"To the back room. It'll be empty right about now."

"W-why?" he asked, following her.

"So I can show you a thing or two about how I treat my men. Unless, that is, you're all talk and no game."

Boar War

Despite the change in weather, Martin was feeling mighty fine as he strolled back to the Dodge. Getting his dick waxed twice in one day was a good way to brighten an already sunny mood. Not hurting was that Lily, he refused to think of her as Laura, was not only a piece of ass but one capable of sucking the whitewall off a tire.

He'd been right to heed his instincts. Originally, his plan had been to head toward Kettelbury to try his luck, but he'd instead decided to keep going, on toward Brewerton. It wasn't exactly a city, but was big enough that you didn't feel like you were in the sticks anymore. He figured that would be as good a place as any to cast his net, and he sure as shit hadn't been wrong on that end.

Best yet, Lily hadn't freaked when he'd not so subtly suggested she was the kind of chick dudes would pay top dollar for.

Normally, that would've been the point where he jumped on that shit like white on rice, but this situation required a bit of patience on his part. Lily already had a gig that was paying the rent, so she was going to need a little more convincing to join his flavor stable. More importantly, Martin had nowhere for her to stay, at least not yet.

It's not like he could just stuff her in the barn, not without Bert and Lin asking a whole shitload of uncomfortable questions. As for the soon-to-be chalet, Lene had made decent progress, true, more than he'd expected, but it was still going to take some time before they were ready to use it – much less allow a foxy lady like Lily to live there as a permanent resident.

He had no doubt he could make it work. With the price of gas and other shit on the rise, a rent-free abode wasn't anything to sneeze at. But he wasn't naïve enough to expect his newest top flavor to live in a shit-hole and be happy about it.

Charlene might've been okay with it, but he wasn't about to risk Lily telling him to go fuck himself. He'd learned his lesson in Nashville. Once he had his flavors up and running again, he had no intention of letting them get away this time. That meant having a firm hand with them, but making sure they were treated well – or at least well enough to not be on the lookout for the next Big Daddy.

He looked up, those thoughts trailing off as something fell upon his shoulder. At first he thought it might've been a bird taking a shit on him, but then he saw the dark clouds looming overhead.

A moment later he felt another drop of water, then another.

Rain. Holy shit, it's finally fucking raining!

It wasn't much, just a tiny drizzle but far as he was concerned it was almost as welcome a thing as Lily slurping on his sausage. Well, maybe not that good, but after weeks of godawful heat, it was nice to feel the pitter patter of rain on his face.

Martin hopped in the car and turned the key, once more enjoying the roar of the engine. He flipped on the wipers and peeled out of the parking lot – not worrying about either the weather or the long drive ahead as he got on the highway and turned east, headed toward the direction of Cooper's Bluff.

Hopefully Bert was still slogging ass out in the woods, but if not Martin was sure he'd think of something to say to excuse his long absence. Worst case, he could tell Charlene to fake a limp or something, then make up some bullshit about taking her to the doctor.

Yeah, that could work.

Even as the rain started to fall a little harder, Martin saw nothing but sunny days ahead – punctuated by a rainbow of flavors and all the greenbacks they were sure to produce.

28

Byron somehow managed to bide his time, forcing himself to sit tight and not jump the gun. Fortunately, there was still work to be done. And with him on site at least the men wouldn't dare slack off.

It was especially important to be seen now, as word of what had been found in the woods began to spread like wildfire. He could tell the men wanted to do nothing more than stand around gossiping like a bunch of hens, so he made it a point to step out of the foreman's trailer at regular intervals to make sure they weren't goofing off.

Behind the closed doors of the trailer, though, his focus was turned toward something else entirely.

He'd long since learned the usefulness of equipping his company's trucks with CB radios. They'd proven useful, especially for survey teams heading into wetlands or heavy brush. More importantly, such devices had planted seeds in his imagination of new and interesting ways to use modern technology to his benefit.

He'd made contacts in several industries over the years, a direct result of the many projects he'd spearheaded.

Boar War

Recently, one of those contacts had paid off. Sitting on his desk was a top of the line police scanner – a tunable prototype that wasn't slated to be out on the market until next year. However, thanks to some pulled strings and a few greased pockets, he'd been able to get a hold of one early.

The wonderful device had already paid for itself on some of his other projects, in terms of fines and tickets he'd managed to avoid simply by keeping his ears open.

Now he found himself eagerly tuned in as the day passed, listening to the drama gripping the town – of which there was no small amount.

In short order, he'd learned several items of interest.

As expected, Sheriff Heller was being taken to the hospital over in Kettlebury. At the very least, they expected him to be kept overnight for observation. It was music to Byron's ears.

He'd also discovered that one of the reasons their search party had seen so many damned delays was that another body had been found earlier. He heard mention of a name he didn't recognize, Patty Something-or-other. Probably either the wife or sister of one of the searchers. Either way that was likely the reason the sheriff had tried to keep it on the sly. According to the radio chatter it also sounded like she'd been found partly eaten. That didn't necessarily mean their monster pig was the cause, but he doubted it was a coincidence.

Perhaps most important of all was that the day hadn't been finished throwing the town its share of tragedies. That deputy the sheriff had sent back to town, McCoy. Turned out he never made it. Instead the folks from the coroner's office, enroute to where the standoff with the pig occurred, had spied something in the brush and come across the broken remains of his body.

It was ironic in a way since he was the same shit-kicker

who'd given Byron crap just the day before. Though he hadn't wished anything like this upon the man, he wouldn't shed any tears over it either. Just another dead yokel as far as Byron was concerned. However, what piqued his interest was how it left the sheriff's office severely undermanned.

There was no way that other deputy, Hendricks if Byron's memory served him right, could be expected to stick around in the woods playing nursemaid to a pig corpse, not with two men down.

Best yet, the weather was rapidly deteriorating. Already, big drops of rain were starting to fall. Sheriff's orders or not, he doubted anyone was going to want to stand around a forest clearing while Mother Nature took a great big piss all over them.

He glanced toward the trailer's window. Soon enough the construction site was going to be too much of a mess for the heavy machinery to keep running. The lighter indoor work could continue, but the rest would need to be postponed.

Normally another delay such as this, especially when they were already behind, would send Byron flying into a rage. However, this time he realized the opportunity it presented.

All it would take was a few volunteers, the promise of some overtime pay, and perhaps a little bonus to ensure they kept their mouths shut. It was an unfortunate expense, but one he was certain would be paid back a hundredfold given a little luck.

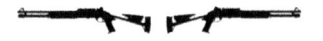

Had Cooper's Bluff been a bigger town, Byron might have been worried about such a small window of opportunity.

Boar War

But a tiny burg like this one boasted limited manpower when it came to public works. People would volunteer for certain endeavors, such as the search for his missing crew, but there was only so much that could be asked of them, especially when they had their own bills to pay.

As for Reg and Grant, he was now fully convinced both had ended up as pig chow. It was regrettable but a done deal as far as he was concerned, not that he was about to say anything in front of the team he'd conscripted for this job.

He'd brought four able bodied men along with him, all of them from the heavy loader crew – each possessing a strong back and mouths to feed back home. Just the sort who'd be more than up for a little under-the-table assignment.

It seemed a safe number. Any fewer and there'd be no way they could handle the hog's body. More and, well, there was that old saying about loose lips sinking ships. Fortunately, he didn't need the whole damned thing. The head, tusks, and hooves would more than suffice. They would serve as proof of the massive beast's existence as well as give a taxidermist enough to recreate a life-sized model.

And that was just the beginning.

First things first, though. They needed to get to that pig, preferably while the body was still fresh.

The rain was coming down harder now and, judging by the color of the clouds to the west, it was only going to get worse. That was fine, though. There'd be plenty of time to dry off later back at his hotel room. Once there, he could order some room service and raise a toast to his own business acumen.

"Shouldn't we be heading back in, Mr. Hoffsteader?" One of the men, a backhoe operator named Guiterrez, asked. "It's starting to get kinda heavy."

Byron had been ready for the whining, assuming it a case of *when* not if. "What's the matter? Afraid of a little rain? Tell me, did your folks complain about getting wet back when they were dogpaddling across the Rio Grande?" Byron locked eyes with the man, practically daring him to say something. Then, with no challenge forthcoming, he turned to the rest. "Let's be clear about one thing. This job is all in. You stick with me through the end and you get paid. If not, you're free to head back on your own. But don't come crying to me later."

As expected, that shut them up right and proper, allowing him to focus on leading them.

Despite the rain, he'd been able to identify the markers he'd committed to memory earlier. Better yet, they hadn't spotted a single soul since entering the woods. Between the weather and the various other debacles going on in town, it was a near perfect storm. Hell, it was practically a mandate from Heaven – one the town would eventually thank him for.

Byron raised a hand, telling the others to stop. If he wasn't mistaken, just up ahead was the clearing where the boar had been killed. He couldn't see any movement in the rapidly darkening woods nor was there any sound other than the rain falling around them.

He wasn't about to be stupid about this, though, not now. In his pocket, wrapped in plastic, was a small stack of fifties. It was a last resort in case they were spotted, but he preferred not to have to use it. The men who worked for him were one thing, but he wouldn't put it past any of the locals to take his money and then rat him out after.

Byron threw a quick warning at his crew to stay put and be quiet, then began to creep slowly forward. Fortunately, the now heavy rain served to mask his footsteps nicely.

Boar War

Finally, he poked his head around the last batch of trees. The clearing appeared to be empty. Not only had the bodies from earlier been removed but there was also no sign of anyone standing guard. Only one thing remained but its presence was enough to put a grin on Byron's face.

Near the edge of the clearing, at the same spot where they'd felled the beast, was a massive hump of dirt – twenty feet long and probably six wide, piled at least three feet high. It was the biggest grave marker Byron had ever seen and the only that had ever excited him.

It was obvious how hastily it had been made. He'd been right. There hadn't been enough men to go around. Between McCoy and that woman who'd been killed, the authorities had been spread too thin.

It painted a clear picture for him – the men setting to work to dig a ditch right next to where the massive boar had died. They'd done as much as they could given the time and resources they had. Then they'd labored to roll the beast into it before covering it as quickly as they could so as to beat feet back to town.

Hell, there was probably no more than a foot of fresh dirt between him and his prize. The rain was likely going to make unearthing it again a bit more difficult than it might've been otherwise, but that wasn't his problem.

After all, it wasn't like he'd be doing the digging.

Byron took one last look around, making sure the coast was clear. Then he turned and whistled for his crew.

"All right, let's go! Bring those shovels and that hacksaw up here. It's time to get to work. Ándale! Time is money you know."

29

The work to uncover the pig's corpse progressed quickly, although the storm seemed intent on making the task as difficult as possible, increasing in intensity with no end in sight. By the time they were finished unearthing the mammoth beast, the rain was coming down in buckets.

Byron wasn't worried about that, busying himself instead with the all-important task of supervision. There was little doubt that whoever had buried this damned thing had cut as many corners as possible to get the job done – and now the rain was doing the rest, washing away the mud and dirt that remained.

One of the men prepared the tarp they'd brought so they could cart it all back when finished, while the other three got to work with their saws.

Byron realized the head was going to be the tricky part. The boar's neck was thick with muscle and tendons, making the effort to hack through it both bloody and maddeningly slow. Even minus its tusks it looked ridiculously heavy. He was sure it was going to take at least two, maybe three of them working in tandem to carry it back – not that he was all too worried about it. After all, that was what he was paying them for. At least this way they'd truly be earning their money.

To the west, lightning flashed in the sky followed by the distant rumble of thunder. All around them, tree branches and bushes whipped in the wind. The longer they were out there, the riskier this would become. He wasn't about to say anything about that, though. The men, especially that Guiterrez fellow, needed to know he was adamant that they finish what they'd set out to do. If he allowed them to second guess him, they'd no doubt insist on cutting this short – robbing him of everything he was there for. That was unacceptable, especially since he suspected this was his only chance.

Byron considered the haphazard way the creature had been *buried*. He wouldn't put it past the sheriff to send some more men out later to do a more thorough job, after all the other ruckuses were dealt with. As it stood, a blind man would be able to tell someone else had been out there mucking with the body. Once the locals figured it out, there was no doubt all suspicion would be dropped right in his lap.

He had no intention of making it that easy for them, though. So, as soon as his men were finished excising the parts of the boar he wanted, he planned to order them to cover it back up. They wouldn't like that, but once again that was their problem to deal with. Besides which, they were all thoroughly soaked by that point. A little bit more wouldn't matter.

Hell, if anything, the rain was a godsend. Not only was it masking their presence, but it was also doing a good job of minimizing the stench rising off the dead pig. The blasted thing still stunk to high heaven but not nearly as bad as if they'd been out there under the heat of the blazing sun.

"Mr. Hoffsteader, sir," one of them, a fellow named Benedict, called out, his voice just barely audible over the storm. "Do you think you could maybe prop this leg up while I work on the hoof?"

Under normal circumstances, Byron would've shot him a withering gaze and held it long enough to convey what he thought of that idea. However, even he was beginning to realize just how bad the weather was getting. The last thing he wanted was to take too long and for one of these ditchdiggers to get struck by lightning or hit by a falling tree branch. That was the sort of headache he didn't need. The ongoing construction already had him popping Tylenol by the handful, with a few quaaludes thrown in after hours.

Much as he didn't care to dirty his hands on the dead beast, he stepped in and grabbed hold of the leg Benedict was indicating. "Get to it then and be quick about it."

"Yes, sir."

The creature's tusks along with a pair of hooves were already laid out and ready to go. All they needed was the remaining two and for the head to be finished. Then they could...

"Madre de Dios!" Guiterrez gasped from the pig's other end.

Byron looked up to see the gore-splattered fool drop his hacksaw and begin backing away.

"Be squeamish on your own dime," he growled. "I mean it, you greaseball son of a..."

There came a heavy snort from somewhere behind him, loud enough to be heard over the falling rain.

It's just the echo of thunder, nothing more. "It's ... only thunder!" he repeated, this time out loud, although his voice didn't convey nearly the authority he'd meant it to.

A bolt of lightning flashed high above, momentarily illuminating the clearing and the woods surrounding them – giving him a mercifully brief glimpse of massive humped figures visible through the undergrowth.

It's an illusion. My eyes must be playing tricks. There's no way it could be...

Guiterrez let out a screech of fright and took off running. He'd barely made it to the tree line when an enormous brown shape burst from the bushes and slammed into him – trampling him beneath its feet.

His screams were cut short as the life was crushed from his body, but the rumble of thunder quickly took its place – the deep bass of nature's fury reverberating in Byron's bones. Loud as it was, it wasn't enough to drown out the angry squeals which filled the air, seeming to come from everywhere at once.

As cries of disbelief rose up from the rest of his crew, Byron turned around – terrified to look but unable not to. Perhaps it was a good thing he was already soaked from the rain because his bladder released less than a second later.

Byron had always considered himself the most rational of men. It was his ability to cut through the bullshit which had helped him succeed where others had failed. However, the downside was that he quickly realized there was no fooling himself about this particular situation. He was thoroughly fucked. Or at least he would be, unless he and the remainder of his crew could...

It was too late for that, though.

The nerve of the three other men broke at the same time. As Byron stood there, terrified and pissing himself in the rain, they scattered.

Had they opted to try climbing one of the many trees within reach, even with the ensuing downpour, one or more of them might have survived. Sadly, each took off running instead, far too panicked to realize they were already surrounded.

There was no way for Byron to know whether these monsters had been attracted to the smell of death, the noise the men had been making, or had simply been riled up by the break in the heat the storm represented.

In truth, it probably didn't matter.

He stood there, too frightened to move or even breathe. All he could do was watch his men die.

Benedict was the first to fall, his steaming intestines splayed along the ground as one of the monstrous pigs gored his midsection with a swipe of its ungodly head.

The next thirty seconds were enough to completely unhinge Byron's mind as a half dozen of the abominations converged on the other two survivors – running them into the ground and descending upon them with tusks, hooves, and teeth.

Driven into a frenzy by the scent of fresh blood, the beasts gored one another in their fervor to devour the crushed and broken remnants of what had been men barely a minute earlier.

And still Byron stood there, miraculously untouched as all this unfolded mere yards away from him. Maybe it was his proximity to the dead pig, or perhaps it was the stinking aroma of piss and shit surrounding him as his bowels were next to let go. Either way, he stood there a mute witness to the carnage that would soon be visited upon the rest of Cooper's Bluff.

A minute passed, then another. Deep within the reptilian portion of Byron's brain some small portion of sanity must've remained, one desperate to survive, because he finally dropped to his hands and knees on the muddy ground and forced himself to turn away.

Reduced to little more than an animal, he tried to make himself as small and unnoticeable as possible while he tried to crawl to safety – silently praying that the driving rain was enough to cover his escape.

He was almost right.

Byron made it to the very edge of the clearing before something impossibly strong and heavy slammed into him from behind. There came one brief moment of pain as something sharp tore through the flesh and muscle of his back, then it all went numb as he collapsed face-first into the mud.

Lying there and unable to move, he was mercifully no longer able to feel anything below his chest. However, the sound of frantic chewing that reached his ears was more than enough to make up for this as the beasts began to gorge themselves on his still living flesh.

30

Deep within the former Piedmont Creek Facility, Charlene cheered as the massive generator coughed and sputtered for a few seconds before finally roaring to life.

Moments later, fluorescent bulbs began to flicker overhead – slowly filling the cavernous space with light.

Though her exploration hadn't turned up the floor buffer she'd been hoping for, there was no doubt that this was far better. Though her efforts to actually get some cleaning done had been subpar compared to what she'd planned, she was hoping this find would be more than enough to put Martin in a forgiving mood.

She'd steadily gone from room to room – stopping in each to take careful note of anything that might be of use for the soon-to-be Koolaid Chalet. It had mostly proven a fruitless effort, save for one large space that had probably once served as a laboratory or something fancy like that.

Inside there'd been some dusty glass beakers as well as a filing cabinet filled with more old papers – ones that she'd dutifully piled to the side for disposal as Martin had instructed. Of far greater interest, though, had been the rows of sturdy tables still set up within.

Darla had once told her that all the upscale whore houses, the ones in classy cities like New York for instance, offered Johns the option to pay extra for a massage before getting their shafts waxed.

Well, shit, most of their clientele would be coming from all that construction going on at the south end of town. She couldn't think of anyone who'd want a massage more than some poor schmuck who'd been breaking rocks with a jackhammer all day.

"Fuck yeah," she'd told herself in Koolaid's voice. "Charge them once to rub their backs then again to rub their cocks. Now you're thinking, girl."

She'd thanked *him* thoroughly for the praise before moving on, thinking that was almost certainly the best find she'd be making this day.

She'd been wrong. Not long after, she'd come across this section of the base. It was the biggest space she'd seen in the facility so far. A wide padlocked roller door sat at one end, telling her it was likely some sort of loading dock.

However, that didn't explain the rest. A row of what looked to be furnaces lined one end of the expansive bay, all of them long since extinguished. What truly caught her attention, though, were two massive metal tanks next to what appeared to be a row of industrial-sized generators.

Back home, she and her father hadn't owned much but there had been an old genny out back for those times when their power got cut off – which was often. She'd spent many a night siphoning gas out of neighborhood cars to keep it running.

These were obviously much larger and more powerful – although likely just as old as theirs had been. She wasn't sure if they ran on the same fuel or not, but a quick tap on the tanks seemed to indicate they were mostly full.

Figuring she had nothing to lose, Charlene had ended her exploration in favor of taking some time to look things over – finding these generators more complex but still vaguely familiar to the one she remembered.

She'd immediately set to work seeing if there was any shot at getting them running again.

Several false starts later, she was about to give up and write it off as a lost cause when she decided to give it one last try. It had been worth it as the base was now returning to life for the first time in twenty years.

At the very least, she could see again – a small miracle considering how dark it had become in the aged army base. The weather outside had gone from bad to worse in the last few hours, meaning she couldn't even count on the meager illumination streaming through the boarded up windows. In the bleakness of the interior, her flashlight had begun to feel wholly inadequate.

Now, though, she finally got a sense of the entire space. In truth, it was no small relief to be able to see every nook and cranny. Though *Koolaid* had been sure to speak up every time she'd found herself a bit spooked, reminding her how stupid she was being, it was nice for her eyes to confirm that he'd been right all along...

"What the fuck, Lene?"

"Sorry, Koolaid. I should've listened to you to begin with," she instantly replied, realizing a second or two later that the question hadn't come from her lips.

"Yo! You here or what?" Martin called out again, his voice coming from elsewhere in the facility.

Charlene's eyes opened wide. She knew she'd spent a bit of time exploring the base's interior but hadn't realized how much until right then. If he was back, then that meant she'd wasted the entire day dicking around when she should've been focused on scrubbing the floors and making this place shine.

Knowing in her heart she'd failed him but hoping to mitigate his disappointment nonetheless, she quickly grabbed hold of the push broom and began sweeping the dust on the floor as she called out. "I'm in here, Koolaid!"

"In where?" he cried, closer this time.

"Back here!"

A few minutes passed and then he finally stepped in to find her diligently shifting dirt from one side of the open space to the other.

He was soaked head to tail, his hair flopping in his face.

"Oh my god, Koolaid, what happened?"

"I stopped at the Y to take a swim. What the fuck do you think happened? It's raining cats and dogs outside." He glanced at her, shook his head, then looked around. "What the fuck is this place?"

"Um, boiler room, I think."

He ignored her response, continuing to take it all in. "Hold on. Did you actually manage to get the lights working in this dump?"

"Uh huh. The generators have still got some juice in them. Ain't it great? We got lights now and even running water too."

"No shit? Goddamn, girl, you've been busy."

"Really, Koolaid?" she replied, grinning ear to ear. "I mean, yeah I have."

He raised an eyebrow. "There's only one problem."

Her heart immediately sank. This was it. He was going to lay into her for being a lazy Susan. "What is it, Koolaid?"

"The lights outside. They're all on too. I was pulling in

when suddenly this place lit up like the inside of a disco. Good thing it's pouring like a motherfucker out there, otherwise someone would probably see it and know what's up."

"Oh! I didn't realize."

He shook his head. "No big deal. We just gotta figure out where the switch is, or maybe bring a ladder next time so you can unscrew the bulbs."

"Okay," she quickly replied, barely able to mask the relief in her voice. "So ... how many new flavors did you score?"

He seemed to appreciate the change in topic. "Just the one for now but she's a real piece. I tell you, Lene, the Johns are gonna be lining up from here to Frontier Road to fuck this chick's brains out. We're talking top dollar, oh yeah!"

"That's great, Koolaid."

"Fuck yeah it is. And now that we got lights in this shit hole, you oughta be able to clean it out twice as fast."

"That's exactly what I was thinking," she replied.

"That's what I like to see, baby, a little bit of that entrepreneurial spirit. Who knows, maybe I'm rubbing off on you after all."

"You really think so, Koolaid?"

"Sure, why not," he said dismissively. "Either that or it's just a case of the blind squirrel finding an acorn." He looked past her. "The fuck is up with those things?"

She followed his gaze. "Oh, those are the boilers I mentioned. I was thinking, maybe we can fix them up for once winter gets here. If you think that's a good idea, that is."

He shook his head. "Pretty sure those aren't boilers, babe. They look like trash incinerators." At her confused look he explained, "My old man worked at a junkyard for a while. Question is, what the fuck were they incinerating here?"

"Papers maybe?"

"Papers? Open your eyes, Lene. The goddamned things are big enough to drive a jeep into." He turned her way. "Why the fuck would you say that anyway?"

"Because I found another stack of them back in the..."

"You throw them out like I told you to?"

She instantly averted her gaze. "No, Koolaid. Sorry, I kinda forgot."

If he was mad at her, he didn't show it. "Fuck it. Grab a stack on the way out. Maybe we can find out what the fuck they were actually doing in this place."

"Really?"

He shrugged. "Might as well. This storm don't look like it's ending anytime soon. It'll give me something to do while we wait for it to pass. Anything's gotta be better than sitting downstairs and listening to a sermon from Bert expounding upon the virtues of shit shoveling."

"You got it, Koolaid."

"Speaking of which, shut this shit down so we can get our asses moving."

"Don't you want me to give you the tour first?" she asked. "I found this spot we could use for..."

"Save it. Half the roads leading into town are already flooded. I want to get back to the farm before we end up stuck in a ditch. Last thing I need is to be bitched out because I got mud all over Uncle Bert's *baby*."

31

The last thing Bert wanted to be at that moment was strong.

The day had seen so many conflicting emotions – fear perhaps the worst among them – that he wasn't even sure how to begin processing them all.

However, despite everything that he had to deal with, Lin came first.

Neither of them had suspected how badly things would turn out when they'd gotten up this morning. If he'd had even the first clue that something had happened to Patty Gantry, he'd have stuck around to be there for Linda – search party be damned.

Of course, that was stupid to think now. Why would he have dropped her off there in the first place if that were the case? Trauma certainly had a strange way of causing one to consider weirdly implausible what-ifs.

Fortunately, Lin finally seemed to be calming down. They were sitting in the parlor drinking Irish coffees – both cups fortified with two extra shots each. The weather had gotten bad enough that TV reception was non-existent, so instead they just listened to the sound of the rain outside as Milo snoozed on the floor in front of them.

The downpour was such a stark contrast to the weather of the past month. Perhaps under different circumstances it would've given them more than enough to talk about as they whiled away the evening. Hell, they would've probably been sitting out on the porch enjoying it, not caring a lick about how wet they were getting.

Today had been a real boot in the ass, though.

"I just can't believe it," Lin said, starting again. "How that thing ... ate her. How it could have gotten..."

"Except it didn't get me, Lin," Bert interrupted. "Didn't even come close. I'm right here, fine as can be. See for yourself."

In actuality, he wasn't fine, far from it as a matter of fact, but she didn't need to know that. Some burdens were for him alone to bear. Fear was only a part of it, however.

The truth was, he wanted to be pissed as hell at both Wilbur and Alan for keeping the truth from him when they'd first learned about what had happened at the Gantry's. They had their reasons, sure, but keeping a man from his wife when she needed him wasn't right. Sadly, that anger was a dead end as Alan was in the hospital with a busted leg, while poor Wilbur had fared far worse.

That thing had found and killed him before he'd even made it halfway back. Bert hadn't seen it himself, thank goodness, but from what he'd heard Wilbur's body had been mutilated nearly beyond recognition.

Sadly, he wasn't the only victim the beast had claimed that day.

God, what a nightmare.

Despite his reassurances to her, Lin was right. That thing had almost gotten him the same way it had gotten Jake Debkins and George Anders, the latter only identifiable thanks to the driver's license in his back pocket. The beast would've succeeded too had Luther and his team not shown up when they had. He'd hesitated at the worst possible moment and it had almost cost him everything.

Bert knew he shouldn't blame himself. After all, the shock of seeing a familiar animal blown up to the size of a Buick was no small thing. It would be like coming home to find Milo was now the size of a moose.

In the weeks to come there would no doubt be endless speculation as to how something that looked like a run-of-the-mill feral hog could've grown so large. He could imagine the questions. What had caused it? Was it radiation, little green men, or just a freak of nature?

Maybe by then Bert would even care. For now, there was a bigger question. How many had fallen victim to it in the days before they'd managed to bring it down?

Obviously, there'd been Patty, but were there others they just didn't know about yet? Those missing men were likely candidates, true, but was it possible there'd been others, people who'd slipped through the cracks? Cooper's Bluff was normally a tight-knit community, but between the economy, the seemingly unending heat wave, and the construction going on at the south end, nerves in the tiny town had been at the end of their rope.

People who might've otherwise been sociable during better times were keeping to themselves, focused on their own affairs. It wasn't like he was immune to it himself. Bert had mostly kept busy trying to keep the farm running while babysitting his fool nephew. Sure, he occasionally called Scooter to shoot the shit but otherwise he'd been mostly concerned with his own business.

Scooter.

He still needed to call his friend. He'd meant to when they got back, but tending to his wife had taken priority, causing it to slip his mind. Regardless, Scoot and Irma deserved some closure for their slaughtered pigs. It wasn't much compared to the damage that freakish beast had caused, but at least maybe someone could take some comfort in its death.

Thinking it through a bit more, he decided that's exactly what he would do – give Scooter a call, albeit he'd keep it quick for now. Much as he wanted to unburden himself to his friend, he didn't want to run the risk of Lin overhearing. She had enough on her plate right now without learning how right she was to be afraid for him.

At the very least, he could let Scoot know what had happened, as well as check in to make sure everything was okay on their end with this crazy storm blowing through. That assumed the phone lines were still working, of course.

He stood up and turned toward the front windows. It was dark as pitch out there aside from the occasional flash of lightning, but it was hard to miss the sound of wind and rain whipping about outside. Sure as hell, this storm was looking to be one for the record books.

"What's wrong?" Linda asked.

"Nothing at all, Hun," he replied, facing her. "Just figured I'd give Scoot a call, make sure all's well with him and Irma."

"That thing, it's what got their pigs, isn't it?"

Bert wanted to lie, to give her something to think about other than that blasted boar and the trouble it had caused them all, but that would've been unfair to her. So instead he simply nodded. "Yeah. No way to know for certain, of course, but if I was a betting man that's where my money would be."

"I know it's silly of me to say, but I hope it helps Irma

... to at least know that thing is dead, I mean. The poor dear was so upset when last we spoke."

"Hopefully," he said, stepping toward her. "Listen. You do know none of this is your fault, right."

Linda looked up at him, meeting his gaze. "I know. It's just ... they ... the coroner told me Patty had been out there for a couple of days at least."

"There's nothing you could have..."

"You think I don't know that?" she snapped just as the lights flickered, almost as if they were in tune with her mood. "Sorry. It's just, I can't help but think that if I'd only checked in on her sooner..."

"Don't do this to yourself."

"I know I couldn't have saved her. I'm not that big a fool, Bert. But maybe if I'd thought to call, realized something was up, I could've alerted the sheriff and the whole town would've been, I don't know, more prepared I suppose."

"I know what you mean, but we can't torture ourselves with maybes. We had no way of knowing what was out there and we can't change what happened. We can only move forward and try to make sense of this so it doesn't happen again."

"You're right. I know that much, but still..." She lowered her head for several long seconds, as if thinking it over. Then, without warning, she stood up and put her arms around his neck. "Here's an idea. Rather than the both of us sitting here grousing like a couple of old hens, you go call Scooter. Then, when you're done, you can come meet me upstairs. How's that sound?"

He raised an eyebrow, caught completely off guard. "Are you sure?"

"Positive. I don't know about you, but I could use a little something to take my mind off things, something to remind me that we're both still alive and kicking. How about it, mister, you think you're up for a *little something*?"

He grinned. Hell, a bit of sweaty distraction with his favorite person in the whole wide world sounded better than okay. "I think I could muster up the energy."

"Good," she replied, pulling away. "Grab a few candles on your way up. I have a feeling we're going to need them before the night is..."

Almost as if on cue, the power blinked again before cutting completely out, instantly dousing them in darkness.

Linda let out a gasp, but then she started to giggle. "Guess I spoke too soon."

"You do have a way with words," Bert replied, also with a laugh. "Although speaking of which, I'm thinking maybe there's no reason for us to head upstairs after all."

"Oh? Change your mind?"

"Not at all. It's just there's a perfectly good couch right here."

"What about your call?" she purred, once again stepping in close.

"It can wait. Phone lines are probably down too."

"What a shame."

"Yeah, it is..."

Before their lips could meet, however, the darkness was momentarily dispelled, although it had nothing to do with the power coming back on. A set of bright headlights flashed from outside as a car pulled up in front of the house. It was accompanied by a familiar rumble that most certainly wasn't thunder.

The Dodge!

Realization hit. Amidst all the chaos of the day, he'd failed to notice that neither Martin nor Charlene were home yet. Hell, there'd been no word from either of them since he and Lin had gotten back to the house, which had been some time ago.

"That little car-snatching weasel."

"Be nice, Bert," Linda told him. "You're the one who said he could borrow it."

"Yeah, to pick his girlfriend up from work, not go on some joyride."

"Maybe he was taking it slow on account of the storm."

Bert highly doubted that. When he imagined slow and responsible driving, Martin's was the last face that came to mind. Still, Lin had a point. He *had* given the kid permission ... sorta.

"Maybe you're right." He let out a huff. "I suppose this means the couch is out."

She leaned in for a quick kiss. "For tonight anyway."

They let go of each other and he stepped to the door, opening it just as his two wayward boarders were running toward the porch.

"Holy shit," Martin cried, soaked from head to tail. "It's coming down like a bitch out there."

"That bad?" Bert asked conversationally, trying to keep his cool.

"Hell yeah. I didn't think we were gonna make it back. It's like every goddamned road between here and Kettelbury is flooded."

"What were you doing over in...?" Bert took a breath then pushed the angry retort away. There was no point in getting worked up over hyperbole. Linda was probably right after all. Considering the weather, Martin had almost certainly been forced to take it slow and...

The sharp crack of splintering wood dispelled those thoughts as it cut through the roar of the storm – coming from the direction of the barn.

What in hell?

Bert turned that way only to realized it was accompanied by the panicked neighing of horses as well as the cries from their remaining cows. No doubt about it. Something had the animals all in an uproar.

He instinctively reached for his rain slicker on the hook next to the door when all the fear from earlier came rushing back in a hot second, causing him to hesitate.

"You gonna let us in or what?" Martin asked, still standing outside.

You're being stupid. That goddamned pig is dead and you know it.

"Earth to Uncle Bert. We're kinda drowning out here."

Back toward the barn, the cacophony continued.

That stupid boar is dead, he silently repeated, as if trying to convince himself it was true.

Either way, he knew he had to check on what was going on, but that didn't mean he needed to be stupid about it.

Bert stepped aside and gestured toward Charlene. "You, in the house." Then to Martin he said, "You're with me."

"What for?"

"Remember when I used to take you hunting as a kid?"

"Yeah, so?"

"Well, it's time for us to see if you still remember how to handle a shotgun."

32

"Did you fix it yet, Harold?"

Harold "Scooter" McNeil let out a sigh as he turned toward his son in the glow of the lantern.

Both of them were standing in the corner of the attic, watching as the rain continued to pour in while his wife Irma called to them from the bottom of the narrow staircase.

"Don't suppose you want to be the one to break the news to her."

Mikey was quick to shake his head. "All yours, Pa."

"Kinda what I figured." Scooter glanced back toward the stairs then raised his voice. "Nope, not yet."

"Then you'd best hurry things up," she called back. "My knitting room's getting soaked."

Rather than say the retort he wanted, he bit his tongue. This was mostly his fault anyway. There was an old sycamore just behind the house, too close to it in his opinion. He'd been looking for an excuse to cut that damned tree down for years now but Irma had argued against it.

So, of course, he'd capitulated each and every time because it just wasn't worth fighting over.

At the very least, he should've pruned the branches back. Sadly, he wasn't as spry as he used to be.

Had James still lived at home, he would've taken care of it, but Mikey was still too young to handle that kind of work, or so Irma believed. He was her *baby* after all. She would've likely tanned both their hides if she ever found him fifty feet up in the tree sawing through branches.

It was too bad because now they were paying the price.

Scooter's original plan for the evening was to maybe grab a few beers with Bert after the day's chores were done and ask him if the search party had turned up anything. He'd briefly considered joining them, but had managed to convince himself there was work to be done that couldn't be put off.

It was a lie, nothing more. The last few days had left him spooked in ways he hadn't felt in years. The truth was, he needed a day of normalcy – a few hours where he could pretend nothing out of the ordinary had happened, that his mind had been playing tricks the night Irma's hogs had been slaughtered.

As his father used to tell him, good honest labor had a way of clearing a man's mind.

That had proven excellent advice, for the first half of the day anyway. Then the storm had rolled in and all thoughts of anything else had washed away with the first few drops of rain.

It had been the most welcome change of weather he could remember. However, as the storm increased in intensity his opinion on that slowly changed. It was like the clouds had decided to make up for their absence all at once.

First the power had gone out – a not entirely unexpected occurrence – then there'd come a heavy *thunk* from above as something landed on the roof, a branch from that damned sycamore. Initially it hadn't seemed like much of a worry, but then they'd heard the sound of dripping from above – loud enough to tell it was coming from inside.

He and Mikey had gone up to investigate only to find that the branch had been heavy enough to puncture the shingles. The damage wasn't too bad, but there was no way anyone was getting up onto the roof to patch it tonight – not with the wind howling like it was and lightning still flashing across the sky.

Scooter respected Irma's concern over her knitting room, but not enough to get his fool ass killed over it.

No, the best thing to do would be to staunch the leak best they could for now and then wait for the storm to pass.

"Come with me, boy," he said, turning toward the staircase.

The last thing he wanted after a long day was to be popping up and down the stairs like some blasted jack-in-the-box, but it was either a few hours of discomfort now or he and Mikey dealing with a major repair tomorrow.

"I'm working on it," he muttered to his wife as he passed her by in the candle-lit hallway. There'd be plenty of time to give her the details later. For now there was work to be done.

With Mikey hot on his heels, he made it to the kitchen where he set the lantern on the counter and began looking around.

He spied several of their smaller pots and pans, but those wouldn't do. If he tried to use them to catch the water streaming in they'd end up having to switch them out every five minutes. *There*! He plucked their old cast iron Dutch oven off the stovetop, but still didn't see what he was looking for.

"Irma! Where's...?"

"You don't have to shout, I'm right here," she said from the doorway, nearly scaring the bejesus out of him.

"Don't sneak up on a man like that," he groused before asking, "Your big stew pot. Where's it at?"

She shrugged sheepishly in response. "I loaned it out to Norma Claverman last week. She was canning this big batch of jam and I guess I forgot to ask for it back."

"Wonderful." Scooter shook his head. It was just his luck. *That had better be some damned fine jam.*

"What about the slop pails out in the barn?" Mikey asked. "We could use those instead."

Scooter considered it for a second or two. "Yeah, that should work. I'll go and…"

"Let me, Pa," his son dutifully offered instead. "It's no problem at all. I can be back lickety split."

Scooter was about to disagree, but the truth was he didn't fancy stepping outside in this mess. The last thing he needed was to catch a chill and be laid up. Mikey on the other hand was young and strong. A little water wasn't likely to bother him none. Still… "Fine, but put on your rain slicker first, otherwise you'll end up a drowned rat before you can take three steps in this shit."

"Harold!" Irma chided.

"Sorry, I meant out in this storm." He blew a breath through his teeth before turning back toward his son. "Keep your head down and be quick about it. No screwing around, okay?"

"You got it, Pa!" Mikey stepped past him, sounding like he was looking forward to this little adventure far more then common sense warranted.

Ah, to be young again. "And take the flashlight with

you," Scooter called after him. "Your mom and I don't need you getting lost in your own yard."

"Will do!"

That settled, he turned to Irma. "Go wait at the door for him. I'm gonna run this upstairs and hope to high heaven it doesn't fill up before he gets back."

Scooter was starting to grow impatient. Fifteen minutes had passed. The pot was less than halfway full which was fine for now, but he didn't fancy carrying it downstairs once it was topped off.

I swear, if he stopped to play with those damned barn cats...

Realizing he needed to go see what the holdup was, Scooter started back down the stairs when there came a heavy crash from below. Irma's panicked shrieks reached his ears in the moment before the whole blasted house seemed to rattle in its foundation.

He lost his footing and fell, just barely managing to catch hold of the railing before he took a bad tumble – wrenching his shoulder in the process but managing to stop before he could really hurt himself.

"What in hell?" he growled, holding on until he managed to get his feet back beneath him.

The goddamned tree! It had to be. The storm must've knocked it over onto the house.

So much for this being an easy fix, he thought, finally making it to the second floor. Depending on how bad the damage was, they might have to finish the night down in the storm cellar – something he was very much not looking forward to. "You all right, Irma?"

There came a second crash from below, the sound like

a dozen logs being split. He felt the floor shudder beneath his feet, but thankfully this one wasn't as severe as the first had been. "Irma!"

No answer reached his ears, causing him to double-time it to the main staircase as he called his wife's name again.

All that he heard in return was the thunder and whipping wind of the storm outside, louder now – as if the walls of the house were no longer keeping it at bay. *Shit!* "Hold on, Irma, I'm coming!"

Scooter made it about halfway down before stopping dead in his tracks at the sight that awaited him. The front door and most of the wall it was attached to had been smashed to kindling – like someone had driven a truck through it.

There was no truck or tree to be seen, though, nor was there any sign of his wife. The damage itself was bad enough, but what truly caused his heart to skip a beat was the thick trail of blood splattered across what had been the threshold of his home just minutes earlier – the red smear rapidly growing in size thanks to the rain now pouring in from outside.

33

Had anyone been around to ask, Scooter McNeil would've told them he honestly had no idea how he'd managed to get to the bottom of the stairs without breaking his neck.

One moment he was standing there about halfway down – his brain refusing to acknowledge the nightmare below him. The next, he was on his knees in a pool of blood as the wind and rain from outside raged against him.

The entire front wall of his home had been caved in, splintered like it was nothing more than kindling. Far worse, though, was the smear of ichor where his front door had previously been – the same spot where his wife Irma had been waiting for Michael, their youngest, to return from the barn.

Scooter looked around, still not believing what his eyes were telling him. He then spied one of Irma's slippers amongst the wreckage – lying there as if to drive home the terrifying reality of what had happened.

His first thought upon hearing the commotion downstairs was that the old sycamore in their yard had come down and struck the house. The problem with that theory was manyfold, however, not the least of which being that the blasted tree in question was *behind* their home.

For one insane moment Scooter envisioned the old tree coming to life – uprooting itself like an angry god to claim his wife as revenge for the fact that he'd argued for cutting it down.

A bark of unhinged laughter escaped his lips seemingly of its own accord – his tortured mind attempting to retreat into absurdity rather than face this grim reality.

Lightning flashed outside, bright enough to make him shield his eyes. In the moment before he turned away, though, he sensed a wrongness out there that couldn't be denied.

He knew his property like the back of his hand, his whole family did. Any one of them could've walked end to end blindfolded without ever tripping once. But in the second before the oppressive darkness once again descended, he was certain he saw things that didn't belong – massive figures silhouetted against the night, standing there as if in judgement.

He knew it was probably his imagination playing cruel tricks on him. Nevertheless, his memories instantly turned back to the other night and the thing he'd seen. There was only one conclusion to be drawn.

Whatever had killed Irma's hogs had returned to take her as well.

It told him what a fool he'd been. He should've taken precautions when he'd had the chance. He should've worked tirelessly to protect his family and land against a creature that was unlike anything he'd ever seen before. But instead he'd chosen to believe those who told him there was nothing to worry about. That it was no more than a hungry bear or rogue mountain lion.

All at once Scooter felt very old. Though he still carried a gun at night, it was more out of habit. He hadn't realized until that moment how much the years had served to dull the abject terror he'd once felt. He'd moved on with his life rather than truly prepare for the possibility that one day he'd come face to face with the unthinkable again.

Now he was paying the price for his hubris as...

An eerie cry from outside dragged him from his rapidly darkening thoughts, a screeching animalistic roar that could no way be thunder. To his ears it seemed to be both challenging and mocking him at once.

That finally got him moving.

Scooter scrambled to his feet, praying it wasn't too late. Maybe Irma was still alive, injured but not yet...

He refused to let himself finish that thought, not until he knew for certain.

Then there was Mikey to consider. The boy was still out there somewhere in the dark – his life in mortal danger for no other reason than his father hadn't wanted to get his precious tootsies wet.

Holding onto the image of their faces like a life preserver thrown to a drowning man, Scooter embraced the anger, outrage, and self-loathing that was building up inside him. It was a bitter pill to swallow but more than enough to overpower the fear dictating that he should turn and run.

He took a single step out into the downpour before forcing himself to stop. Scooter desperately understood that he needed to move quickly, but he was old and wise enough to know that acting rashly wouldn't help anyone.

Instead, he turned and raced to his gun cabinet in the next room over – pulling out his twelve gauge along with a box of buckshot. In his haste to ensure the weapon was fully loaded he dropped several shells to the floor, not bothering to stop and pick them up.

If what was already in the magazine wasn't enough then a few more probably wouldn't make a difference. Besides, he'd wasted enough time.

Now duly armed, Scooter stepped back out into the storm. The darkness alone was challenging enough, but the driving rain was nearly blinding in its ferocity. As such, he had no choice but to keep his head down – waiting for the intermittent flashes of light to guide his way.

"Irma! Michael!" he called repeatedly, although he may as well have been whispering for all the good it did against the howling wind.

Lightning flashed high above. Scooter used the opportunity to scan the ground around him for any sign of footprints or drag marks. It was pointless, though. Any tracks had been instantly washed away in the deluge. Hell, it was like his entire front yard was now a lake of ankle-deep water.

Alas it was also a lake filled with unknown dangers as once more there came a piercing bellow from the blackness that had nothing to do with the weather. It sounded familiar in a way, almost recognizable. He knew it was possible he was maybe hearing a cow or horse in distress, but deep down in his gut Scooter didn't believe that.

"Irma!" he cried, continuing to trudge forward.

Once again, lightning crackled across the sky, but this time something caught his attention. There was a small object on the ground nearby, momentarily visible in the bright glare from the flash above.

He turned that way, toward the direction of their barn – continuing to shout the names of his family despite being overpowered by the wind and thunder. He stopped and crouched low, his heart breaking at the sight of the flashlight lying partially submerged in the mud.

No!

Half-crazed with grief and fear, Scooter began to sprint wildly – racing first one way then another as he tried to find something, anything that would tell him he was wrong, that his worst fears simply weren't true.

The distorted sounds of frantic grunting reached his ears as he barreled forward in the darkness, although in his panic he couldn't be certain what was real and what was the storm.

Then, before he could find the source of the disturbing ruckus, his foot slammed into something hard – the stump he and Mikey had spent many an afternoon chopping firewood at. Scooter felt more than heard the sharp crack of at least two of his toes breaking in the moment before he toppled over face-first into the mud.

Choking on the foul tasting muck, he pushed himself up to his hands and knees just as another bolt of lightning flashed high overhead, illuminating the yard before him.

His first thought was to wonder how their cows had gotten out of the barn and why they were stupid enough to be grazing in this crazed maelstrom.

The illusion lasted less than a second before he realized that, big as they were, the shapes of the creatures less than forty feet away were all wrong.

Their faces were indeed planted to the ground, but there was a desperate almost frantic quality to the way they were rooting around.

Steadying himself on his knees, Scooter wiped the mud from his eyes and then took aim as he waited for the next flash. A part of him was certain his eyes were playing tricks on him but he was through taking chances.

Barely a minute later, the field lit up from above once again.

He saw in an instant that this was no mirage or trick of the light. He'd been right all along. The beast that had killed their hogs was no bear.

Nor was it apparently alone.

At least three of the behemoths were gathered in a cluster – nightmares given form, grunting and shoving each other out of the way as they tore into something on the ground.

Then, just before the light faded, he saw it – barely two yards ahead of him, so close he could've almost reached out and grabbed it.

Irma's other slipper.

There was no blood, at least that he could see. The rain had taken care of that, but it had been impossible to miss the severed foot, sheered off at the ankle, on the ground next to it.

Fighting back tears of anguish, Scooter chambered a round as he held the gun in his trembling arms. It was too late, though. All the fight had already gone out of him as the horrifying realization set in.

Irma and Mikey were gone, both having met a fate that was too terrible for him to ever want to consider.

As he knelt there feeling all sense of hope drain away, lightning flashed again. In that time, he numbly saw one of the beasts turn his way, as if finally noticing he was there.

That was what decided it for him. Even if he survived the next few minutes, a dubious proposition at best, then what? Did he truly want to be forever haunted by his wife and son's deaths – a memory he'd be forced to relive until the end of his days?

Deep down he already knew the answer.

Scooter planted the butt of the shotgun into the mud. With a resolved sob he placed his chin atop the barrel and then reached out until his thumb was pressed against the trigger.

To his credit there was no hesitation on his part.

A moment later the shotgun's roar filled the air, just as thunder rumbled high above – almost as if the heavens chose to acknowledge his sacrifice.

The sharp report served to catch the attention of the monster pigs, for a moment anyway before they resumed devouring the last remnants of their awful meal.

Deep inside the dark barn, Michael McNeil cocked his head and listened. It really was a wild one out there. Despite his assurances to both his parents, he almost had gotten lost on the way when a gust of wind had caused him to stumble – sending his flashlight tumbling out of his grasp and into a puddle, where it promptly died.

Realizing it was pointless to retrieve the stupid thing, he'd soldiered on – finally making it to the barn, where he'd closed the doors behind him.

Mikey was a kind boy at heart. Despite knowing he should've hurried back with those pails he'd promised his pa, he first made it a point to check on their milking cows – making sure they were all tucked safe in their stalls. Then, just as he'd been about to head back out, he'd heard the most pathetic mewing imaginable coming from the far corner of the barn.

He knew at once there was no way he could just ignore it.

Sadie, one of their barn cats, had recently given birth to a litter. It seemed only right to check on her and her kittens. Sure enough, they were all safe and dry, but he'd made it a point to give each of them a bit of attention in turn.

It was only as the sound of thunder once more crackled outside, sounding almost like the report of a gun, he realized he'd stuck around far longer than he'd intended to.

His parents were almost certainly going to be cross.

Then, realizing the damage had already been done and that a few more minutes likely wouldn't matter, he picked up the next kitten in line and began to dote over it.

34

Martin was pretty sure that Bert had lost his dung-addled mind. He'd expected to be yelled at when they'd gotten back, maybe even completely bitched out over his unsanctioned use of the Dodge. Instead, he'd been handed a loaded shotgun and ordered to follow as his uncle tore ass across the yard in the middle of the fucking deluge that was coming down.

He'd already been soaked to the bone, but he felt like little more than a dish rag by the time they reached the barn and the ruckus coming from inside.

Bert then ordered him to stand at the ready, gun raised, as he prepared to open the door. Martin was tempted to ask what the fuck was going on, assuming he could even be heard over this fucking storm, but his uncle's tone didn't leave much room for protest. So, rather than argue, he did as told, trying not to freak out over the fact that Bert was clearly spooked to high hell and back.

Balancing his own gun in one hand along with the

flashlight he'd brought, Bert yanked the door open then quickly shined the meager light inside.

From the sound of the animals within, you'd have thought they were all being stuffed into a thresher, but Martin had spent enough summers at the farm as a kid to know how easily livestock could be set off. Once one started in, the rest tended to follow.

After several long seconds of his uncle checking in seemingly every direction, it became pretty evident what had happened. One of the cows – he'd never bothered to remember their names – had partially broken through the front of its stall, likely spooked by nothing more than the weather. The stupid thing had gotten tangled up in the mess and panicked, which was causing everything else in there to likewise throw a shit fit.

As Bert continued to frantically scan the barn, as if expecting to find something else inside, Martin finally asked, "So, did we come out here to shoot the cow or something?"

"Huh? No, of course we're not shooting Bessie."

"Just asking, man. You're the one who dragged us out into this shit like it's hunting season."

Bert glared at him for a moment, before stepping inside. "Come on. Let's get her and the others calmed down before they hurt themselves."

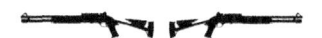

Martin found himself not only soaking wet but down on his knees as he hammered the last few nails of the makeshift stall repair – all while his uncle worked to calm down the agitated animals within the barn.

Knowing my luck I'll catch pneumonia and die right

before the goddamned chalet opens, he groused to himself as he finished. "So, are you going to tell me what's up?"

"What do you mean?" Bert replied.

"I mean, were you and Auntie Lin like dropping acid earlier or maybe popping some ludes? Because if so you might want to cut back."

"No," his uncle said, throwing Martin some side eye.

"Hey, no judgement if you were. It's all good. I understand. You guys were home alone, the lights were out, and you were looking to pass the time. I get it. You just gotta watch that shit. You guys aren't as young as you used to be, and too much will..."

"We were *not* doing LSD," he snapped.

"It's cool, man. Just saying." Martin glanced over at the two guns now leaning against the wall. "So, if that's the case then why are we out here packing like Five-O?"

Bert ignored him at first, continuing to soothe the damned cow. Whatever was going on, he could tell his uncle was every bit as agitated as the dumb animal. All the same, it couldn't just be because of the storm, bad as it was. Hell, if anything, he should've been glad to finally be getting some rain.

No, agitated isn't the word. He's acting like he's scared of something.

That wasn't like him.

Martin knew about what had happened over at Old Man McNeil's place a few days back, but far as he'd heard it had been a bear or maybe a mountain lion. Either way, it was nothing to get worked up over. Maybe his uncle's mood had to do with that search party from earlier. Was it possible they'd uncovered something unexpected? Either way, something was eating at him – enough for them to treat the trek to the barn like they were preparing to storm the beaches of Normandy.

"So then what gives?" he asked, trying again. "We talking a jailbreak here? Maybe a couple psychos escaped from the looney bin? What's up?"

Bert turned his way and inclined his head, as if debating whether he should say anything. Then, just as Martin was sure he was going to be ignored again, he said, "I don't know. I ... guess that damned pig's got me all riled up."

"The pigs? Why's that? You growing something in your garden you ain't supposed to be?"

Bert raised an eyebrow. "I'm not talking about the police, you moron. I'm talking about... Hold on. I guess you didn't hear."

"Hear what?"

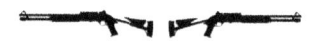

Ten minutes later found Martin leaning against the freshly repaired stall as Bert finished relaying a tale that sounded more like the bullshit the dried up old fucks sitting outside the general store liked to tell.

"You're shitting me."

Bert, however, shook his head. "I shit you not. Was bigger than Bessie over there and ten times as mean."

"That's fucking wild."

"Wild is one word for it," Bert replied with a tired sigh. "Listen, Martin, I'm sorry for dragging you out here like I did. I may have ... overreacted. It's just..."

"You think there's more of them out there?"

"What? No. This thing was a freak of nature. Had to be. But... I dunno. It's hard to explain. It's just when you see something like that, something that's so wrong compared to what you think you know. Well, I guess it just rattled me worse than I thought."

"Uh huh. But you guys killed it, right?"

Bert nodded. "No doubt about that. We put at least three rounds into its head after it was already down."

"Okay, so no problem then."

"You're not listening. It's..."

"Nah, I get it, man. If I saw something like ... what's it called? Oh yeah, if I saw something like the Loch Ness Monster I'd probably be a bit messed up about it too."

"Yeah, I suppose."

"So how about this? After the storm passes, the both of us can go out there and double check to make sure it's good and dead. Maybe that'll help you sleep at night."

Bert shook his head. "No can do. They already buried it."

"What, and we don't have any shovels around here? C'mon, Uncle Bert. We can dig it back up, maybe bring Aunt Lin's Kodak with us and take a few pictures while we're at it. Imagine that shit in the family album."

"Pretty sure the sheriff wouldn't like that."

Martin almost laughed. Of all the things he was doing that the sheriff wouldn't appreciate, taking photos of a dead pig was probably the least of his worries.

Still, it was worth considering, even if his uncle didn't like the idea. At the very least it would make for a hell of a portrait to hang in the new Koolaid Chalet. Maybe he could even design a room around it – an exotic safari experience he could charge extra for.

Oh yeah! He definitely liked the sound of that.

"...where it came from and how it got here."

He suddenly realized his uncle was still talking. "Huh, what was that?"

"I just said I only wish I knew where the damned thing had come from."

As his uncle's words sunk in, a proverbial lightbulb

turned on in Martin's head. He immediately glanced toward the barn doors, closed now to keep the worst of the storm out. Beyond them lay his uncle's Dodge as well as the stack of papers he'd had Charlene toss into the trunk.

He hadn't thought much of it since then, being far more focused on the progress she'd made in getting his new love motel up and running, but hadn't Lene said there'd been something in those papers about pigs?

Now, hearing his uncle's tale of a monster boar larger than anything he'd ever imagined, the thought gave him pause.

"Yo, Uncle Bert, I think there's something you..."

Martin trailed off as he began thinking this through more carefully. Yeah, he supposed it was possible the government had been breeding giant hogs out in that facility. That would certainly explain the size of those incinerators. But for what purpose? It sounded more like the plot of a bad drive-in movie than anything.

More importantly, sharing those papers could turn out badly for him. He sincerely doubted there was any chance Bert would keep that knowledge to himself. No, he'd almost certainly bring that shit to the cops, who would then turn their attention toward the not-so-abandoned army base. Not only would all his hard work be wasted, but what if Charlene had left something behind that would lead the fuzz straight to them?

It would be just his luck to get busted while trying to do the right thing.

Fuck that shit.

Worst of all, it would be for nothing.

Even if the pig his uncle was describing had been real, it was dead now. This ordeal was over, done. So what was the harm in keeping this his and Charlene's little secret?

"Huh?" Bert asked, turning his way. "Something I what?"

"Never mind," Martin was quick to reply. "It's nothing that won't hold until the storm passes."

He had no idea how so very wrong that decision would turn out to be.

35

Acting-Sheriff Luthor Hendricks never thought he'd be so glad to see downtown such a mess.

He stood there at the front window of the tiny police station silently counting to himself between each flash until there came the roar of thunder. It was a trick his grandmother had taught him as a child, a way to tell when a storm was finally blowing over. Too bad this one wasn't showing any signs of slowing down yet.

Lightning flashed again, revealing the street beyond – if it could even be called that anymore. From his vantage point it was more like they were perched on the edge of a raging river.

The power had gone out some time ago, leaving them at the mercy of the diesel generator out back. Fortunately, it was fueled for the long haul if it came to that. A few other buildings along High Street likewise had backup power – tiny islands of light within a sea of darkness. One of them was Dusty's Garage. There was a two man overnight crew on shift there, manning the radio in case their wrecker was needed.

Hopefully that wouldn't be the case. With any luck, people across both Cooper's Bluff and Piedmont Creek were hunkered down with their shutters closed and plenty of candles to make it through this storm.

So far, aside from the wind and rain, it had been quiet – not a soul to be seen outside, not that visibility was all that great even with lightning flaring high above.

"You do realize staring at this crap ain't gonna make it blow over any quicker, right?"

"Not sure I want it to," Luthor whispered beneath his breath, stealing a glance at the aged man standing behind him – his wrinkled reflection visible in the glass.

Cassius Danvers had once been a deputy in the shared township, serving for over thirty years before hanging up his badge. His retirement had lasted all of maybe six months before boredom had set in and he'd returned to work, not in an official capacity but doing odd jobs for the department and pitching in where needed.

Earlier, Luthor had tried to convince both him and their dispatcher Ellie Kent to go home but both had steadfastly refused.

He couldn't say he was unhappy to have the company. Without them there, it would've been just him – with no backup or anyone to talk to. Though mostly lost in his own thoughts, replaying the events of the day, Luthor didn't want to be alone with them. The presence of others meant he had no choice but to keep his shit together. Someone needed to be in charge and as the ranking deputy he...

Correction, the only *deputy.*

Luthor gritted his teeth, fighting the emotions that warred within him. Wilbur McCoy had been his colleague as well as friend – the kind of man you could work a

Boar War

twelve hour shift alongside then happily grab a beer with after.

And now he was nothing but a stiff taking up a slab in the morgue, and he wasn't alone. Hell, it was only by God's good grace that Alan hadn't ended up there beside him.

Sadly, the sheriff hadn't walked away unscathed.

His leg had been busted up pretty bad by that monster. Despite that, he'd insisted on sticking around and doing his job for far longer than he should have. Hell, it had only been an hour or so since Ellie had finally convinced him to let the frazzled attendants finally load him into the waiting ambulance.

Luthor most certainly didn't envy what was sure to be a slow miserable ride to Kettelbury in this downpour.

The whole thing was almost like a bad joke without a punchline. One of his friends was dead and the other on his way to the hospital for a long stay, all while that son of a bitch Hoffsteader barely had a scratch on him.

Luthor didn't blame him for them being out there in the woods this morning. After all, that was their job. However, his attitude and utter contempt toward them had been a bitter pill to swallow. Then, while they were still surrounded by bodies bleeding out onto the ground, the bastard had the nerve to suggest they haul that pig back to town – hoping to make a buck off it.

That was his only real regret about the storm. Had it remained clear, he'd have happily camped out in the woods next to that blasted beast – just waiting to see if Hoffsteader was stupid enough to try something. It would've given him no small amount of satisfaction to not only bust that heartless SOB but to be none-too-gentle while dragging his ass to lockup.

I'll need to check back out there again tomorrow, he told

himself, being mindful of Alan's orders. At least he didn't have to worry about it tonight. Nobody would be stupid enough to try anything in this weather, not even that greedy motherfucker.

"All right, that's enough grousing, Luthor," Cassius said, putting a hand on the larger man's shoulder. "Come sit with me and Ellie. Maybe I'll even let you win a hand of pinochle, although I wouldn't put money on that."

"Yeah, you're probably right, Cass. Staring at this rain ain't gonna make it go away."

"You got that right, son. Now come on, take a load off."

Luthor didn't particularly care for pinochle but he realized a distraction from the day's awfulness might not be the worst idea in the world, especially since he doubted there'd be too many breaks in the days ahead.

Maybe it was best to get a few minutes of peace while he still could.

Unfortunately, just as Cassius was pulling the card table from the broom closet, the radio on Ellie's desk squawked to life.

She donned her headset and answered it without any hesitation.

"Say that again," she said into the receiver, making a preemptive shush motion to the two men in the room. "I can barely hear you."

Ellie grabbed the pad of paper next to her and started furiously scribbling. "Okay. Go on. Uh huh. Did you say Briar Crossing? Got it. Is everyone okay? All right. Sit tight. I said sit tight, we'll be out there soon as we can. Over."

Before Luthor could ask, he saw the look on her face – worry mixed with a healthy dollop of exasperation. "What's wrong?"

"It's the ambulance, the one Alan's in," she said. "They hit a deep patch of water about two miles outside of town, over on Briar Crossing. Sounds like they're stuck in a ditch on the side of the road. Can't get any traction because of all the mud."

"Anyone hurt?"

She shook her head. "No. At least not more than they already are. I swear, if that darned fool had just left when we told him to."

Luthor put a hand on her shoulder. "That's Alan for you. Never did listen to anyone save the man in the mirror. All right. Get on the horn with Dusty's and let them know what's going on. I think Cal Summer's on shift tonight. Tell him I'll meet them out there."

"You actually going out in this mess?" Cassius asked.

"Don't see how I've got much choice."

"Then let me grab my rain slicker," the older man said. "Better to be a pair of fools out there than just the one."

"You sure about that?"

Cassius nodded. "Yup. If'n anyone asks, you can just tell them you were escorting this old coot home."

"Yeah, but Ellie might need…"

"Don't you worry none about me," she interrupted. "I'll be fine here. Snug as a bug in a rug. You two look out for each other. Make sure Alan gets where he needs to be and don't take any lip from him if he insists on coming back."

Luthor couldn't help but smile. "Yes, ma'am."

He couldn't say he wasn't glad to have the company. Even with an extra set of eyes, it would be slow going. Hell, it would be a damned miracle if they didn't end up stranded themselves, but if so at least he'd have someone to talk to.

Either way, it was time to do his duty.

Alan Heller had never felt more useless than he did at that moment, and the pain wasn't even the worst of it.

It seemed every decision he'd made in the last few days was coming back to bite him in the rear. First he'd bawled out his own son – grounding him for telling lies rather than even consider he might've been telling the truth about a monster in the woods.

As a result, good men – some of them his friends – were dead because of the calls he'd made. To top it all off, the ambulance transporting him to the hospital was stuck fast because he'd refused to leave until long after common sense dictated they should've been on their way.

None of this needed to have happened.

He understood that was hindsight talking, but it still didn't make him feel better.

His busted leg wasn't helping matters either. Roger and Avery, the two ambulance attendants sent to pick him up, had offered pain killers to make the ride easier but he'd refused anything stronger than a couple aspirin.

It was a decision he'd regretted almost immediately as the wet roads had rapidly given way to increasingly deeper patches of water.

He'd known the exact moment the two men had lost control of the vehicle – feeling every swerve and bump as it reverberated in his leg. Sadly, he'd been too busy trying not to bite through his own tongue to offer much in the way of advice as the ambulance finally skidded to a halt at a fifteen degree angle – the wheels on the passenger side stuck fast in the mud.

Avery had gone out into the storm to assess the situation while Roger began trying to hail someone on the radio.

Long minutes passed, most of them a pained blur for Alan. It was punctuated by shrill static from the radio, Avery occasionally pounding on the side while yelling to turn the wheel and give it gas, and Roger occasionally offering him platitudes that everything was going to be okay.

Alan's head was starting to swim – the stress, pain, and events of the day finally catching up to him – when he heard Ellie's voice, garbled but there, coming from the radio. After a bit of back and forth, Roger said, "Good news, Sheriff. Help's on the way."

"Glad to hear it," he wearily replied, although he could only imagine what Ellie was probably saying to the others.

Other, he corrected himself. Luthor was the only deputy left. He'd sent Wilbur to his death, yet another decision that had...

"Sure you don't want to reconsider?" the medic asked, interrupting Alan's inner self-loathing.

"Huh?"

"I could give you a shot of Numorphan. I guarantee it'll make the wait a lot more bearable."

"I..." He was about to refuse again, but instead said, "I'll give it some thought."

"You do that," Roger replied before calling out, "Yo, Aves, they're sending a truck. Get your wet ass back inside!"

There came no response save the crack of thunder.

Alan was about to rebuke the younger man for his language when the ambulance suddenly lurched to the side, followed by the heavy *crunch* of metal.

He felt the vehicle begin to tilt before the driver's side once more slammed back down onto the ground, the jolt hard enough to instantly scatter any thoughts he might've had toward scolding the driver.

Son of a bitch!

"The fuck is that idiot doing?" Roger cried, pushing open his door against the force of the wind, exposing them both to the full fury of the squall before hopping out and shutting it behind him.

"Avery!" he called out, his voice just barely audible over the storm. "Where the hell are…?"

Before Roger could finish, his words became a garbled cry, rising in pitch until they became nothing but a shrill scream.

Alan tried to sit up before remembering he'd been strapped in place so as to keep his leg immobilized. As he fumbled with the belt holding him down, he saw the driver's side door get yanked open again.

He caught a brief glimpse of Roger's hands as the man frantically tried to scramble back in, then something slammed into that side of the ambulance with the force of a freight train.

A spray of blood shot across the front seat as there came the crunch of broken bone and metal. The stricken vehicle pitched hard to the right, where it balanced on two wheels for a precarious moment before finally rolling over onto its side.

Alan let out a scream as the ambulance toppled over, the bones of his injured leg grinding against each other. The subsequent explosion of pain sent all other thoughts fleeing to the dark recesses of his mind.

It was too much. He felt himself slipping away.

As his consciousness faded, one of the ambulance's back doors fell open. His last sight before the darkness claimed him was the stuff of nightmares – a flash of lightning, momentarily illuminating the massive tusked head waiting outside.

36

Gary Higgins slammed the front door shut behind him or at least he tried to. With the wind blowing like it was, he had to struggle just to pull it closed – finally cutting off the sound of his wife's incessant bitching.

She'd been riding him extra hard this evening. With the power out and the unending drip of water from their leaky roof to egg her on, she'd apparently decided it was the perfect time to crawl up his ass.

It was the same shit as always. He needed to find a steady job, and God forbid he decide to have a couple drinks at the end of the day to settle his nerves. It was like she got pleasure in berating him, and always with Billy in the room – as if she took extra joy in cutting him down to size in front of his own son.

It wasn't his fault the economy sucked or that the blasted heatwave had left half the farms in town on the verge of welfare. He took odd jobs as a handyman whenever he could, but it was difficult to find work when nobody had any fucking money to spend.

Gary gripped the threadbare rainslicker more tightly around him as he trudged away from the house, for all the good it did. The weather tonight really was something else, more like a biblical plague sent by the good Lord himself than a passing summer storm.

Either way, he wished he'd had the foresight to ride it out down at Morty's instead of coming home to leftover meatloaf and a side helping of Bernice's attitude.

Hell, she should've been proud of him. He'd done exactly as he'd promised. The day before, she'd pleaded with him to lay off the liquor and show up bright and early for that goddamned search party. She said it would show he was reliable in a pinch – that it was the sort of thing that would convince more of the townsfolk to throw some work his way. So he'd done just that, traipsed through the fucking woods despite a headache pounding away behind his eyes.

And what good had it done him? Not a damned bit, save almost getting him killed by that fucking pig. Not only had he returned home needing to change his damned pants but he doubted anyone even remembered he'd been there at all.

So of course it figured that it would pick today to rain. Between the storm and that damned hog, he doubted the town would talk about anything else for days to come. His effort to make a good impression had amounted to nothing more than a colossal waste of time – one that had almost ended with him maimed or worse.

He shook his head, sending droplets of water flying. Nobody in their right mind would blame him one bit for needing a drink after a day like he'd had, but that was apparently giving his shrew of a wife too much credit.

He'd barely cracked open his second Schlitz when she'd decided to jump down his throat.

Boar War

After several minutes of her bullshit, Gary had enough. It was either brave the weather or go nuts listening to her. So he'd made up a lie – that he needed to go check on the chicken coop, make sure it was still standing in this gale.

Regardless, that hadn't stopped her from nearly following him out into it.

Had it still been daylight, he was certain she would've – rain or not – but Bernice didn't like the dark. She'd had a bad experience in the woods as a child, something she refused to go into detail about despite their years together. Whatever the case, she didn't like venturing outside after nightfall, especially in the back where their property bordered the marsh.

Thankfully, her phobia was his salvation.

In truth, he couldn't have given a shit less about their chickens. Let the damned things drown for all he cared. He had more important matters to attend to.

Gary stomped past the coop, his feet nearly sinking up to his ankles in the mud. It was so goddamned dark he could barely see his hand in front of his face. With the wind whipping about like it was, it was a near miracle that he didn't fall and break his neck.

He only stopped once he reached the tree line, the rain soaking him every bit as much as if he'd jumped in Berryman Lake fully clothed. Finally, there came a flash of lightning. The night sky lit up, illuminating the overgrown spot he'd been looking for – the one that marked a concealed trailhead leading into the woods beyond.

He heard the sharp echo of a tree falling from further ahead, audible even above the ruckus. From the sound of things, it had been a big one. There was little doubt there'd be many more before this shit was over and done with. The very real threat of being either electrocuted or crushed to death gave him pause as he stood there debating on his course of action – but only for a moment.

Between the fuckery of earlier and Bernice's harping, his nerves were shot. The need within him was simply too great to ignore. In truth, there was likely no amount of danger that would've dissuaded him at this point. Even had he known what was happening elsewhere in Cooper's Bluff, it's debatable whether he would've been swayed.

Heeding the call of the monkey on his back, he pushed through the wet brush and stepped into the woods. Between the wind and rain he couldn't see a damned thing, but that didn't deter him in the slightest. This trail was one well known to him. Once on it, he could've followed it blind drunk – something he'd done more than once over the years.

Navigating the path with a surety born of someone who'd tripped over every root and rock enough times to know exactly where they were, Gary made surprisingly quick progress.

He began to lick his lips in anticipation of the prize awaiting him.

Soon enough, none of the perils of the woods mattered in the slightest. The only thing that bothered him even remotely in the back of his mind was the constant roar of thunder echoing through the trees.

To his ears it sounded almost like a living thing, reminding him of that blasted pig. It forced him to wonder what else might be lurking out there in the darkness.

Gary slowed down, disgusted with himself – although perhaps not for the reasons he should've been. *Christ on a cracker, Bernice must be rubbing off on me.*

He pushed away those thoughts best he could,

focusing instead on what awaited ahead. It wasn't far now, maybe a few dozen paces at most. With that in mind, he continued onward.

Almost as if heralding his arrival, the sky lit up again just as he reached his destination – his own personal nirvana. It was like a great weight lifted from his chest as he stepped into the clearing, the one place in the entire goddamned town where he could relax without having to worry about some son of a bitch casting judgement on him.

This was his secret spot, the one nobody else knew about. Well, okay, maybe that wasn't entirely true, he considered. There was a good chance Billy was aware of it. After all, he and his friends spent a lot of their free time either fishing or exploring. It was simply what kids in Cooper's Bluff did when they were bored.

However, if he had ever found this place, he'd at least had the good graces to never mention it to his mom.

Far as Gary was concerned, that practically made the kid a hero, but enough of that. His focus currently lay elsewhere.

On the far side of the clearing was a lean-to he'd built years earlier and had spent many a night passed out beneath. It was wide and deep enough to keep the worst of the storm at bay, which was all that mattered.

Of far greater interest to him, though, was what awaited opposite the crude structure. He turned that way, waiting for lightning to flash once again.

There!

Hanging from a rope, perhaps seven feet off the ground, was a sealed plastic bucket. Inside it: his own personal version of heaven.

Awhile back he'd been talking to old Al Lisbon when

the concept of prison hooch had come up. Al had done time for armed robbery years ago, so it was a concept he was well familiar with. The thing was, as Al had explained, men were men regardless of whether they were free or locked up. And some men had a powerful thirst that not even the thickest bars could quench.

Where there was a will, there was a way.

Gary's first attempt at brewing the potent concoction had been questionable at best, leaving him mostly-blind for nearly an hour. But eventually he'd gotten the hang of it. Pulped fruit, bread, and plenty of sugar. Leave it for a week or so and voila – cheaper than Morty's and the company was twice as good, there being no one around to give him shit for it.

As for the rope, Gary had learned that lesson the hard way when some racoons had discovered his secret stash and gotten piss drunk while ruining his hard work.

Thunder rumbled again, pulling him from his reverie – the sound distorted by the forest, once more reminding him of the growl of some ravenous beast.

A chill crept up his spine that had nothing to do with the rain, but his course was set. Gary took off toward the bucket. He kept a tin cup in the lean-to as well as a few old blankets. That would be more than enough to ensure he rode out the rest of this storm in both peace and comfortable numbness.

Making his way forward more by memory than sight, he fumbled about a bit until his hand finally grabbed onto the rope holding the precious nectar aloft.

Practically salivating, he frantically worked to untie the knot wrapped around the tree trunk. A few minutes passed, most of it punctuated by cursing and yelling, but still the bucket remained suspended. After nearly working himself into a froth, he forced himself to take a deep breath and think this through.

Once he did, the reason for his failure became obvious. The damned rope was soaked through from the rain and had swelled to the point where the knot was stuck tight. Fumbling with it in the dark was doing nothing save make him ever more desperate for a drink.

He tried to take it more slowly, letting the glow from the lightning guide his hand, but his progress was only marginally better. He'd get a momentary glimpse of what needed to be done, only to quickly lose his way again as his mind couldn't seem to focus on anything but the fermented goodness waiting to be savored.

Fuck it!

He hadn't brought anything to cut the rope and he sure as shit wasn't going to try climbing the tree. Fortunately, the bucket was still within reach which meant he wasn't finished yet.

He tromped over to the lean-to, enjoying the momentary respite from the rain, found his cup in the back corner where he'd left it, and then trudged back to the hanging bucket as quickly as the weather allowed.

Gary's plan was simplicity itself – pry the lid off just enough so he could tip it over and fill his cup. True, this way would be slower, more wasteful, and require several trips back and forth, but it's not like he wasn't already soaked to the bone.

Besides which, after a couple of good swigs he wasn't likely to even notice the rain anymore.

Puckering his lips in anticipation of the sweet numbness to come, he braced himself against the wind then stood as high as he could on his tippy toes and grasped hold of the bucket.

Unsurprisingly, it was both wet and slippery, almost

causing him to lose his grip and fall, but he held tight with the manic strength of a man firmly in the thrall of his personal demons.

Holding himself steady, he managed to reach one hand to the top where he was able to grasp the lid. Slowly, he worked to pry it open.

Just a little more.

He could almost taste the bitter-sweet liquid within. He'd drink his fill and then take a well-deserved snooze. And if he happened to go blind guzzling it down, then so be it. It's not like there was a lot to see anyway.

Or so he thought.

Lightning flashed again, illuminating the space before him. That's when he realized he wasn't nearly as alone as he'd thought.

Standing there, glaring at him from barely a dozen feet away – it's head held high enough to look him in the eye – was another nightmare pig, every bit as large and terrifying as the one they'd just barely managed to kill.

Impossible!

Gary had seen things before whilst in the grip of his wondrous ambrosia, things that weren't there. Hell, he'd had whole conversations with people who in the end had only existed in his mind. Problem was, he'd been tanked to the gills each time it had happened. Right at that moment, though, he was damned near sober and the beast in front of him looked way too real.

Thunder boomed and the creature let out a roar of rage to accompany it.

Oh God!

Gary screamed as well, partially out of sheer terror but also because in that same moment he lost his footing. His feet slid out from under him. In a panic, he grabbed hold of the only thing within reach, the bucket – upending and spilling its sticky sweet contents all over him as he fell to the ground.

He landed on his back, ironically choking on the heavy splash of hooch that fell in his mouth.

It's all in my mind! There's nothing there!

However, even as he tried to rationalize it away, he felt a series of dull vibrations from the ground beneath him. This monstrosity was not only real but quickly approaching. There came a snuffling sound near his leg, erasing any hope of escape. This was it. He was mere moments away from dying.

Tears filled his eyes and his bowels released as the realization hit home, filling his pants with steaming shit born of fear and his wife's bad cooking.

Gary began to whimper as the snuffling intensified, the beast's wet nose working its way up his body.

Lightning once more flared above, revealing the massive boar that now towered over him – its tusks long enough to run him through. The creature looked down at him as it took one last sniff, as if letting him know his fate.

I'm sorry, Bernice! I should've listened!

The dire beast raised its head high … and then made a coughing sound, hacking a wad of vile phlegm onto his chest.

Gary closed his eyes, praying the end would be quick, but instead the snuffling sounds began to grow fainter – until once again all he could hear was the storm whipping through the woods.

Cracking one eye open just as the sky lit up once more, he realized the boar was nowhere to be seen. For some reason the beast had spared him.

Fearing it was nothing more than a ruse, he lay there in his own filth for several more minutes until his nerve finally broke. Reeking of mud, shit, and liquor, Gary scrambled to his feet and made a mad dash for his house.

Ironically, it was the first time in many years where the thought of going home and being with his family far outweighed any desire for a drink.

37

Luthor was beginning to suspect he and Cassius would've been better served commandeering a rowboat.

His police cruiser was tough, dependable, and well maintained, but driving at any speed beyond a snail's pace was proving to be near suicidal.

"Don't forget to pump the brakes," Cassius said as they drove through a pool of water nearly deep enough to go fishing in.

"I know how to drive, old man."

"You call me old man again and that ambulance is gonna be hustling *two* patients over to Kettelbury."

Luthor let out a chuckle. It was good to have someone to talk to. It made the drive somewhat less nerve wracking. On a clear day, it would've taken him maybe ten minutes to get out to where the ambulance carrying his boss had broken down. Of course, on a good day it probably wouldn't have ended up in a ditch to begin with.

There'd been no update from Ellie since he'd left, other than to let him know the wrecker wasn't too far behind.

Finally, after what felt like an interminably long time, Cassius pointed toward the windshield. "There! Lights ahead. I think that's them."

Luthor had no idea how he was able to see that when he himself could barely make out the road directly ahead of them, but a few moments later proved the older man correct. He finally made out lights on the side of the road, but there was something off about their placement.

"Oh shit," Cassius said. "I think it's on its side."

"How the hell did that happen?" Luthor asked. "Ellie said they just bottomed out in a ditch."

"Maybe Ellie heard wrong."

"Guess so." He picked up the radio's mic and pressed the button. "Cal, you got your ears on? This is Luthor. Over."

A few moments passed then the radio crackled to life. "*Yeah, Luthor, come on. Over.*"

"You'd best get a move on. We just arrived at the scene to find the ambulance on its side. I'm gonna make sure everyone is okay but we could use some muscle."

"*On its side?*" Cal Summers responded. "*Okay, hold tight. Doing the best I can to get out there.*"

"Do better. Over."

Luthor pulled over as much as he dared, not that there appeared to be much risk from other cars in this shit weather. "Stay here."

"You sure?" Cassius replied.

Luthor nodded. "Yeah, stay with the radio just in case. Besides, no point in both of us drowning out there."

"All right, just be careful."

"You know it."

Luthor opened the door, almost losing his hat to the wind. He secured it then stepped out into the downpour.

The first thing he noticed upon approaching was that one of the ambulance's back doors had fallen open.

"Everyone okay in there?" he cried, although there came no answer save the rumble of thunder.

The road here was higher than the ditch running along the side, so the top of the ambulance was canted downward, lying in about a foot of water. That was bad enough, but fortunately it didn't look like any had reached the interior yet.

Either way, he quickly saw there likely wasn't much Cal was gonna be able to do in terms of righting this mess. They were going to need another ambulance, although whether the hospital would risk sending another before the storm was over was debatable. Hell, at this point, he might end up driving Alan there himself – a less than ideal scenario as that would leave the town without police backup.

Luthor reached the stricken vehicle and yanked the other door open.

"Anyone home?" he asked, shining his light inside. "Oh shit!"

Though there was no sign of the attendees, his light immediately fell upon Alan – lying on his side, still strapped to a stretcher. His eyes were closed and he was unmoving.

Luthor took a quick look around before clambering inside. *Where the fuck are the drivers?*

He placed two fingers to the side of Alan's neck, thankfully finding his pulse both strong and steady. His friend was unconscious, although Luthor had no way of knowing what had caused it. He could've hit his head when the ambulance tipped or it might've simply been the result of a sedative he'd been given.

All he knew was he couldn't leave the sheriff lying like that.

There wasn't a lot of room to maneuver at this angle, but Luthor managed to get Alan's stretcher mostly righted – eliciting a pained groan from the man.

"You'll be okay, boss," he said. "Back in a jiffy."

His first thought was the two attendees must've been injured in the accident, but if so then where the hell were they?

And why had they left Alan all alone?

It made no sense, especially since there'd been two of them. Hell, they'd radioed Ellie. They knew damned well someone was on the way. So why leave?

Sure, Alan didn't look great and Luthor certainly was no doctor, but he didn't appear to be in the sort of critical condition that would warrant racing out blindly into this storm.

Whatever the reason, he needed to check and see if they were still close by. Luthor crawled from the back of the ambulance. He waved his flashlight toward Cassius to let him know to hang tight for the moment while he assessed the situation.

"Anyone out there?" he cried into the storm, the whipping wind the only answer his ears could discern.

He started toward the front of the ambulance, sweeping the ground with his flashlight for signs of the two men, when the sky lit up from above.

What the?

He whipped toward the vehicle, certain the shadows were playing tricks on his eyes, only to discover the horrific truth. The cab on the driver's side had been nearly crushed.

The door was bent off its hinge and the frame was a crumpled mess.

Had another vehicle collided with them? If so then where was it? The road ahead was clear, far as he could see anyway, and neither he nor Cass had noticed anyone else on the way in. He was likewise certain there was no place to turn off from this stretch that wasn't already flooded.

It didn't seem likely that anything less than a big rig could hit an ambulance with enough force to knock it over yet still be fine to drive away.

And that still didn't answer the question of where the attendees had...

A sound, not unlike that of a wrecking ball smashing into the side of a building, ripped through the night. Luthor nearly jumped out of his pants as he spun back toward the patrol car, only to find its front end pointed nearly perpendicular to the road.

What in Hell? Had Cal accidentally hit his cruiser on the way in?

He started that way, shining his flashlight before him. Sure enough, something had knocked the police car askew. There was no sign of Cal's wrecker, though. Instead, the beam of light fell upon a massive shape standing behind the vehicle, something that was most certainly neither car nor truck.

No fucking way. It can't be.

The passenger door of the cruiser opened and Cassius stumbled out holding his head.

"No! Get back inside!" Luthor screamed even as his voice was drowned out by the rumble of thunder.

Cassius staggered a few steps away from the vehicle just as the massive beast stepped around to that side.

Lightning flashed again, fully revealing the nightmare given flesh that was the monstrous pig.

Luthor's first thought was that he must be seeing a

ghost, but his next realization was far worse. The pig they'd killed, it hadn't been alone.

"Cass! Run!"

The older man turned just as the pig charged him. He had time for one high-pitched scream and then was trampled like he was no more than a ragdoll, his broken body disappearing into the muddy water beneath the beast's hooves.

Luthor stared in horror as the boar stomped the life from his friend, frozen in place for one shocked second before remembering he had his sidearm. He desperately pulled it from its holster and fired twice at the massive creature.

An angry squeal erupted from its throat, telling him he'd hit it at least once. Sadly, it was not only still standing, but he now had its full attention.

Crap on a cracker!

The gigantic hog barreled straight at him, a freight train on legs – heavy enough that he felt the impact of its hooves through the soles of his shoes.

Knowing he had a choice between taking a stand or moving, he chose the latter – the S&W 19 in his hands suddenly feeling way too inadequate for the task.

There was zero chance of him beating this thing in a footrace, so instead he turned toward the ambulance. Luthor nearly lost his footing in the muddy runoff covering the road, but managed to slide around the front of the fallen vehicle just as the behemoth thundered past him.

The storm wasn't making it easy on him, but he highly doubted the murderous beast was about to give up so easily so he forced himself to keep moving. There came the groan of metal and the ambulance lurched in place next to him. Luthor turned to find the pig rounding the front, same as he had, its sheer bulk more than enough to rock the vehicle simply with a glancing blow.

He no longer had any question as to what had happened to the attendees. Poor Cassius was likewise beyond help, trampled to death where he stood. He and Alan were still alive, though, and he planned to keep it that way.

The question was how.

He could try and run, but his friend was trapped inside. If this beast decided it wanted in there, he had no doubt it could turn the ambulance into a mangled heap in the process.

He couldn't risk that happening. Luthor knew he had no choice but to make a stand and hope he could get a lucky shot in before...

The cruiser!

All at once he felt like a danged fool. There was a loaded shotgun in the trunk. If he could get to it, the weapon would go a long way toward evening the odds against this monster.

It was a straight run back to the car from where he stood, but there was little chance he'd get there before the boar was upon him.

So he broke hard right instead – deciding on another round of Ring Around the Rosie, hoping he could put enough distance between himself and the...

Luthor heard more than saw the pig break off its pursuit of him.

Knowing he should've kept moving but unable to help himself, he glanced over his shoulder only to hear the pig let out a roar of rage as it turned its attention elsewhere. A moment later, he spotted the reason why – approaching headlights.

It was the wrecker and it looked to be hauling ass.

Guess Cal had taken it to heart when he'd told him to step on it.

Without warning, the angry boar took off running, barreling straight toward the oncoming truck.

Oh no. Cal!

Luthor raised his arms and shouted, trying once more to get the enraged beast's attention. He fired two shots into the air but still the pig ignored him.

"Come on! I'm right over here, you son of a..."

Anything else he had to say was lost to the sound of screeching tires, shattering glass, and crumpled metal. The worst was a high-pitched shriek that rent the night air before abruptly falling silent, like the gates of Hell itself being thrown open.

Luthor stood there for several minutes, soaked to the bone as he tried to make sense of what had just happened. He waited for any more signs of movement, but all he could see through the rain was a single flickering headlight of the wrecker as it faltered and went out.

Then lightning flashed, revealing the true horror of what had happened.

The boar lay dead, its neck snapped from the head-on collision. Sadly, the truck hadn't fared much better. It was a wreck of blood and twisted metal. The body of Cal Summers hung partway out the shattered windscreen. Within seconds the gut-wrenching scene was mercifully swallowed back up by the blackness, but it had been enough to tell Luthor all he needed to know.

Soaked and in shock, he numbly walked back to the police cruiser only to find it undrivable and the radio dead.

Understanding that nothing but death awaited him in the darkness while the storm continued to rage high above, he climbed into the back of the ambulance and sat down next to Alan. There, he kept the barrel of his gun pointed toward the opening while praying that God might keep them mercifully hidden from the eyes of any more such abominations stalking the shadows that night.

38

Bert lifted his head against the rain as they neared the house. The sound of frantic barking from inside had caught his attention. It was hard to make out above the wind and thunder but there was no doubt something had set Milo off.

With the work in the barn done and Bessie once again secure in her stall, he hadn't relished stepping out into the rain again. However, sleeping in his own bed next to Lin was far preferable to riding out the storm in a pile of hay alongside his nephew.

"What in hell is that stupid dog yapping about?" Martin cried from behind him as they trudged through the sodden yard.

Bert bit his tongue against the response he wanted to make. Martin had helped him get things settled with Bessie after all. Nevertheless, with his nerves already frayed, even he had to admit the incessant barking was a bit grating.

Milo had been his pet ever since he was a pup and he'd never once been prone to being spooked by thunder. But he also wasn't a young dog anymore and this storm was no walk in the park, so perhaps he was owed some slack on that one.

They reached the front porch, where Bert kicked the mud from his boots as best he could then opened the door ... only for Milo to race out past him snarling.

"What the hell?"

"Sorry," Lin said from just inside. "He bolted before I could grab him. I swear, I don't know what's gotten into that dog."

"Maybe he's just, y'know, gotta take a dump," Martin offered, stepping past her.

Bert threw him some side-eye but didn't immediately follow. Instead, he turned back toward the yard where Milo had disappeared – shining his flashlight that way despite the beam barely cutting through the darkness.

Somewhere out there, beyond where he could see, Milo started barking again.

Despite the heavy rain still coming down, Lin stepped out beside her husband. "What do you think's gotten him all into a tizzy?"

"I have no..."

The words caught in Bert's throat as an angry squealing roar rose up over the storm. He would've been able to identify such a cry in his sleep, although he instantly understood it hadn't come from any pig that he had ever owned.

No. This was louder and far more ominous than anything they were capable of.

Oh God, there's another one out there. "Get inside, Lin."

"What was that?" his wife asked.

"I said get inside," he snapped. "Grab Martin and Charlene and get your asses down into the root cellar." He took a deep breath. "*Please*. Trust me on this, okay?"

She fixed him with a curious stare but simply nodded. "Always."

"Good. I don't mean to yell, but this is…"

She put a hand on his chest. "Just tell me what you're going to do."

He considered the rifle still hanging off his shoulder. "That one's easy. I'm going back out there to find our dog."

Before Bert could take a single step back out into the driving rain, Milo's barks became a high pitched yelp.

No! "Milo!" His heart leapt into his throat as visions of the unthinkable assaulted his mind's eye … for a moment anyway. Then his flashlight beam picked up the old dog tearing ass back toward them, as if the devil himself was on his heels.

"Come on, boy!" he shouted with desperate relief, not that Milo seemed to need any encouragement.

Tail between his legs, he raced past both of them and into the house.

Bert knew that should've sealed it – that he should go inside with Lin, hunker down in the cellar, and pray the rest of the night was uneventful.

If there truly was another of those blasted things out there, it would be best to wait it out. Then, when the sun was shining again, they could all drive over to Scooter's, gather everyone there, and then head into town to see who they could round up to hunt this other monster down.

Yeah, that would've been the smart thing to do, but Bert couldn't stop thinking about earlier. Out in the woods he'd hesitated, almost getting his fool ass killed in the process. But this was his property, his *home*. Despite

Boar War

knowing the grave danger likely lurking just outside his line of sight, he wasn't so eager to turn tail and let some oversized hog run roughshod over everything he and Lin had worked so hard for.

"Bert?"

"Go inside. I'll be there in just a bit."

"Don't you dare give me that tone, Bert Cooper," she shot back. "If you're aiming to do something stupid, you can at least come right out and tell me. You..."

He turned toward his wife, curious as to why she'd trailed off. That usually wasn't like her when she was in the mood for a tongue lashing. But then he heard it, heavy grunting – the same kind he might hear on any given day while he was slinging slop into the pigpen.

Too bad the pen was on the opposite side of the yard.

"Get into the cellar," he repeated, once more shining his light out into the darkness beyond the porch.

There!

Reflecting in the beam he caught the dull glow of red eyes.

Bert was about to unsling the gun from his shoulder when the flashlight caught another set, then a third. But that was impossible. It would've meant there were at least *three* of those things out there.

The fuck?!

Lightning flashed in that same moment, illuminating their yard along with the trio of monstrous boars tearing up the muddy earth. Sadly for them, this door swung both ways.

As the first of the beasts turned its head their way, all the fight drained out of him. "Run," he hissed, grabbing his wife by the arm.

"Oh my God. Those monsters," Lin gasped. "They're what killed Patty, aren't they?"

"There's no time for that. Move!"

He was about to direct her to the cellar as planned but then hesitated. Yes, their root cellar *might* provide them sanctuary, but if all three of those abominations managed to get inside at once there was a good chance of the floor caving in atop them.

If that happened, they'd be dead before they even knew what hit them.

"Out the back," he shouted instead. "That means everyone!"

Bert shuffled his wife back inside than slammed the door behind him, despite knowing it wouldn't do dick to slow down the monsters coming for them. He grabbed the shotgun his somewhat confused looking nephew was still holding and jammed it into Lin's hands. "Take this. Use it if you need to."

"Something wrong?" Martin asked, sounding dumbfounded. "You're kinda acting all freaky deaky."

"Remember that pig I was telling you about?"

"Yeah, what of it?"

"Well, it brought some friends to the party."

"You're shitting me."

"Let's just say I wouldn't recommend going out the front to find out." Bert looked around. "Where's Charlene?"

"She went upstairs to get changed," Lin said.

Crap! "Okay, I'll go get her. You two out the back. Whatever you hear or see, don't stop to gawk. Trust me on this." Lin opened her mouth to say something, but he cut her off by putting two fingers into his mouth and letting out a shrill whistle. A second later, Milo slid out from beneath the table he'd been hiding under. "Good boy." Then to Lin, he said, "Take him with you. No time for questions, just go!"

He waited to see if there would be any argument but fortunately they both seemed to understand how serious this was. Lin grabbed Milo by the collar then motioned for Martin to follow as she turned toward the back.

Seeing they were on the move, Bert bolted upstairs.

There came the faint but familiar creak of the back door just as he reached the top of the stairs. "Charlene!"

"Just a minute," her voice carried to him from behind a shut door at the far end of the hall.

"We need to leave now!"

His shout was somehow both punctuated and simultaneously drowned out by the shattering crash of one or more of those damned monsters bulldozing through the front door.

The entire house shuddered around him. Bert grabbed hold of the banister just in time to keep from tumbling back down the stairs. Thank goodness too as one glance in that direction told him that would be an instant death sentence.

The pig he spied was slightly smaller than the one from earlier, although not enough to make much of a difference. It swung its head, knocking a hole through the foyer wall before looking up and locking its malevolent eyes on him. They held each other's gaze for a moment, then it opened its mouth and bellowed.

Shit!

The beast was almost certainly too large to force its way up the staircase, although it looked like it was willing to try. Staying put was no longer an option, especially if these monsters caused enough damage for the second floor to collapse – something that was beginning to feel disturbingly likely the way the once-cozy home was shaking.

"Okay, I'm coming," Charlene complained, throwing open the door. "You don't have to knock so loud."

"Yeah, well it's about to get even louder." Bert cried, readying his rifle as fast as possible before squeezing the trigger.

Charlene yelped as the roar of gunfire filled the air. Down below, the boar staggered as one of its ears was blown completely off, along with a good chunk of bloody scalp.

It was a good shot, just not good enough.

Bert didn't waste any time. He chambered another round and fired again. This time he scored a direct hit. The massive hog shuddered once before collapsing dead at the foot of the stairs. That still left two more, but at least this one's body had blocked the way for the others.

It was a small victory, but they weren't out of the woods yet.

He got up, slung the rifle back over his shoulder, and raced down the hall to where Charlene waited.

"Have you gone crazy?" she cried. "You shot at…"

"Something that shouldn't exist," he interrupted. "Something that isn't alone. I'll explain later. Right now, we need to get the hell out of here. Come on."

He steered her back toward the room she'd emerged from.

"Wait, the stairs are back that way."

"We're not using the stairs."

"We're not?"

Thankfully, the window in Charlene's room opened up over their kitchen. There was a small overhang there, just wide enough for someone to stand on and hopefully lower themselves most of the way to the ground with.

It would have to be good enough.

Another crash came from downstairs, this one accompanied by the disturbing sound of overstressed wood starting to splinter. This time it felt like the whole house began to tilt.

Guess that one was load bearing, Bert silently remarked, throwing the window wide open and letting in the fury of the storm outside.

He tried not to think of all the history and memories that would be irrevocably lost as those monsters continued their rampage. There would be time enough for that later ... but first they had to survive. "Come on. We need to jump."

"But why? You haven't told me what's happening!"

"Fine. There's about two tons of pig downstairs tearing the place apart to get to us. Happy now?"

"Pigs?"

"Yeah and believe me they aren't the friendly kind that go to market or sit down and have roast beef. Now let's *go*."

"I ... can't," Charlene screeched, backing up. "It's too high."

"Yes, you can. I'll go first and catch you."

"But Koolaid..."

"Koolaid ... *Martin* is already outside, which is where we need to..."

The room shook and there came a heavy *crack* from below. Then the floor close to the doorframe caved in – taking the nearby dresser with it.

Fuck!

There came another crash from below, followed by an angry bellow and more sounds of destruction. They didn't have long before the whole place was turned into kindling.

"Any more questions?" Bert growled, gritting his teeth.

She numbly shook her head in response.

"Good. Then let's get moving. This place isn't going to take much more."

She glanced out the window than back at him. "You promise you'll catch me."

"Cross my heart and hope to…" The floorboards groaned beneath them. "You know the rest."

She nodded, looking back wide-eyed at the hole in the floor.

"Let's go." Hoping she took the hint, Bert climbed out the window. He steadied his footing against the gusting wind and prepared to lower himself the rest of the way, when something heavy slammed into the wall directly beneath him.

The kitchen window shattered from the force of the blow and once more the house seemed to shift on its foundation.

Bert lost his balance. He pinwheeled on the edge of space for a moment or two and then found himself airborne.

Oof!

He landed hard – the rifle digging into his back and the wind knocked out of him – but thankfully the mud from all the rain had cushioned the worst of it.

"I'm coming down now. Don't forget to catch me!"

Bert looked up to see Charlene blindly scrambling out the window.

"Wuh … wait."

Fortunately, her exit proved somewhat more graceful than his. She dropped to the ground, slipping a tiny bit but otherwise landing on her feet.

"You were right, that *was* easier than it looked."

"Yeah," Bert gasped, sitting up. "Easy as pie. Now come on. We need to find…"

Their little section of yard suddenly lit up. Bert turned

Boar War

to see a pair of malevolent glowing eyes bearing down on them, followed by a throaty roar.

His insides clenched in the moment before he realized it sounded nothing like those monsters.

The Dodge!

Sure enough, the car pulled up alongside them – revealing Martin behind the wheel, Lin in the passenger seat, and Milo happily curled up in back.

"Going our way, sailor?" Lin asked, opening the door.

Bert shook his head, amazed. "But how?"

"I remembered I still had the keys in my pocket," Martin proudly proclaimed.

"Good thinking, kid," Bert replied. "But first things first. Out of the driver's seat."

Just then there came another heavy crash from inside.

"No offense, man, but we could either stand here debating who drives, or we could get the hell out of here while we still can. Your choice."

Sadly, Martin was right. There wasn't any real debate on the matter.

"Move on over, boy," Bert said to his dog before gesturing for Charlene to climb in first. "It's gonna be a tight squeeze back there."

39

The roads were more like rivers, visibility was near zero, and they were running for their lives, but deep down Martin was having the time of his life.

It had taken his best efforts just to get Bert to relinquish the keys to his precious Challenger. Now, not only was his uncle sitting in the back as Martin drove but he was actively imploring his nephew to floor it.

Sadly, much as he might've wanted to, he couldn't give the meaty V8 everything it had. There were too many spots along these country roads that were completely washed out. Powerful as the engine was, it would be disastrous if he ended up plowing them nose first into four feet of water.

Speaking of which...

"So, where exactly are we going?"

Silence met his question for a moment or two. Obviously, everyone had been in too big of a hurry to think things through as they bugged out of the farm, but whatever danger they'd been in was in the past. They were all alone out there on the saturated road, at least as far as he could tell. And even if they weren't he had more than four-hundred horsepower at his disposal, enough to leave anything in the dust.

After another thirty seconds or so, Bert finally said, "Head into town, to the sheriff's office. Night like this, someone's bound to be there."

Martin nodded, although he was personally doubtful. From what his uncle had told him, the town was down not one but two of its coppers – not that he cared much for their fate. However, he was definitely curious as to what had set them running in the first place.

"So, mind telling me what the hell really happened back there?"

"What *really* happened?" Bert replied. "Are you kidding me? I already told you."

Martin let out a sigh. With both Bert and Auntie Lin obviously freaking the fuck out, he hadn't bothered to ask a lot of questions at the time. He knew real fear when he saw it. After all, he'd gotten his ass kicked badly enough in Nashville to know that sometimes it was best to beat feet first and ask questions later.

True, once they'd gotten outside he'd heard the ruckus going on within – sounding like a bulldozer was running wild through the place. There was no doubt in his mind that something nasty had busted through the front door.

But a giant man-eating pig?

That was a bit too far out for him to swallow. The hicks might've been quick to believe in the boogeyman, but Martin considered himself a step above. "Seriously, though, what's the real deal? We talking a grizzly here, or maybe a...?"

"It wasn't a bear. I'm telling you..."

"Yeah, yeah, giant pigs on the loose, just like you said.

No offense, but when you told me that story I sorta figured you were..."

"Were what?"

"Pulling my leg, man. I mean, for real, think about how that sounds."

"Wait," Charlene replied from behind him. "You were serious about it being a pig?"

"Dead serious," Bert said. "And not *a* pig, *pigs* plural."

Lin turned toward Martin. "I know how it sounds, but I saw them too." She shook her head. "I can barely believe it myself, but I saw what that thing did to poor Patty. And now to find out there are three more of those monsters out there."

"Two," Bert corrected with a finality that made Martin understand what those gunshots he'd heard had been about.

"Okay," he said, "so then why are we running scared instead of going back and popping the rest?"

"I don't think you're grasping the situation here, kid. We're not talking some fattened up hog that escaped the pigpen. Every single one of these things is bigger than this whole damned car."

"Okay," Martin replied, trying to sound as placating as possible so as to not set his uncle off again. "If you say that's what happened, then that's what happened."

He still refused to believe it, though. He was convinced his uncle was either pulling his leg in some sort of sick joke or he'd simply hallucinated it. Hell, maybe the storm had somehow played tricks with his mind – making those things look bigger in the glare from the lightning.

Martin was no meteorologist but he supposed that was possible.

At least he knew better than to argue. Whether it was the storm, a trick of the light, or a bad drug trip, there was little doubt both Bert and Lin were scared outta their gourds,

"Hey, Koolaid," Charlene said after a moment or two, her voice low, almost a conspiratorial whisper – not that it mattered much in the packed car. "Do you remember those papers we found? Do you maybe think...?"

"Not now, Lene," he snapped, his eyes opening wide at the realization of what she was about to spill.

"But..."

"I said *not now*."

"What papers?" Lin asked.

Goddamn it! "It's nothing," he replied, thinking quickly. "We had to run to the library earlier ... because of her job, to look up some stuff in the old issues of the Gazette they keep on file. Anyway, they had an article from a few years back about a prize-winning hog at the county fair. There was a picture, too. Was one hell of a big sucker." He glanced in the mirror catching Charlene's eye. "Isn't that *right*, Lene?"

It took her a moment or two, but finally she nodded. "Oh, yeah. Guess I just remembered it now ... because we're running from another big pig."

Martin blew out a breath through gritted teeth. The last thing he needed was her dumb ass spilling the beans on the old army base. So what if there were a few fat porkers running around the Bluff? It would all get sorted out. Hell, who was to say they even had anything to do with whatever the government had been fucking around with there? It could've been nothing but a coincidence for all he knew.

But if she blabbed about the papers they'd found, the same ones still in the trunk of the goddamned car they were driving, it would be all over.

There was no way the pigs, the uniformed ones that is,

would keep their noses out of his business. They'd go out to the base and poke around, even if for no other reason than to justify their paychecks. If that happened, there'd be zero chance that they'd fail to notice all the cleaning and rearranging that had been done.

Though hopefully there was nothing there to connect it back to him, they'd almost certainly keep a close eye on the place for the foreseeable future. All of his grandiose plans would go up in smoke.

First thing I'm doing when we stop this car is tossing those fucking papers into the nearest mud puddle.

It seemed the chances of that happening sooner rather than later were higher than he expected, as Martin took his focus off the road just long enough to hit a deep patch of water – causing him to almost smack his head into the damned steering wheel as the car lurched.

"Watch it!" Bert roared from the back.

"Sorry," Martin was quick to respond, turning the wheel and steering them toward the high part of the road – which still left them driving through at least six inches of water.

He pushed those damnable army papers to the back of his mind for the moment as he focused on driving, even though he was still convinced there was a rational explanation other than truck-sized pigs terrorizing Cooper's Bluff.

Sure, there was no denying something big had busted into the house, but that didn't mean it was a pig. Hell, it could've been Bert's missing cow for all Martin knew, save that his uncle was too busy losing his shit to realize it.

Whatever the case, Martin needed to take it slow if they wanted to reach the sheriff's office alive.

The good thing, though, was it gave them all a chance to calm down a bit before then, as well as giving him some time to think through how best to keep Charlene from spilling the beans on the Koolaid Chalet.

That was the key to it all. A little bit of time to figure out how to come out of this mess smelling, perhaps not like a rose, but better than a pig.

40

Ellie Kent had worked for the combined Cooper's Bluff / Piedmont Creek constabulary for over three decades. Over the course of her tenure as dispatcher, she'd raised a family, buried a husband, and survived more friends than she cared to remember. She'd been there long enough to remember operating the old switchboard, conducting air raid drills, and organizing the monthly scrap metal drive.

All of that was now in the past but she remained, a fixture in the tiny sheriff's office – doing a job she knew by heart and serving the town she loved. Her eyes weren't as sharp as they used to be and she had to turn the volume on her headset up to properly hear it, but otherwise she fully intended to keep performing her duties until such time as the good Lord decided otherwise. With her kids grown and her house now empty, it gave her purpose.

Alas, that purpose was seemingly more important than ever now. The horrors of that day had changed everything. Sheriff Heller had gotten maimed by that ... creature, and poor Wilbur...

Boar War

She didn't want to think about it.

If anything, she dreaded finally going home. She'd long since learned to separate her feelings while at work. It was a necessary part of the job. Once she got home, though, that would all change. She wouldn't be able to stop the tears from falling, and sadly there was nobody waiting there to comfort her grief.

In some ways, she'd been secretly glad for the storm that continued to rage outside. It gave her a reason to stay where she was and keep those demons at bay for a little while longer.

Sadly, it seemed they'd found her nevertheless – eating away at her stalwart resolve, not with sadness and loss, but in the form of deafening silence.

She'd been trying to raise Luthor for well over an hour, only to hear nothing but static in response. Her last communique with him had been a quick check in as he neared the spot where Sheriff Heller's ambulance had gone off the road. Since then, nothing.

If that had been it, she might not have worried as much. After all, whatever had happened out there was likely to keep him busy for a while, but his wasn't the only silence weighing upon her.

First she'd failed to reach the ambulance again, to let them know help was on the way. Shortly thereafter she'd received Luthor's last check-in. Now neither he nor that old coot Cassius were picking up. The last update she'd gotten had been from Cal Summers, letting her know he too was nearing the location of the wreck.

Now he wasn't answering and apparently it wasn't just on her end. Red Graven who worked the overnight at Dusty's hadn't been able to get through to Cal either.

It was as if the storm had transformed Briar Crossing

from a simple country road into some sort of black hole, where those who entered were never heard from again.

That was a silly thought and she knew it. Interference from the storm was likely to blame, or so she told herself. In the back of her mind, though, she didn't quite believe that. Though the phone lines were down, Ellie had been monitoring the radio all night. True, the weather was certainly playing havoc, but she'd been able to touch base with her counterpart all the way over at the Kettelbury PD – which was well past where the ambulance had broken down.

In fact, despite all the static from the storm, there seemed to be no shortage of chatter on the old squawk box – except from those she was actively trying to reach.

It made no sense. Even if the situation with the ambulance was worse than they'd been told, there should've been enough men on the scene for at least someone to answer her.

Not wanting to come across as a worrywart, she had tried to pass the time with a few hands of solitaire but it was hard to focus. Anything, even a quick check-in, would have set her at ease. So she'd taken to pacing instead, not the most comfortable thing in the world with her aged hips.

She alternated between the window facing the street, not that there was much to be seen there, and staring at the radio as if trying to force a response by sheer will alone.

As the wind gusted outside, Ellie began to consider her options. More than once she'd envisioned picking up the mic and calling Kettelbury to see if they could spare a patrol car to help them out. After all, it's not as if cooperation between the two departments was a foreign concept.

However, she hesitated from doing so. From all the

various radio chatter, it sounded as if they had their hands full between stranded motorists and downed trees. It likely wasn't untrue to say the entire region was currently a disaster zone.

Because of that, Ellie decided to wait. Calling them was still an option but only as a last resort. She'd give Luthor and Cal a bit more time, trust that they knew what they were doing and were likely just hard at work.

Another hour, she told herself. If neither she nor Red heard anything by that point she'd ring up Kettelbury. Hopefully by then they'd get a break from this blasted storm.

Speaking of which, this was certainly one for the ages. She couldn't remember anything as bad since back when she was a little girl and a string of tornados had touched down just outside town, forcing her family to ride it out in the root cellar until the all-clear was…

A sound from outside caught her attention, causing Ellie to turn back toward the front. There was no way to tell what it had been, save that it had been loud enough to be heard above both the wind and the hum of the genny out back.

Curious, she stepped to the front window – seeing nothing but the rain hitting the glass and an endless sea of darkness beyond it.

Heck, she might as well have fallen off the face of the Earth itself, judging by…

Wait.

Ellie looked again, wondering what had caught her eye since there was literally nothing to be seen.

That's when it hit her.

The sheriff's office wasn't the only building downtown with a generator, yet none of the others were currently visible. It was possible, likely even, that as it got later in the evening some might've shut down to conserve fuel. But Dusty's wouldn't have been one of them, especially not with their wrecker still in the field.

Ellie turned back toward the radio. If Red was having electrical problems then she really ought to check in with him. However, she stopped halfway there, chiding herself. If their generator was out then so too would be their radio.

That should've been obvious but she tried not to be too hard on herself. After all, it's not as if the day hadn't left her rattled to her core. While Luthor and Cassius were there, it had been easy to keep herself composed. But with them both gone, it was becoming harder and harder.

Ellie couldn't help but realize the joyless irony. She had both power and a working radio, yet still felt completely isolated.

She glanced again at the front window. It truly was coming down like cats and dogs out there. There was little doubt it would be the height of foolishness for her to venture into this maelstrom. She'd be lucky to not be knocked to the ground the second she stepped out the door.

And even if she made it to Dusty's, then what? It's not like she could do much to help. Besides, Red was no fool. If his generator was down, he was likely already on his way to her. He could run his dispatch just as well from her radio as his own and it's not like she'd send him away on a night like this.

But what if something else had happened? If he was in trouble over there...

She thought back to the events of earlier. In hindsight, it was hard to not think this day had been cursed. But if so, then who was to say whatever evil had visited their small town was finished with them?

Once more she looked back toward the radio.

Boar War

Reaching out to Kettelbury was almost certainly the wise decision. Surely they could spare a few officers to help them out.

However, there was also no guarantee they'd be able to make it with the roads being what they were – and even if they did, it would likely take them some time.

That settled it. A little wind and rain wasn't going to deter her from checking on a friend. She'd been through worse after all. Then, once she was certain Red was okay, she'd check in with Luthor once more. If at that point he didn't respond then she'd finally radio for help.

Her mind made up, Ellie stepped to the coat closet and pulled out Sheriff Heller's rain slicker. It was far too big for her but that was fine so long as it kept the worst of the storm at bay.

Sliding it on and grabbing a flashlight from her desk, Ellie walked to the front door intent on her course of action. The darkness beyond seemed nearly absolute, swallowing the meager light from inside the station before it reached more than a few feet beyond the window.

She knew it was nothing but an illusion. Once outside, her eyes would quickly adjust. And it's not as if she didn't know the way.

Illusion or not, though, the darkness served a singular purpose she wasn't aware of, one that had already damned far too many in the small country township.

It ensured Ellie had no warning as to what happened next.

As she reached for the handle of the door, she caught a flash of movement beyond it, coupled with a glimpse of something that shattered her sanity in a single instant.

Sadly, by then it was too late.

The massive beast plowed through the front of the

police station – sending razor sharp slivers of wood and glass flying from the impact.

A three inch shard lanced Ellie's face, puncturing her right eye, but she barely had time to register the overwhelming pain before she was thrown to the side like little more than a ragdoll.

Though it was barely a glancing blow as far as the twelve-hundred-pound rampaging hog was concerned, nearly all of Ellie's ribs were instantly pulverized. She slammed into the wall then crumpled to the floor, a twitching bloody heap.

Ellie landed near the very same closet she'd just come from, half-blind and unable to draw a breath due to her lungs being punctured in half a dozen places. She was only vaguely aware of the monstrous pig as it tore past her, pulverizing the dispatch desk like kindling and sending the radio atop it clattering to the floor beside her.

The ... radio.

Her lifeforce ebbing away as the sounds of destruction continued to ring in her ears, she feebly reached for the microphone just inches away. Her fingers managed to brush against the edge of the device, a cruel jest on the part of destiny, allowing her a final moment of false hope.

Then lightning flashed outside, giving her one last glimpse of her beloved Cooper's Bluff, although not in any way she had ever hoped to see it. In that same instant, the trauma of her injuries became too much for Ellie Kent's aged body.

She died with an image straight from Hell itself burned into her remaining retina – one of monstrous tusked beasts as they rampaged through the town beyond, destroying everything in their path.

41

Bert sat in the backseat of the Challenger, his eyes shut and Milo's head on his lap as the car jostled through a seemingly endless succession of deep puddles.

It was the only way to hold onto his sanity while Martin was behind the wheel.

Under any other circumstance, literally *any* other, he would've long since demanded his nephew pull over and relinquish the driver's seat. But this wasn't like any situation Bert had ever experienced. Living on a farm often meant having contingency plans. He always had to take into account the consequences of bad luck, whether it involved the weather, disease, or the price of feed going through the roof.

However, never once had he considered that he might need to deal with an attack by giant mutant hogs. That was the sort of ridiculous fluff you found in those science fiction movies from the fifties, not in real life. And yet there was no denying his family home was now likely little more than rubble on account of wild boars the size of a pickup.

There was no two ways about it. Bert was scared. And though it was rational to conclude they'd long since escaped the danger back at the farm, fear didn't succumb so easily to rationality. That was the real reason he hadn't told Martin to stop. It had nothing to do with the storm so much as not knowing what might be lurking out there in the darkness. Try as he might, he couldn't stop imagining what might happen if they stopped, envisioning something racing out of the shadows and claiming Lin – all because his ego demanded he should be the one driving.

So instead he sat there, doing his best to keep his mouth shut. At least his nephew had ceased his asinine line of questioning. What the hell did he think had caused all that damage to the house, a fucking cow? Even if Bert had been wrong, his response to it hadn't been. If something was powerful enough to tear a house apart like cardboard, then you made it a point to get as far away as possible, plain and simple.

Either way you looked at it, they were in over their heads. He'd managed to get lucky by killing one of those monsters, but even the best of luck had limits. To think they could put the other two down without anyone being hurt or worse was both arrogant and crazy. Bottom line was Martin hadn't been out in the woods with him earlier that day. He hadn't seen firsthand what that creature had done. Sadly, he was beginning to realize that stories simply couldn't do it justice.

Regular run-of-the-mill boar could be mean sons of bitches. Cornering one in the woods was a dicey proposition at best, even while armed. But these things... it was like that meanness was amplified along with their size.

That wasn't even taking into account the monstrous appetite something that big would have. Hogs were omnivores and not particularly picky about it either. When they were hungry, they didn't care much what they ate.

And despite what some might've thought, they were smart too. Sometimes a little too damned smart.

He'd been around pigs all his life, more than enough to know to respect them. When you were working in the pen, you didn't let your guard down for a single instant. A herd of swine might be happily munching on their slop one minute, but if you turned your back at the wrong moment you could easily end up next on the menu.

And that was just normal sized hogs. These things were a whole other story. Bert couldn't imagine how much they probably needed to eat. It would've had to have been...

He cocked his head as a revelation hit him. Maybe that finally explained all the deaths. This summer had been a scorcher – so bad that even the marshes were mostly dried out. There was no doubt that had affected the food chain.

That would also explain why nobody had seen these damned things before now. When food was plentiful, they'd probably lived deep enough in the woods that encounters were unlikely. After all, normal feral hogs knew to avoid people, so why not these bastards too. But now things were becoming desperate. These beasts were hungry. So they were growing bolder, venturing to wherever they could find new food sources.

That explained Scooter's hogs. Sadly, it also accounted for Patty Gantry and those men they'd been looking for. And now ... well, it seemed all pretense for caution was gone. Starving for food and driven into a frenzy by this freak storm, these things were now running hog wild.

"You okay, Mr. Cooper?" Charlene asked from the corner of the backseat.

"Huh?"

"It's just that your eyes were all scrunched up, like you had a headache."

Bert shook his head. "Sorry. Just thinking, that's all."

"About anything good?" Lin asked, turning around in the passenger seat to face him, although the tone of her voice wasn't overly hopeful.

"Just that we need to get to the sheriff's office pronto so we can let them know what the hell's going on."

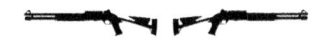

"What the hell?"

Bert perked up in the backseat at the sound of his nephew's voice. Before now, the kid had been mostly dismissive about the danger – as if he were too cool to believe in monsters, no matter how real they might be. But something in his voice now said otherwise. "What's wrong? Are we there yet?"

"Almost," Martin replied. "We just turned onto High Street, not that you'd ever know it."

He wasn't wrong. Endless darkness stretched out ahead of them, making it feel more like they were in an abandoned ghost town than the main stretch of the Bluff.

Bert wasn't surprised to find the power was out there too, but what was far more worrying was the lack of any light at all. He knew for a fact that several buildings there had backup generators. And even if they didn't, he'd have at least expected to see some candlelight shining from the windows.

But there was nothing to be...

Boar War

"Watch out," Lin cried, just as they swerved past some debris in the road.

"Is it me or was that the sign that used to hang off the diner?" Martin asked.

Bert had only caught a glimpse from the back, but it certainly hadn't looked like any branch or tree limb.

All of a sudden, he felt his stomach drop as a thought hit him. *No, it can't be. It's gotta be from the storm.*

There was only one way to be certain.

"Pull in closer to the sidewalk," he ordered.

"Why?"

"Just go slow. You'll be fine. I doubt there's anyone crazy enough to be parked out in the open along this stretch right now."

"Okay, if you say so," his nephew answered dubiously.

Bert then turned to his wife. "Here, take my flashlight. Roll down the window and shine it that way."

She raised an eyebrow but then cranked the window down as asked, allowing the rain in – where it began to soak the leather seats.

Much as it pained Bert to be so careless with his pride and joy, it was far more alarming to see what the meager beam of light had picked up.

"Oh my God," Lin cried. "What happened to the post office?"

Bert had hoped his fears were nothing but an overactive imagination at work, but instead his heart sank into his chest. It was like a bomb had gone off inside the building. "P-point the light up will ya, hun."

She again did as asked, which only served to further prove his point. This damage hadn't been caused by any falling tree. No, it was more like something had rammed the building straight on, save there was no sign of any crashed vehicle.

He had no way of knowing how long ago this had happened. It was entirely possible it had been caused by the same monsters he'd seen at his farm, but somehow he didn't believe that. It felt a little too ... convenient.

There's more of them. Dear God, there's more. "Get us to the sheriff's office."

For once, Martin didn't have any comment to make.

As they continued down High Street – situated right at the border between Cooper's Bluff and Piedmont Creek, and undoubtedly the heart of both towns – Lin continued to shine the flashlight.

No one said a word. The only sounds to be heard were the rain hitting the ground, the rumble of thunder, and the growl of the engine as they passed one ruined building after another.

"Should we like stop and see if anyone is hurt?" Charlene asked, breaking the silence.

"Keep going," Bert said, unable to take his eyes off the destruction.

The post office, Ned's Appliance Warehouse, and even Kelly's Diner, all of them had been wrecked. The only mercy was their light's meager beam didn't carry far inside any of the once familiar shops, sparing them the knowledge of whether anyone had been inside at the time.

While it was after hours, meaning most would've been empty, Bert knew it was too much to hope that for all of them. Kelly's Diner for instance was usually open late. Even with the power out, Bert could easily picture Seamus staying close to his grill so as to support those on duty tonight.

No longer, though. The interior looked like a truck had been driven through it. Bert could only hope Seamus had chosen to take the night off in light of what had happened in the woods earlier.

"Um, Uncle Bert," Martin said, interrupting that solemn train of thought. "I hate to be the bearer of bad news, but I think we're gonna need a plan B."

A few moments later, the Dodge pulled up outside what used to be the sheriff's office that served both towns. Now it was nothing more than another destroyed hovel, barely distinguished from the rest, save for a cracked shard of window glass that remained, displaying a partial image of a badge.

No!

It was as if any hope he might've felt had instantly been erased in one fell swoop. However, much as he wanted to do nothing more than order Martin to drive and just keep going, no matter the direction, he realized that would almost certainly be condemning others to the same fate as this once vibrant stretch of road. "Hand me the flashlight. I need to check inside."

"I'll go with..."

"No!" he snapped before softening his tone. "You stay with the car. Martin, keep the engine running. I'll just be a minute. I need to ... see if anyone's left."

In truth, he didn't expect to find any survivors, not the way this place looked, but that wasn't his real goal. He just didn't want to sound callous by voicing the truth, that he was hoping to find a working radio. With the power out and the phone lines down, it was likely their only chance of summoning help.

Normally he would've expected Lin to protest, but he could tell she was just as scared as him. Rather than argue, she lifted the shotgun still sitting in her lap. "Go. I'll cover you."

Bert nodded. "Fine, but from the car. And only shoot if you need to. I don't fancy an ass full of buckshot."

His comment was meant to lighten the mood a bit,

but seemed to have the opposite effect. If anything, he could feel a cloud of hopelessness hovering just above them, waiting to descend and smother any idea that things would ever be right again.

So, rather than put his foot in his mouth again, he waited for his wife to scoot her seat up. Then Bert stepped out into the pouring rain, hoping his desire to save them all wouldn't prove a fatal mistake instead.

42

"Keep that engine running," Bert commanded. "Got it?"

"Got it," Martin repeated, letting the muscle car idle.

Bert nodded then took a deep breath, steeling his nerves to step away from the vehicle and toward the ruined sheriff's office.

It was a calculated risk. Leaving the Dodge running would essentially make it a beacon on the otherwise dark street. However, it would also be a necessity should the need for a quick exit arise – something he wasn't about to rule out.

There was no telling how long ago this damage had occurred, at least not from what he could see. Sadly, the cloak of night offered no insight into whether the perpetrator was long gone or still in the area. Hence why he had both a flashlight and his rifle with him, with Lin backing him up from the car if need be.

Now to hope it was enough.

With a shaking hand, he shined the beam of light into

the interior of the wrecked office front – terrified that the last thing he'd see would be a pair of malevolent red eyes, right before being gored to death.

Instead, all he saw was the aftermath of destruction – smashed furniture, a collapsed wall, and overturned file cabinets. From the look of things, whatever had barreled through the front had kept on going – like a runaway train. The strong stench of diesel permeating the air seemed to back that notion up, although with any luck he wouldn't have any need to investigate that far.

There's no way just three of those things did all this. The majority of High Street had seemingly been reduced to rubble. It was more what he would've expected from a tornado, but there was nothing natural about this kind of disaster. He turned the beam of light toward the floor, as if seeking confirmation, only to spy a chaotic assortment of muddy hoof prints the size of dinner plates.

That wasn't all he saw, though.

A smear of blood lay near one print, still red enough to be fresh.

Had Luthor or perhaps someone else tried to fight back as the beast tore through the place? If so, he didn't care to guess at the outcome – especially since he saw no giant pig corpses lying around, something that would've been hard to miss.

Sadly, the answer to his question came moments later as he continued onward, his feet crunching on broken glass and splintered wood.

There, lying half buried in the debris, was the body of Ellie Kent, a beloved fixture in the Cooper's Bluff PD since he was a child.

Gritting his teeth against the cry that wanted to escape, Bert positioned himself between her and where Lin was watching his back from. She'd seen enough this day. If he could spare her even this much, he would.

Regrettably, it was the space of a few seconds, no more, for him to tell there was no hope to be had in this forsaken place. Ellie's body was completely mangled. Some of her injuries had no doubt been sustained when the creature had first slammed through the front of the office, but the ragged stump of her missing right arm suggested that hadn't been the end of it.

"I'm so sorry," he whispered.

"See anything?" Lin called to him in the next moment.

"Not yet," he replied, forcing his tone to remain steady.

By choosing to come inside, he'd known this had been a likely possibility but that didn't make it any better. Ellie's death was a true tragedy, but what came next potentially sealed the fate of all those still left to fend for themselves on this accursed night.

Forcing his eyes away from Ellie, he continued his search, realizing mere seconds later that whatever gods bestowed their fortune upon small towns were almost certainly looking elsewhere this evening.

Goddamn it all!

The beam of his flashlight had fallen upon the radio lying on the floor, or at least what was left of it. One side had been crushed beyond all hope of repair.

Seeing it in that state, Bert's remaining hope turned to dust in the wind. He found himself split on what to do next. A part of him wanted to cut their losses, get back in the car and keep going until they ran out of gas, then pray it was far enough. But what if Ellie hadn't been alone? Shouldn't he at least make sure?

Besides, even if the radio was destroyed that didn't mean there wasn't anything there they could use. At the very least, there was probably a weapons locker in the back. Though already armed, he wasn't fool enough to turn down some extra firepower.

If so, that would up their odds a bit as they...

Thunder rumbled outside, but along with it came another sound that caught his ear. Milo had started up again, a frantic baying from the back of the Dodge that told Bert they'd used up what little time they had.

Oh no!

He spun back toward the entrance a moment too late – just in time to see a massive form come racing out of the darkness. The beast slammed into the rear of the Dodge, hard enough to shove the car's back wheels up onto the sidewalk and send the spoiler flying in two directions.

Lin's shotgun went off as the vehicle jerked to the side, causing a section of wall disturbingly close to where Bert stood to be peppered with buckshot.

Jesus!

There was no time to worry about how close he'd just come to buying the farm, though, as the pig shoved its way past the vehicle and turned its attention toward him.

With nowhere to run and little room to maneuver, Bert threw his flashlight toward the far wall. The charging boar turned its head to follow, giving him just enough time to shoot from the hip.

There must've been some guardian angel watching over him because the bullet struck home – shattering bone as it buried itself in the beast's front leg.

The pig let out a godawful screech as it tumbled to the floor amidst the rubble, sliding into the remains of what had once been the dispatch desk.

It was down but by no means out. Bert briefly considered chambering another round and finishing it off, but some primal instinct in the back of his mind was screaming for him to run instead.

It was a warning he decided to heed, perhaps mercifully so.

He turned back toward the car just as lightning flashed overhead. It was only for an instant, no more, but in that moment he saw just how fucked they were. Monstrous, humpbacked shapes could be seen rooting through the muck and debris of High Street – more than he could count in the short time he had, an entire herd of the godforsaken things.

If he'd had any illusions toward staying to fight, they were instantly erased.

"Oh my goodness, are you okay?" Lin cried as Bert reached the car.

Rather than answer, he instead shoved his upper body through the window as he tried to scramble inside.

"Don't just sit there. Drive!"

Charlene wasn't sure whether to scream or cry. She was convinced they were as good as dead, that the car had been struck hard enough to damage it beyond all hope of escape. Now, though, with Bert hanging half out the car's window while his dog went nuts next to her, she realized neither would do this situation proper justice.

Martin hit the gas and for a moment nothing happened, as she feared. Then the car lurched forward, bringing with it an insanely loud screech that finally gave her the motivation she'd been looking for. She let out a cry of pure panic, certain another of those monsters was about to finish the job the first one had started.

"Zip it, Lene!" Martin roared from up front, turning

the wheel even as he continued to accelerate. "I'm trying to focus here."

However, the screeching continued, both from within and outside of the car. "But...!"

"It's just the fender rubbing against the rim," he snapped, seeming to understand what had set her off. "Fucking thing must've bent the shit out of it."

Charlene didn't immediately respond, but as she listened she realized he was right. The high-pitched squeal coming from close by sounded nothing like the beast that had attacked them.

"Just pray we don't shred a tire in the process," Bert said, finally dragging himself all the way in.

"Let's hope not," Martin replied, "because I sure as shit ain't getting out to fix it."

As Bert righted himself in the backseat, Milo was all over him. "All right, boy. Settle down. I'm fine. We all are."

Sadly, his words proved somewhat less than prophetic.

"Watch out!" Lin shrieked from the passenger seat, just as Martin spun the wheel – barely dodging another monster boar that had appeared in the beam of their headlights.

"We need to get out of here," Bert said, his face ghostly white in the meager glow cast from the dashboard.

"No shit, Sherlock," Martin cried, trying to look everywhere at once. "But where to? It's not like this fucking storm's giving us a lot of options."

Everyone fell silent for several seconds, leaving only the roar of the engine and the damnable squeal from the wheel well as Martin once again swerved.

Finally Bert said, "Head to Scooter's place. We should be able to regroup there."

"Regroup? For what?" Martin asked. "Did you see the size of that fucking thing?"

"Trust me, kid, it was kinda hard to miss. But unless you've got a better idea..."

Bert's statement hung in the air as the car continued to jostle back and forth, partly from the wet roads but mostly because Martin was steering frantically. It was like the entire street was suddenly full of those things – a fact probably not helped by the high-pitched whine still coming from the car, almost certainly the equivalent of ringing the dinner bell for the monsters after them.

"All right, first things first," Bert said after another moment or two. "Is everyone okay?"

His voice was a bit shaky but Charlene took some comfort in noting that he wasn't outright panicking. It wasn't much, but it gave her something to latch onto.

"Does shitting my pants count?" Martin remarked.

"We're fine up here," Lin stated, throwing her nephew a glare. "Charlene, honey, what about you?"

"I... I'm..."

"Don't worry about Lene," Martin interrupted. "She's tough."

Charlene's heart swelled even as his aunt rebuked him. "I'd like to hear it from her if you don't mind."

"I'm..." Good wasn't quite the word she was looking for. No, definitely not, since they were facing pigs the size of *Mighty Joe Young*, one of her favorite movies as a child.

Pigs the size of...

Martin had silenced her earlier when she'd tried to talk about it, but surely he understood things were different now. He'd finally seen those monsters with his own eyes. They all had. Rather than answer Lin, she said, "We need to tell them, Koolaid."

"Huh? Tell us what?" Bert replied.

"It's nothing," Martin barked. "Isn't that *right*, Lene."

"Will you please let the poor girl talk," Lin admonished.

"There's nothing to be said, Auntie Lin. Trust me on this. It's just a ... *misunderstanding*. Nothing more."

Charlene's first instinct was to agree with him. After all, he was Koolaid. He was her man, true, but more importantly he was almost always right. Who was she to argue with him once he made a decision?

However, just then he swerved the car again, nearly spinning them out of control. In that same instant, she caught a fleeting glimpse of tusks bigger than railroad spikes as they just barely avoided another of those things.

That did it.

"N-no! It's not a misunderstanding. I'm sorry, Koolaid, but you've seen those monsters. This ... well, it could be important!"

"Lene," he warned again.

"That's enough," Bert said. "You, eyes on the road and mouth shut." He then turned toward her. "And you, if you have something to say, say it."

"I..." She hesitated, noticing Martin's eyes glaring at her in the rearview, but after a moment she swallowed hard and decided this was one bull that needed to be taken by the horns. "I think I might know where these things came from."

"You do? How?"

She nodded. "Remember that old army base, the one just a few miles from here? I think ... they were doing things to pigs there. You know, like experiments and stuff."

"We don't know that for sure," Martin growled.

"Then how come they have all those labs and those big

incinerator things? And what about those papers we found?"

"Hold on," Bert said. "What papers?"

Lin held up a hand. "I'm more interested in what exactly you were both doing out there. You do know that place has been off-limits for years, right?"

Charlene shrugged uncomfortably, not sure how to answer. "Um…"

"We've been cleaning it up," Martin interrupted, jumping back in. "I had an idea to … make it into one of those youth centers."

"Youth centers?"

"Yeah. Just like the ones down in Nashville," he continued, not missing a beat. "It's a place where kids can go to meet new friends, hang out, shit like that – so that their parents don't have to worry about where they are. Lene and I saw that old dump and thought, y'know, with all the construction going on maybe the Bluff could use a place like that too. *Ain't that right, Lene?*"

Charlene blinked a few times, trying to take this all in. Then she quickly nodded, perhaps a little too vigorously. "That's it exactly, Koolaid."

"Okay, whatever," Bert replied, sounding as if he couldn't have cared less. "We can talk about that later. I want to know more about those papers you mentioned."

"Oh those? You can see for yourself. There's a whole bunch in the trunk."

"*The trunk*? And why are we just hearing about this now?" Bert paused to take a deep breath. "You know what? Never mind. We'll take a look when we get to Scoot's. For now, let's just keep focused on the road and making sure we don't run into any more of those damned things."

43

"I just wanted to spend a little time with our cats, that's all. I ... didn't mean for anything bad to happen."

Bert listened silently as Lin attempted to console Mikey McNeil in the battered living room of the darkened house. He couldn't begin to understand what the boy must be going through – to have lost everything to those monsters.

At the same time, he was also being forced to deal with his own grief – making him thankful that Lin was there. Comforting poor Mikey while trying to come to grips with his own feelings of loss was too much. He simply didn't have enough in him to do that and remain functional.

And right then he needed to keep his eye on the ball. They all did.

So instead he and Martin stood guard just within the destroyed front façade of the McNeil home – guns at the ready, tensing up with every flash of lightning that lit up the yard beyond.

What a fool he'd been. The second, *the absolute second* he'd realized there were more of those things, his thoughts should have turned toward his friend. There was no doubt now that one of those monster boars had been responsible for killing Irma's pigs. That meant they likely already associated the McNeil place with food. Of course they would have come back.

If only he'd thought of that sooner then maybe Scooter would...

But the awful truth was he hadn't. All the what-ifs in the world couldn't change that. Nor would he try to fool himself with the false hope that maybe Scoot or his wife had gotten away and were instead hiding somewhere. His friend had been capable of many things, but there was no way he'd have left Mikey behind to save himself.

Sadly, the only thing left for Bert to hold onto was the hope that it had been quick.

He let out a heavy sigh, glad for the whipping rain peppering him as it hid the tears that rolled down his cheeks.

This was no time for proper grieving, though. He knew they couldn't stay there for long. If those fucking monsters had come back once, there was nothing to stop them from doing so again. If that happened, they might be able to stop one or two on their own, but if there were more...

No, what they needed was a plan – either a place to hide or some way to stop these things before all of Cooper's Bluff was reduced to nothing more than a muddy graveyard.

At least Martin had stopped his incessant whining for the time being, seeming to finally take this seriously.

Bert glanced at him from the corner of his eye as they waited. He hadn't said anything in the car, but the truth was he didn't believe for a second that his nephew was planning on turning the old Piedmont Creek base into some sort of half-assed YMCA.

Nothing Bert had seen of either the young man's attitude or work ethic had suggested there was that sort of altruism lurking just beneath the surface. Sure, it was possible he'd been wrong about him, but somehow he didn't quite believe that. More than likely it was nothing more than a bullshit story to cover the fact they'd snuck into the old base looking for a quiet spot to do the horizontal mambo and maybe smoke a little dope.

But if so, then why snatch a bunch of papers? And what was that talk earlier about incinerators? That seemed a bit strange for two kids in search of a quick lay. An abandoned building teeming with mice didn't sound like the sort of place one would want to stick around longer than it took to do the deed.

Curious as it was, none of that was important at the moment. They could talk all that out once this was over. For now, he scanned the yard one more time as lightning flashed high above, noting with no small amount of relief that it was still clear.

Thank goodness too, for in that same instant Charlene slammed the trunk of the Dodge closed before racing back inside with the stack of papers she'd retrieved.

She threw Martin an apologetic glance, one he didn't seem inclined to acknowledge, then handed them to Bert.

He took them then motioned her toward one of the end tables that hadn't been destroyed, upon which lay an old Winchester repeater and a Colt six shooter, both loaded. Bert felt like a ghoul raiding Scooter's gun cabinet, but he also knew it was something his friend would've wholeheartedly approved of had he been there. "You know how to use either of these?"

Charlene hesitated for a moment before gingerly picking up the Colt.

"Okay, that'll work." He leaned in and lowered his voice. "Only if you absolutely need to ... *and* you're certain you won't miss. Got it?"

"Got it," she repeated.

Bert nodded, hoping he hadn't just made a mistake. Then he turned away from her, toward where Lin continued to comfort Mikey. He considered saying something, but ended up biting his tongue instead.

Let the boy have a bit more time, he told himself. Unfortunately, a bit was likely all he was going to get. Horrible as it was to even think considering what had happened, he was going to have to ask Mikey to push it all down – at least for now. They couldn't leave him there, no way was that happening, but Bert was a realist. If Mikey couldn't get himself under control, it could very well jeopardize their chances of surviving the night.

It was more than he wanted to ask the poor kid, but it needed to be done for all their sakes.

So, rather than say anything to either of them, at least for now, he instead turned back toward where his nephew stood guard. "You're in charge while I'm gone. Keep your eyes and ears open. If you see anything out of the ordinary, if even a single goddamned leaf falls to the ground the wrong way, you send Lin to come get me."

"And then what?" Martin asked.

"*Then*, you open fire and make it a point not to miss whatever you're aiming at."

Bert locked himself in the McNeil's bathroom then pulled the curtains on the lone window shut before finally switching on his flashlight. On any other given day he'd have felt foolish doing so, but pigs had excellent senses. That meant they were in danger regardless of the precautions he was taking, but he also saw no reason to ring the proverbial dinner bell by lighting the place up for all to see.

That done, he sat on the toilet and began to leaf through the stack of papers Charlene had handed over. They were yellow and discolored, many of them so stained as to be unreadable save for a few words here and there.

He flipped through the first couple of pages, seeing nothing of pertinent interest, and was beginning to think this would prove nothing but a dead end when a phrase caught his eye.

Porcine growth hormone.

His curiosity piqued, he kept reading, thankful he hadn't dismissed it out of hand. Noticing more and more as he went on, soon the old pile of notes and status reports had his undivided attention. The narrative contained within was incomplete, reports scattered across a few years – most of their contents dry as fuck. These were scientists working for Uncle Sam after all. It was doubtful they'd been hired for their ability to write gripping prose, yet Bert found himself unable to look away nevertheless.

Son of a bitch. What the hell were they doing out there?

Little by little, the pages began to paint a picture. It was the years following the war and the US was facing a dramatic baby boom – meaning tons of new mouths to feed. It was a time of prosperity, true, but science was already looking ahead toward a future where new food sources might one day be needed. Breeding bigger, hardier livestock was certainly one potential solution.

Whatever the case, they'd apparently succeeded in spades. Bert was no scientist, so a good deal of what was written down before him made no sense, but there were clear mentions of two-hundred and even three-hundred percent increase in bone and tissue density among the test subjects.

He wasn't exactly sure what they'd done to the pigs they'd kept at the Piedmont Creek base, but it sure as hell sounded like they'd managed to grow them freakishly big.

Sadly, that was about all he could glean from what was there. The last few pages made mention about personnel being reassigned but didn't say why.

Bert paged through the stack a second time, finding a bit more scraps of information but nothing that gave him any insight into that last part. It made no sense. If their experiments had truly been such a remarkable success, then why hadn't anyone heard of it before now?

Though he'd only been a kid at the time, he couldn't recall any emergencies, accidents, or scandals related to the base. Far as he could remember, the government had simply shut it down on short notice and moved on.

There had to have been a reason, though. Had the pigs been sickly or perhaps their meat somehow toxic? Hell, maybe there'd been some sort of competition with the Russians that hadn't panned out. Either way, he was left with nothing but speculation as to the cause.

However, it did give him some ideas of what might have happened next. True, there was no mention of wild boar within the notes he'd read. All the experiments seemed to involve domesticated stock, but that didn't necessarily matter. Pigs weren't picky when it came to their partners, and feral hogs had never been in short supply in the woods surrounding the Bluff.

That's it! It has to be!

Some of their experimental animals must've either escaped or been set loose when the base shut down – likely the former, since he couldn't imagine anyone being so grossly incompetent as to simply let a bunch of mutant pigs run free. Regardless, that had to be what they were now facing – the feral descendants of these original creatures.

That meant there was an entire breeding population of these monsters out there. Worse, they were large enough to have no natural predators that he could think of. They were literally sitting at the top of the food chain. And now, thanks to the goddamned drought, they'd set their hungry eyes on his town.

All that was bad enough. But what would happen once they were done consuming everything they could get their teeth on? Would they then disappear back into the woods, leaving the authorities to wonder what had happened here?

He considered that unlikely. Desperation might've initially drove these monsters from the depths of the bog they'd called home, but if they came to recognize humans as a food source then who was to say where else they might turn their attention.

That was what frightened Bert Cooper most of all.

If these abominations were left unchecked long enough – eating everything in their path while continuing to breed even more of their unnatural offspring – they might soon prove to be unstoppable.

44

"C'mon, Koolaid," Charlene whispered. "I told you I was sorry. Please say something."

In truth, Martin wasn't angry at her, at least not after having some time to think it through. Although, that didn't stop him from turning his head ever so slightly and giving her the stink eye. It was just the way things had to be. He was her pimp after all. Hoes like her needed to be constantly reminded there were consequences to their actions.

It was like an unwritten law of the urban jungle.

Martin wasn't stupid, though. Their harrowing escape from High Street and the horde of monsters swarming it had gone a long way toward convincing him that the Koolaid Chalet was, at best, a secondary concern compared to surviving this mess.

Awesome a dream as his love motel had been, there was no denying the chances of salvaging it at this point were slim. Had there only been one of those pigs, it would've been a cool novelty – the sort of tourist attraction that would draw people far and wide, many of whom would be happy to wet their wicks at the end of the day. But a whole herd of those fucking monsters? That was going to draw an entirely different brand of scrutiny – the kind that wore badges and carried guns.

As for the army base, he realized now that even had Charlene kept her trap shut, it would've only been a matter of time before someone put two and two together. Uncle Sam would then be faced with a choice – either admit they had a hand in this shit or say, "fuck it," and give everyone involved the Agent Orange treatment. He had a feeling which one those jackbooted pricks would probably pick.

The big question was how much of that scrutiny would potentially turn his way if that happened. He didn't fancy ending up as the town's scapegoat, but he liked the idea of disappearing without a trace even less. The last thing he needed was some government spook deciding he knew too much.

Fuck that shit.

At least he didn't need to worry about either Bert or Lin ratting him out. They might've been squares but they weren't stool pigeons. Family was a powerful thing around these parts after all. But if *the man* ended up scouring the base for clues, hell, even if they did no more than dust for fingerprints, he was as good as toast.

Though he wasn't particularly fond of the idea of going to jail, he'd fully understood the risks when he'd embarked on his career into pimping. But there was a vast difference between doing time in the county slammer versus being on Uncle Sam's shit list.

Talk about a rock and a hard place. More and more, it seemed like he might be forced to choose between getting trampled by a monster boar or ending up with a bullet to the back of his head, courtesy of a different kind of pig.

There had to be another option.

He needed to figure out some way to make it through this that left no ties between him and...

A sound caught his ear, causing him to flinch and almost pull the trigger of the rifle he was holding. However, aside from the rain still coming down outside – which finally seemed to be letting up a tiny bit – the yard ahead remained clear.

That's when he realized the noise had come from inside.

Martin turned in time to see Bert douse his flashlight as he stepped from the bathroom. At least the darkness gave him a chance to bite down the sigh of relief that wanted to escape his lips at realizing it was just his uncle.

Next to him, Charlene opened her mouth but then quickly closed it again – throwing him another glance, as if afraid to say anything.

Fuck it. Right as she was to do so, they had enough shit to deal with at that moment. They could always have a good long talk about who was in charge once this was over. "Find anything useful?" he asked, breaking the silence.

Bert approached them slowly from the dark hallway. "Too much and not nearly enough."

"Wuh-what do you mean?" Charlene asked gingerly, no doubt testing the waters to see if she'd be yelled at.

"You two were right. There's almost no doubt those things came from that base."

"Okay, but why?" Martin asked. "Were those fascist fucks trying to breed war pigs or something?"

Bert shook his head. "Of course not. From what I could tell, they were conducting experiments to increase the size of domestic pigs for the purpose of breeding a heartier food stock."

"So then what the fuck happened? Did their science projects turn that shit around and eat them instead?"

"No idea," Bert replied, putting the stack of papers down. "That's the bad news. There's nothing here about anything going wrong."

"Well, ain't that a kick in the..."

"Please tell me you found something," Lin interrupted, appearing in the doorway leading to the parlor, her face ensconced in shadow.

"Nothing that's of any use," her husband replied. "How's Mikey doing?"

"As best can be expected I suppose. He's lying down with a cold compress over his eyes. Milo's keeping him company."

Hell of a time for a rest break, Martin thought, although he kept it to himself. "So back to these giant hogs. Where exactly does that leave us?"

"Honestly? Probably up Shit Creek without a paddle."

Lin stepped in and hugged her husband, probably for her benefit as much as his. "There's gotta be something in there we can use."

"I wish there was, hon, I really do, but it's just pages and pages of notes, nothing more."

A depressing silence descended for several long minutes as his words sank in. Once again, Martin found himself debating the merits of becoming pig slop versus eating a sniper's bullet.

Then, just as he was about to conclude how royally fucked he truly was, Lin turned toward him and Charlene. "Listen up, you two. I need the both of you to think real hard. Did you see anything in that place that might help us? And I mean anything at all."

"Lin..."

She held up a hand, silencing her husband. "We have to at least try. We can do that much, can't we?" Then, when there came no protest, she continued. "I want you to tell us everything, even if it didn't seem important at the time."

Charlene looked at Martin expectantly, her doe-eyed question more than clear even in the dark. After another moment, he nodded. *What the fuck could it hurt at this point?* "Go ahead. Tell them."

"Thanks, Koolaid. You're the best!" she replied before facing Lin. "Okay, so there were a lot of old desks and filing cabinets in the first couple of rooms. Like we're talking everywhere. Mice too."

Lin inclined her head. "What else?"

One of the sinks still works. Can you believe that? Surprised the heck out of me. Although just between us, I wouldn't drink from it if I were..."

Bert motioned her to hurry it along.

"Sorry." She paused for a moment, probably to get her scattered thoughts in order. "There were these big rooms full of tables, like they have in those fancy massage parlors up in..."

"Those were probably the labs were they conducted all their voodoo bullshit," Martin interrupted, gritting his teeth.

"Yeah, probably," she acknowledged. "Either way, they were all pretty empty. Oh, and there was a loading dock too. That's where we found those big incinerators I was telling you about."

That seemed to perk Bert up. "Exactly how big? Are we talking large enough to fit one of those pigs inside?"

Martin hadn't considered that before. He rolled it around in his head for a moment then jumped back in. "Yeah, I'd say so. At first, I figured they just had a lot of trash to get rid of, but now that you mention it that probably makes a lot more sense."

"That's gotta be what they were for," Bert said. "Disposing of the bodies."

"Fat lot of good that'll do us now, unless you've got a plan to march those things in there single file."

Lin blew out a frustrated breath. "Even if we could, what then? I doubt anything in that old place works anymore."

"Not true," Charlene replied. "Like I said, the water's still on."

"That's not what I..."

"And we even managed to get the lights working again."

Bert cocked his head. "Wait. Are you telling us that place still has power?"

"Not like normal. But there's a bunch of generators inside and those still work."

"Hold on, generators?"

"Yeah, a whole mess of them," Martin added. "They're attached to these two bus-sized tanks. Hell, even if those babies are only half full of diesel they could probably run that place for a month straight."

Bert put a hand beneath his chin. "No. They couldn't."

"Sure they can," Charlene replied. "We saw em with our own two eyes."

He waved her off though. "No, I mean diesel wouldn't work, at least not anymore. It doesn't last that long. A year, maybe two at most, but not twenty. Those gennies would be dead as doornails."

"But they're not."

"Relax. I'm not saying you're wrong. That just means there's something else in those tanks."

After a moment or two, Martin snapped his fingers as

a thought hit him. "Propane!" Then, when everyone turned his way, he added, "Remember when I told you my old man used to work at a junkyard?"

Unsurprisingly, Charlene nodded vigorously.

"Well, they'd occasionally get called to pick up these big metal tanks that places didn't want anymore. He mentioned once that if they weren't rusted through yet, there'd sometimes be fuel left in them. It would still be good to use because apparently that shit lasts forever."

"Isn't that, like dangerous?" Charlene asked.

He was about to answer when his eyes opened wide with realization. She was right. It *was* dangerous. That was it – the solution to both his problems. It had to be! And best of all, judging by the look on the other's faces, they were coming to the exact same conclusion.

"It can be," Bert said, his eyes also wide. "Especially if you aren't careful or the tanks are old and starting to corrode. Or ... if one were to do something to them."

"You can't be serious," Lin replied.

"What choice do we have?" he asked her. "It might be the only shot we have."

"I don't get it," Charlene said after a few seconds.

Martin turned to her and grinned, probably his first real smile since they'd been driven from the farm.

"It's simple, baby. We don't need to worry about those incinerators because we're gonna turn that moldy old base into one. All we have to do is figure out how to get those fucking monsters back there. Then we blow those tanks and *boom*! The entire building becomes a giant pig roast – one big enough for the whole goddamned town to enjoy."

45

Bert listened as his nephew expounded upon the idea of rigging the army base to explode with the pigs inside.

Maybe there's hope for the kid after all.

Or maybe not as Martin was making it sound way too easy, as if they could just holler a few pig calls and the entire drove of monster boars would come running.

If he was indeed right about the generator tanks being at least partially full of propane, then blowing them up would in theory be the easy part of this plan. Surviving the blast, on the other hand, would require no small amount of luck – although probably not as much as luring their targets there.

Sadly, this wasn't something they could just sit back and plan at length. Come morning, there might very well not be a town left to save, and that was assuming the pigs weren't miles away by then.

Whatever they were going to do, it had to be soon. Terrifying as the concept of going back out there was, Bert loved his hometown and the people who lived there too much to stay put and hide. Cooper's Bluff had already lost too many good souls, many of them friends. Hell, he wouldn't blame Scooter one bit for haunting him to the end of his days if he got the inkling that Bert could've done something but had chosen not to.

Oddly enough, that thought brought a tiny smile to his face. That aside, though, the fact remained there were several massive hurdles to overcome in order to make this plan a reality.

"So, how are we gonna get all those pigs over there?" Charlene asked, giving voice to this concern. Amusingly enough, her hopeful tone suggested she actually believed one of them might have a solution.

Silence descended amongst their circle as they stood there in the dark, the rain outside suddenly sounding very loud.

After a moment or two, Lin let out a sigh and said, "I'm gonna go check on Mikey."

Before she could step away, Bert grabbed her gently by the hand. "We can't stay here and we can't leave him behind. Neither is an option."

She nodded sadly. "I know. I'll make sure he's ready."

Bert felt like an absolute shit for saying it, but at least Lin hadn't tried to fight him. She knew what was at stake as well as the boy's odds should they abandon him. Sure, it was possible he'd be okay, *but* that would entail hoping that none of those things were still in the area.

The open maw that used to be the front of Scooter's home, however, was proof enough that being indoors was no protection against those beasts. The fully grown adults were larger and more powerful than a rampaging rhinoceros – while possessing an even worse temper.

"Okay," Martin began after another minute had passed, "let's try to think this shit through. We know these things are tearing ass through town. But the question is why?"

"Why do pigs do anything?" Bert replied. "Food."

"Are you sure about...?"

Bert held up a hand. "Yes. Zero doubt on the matter. Think about it. You've seen how much my pigs eat. Well, the sheer amount of food required to feed something five times that size would be massive. Between that and the heatwave, these things must be ravenous with hunger – enough to put us all on the menu."

Martin grumbled. "I don't suppose anyone here wants to volunteer to cover themselves in A.1. Sauce and let those things chase them back to the base." Charlene let out a giggle, to which he added, "It's not funny, Lene."

"Sorry, Koolaid."

Bert shook his head. He truly had no idea how their relationship worked, nor did he have much interest in gaining insight into it, especially right then.

Lightning flashed outside, so he took a moment to survey the yard beyond. *Still clear, thank God.* Bert turned back toward the others as thunder boomed – feeling the low pitched rumbling in his bones.

The deep bass sound abruptly rose in pitch for several moments, sounding almost more like the wail of some cursed banshee than anything natural. Then it faded away, once again leaving only the wind and the...

Wait!

He looked up to find both his nephew and Charlene staring wide-eyed at him. "Please tell me you heard that."

Martin nodded. "No way was that thunder. At least not at the end."

Shit!

The two men raised their guns, with Charlene following their lead a second later. Bert once more scanned the yard but to no avail. Though his eyes had adjusted to the dark, it was still pitch black beyond the broken façade of the McNeil home. Turning on their flashlights would probably help, but it would also serve as a beacon to whatever was out there.

Goddamn it! Their only choice was to wait for the next bolt of lightning and hope they got lucky.

Sadly, this was only one side of the house. If the beast was elsewhere and decided to plow through one of the other walls...

Bert turned his head, keeping his voice just barely above a whisper. "Lin! Lin, can you hear me?"

There was no answer from her, although Milo begin to whine from the other room.

He briefly considered his options. Much as he wanted to be by his wife's side for whatever happened next, he knew that could prove disastrous. There was no doubt everyone present was taking this seriously but all the same, he didn't quite trust that his nephew and girlfriend were up to the task of defending this spot without him.

Fuck a duck! This was exactly why he needed Mikey back on his feet. It wasn't nice and it wasn't fair but it was necessary if they were to have any hope of avoiding the same fate as...

He kicked that thought to the side, not wanting to finish it. Instead, he tried to focus on what they should do in the here and now. *Martin*. Bert could send him to watch over Lin, while he stood guard with Charlene at the entrance. That way...

Just as he was settling on that course of action, though, there came the distinct sound of wooden planks being shattered like kindling.

Milo let out a single bark as Bert's heart leapt into his throat. An agonizingly long second passed as he waited to see from which direction death would strike, but then he realized it hadn't come from the house.

In the next instant, the screams of livestock reached his ears, loud enough to be easily heard over the storm.

The barn!

Of course. The boars had come to associate the town and outlying farms with food, but that didn't mean they were exclusively after people. He knew pigs. They weren't picky when it came to stuffing their gullets.

Much as Bert felt bad for the helpless livestock trapped in the barn, they were serving as a buffer – letting him and the rest know that the danger was far from over. It was an early warning they could exploit.

He turned to his nephew. "You up for helping me take this asshole out?" He expected hesitation, even reluctance, but to his surprise Martin smirked.

"Fuck yeah."

"What?" Charlene screeched before lowering her voice. "You actually want us to go after that thing?"

"Not *we*," Bert said. "Just Martin and me. I need you to stay here and keep your eyes peeled. If you see anything that isn't us, don't hesitate to shoot it dead. Then you grab Lin and Mikey and run like hell. Got it?"

"But what about...?"

Martin stepped in. "Don't worry about us, babe. Trust in your Koolaid man. Okay?"

Apparently that was all that was needed to calm her nerves and steel her resolve. Bert didn't understand it in the slightest, but he wasn't about to question this gift horse either.

Standing there in the middle of the yard, soaked to the bone and ankle deep in mud, Bert and Martin waited.

Nearby, the frantic shrieking from the barn continued – coupled with angry, high-pitched squeals. In truth, Bert wasn't looking forward to laying eyes on the slaughter happening within. He'd already witnessed enough death for one day. Too bad he had a feeling fate wasn't finished with him in that regard yet.

Either way, he wouldn't have to wait for long.

Lightning flashed and he spun, taking in as much as he could in the time he had. All was clear as far as he could see. There didn't appear to be any more of those things lurking within sight.

As the darkness reasserted itself and there came the thrum of thunder, he looked at Martin and mouthed a single word.

Now!

Bert led the way, keeping his ears open. So long as panicked bleating continued to be heard from the barn, it meant that the monster inside was still busy.

That, of course, assumed there was just the one.

He said a silent prayer in that hope. If he was wrong, then they'd be faced with two choices – either get supremely lucky or, failing that, try to keep these bastards busy long enough for those still in the house to escape.

Regardless, it was too late to back out now. They reached the set of barn doors. As previously instructed, Martin moved to the side waiting for the signal to pull one open. Bert nodded before turning on his flashlight and setting it on the ground just outside – the beam playing out ahead of them. Then he lifted his rifle, took aim, and shouted, "Do it!"

Please, God, let this work.

The barn was old, but thankfully Scooter and his

family had kept it in good repair. The door pulled open with minimal sound or effort.

That was the easy part.

As for the rest, it would all be decided in the next few moments – one way or the other.

46

As Martin stepped to the open doorway with his rifle raised, he felt a chill creep down his spine. It was painfully obvious that the flashlight beam didn't penetrate very far into the large barn – leaving the far corners enmeshed in shadow and giving the whole place a distinct haunted house vibe.

Thankfully, he didn't need to see it all. There was no mistaking the monster tearing up shit inside. It was positively enormous, impossible to miss even with the tiny bit of light at their disposal.

Time seemed to freeze for the young man.

Martin had seen more than his share of these monstrosities as they'd hauled ass away from the sheriff's office, but this was different. Inside the car, weaving past them on the road, it had felt surreal, almost like watching a drive-in movie that he was also somehow a participant in.

Whatever enthusiasm he might've felt earlier toward taking this thing down was quickly extinguished as the reality of their situation finally hit home.

All at once, he was back in Nashville – duct taped to a chair in a dingy hotel room while Big Daddy threatened to cut his balls off and have them bronzed. It was one of the few times in his life that Martin's fight or flight instinct had kicked in. Needless to say, flight had won that day.

In truth, it almost won again right then and there. His uncle would never know how close he'd come to hauling ass back to the house, grabbing Charlene, and taking off in the Dodge.

Fortunately for them both, Martin had a chip on his shoulder the size of Tennessee regarding the aforementioned incident. He'd once vowed to Charlene that if ever given the chance to do it all over again, he would make sure that things ended differently.

Most of that had been bullshit bluster, or so he'd thought – pimp talk so that she wouldn't lose respect for him. Once bitches lost respect for their *manager*, it was all downhill from there.

However, as the barn doors finished sliding open and Bert took aim, Martin realized this was it. Pig or pimp, it was all the same. This was finally his chance at redemption, at least by his own logic.

As the fear threatened to overwhelm him, he began to chide himself inside his own mind – or, more precisely, his Koolaid voice did.

The fuck you afraid of? Would you be such a pussy if it was that fat fuck Big Daddy waiting in there? Hell no! You'd show that fucker who's boss once and for all. So what you're gonna do is step up and fill that fucking thing full of lead. Nobody fucks with the Koolaid man.

Amazingly enough, treating his terror like it was nothing more than another flavor in his stable did the trick. He stepped in and did as *Koolaid* had ordered, pushing everything else from his mind.

Martin was barely aware of the kick of the Winchester in his hands as he alternated between pulling the trigger and chambering another shell. He just kept firing, confident in the fact that his target was damned near impossible to miss.

The roar of the guns warred with the screeching of the pig inside, a maddening concerto of violence, until finally both sides fell silent.

Long seconds passed, a near eternity. That's when he realized it was over. They'd won.

Oh yeah!

In the end, his uncle's plan had been simple but effective – helped greatly by his subconscious egging him on.

"Yeah, I got you, motherfucker," Martin whispered. "Eat a fat dick, Big Daddy."

"Huh?" Bert asked from alongside him. "What was that?"

"Just a bit of unfinished business," Martin replied. "Nothing important."

The inside of the barn looked like a slaughterhouse – no, it looked worse, Martin considered. Far worse.

After breaking through the far wall, the pig had torn through nearly every living thing within – like they'd owed him money and it was finally payday. As for the few survivors of its rampage, sadly there wasn't much that could be done other than mercifully put them down.

By the time it was all over there was nary a patch of hay to be found that wasn't dripping with blood and offal.

It was less like a wild animal had caused all this and more like a giant lawnmower had been set loose within the barn. The insane amount of carnage the pig had caused made it seem more like a land shark drawn into a feeding frenzy.

As for the beast itself, they made sure to pump a couple extra rounds into its still twitching body just to be safe.

At least these fucking things aren't bulletproof.

He could only imagine how bad shit might've been had those eggheads at the base been trying to make weapons out of these things instead of food.

"Well, will you look at that."

Martin turned at the sound of his uncle's voice, only to realize that the seemingly endless torrent coming down outside finally seemed to be slowing down, having decreased in intensity at some point over the last few minutes to merely a strong drizzle.

"About goddamned time."

To Martin it was almost as if Mother Nature herself was acknowledging their victory – that she knew there was a new pimp daddy in town and his name was Koolaid. He could dig that.

"One down, God knows how many more to go," Bert said, turning back and surveying the slaughter once again.

"How many bullets do you think that's gonna take?"

"A lot more than we have. Hell, probably more than the whole town has." Bert let out a sigh and then stepped toward the dead pig. "Which brings us back to the problem at hand. How in hell are we going to get an entire herd of these things where we need them to go?"

Martin approached the corpse also, although he couldn't help but throw a kick at its massive head. *Ugh!* The goddamned hog still had a hunk of flesh hanging from its mouth. So engrossed had it been in filling its gullet that it hadn't even turned their way until the first volley of shots had been fired. It was likely the only reason they'd been able to put it down so quickly.

It spoke to Bert's earlier advice about these things being entirely motivated by hunger. If only they could somehow use that to their advantage.

Too bad we don't have a dump truck full of pig slop we could use to lure these fuckers back to the base.

Martin's eyes opened wide as an idea began to form. He once again took in the carnage around them. It was nothing but blood, guts, and bleeding bodies. The boar itself was the largest, but the remains of cows and horses littered the floor. Soon enough, they would begin to stink to high heaven.

He abruptly turned and double-timed it back to the still open doorway.

"No shame if you need to vomit," Bert said from inside. "Trust me, I'm pretty close to doing it myself."

Martin ignored him, though. He began to scan the yard outside. The rain had indeed petered off considerably. Had it still been coming down like a bitch, the idea he had in mine wouldn't work. The weather would've played too much havoc with things. But if the storm was truly moving out of the area at long last, then they might have a chance.

Lightning flashed, but it didn't appear to be as close as earlier. *Yeah, we're definitely seeing the ass end of this weather front.* However, as the storm lit up the yard before him, he laid eyes on exactly what he'd been hoping to find.

Fucking A! With a grin he turned back toward his uncle. "Hey, do you know if the truck over on the side of the house still works?"

"Scooter's pickup?" Bert replied. "Yeah, far as I know. Why?"

"Because I might have an idea for how we can lure those fucking monsters to the army base."

"Oh? Do tell."

"Yep. All we need is a full tank of gas, some rope, and maybe a tiny shit load of luck."

47

"This is crazy, absolutely fucking bug-shit crazy," Bert muttered, although he doubted his wife heard him above the unholy mix of mud, blood, and wind continually whipping him in the face.

Sadly, he realized as he held on for dear life, crazy was likely their only option if they were to have any hope of containing this massacre before it spread beyond the borders of their beloved little township.

Martin had explained his idea as they stood there looking at the slaughterhouse that Scooter's barn had become. Bert's first instinct had been to reject it out of hand, partly due to how nuts it sounded, but also because he didn't exactly consider his nephew a shining beacon when it came to good ideas. As he pushed his initial doubt to the side and actually considered it, though, he realized it not only had a shot of working but it was far better than any plan he himself had come up with to that point.

They'd returned to the house and shared it with the others, who, after their initial shock and revulsion, had eventually agreed that this was likely their best shot, short of fleeing and not looking back.

Leaving Milo in the house to watch after Mikey, they'd quickly gotten to work. Time was of the essence after all, not only to stop the threat the pigs represented but to get this done before any of them could realize exactly how insane Martin's plan actually was.

The equipment itself was the easy part. Scooter had an old trailer in the yard he'd once used to bring Irma's pigs to the county fair and back. They were able to connect it to the tow hitch at the back of his pickup with no problem.

That's when the true dirty work got started. The trailer had been built for hauling livestock, but what they'd needed to load it with now no longer qualified as being alive. A chain-fall hooked to the barn's rafters had helped with the heaviest of the bodies – the dead boar and one of Scooter's cows – but they didn't stop there.

Martin's plan wasn't for the faint of heart. In order to guarantee the maximum chance of success, the trailer had to be as full as they could make it.

Needless to say, it wasn't long before all four of them were drenched head to toe in gore.

And they still weren't done yet. Though the floor of the trailer was now ankle deep with offal, they needed to make sure without a doubt that the odor was completely irresistible to those monsters.

So Bert and his nephew, armed with an axe and a gas powered chainsaw they'd found in the shed, had set to work on the largest of the bodies.

By the time they were finally ready to go, the trailer looked like a horror show. More importantly, it stunk to high heaven of blood and guts. They did too, but there wasn't much to be done about it. Showering was the last thing any of them had time for.

Instead, they'd divided up the duties that lay ahead – a brutal necessity if this was to have any chance in hell of working.

In the end, they decided that Martin and Charlene would take the Dodge and head over to the army base. Ultimately, they knew the layout there better than anyone else in town. Their job was to get those lights on again and make the place an unmistakable beacon in the dark, one those pigs wouldn't miss. After that, they would focus on whatever needed to be done to prep those propane tanks to blow.

Though the work needed at the base ultimately held no guarantee of either success or survival, Bert had assigned Mikey to Martin's team as well. It was either that or leave him at the farm, something they'd already concluded wasn't an option.

Dangerous as that was, it was still better than letting the boy join him and Lin in the truck. The risk there was simply too great. If anything went wrong, they'd end up paying with their lives. It was bad enough that his wife insisted on coming with him, but to put Scooter's son in that kind of jeopardy too was unthinkable.

Knowing all that, he'd pulled Martin aside, out of earshot of the rest, and given him one bit of extra direction before their respective groups had headed out.

That left him, along with Lin and Milo, to get this party started.

It was only now, trying like hell to keep from being thrown from the trailer as they weaved through High

Street, that Bert realized they probably couldn't have done a better job of divvying up their respective duties had they tried. All three of them in the truck, even Milo, had their own part to play and so far it was going as well as could be expected.

Lin was behind the wheel, doing her damnedest to stay on the road as well as keep one step ahead of the ravenous beasts hot on their tail.

Much as a part of him wanted her to gun it with everything the Chevy had to give, he knew they couldn't. For this to work, they needed to stay close enough to those damned boars to remain a tempting target.

Bert's job in all of this was to make sure they were indeed as tempting as possible. That was easier said than done, though. As the truck lurched to the left, his feet slipped on the blood-slicked trailer floor for perhaps the hundredth time.

Fortunately for him, the heavy knot of rope tied around his waist kept him from bouncing out and ending up a premature buffet. The other end was looped around the tow hitch, thus ensuring that even if they lost the trailer he wouldn't be left behind. He probably wouldn't survive the ordeal but, oddly enough, the thought of being dragged to his death was still preferable to being eaten alive.

Using the shovel he'd brought as a brace, he pushed himself to his feet. Then he scooped another load of intestines into the blade and flung it out the back.

Almost immediately, one of the boars turned and made a beeline for it. Just as quickly, another changed course and gored the first one in the side.

That's right, kill each other, you greedy fucks!

Being hungry and bad tempered made these things extremely dangerous, but that danger extended to the rest of their kind as well. It was something he was doing his best to use against them. Three of the beasts had already fallen to their fellow hogs – either killed outright or at least badly wounded.

Too bad that left about eight still after them, at least that he could tell. It was difficult to keep track in all the chaos, and it wasn't like he was about to yell to Lin to slow down long enough for him to get an accurate count.

At first, Bert had been worried that as some of the monsters fell to the wayside injured, others would break away to finish them off. Thankfully, that hadn't been the case, though, because it turned out Milo was their unexpected ace in the hole.

The windows in the cab were rolled down – not quite far enough for the pissed off collie to leap out, but more than enough for him to be heard.

In a leap of luck, it turned out his frantic barking had served to enrage the pigs to the point where their attention remained focused on the truck and the bloody trailer being towed behind it.

Speaking of which, Bert grabbed onto the side as the truck swerved hard to the right. Another of those beasts had just appeared on the side of the road, charging them as they passed.

Guess that makes nine.

His nerves nearly shot, Bert turned to the front of the trailer and cried, "Time check!"

Long moments later, Lin leaned her head out of the cab. "An hour left to go!"

Shit!

He was certain he'd been bouncing around in the trailer for far longer than her answer implied. It made him wish he hadn't left his rifle in the cab. A few lucky shots would no doubt improve their odds more, and it's not like they didn't have the time to spare.

Regardless, another hour meant hopefully finding more of these monsters to lead in this macabre Pied Piper parade.

He yelled back, hoping he was heard. "Head toward Berryman Lake! Circle it and let's see if we can find some more of these fuckers to join this dance party."

That done, he planted his feet as well as he could in the slippery mess and threw yet another shovelful of steaming guts overboard.

48

Charlene didn't know the layout of the town quite as well as everyone else in their tiny group, but she'd lived there long enough to know that it would've normally been maybe a five minute drive from the McNeil farm to the army base.

However, that assumed the roads were in fact drivable, which was questionable at best right at that moment. They'd been in the Dodge for over half an hour and were just now starting to make some progress toward their destination.

Martin was behind the wheel, his teeth gritted in annoyance as he tried to keep the muscle car from becoming bogged down in the mud, while also avoiding the downed trees that seemed to bar their progress every hundred yards or so.

Sadly, she realized, that was probably not the only source of his irritation.

It had been an uncomfortably quiet drive following their decision to split their already tiny group. In fact,

Martin hadn't said a word since telling her to plant her ass in the shotgun seat.

With the phone lines down and their quest to find a radio at the sheriff's office ending in near disaster, the two groups had no way to communicate with one another. The best they'd been able to do was agree on a time. Two hours – for Bert and Lin to wrangle as many of those monster pigs as they could, while she and Martin rigged the army base to blow sky high.

It was a stark contrast to their earlier drive, she noted as they passed the spot where Martin had pulled over to make furious love to her in the backseat. Or at least she thought it was the same spot. It was hard to tell in the dark. Nevertheless, that felt like a lifetime ago. Everything had been so bright and cheerful this morning, probably helped by the fact neither of them had been drenched with blood at that point.

It was hard to enjoy even the rumble of the V8 when the entire car smelled like death.

Finally it became too much. Despite wanting nothing more than to curl up into her seat and not cause any more trouble, she mustered the courage to turn toward him. "Please don't be mad at me, Koolaid."

Almost in response, he swerved violently to the left, causing mud and water to spray in a wide arc as he avoided yet another tree limb. Then, after another moment or two, he let out a sigh. "I'm not mad, Lene."

"Are you sure?" she asked carefully.

He glared at her from the corner of his eye. "I *said*..."

"Okay, Koolaid, I get you. Not mad." She found herself not quite as relieved as she would've liked, but if Martin said he wasn't angry then who was she to question him?

That's right, bitch. Don't even think of second guessing your Koolaid man, his voice responded inside her mind.

Just then, Mikey McNeil leaned forward, his face deathly pale in the light from the dashboard, appearing almost like a ghost from the backseat. "Why did you call him that?"

Charlene almost jumped out of her skin. The kid had been so quiet, she'd almost forgotten he was back there. "W-what?"

"Kool-Aid. Why did you call him that?"

"Because I'm the man who brings the flavor, kid," Martin replied, grinning.

"I ... don't know what that means, sir."

"It means talk to me in a few years when you've got some hair on your nut sack. Maybe I'll hook you up with a good time." Before Mikey could say anything to that, Martin added, "Enough with the stupid questions, okay? There's only one that matters right now. Do you, or do you not want to kill the fucking monsters that deep-sixed your folks?"

"Y-yes, sir. I do."

"Good. Then shut up and let Lene and me strategize here." He waited a beat then glanced her way again. This time his tone was far more mellow. "Like I said, I'm not mad. I was at first, but I've had some time to think it through. Don't get me wrong, shit like that wouldn't normally fly with me. You understand what I'm saying?"

She nodded vigorously, feeling her heart swell. She'd been afraid earlier that she might have irrevocably damaged his trust in her, so to hear him talking to her like normal was no small relief.

"But," he continued, "this being extenuating circumstances and all, I think we can let it slide, just *this once*."

He turned her way and met her gaze fully as if to drive home the point.

"I'm really sorry about the chalet," she said, sensing this was a chance to explain herself. "It was a great idea, Koolaid, really it was. The best. I'm telling you right now, if this stupid town wasn't overrun by giant pigs you'd have made a fortune."

"Don't doubt it for a second, baby. Still could happen. But even if you hadn't said shit, it was gonna be a bust. The second the cops put two and two together, they were gonna be all over that army base like white on rice. At least this way, we can ensure there's no trace left for them to connect the dots to us. You catch my drift?"

"I do, Koolaid!"

"Good. Then what say we blow this pop stand to the moon?"

Martin made out the gate up ahead, the metal reflecting off the high beams of the Challenger.

About fucking time.

"Want me to get out and open it?" Charlene asked as they approached.

"No need, babe," he replied, allowing himself a smirk as he stomped the accelerator to the floor.

The powerful engine roared in response.

"What are you...?"

Before she could finish the question, the Dodge plowed through the chain link gate – destroying the latch and sending it flying wide open.

"Wooo!" he cried. "That's how you do it!"

"Oh my god, Koolaid! Your uncle's gonna throw a fit," Charlene cried, sounding horrified at what he'd just done.

Boar War

"So?"

"So, this is like ... his baby or something."

"Then consider me a coat hanger."

"Huh?"

"Never mind." Martin shrugged. "Trust me, baby, if this all works out he won't say shit. And if it doesn't, then who cares because we're probably all fucked anyway."

He slammed on the brakes, causing the car to skid before turning the wheel hard – finally bringing the vehicle to a halt right in front of the doors. The momentary adrenalin rush wasn't nearly as good as boning Lily had been, but it definitely got his heart pumping.

And right then, he most certainly needed it.

Despite his outward bravado, Martin was scared shitless. When this idea had first popped into his head, it had struck him as near brilliant. It still was – on paper anyway.

In practice, however, he was finally beginning to come to terms with how utterly stupid what they were about to do truly was.

Martin's dalliances with the law had been mostly confined to the occasional petty theft, dealing weed on the side, and of course pimping his flavors. A few years back, though, he'd met, through a mutual acquaintance, this dude named Steve who legit worked as a professional firebug.

Shady fuckers would hire this guy to burn down old buildings or failing businesses so they could then collect on the insurance. It was crazy shit, but then so was Steve. No doubt this was a dude who was a few pennies short of a dollar. The thing was, he wasn't a complete psycho, though. While the guy obviously had a hard-on for fire, he'd once mentioned that he had a system to ensure the jobs he worked gave him plenty of time to get out before they burnt to the ground.

Therein lay the problem. If they were merely trapping those fucking pigs inside and setting the place ablaze, that would be one thing. It wouldn't work, though. He'd seen the door to the loading dock. It looked sturdy enough, true, but he didn't doubt for one second that, given enough time, those monsters would tear right through it.

If so, they'd be right back where they fucking started – up shit creek without so much as a paddle.

No. They needed to blow this place to smithereens – to end this nightmare as well as cover his tracks.

After that, well, it would probably be a couple months of slinging pig shit at the farm before the heat died down enough to try again. The only upside was those goddamned hogs had caused so much damage downtown, that he was fairly confident there would be ample window of opportunity even after waiting things out.

Forget that construction on the south side, half the damned town needed to be rebuilt.

In truth, that was the only thing keeping him from telling Charlene to hold onto her seat as he gunned it out of this cursed town. If things worked out, he'd have his cake and eat it too. He just needed to swallow a spoonful of shit first while keeping a smile on his face.

"Are we actually going in there?" Mikey asked from the back.

"*We* is kind of a generous term," he replied, turning and facing the kid as they sat outside the doors of the abandoned army base – the only sound that of the idling engine and the occasional *tap-tap* of sputtering rain as it hit the roof of the vehicle.

Martin turned off the car then tossed the keys to Charlene. "Go grab what we need from the trunk, baby."

"You got it, Koolaid."

"As for you, kid, you have a slightly different part to play in all of this," he continued, once again facing the McNeil boy. "First things first, though. Tell me, have you ever by chance driven your old man's tractor?"

49

That has to be it. It just has to be, Bert thought, as he threw yet another shovelful of innards overboard. *There can't be many more of these godforsaken things out there.*

The trip around Berryman Lake had been a wash, no pun intended. They'd found a handful of the beasts in the area around there, and had enraged them into giving chase along with the rest – a situation that had almost gotten them sideswiped more than once.

Thanks to Lin's quick thinking, though, they'd managed to avoid anything worse than losing one of the trailer's side panels. As a result, Bert had made a silent vow to never again make a crack about women drivers.

Despite gaining a few new followers to their nightmare parade, a couple of the boars had fallen to the wayside as well – gored and crippled by their fellows. That was all well and good. Even if the injured pigs didn't die of their wounds, they'd be easy pickings later.

Hopefully.

One of the maimed pigs must've been a sow because

another of the beasts immediately stopped and attempted to mount it.

He doubted it would be successful, not with the wound that had been ripped into the crippled pig's side, but all the same they couldn't circle back to try and entice it to follow them again. With between eight and ten of those monsters still hot on their tail, it was simply too risky.

Bert tried to tell himself that was okay. They knew going in that the odds of them finishing off every last one of these beasts were slim. So long as they got most of them, that was what counted. A few stragglers could be hunted down with much less risk than a full herd.

What was important was that they killed enough to destroy any chance of a breeding population taking hold again.

At least so he hoped. With any luck, this was the majority of them. With their sheer size and appetite he simply couldn't imagine many more of these things might still be lurking hidden in the deep woods.

That was a problem for tomorrow, though. For now they had a job to finish, one that would hopefully ensure the town had a tomorrow to look forward to.

Ever since their detour to Berryman Lake, Lin had been calling out regular time checks. Between the wind whipping past him and Milo's continued barking, he'd heard maybe a third of them but it was enough. By his estimate, they had maybe half an hour left until Martin would hopefully be ready on his end. The base wasn't far, but the current state of the roads would almost certainly eat up that time and more.

And if it didn't, then they'd simply have to circle the area a few times and hope these hogs didn't grow bored with the chase.

Fortunately, he wasn't really worried about that. These things were hungry and pissed. The bigger issue was that the old truck only had so much gas in its tank. If they ran out before reaching their destination, they'd be as good as dead.

Steadying himself as best he could in the blood slick trailer, he took stock of the situation. After all this time, he was finally starting to run low on guts to shovel. Soon he'd need to start tossing chunks of meat overboard from the hacked up bodies taking up most of the trailer's space. However, after thinking it over, he concluded there was probably no need.

A continual stream of blood was dribbling off the back of the trailer, fed by the stinking piles of meat they'd loaded aboard. That would hopefully be more than enough to keep these fuckers invested in following them the rest of the way.

That was good because he wanted to make sure he was close to Lin for this last leg of the journey, just in case something went wrong.

His mind made up, he threw the shovel down and climbed over the front of the trailer – holding on for dear life.

Nice and steady, baby. Nice and ... now!

Bert leapt for the pickup's bed. In that same moment, however, the truck hit a bump in the road. It lurched to the side as he was airborne, telling him that he was about to miss his mark.

Shit!

He hit the top of the bed's side panel, tried to right himself, and tumbled off instead – managing to grab hold before he could fall to the ground. He was still tethered to the trailer hitch, but that wouldn't save him if he lost his grip.

Sadly, his already perilous position was made all the worse due to the fact that he was literally drenched in blood. His grip on the truck's bed was tenuous at best and slipping fast.

"Bert!" Lin cried.

He craned his neck and saw her staring frantically at him through the side mirror.

"Don't worry about me," he shouted. "Just keep going."

"But..."

"Do it!"

Bert kicked up, trying to hook his leg over the side wall, only for it to slide off. Both of his feet swung down and hit the muddy ground, nearly shaking him loose as he held on for dear life.

One more time, he told himself. *You can do this.* He only wished he believed that, trying his best to ignore how close his left foot was to being sucked under the truck's back wheel. *Don't look at that. Focus instead on...*

A squeal of rage rent the night, one coming from way too close by.

Fuck me!

Bert turned his head to find several of the boars rapidly gaining on the truck. One of them had spotted him and was angling his way, no doubt intent on crushing him against the truck's side.

Double shit! "Speed up, Lin! Do not, I repeat, *do not* slow down!"

Good as her intentions were, she was going to get them both killed if she didn't get this damned heap moving faster.

Thankfully, the message seemed to have gotten through. Bert felt the truck once more begin to pick up speed as the monstrous boar mercifully fell behind again.

It was now or never.

Enough of this crap. He kicked up again, one last effort with everything he had – this time managing to hook his right leg over the truck's bed.

Thank God!

The extra leverage allowed him to pull himself up and over, although not without almost losing his grip twice.

Finally, he tumbled inside, landing on his back and finding himself looking up at the sky.

Huh. Stars. Guess the storm really is breaking up.

"Are you okay?" Lin cried, her panicked voice just barely audible over the din. "Oh for Christ's sake, Milo, shut up for a second."

"It's okay. L-let him bark," Bert gasped, way too softly to be heard. Still trying to catch his breath, he sat up and scooted back until he was leaning against the outside of the cab. They'd had the foresight to knock out the truck's narrow back window before embarking, meaning he was now close enough to be heard without screaming his head off. "I'm fine, Lin."

"You'd better not be lying to me, Bert Cooper." she chided.

"If I'm lying I'm dying." Then, realizing what he'd just said, he quickly added, "Sorry. Bad joke. Anyway, yes, I'm good. Turn toward the base. It's time to bring these little piggies back home."

"Are you sure?"

"Positive. We've been out here long en…" He was interrupted by Milo poking his head out the back window and licking him across the face.

"I know, boy. I taste delicious," he said, pushing the dog back inside.

"Now I'm definitely not kissing you," Lin replied, smiling at him in the rearview mirror.

"I can't see why not. I probably taste like bacon. Everyone likes bacon."

"Eww."

He let out a tired laugh as the truck bounced up and down, still managing to stay a few steps ahead of the angry pigs on their tail. "How are we looking on gas?"

"Could be better, but we should make it."

"Good. Do me a favor."

"Anything," she replied. "Unless you're about to tell me to pull over and let you drive. Then you can take a hike, mister."

"Wouldn't dream of it, Hun. But if you wouldn't mind handing me my rifle, I'll see if maybe I can't thin out this herd a bit before we get where we're going."

50

Martin wouldn't have ever admitted it aloud, some things just weren't said, but deep down he was impressed that Charlene had kept her shit together so well – and it wasn't just about the events of that night.

His visits to the would-be chalet had been mostly brief before today, or make that yesterday. Despite keeping track of how long it had been since they'd parted ways with Bert and Lin, he hadn't given much thought to the actual time of day until that moment.

Anyway, earlier on when he'd picked up Lene, shortly before everything had turned to shit, it had been dark as fuck inside, true, but he'd only ventured a short way in before the old fluorescents had buzzed to life, lighting the way.

That had been her handiwork, and yes it still surprised the fuck out of him.

Now, though, the lights were off again as they slowly made their way back to the loading dock where both the generators and their tanks lay. He was finally getting an idea as to just how spooky this old base could be.

Not only had Lene been left here all by herself for hours on end, but she'd managed to explore a good chunk of the place on her own. Sure, that was time she was supposed to be using to clean but, all things considered, he wasn't about to split hairs over that now.

Under other circumstances, if asked, he would've guessed her more likely to cower in one spot than go off exploring. The sheer number of vermin alone that probably called this place home would've been enough to cement that opinion.

Thus it was surprising to find her not only taking the initiative but being so resourceful as well. Lene was loyal and hardworking, true, but typically Martin was of the mindset that if brains were dynamite, she'd be lucky to blow her nose.

It was something he realized he might have to rethink as she led the way through the warren of labs and offices, using just the beam of a single flashlight.

That was a problem for future Martin, though, as they finally made it to the warehouse-sized loading dock.

"Hold up." He dropped the supplies he'd been carrying and grabbed hold of her arm before she could step away.

"What's wrong, Koolaid?" she asked.

Rather than answer, he took the flashlight from her hands.

Resourceful she might've been, but the girl had all the survival instincts of a caged hamster.

He shined the light around the room, the darkness making the cavernous area feel both foreboding and unwelcoming.

The outside door was still closed and locked – something he'd soon be remedying – but for now that seemed to at least ensure they were alone.

In truth, that should've been obvious, but Martin had seen his share of double features at the drive-in. Even when busy getting his dick waxed, he always tried to pay attention to the plot. No point in letting good money go to waste, after all. The problem was, shit like that had a way of weaseling its way into one's mind.

Were this a movie, there was no doubt how it would play out. The moment they assumed all was well, they'd turn around to find the whole fucking place full of those monsters. It was both stupid and paranoid to think that might happen, but he had no intention of being caught with his pants down.

"What are you looking for, Koolaid?" Charlene asked after a minute or two.

"Nothing. Just making sure the coast is clear, is all."

She appeared confused as he handed her back the flashlight, but apparently sensed it was best to not pursue the matter further. It was rare for her to be so insightful.

Yeah, he might very well have to rethink his opinion on her capabilities ... later.

"All right," he said after another few seconds. "You go and get those lights turned on, while I go and see about getting us some fresh air."

As the lights flickered to life, likely for the last time, Charlene couldn't help but feel a twinge of sadness.

It would've been so great, it really would have.

While she couldn't deny feeling some doubt at first, she'd quickly come to have full faith in Martin's vision. He'd seen the potential here that all others had missed. As she'd worked to clean it up, she'd found herself more and more convinced of it.

She had no doubt that had they gotten this place up and running, there would've been no shortage of Johns lining up outside. Martin's pockets would've been overflowing and he'd have a full set of flavors working for him again. Best of all, she would've been there at his side sharing in his dream.

All of that would've made him happy, damn it, and that was what she wanted most of all.

But now it was all destined to go up in flames. It was necessary, both for the town's safety and keeping the coppers off their tail, but she was sad to see it go all the same. Though she knew there would be more opportunities for a man like Martin, what were the chances of them ever finding prime real estate like this ever again?

Is that doubt I hear in your voice, bitch? he asked from inside her mind. *Have a little faith in your Koolaid man.*

"I will, Koolaid. I'm sorry."

"Sorry about what?" Martin asked, looking up from where he'd been working to cut the lock holding the bay doors shut.

"Um ... sorry it took me so long to get the lights on."

"Don't sweat it, Lene. I mean, for Christ's sake, those gennies are over twenty years old. That you got them working at all is a damned miracle." There came a dull clunk and the heavy lock finally fell off. "About fucking time. It's amazing how much easier this shit is when I can see what I'm doing."

He moved to the chain hoist that controlled the doors and gave them a heave. At first nothing happened. Then slowly, with a squeal of rusted metal, the massive doors began to open – revealing the overgrown gravel drive leading up to it and the darkness beyond.

Thankfully that was all that was out there waiting.

For now, it was quiet, but it wouldn't be for long – at least not if the others were successful in their part of the mission.

Charlene couldn't pretend to have been all that fond of Bert and his wife as the summer had progressed, not the way they seemed intent on ignoring Martin's genius. Nonetheless, she said a silent prayer all was well on their end. Once this was all over, they'd surely have a newfound appreciation of their nephew and his capabilities.

"All right, that's that," Martin said, tossing the bolt cutters to the side and heading back toward her.

"Now what?" she asked, curious. She had a vague idea of what needed to be done, but he hadn't explained much in the way of details to her as they'd prepared back at the farmhouse. There simply hadn't been time.

After helping to fill the trailer, she and Lin had gone back inside. There, as per Martin's instructions, they'd grabbed every bed sheet, blanket, and covering they could find in the old house and had knotted them together, ending up with a rope of linens that must've been over a hundred feet long.

The whole thing was a bloody and stained mess, lying in a heap where Martin had dropped it, but according to him that didn't matter.

He pointed to the final item they'd brought with them – an old gas can, three quarters full thanks to what they'd been able to siphon from Old Man McNeil's tractor.

"Now, you're gonna take that gas can and douse those sheets with it, while I go and work on loosening the fill valve to these here tanks."

She began to get a clue as to what he had in mind, but wanted to hear it from his lips just to be sure. "Then what happens next, Koolaid?"

"Then, baby, we stuff one end of those sheets into the valve and unfurl the rest. If it all works like I think it will, the whole length will act as a giant fuse." He turned and gestured toward the propane tanks. "One hopefully long enough to give us a head start before it ignites the biggest goddamned stick of dynamite this shit-kicking town has ever seen."

51

With the lights back on, the old army base stood out against the darkness like a lighthouse overlooking a stormy ocean.

Even so, it was obvious from a distance that not everything within the old complex had withstood the test of time. Some parts of the building remained dark, while a good many of the outside lights flickered on and off, giving the whole place a distinctly ominous vibe.

Bert didn't care either way so long as the power was on.

Martin had been given two directives and this was easily the most dangerous and important of the two. He and Charlene had been asked to do whatever they could to coax this place back to life one last time. Without that, all their hopes would be for naught.

That wasn't all, though. Before they'd parted ways, he'd pulled his nephew to the side and told him to find a safe place to drop Mikey off first – one not in the path of either the truck or the pigs following it.

There was no doubt they'd succeeded at the first task.

Boar War

As for the second, Bert could only pray. However, there was nothing he could do about that now. All they could do was get to the base, make sure the pigs followed them inside, and then run like hell.

It all couldn't happen soon enough. He was down to only two rounds left. Sadly, his attempts at culling the herd had proven easier said than done while trying to aim from the back of the jostling vehicle.

He'd killed two of the hogs and was moderately certain he'd fatally crippled a third, but all the rest of his shots had either missed or been ineffective in slowing them down.

On the upside, the half dozen or so boars still chasing them were now seriously pissed. Had he been a betting man, he'd have put odds on them following the truck to Hell and back before giving up.

Now came the tricky part, as if everything up until that point had been a cakewalk.

He slung the rifle over his shoulder. Hopefully, he wouldn't need it but Bert was no fool. He wasn't willing to risk leaving it behind and then have things go all to shit.

So far they'd been lucky, but luck had a way of giving out when you needed it most.

Considering how this night has gone, no doubt about it.

Bert took one look back at the trailer still being towed behind them. Quite frankly, it was a miracle it hadn't been pummeled into firewood on the tumultuous ride over.

A small part of him preferred to think that was Scooter at work, doing his part to see them through this nightmare.

Now all the old trailer needed to do was survive another couple of bumps and its job would be done.

"Keep your eyes peeled, Scoot," he said under his breath, far too low to be heard above the wind whipping past him, "because we're about to set off some fireworks that'll put the state fair to shame."

That small *prayer* to his friend said, he leaned over the passenger side, hooked open the door, and then swung a leg over and managed to plant it on the narrow running board.

"Come on, Milo, scooch on over."

Grabbing hold with a death grip, he managed to swing himself inside the vehicle, although he didn't bother shutting the door again. With the end of this crazy ride in sight, there was no point.

"Trying to be the next Evel Knievel, mister?" Lin asked. Her tone was meant to be light, but he could see the harried look about her. It was like the last two hours had aged them both by five years.

"Not at all," he replied. "In fact, if we make it through this, I think we'll have both earned a nice long vacation."

"Then you can bring the tent, because I have a feeling we'll be sleeping in one for a while."

They smiled at each other. In her eyes he could see the love she had for him as well as the worry. Try as he might to focus on the former, he knew the latter was showing through on his face as well.

"You ready for this?" he asked as they approached the fence surrounding the facility.

"No," she said, her voice quivering.

"Neither am I."

Ahead, in the glow of the headlights, he could see the gate lying askew as if something heavy had rammed it open.

Don't think about the Dodge, he told himself. *The Dodge can be replaced. People can't.*

He didn't see his car parked anywhere inside, but that

was probably a good thing. In just a few short minutes, Scooter's truck would be rendered undriveable. Hell, even if it wasn't, chances were they wouldn't be able to get anywhere near it again – not that he had any plans on trying.

It was possible Martin had actually thought ahead and planned on them maybe needing an escape vehicle. Whatever the case, he'd surprised Bert this night both with his ideas and his willingness to see them through.

Prior to all of this, he'd considered his nephew a dreamer, always with his head in the clouds as opposed to focused on the work in front of him.

If they lived through this, he promised to show the kid more respect. Charlene too. They'd both earned it.

First they had to make it, though.

"Remember," he said, for Lin's benefit as well as his own, "throw yourself clear and then roll when you hit the dirt. The ground is soaked through. It should cushion the worst of it. Then I want you to run. Don't worry about me or Milo, just run."

He'd purposely left out anything that might suggest either of them could be left in a condition where they couldn't escape. Now was not the time for negativity, as Lin careened through the gate then turned left – following the overgrown drive as it circled the base and hopefully led toward the loading dock.

Lin hesitated for a moment, no more, before giving him a single nod. Then she reached over and pulled the handle of the driver's side door, unlatching the lock.

"Stay safe," she said.

"You too."

"I love you."

"I love you more."

Before she could say anything else, he grabbed hold of

Milo and pulled the old dog against his chest. "You're with me, buddy. No chasing the pigs!"

Milo let out a whine, although whether in protest of the order he'd been given or anticipation of what was to come, Bert didn't know.

"There," Lin cried. "I see it!"

Up ahead, the drive sloped downward toward a wide open chasm from which bright light spilled out. It looked absolutely massive inside. In fact, it was too big. Bert had been hoping for a space large enough to lead the pigs into, yet tight enough that they'd have trouble escaping even if they sensed something was amiss.

However, from the look of things, this bay had been designed with multiple trucks in mind.

This isn't going to work, not unless...

He made a decision then and there, one he decided it was best to keep to himself.

"Remember," he repeated, "run and don't look back. If anything comes after us, I'll take care of it."

"But..."

"They probably won't," he interrupted. "But in case any of them do, I won't be able to focus on killing it if I'm worried about you."

She looked like she wanted to say something to that, but there was no time – the loading dock was rapidly approaching. Instead, Lin nodded again before speeding up, causing the old truck's engine to roar. Then she jammed the butt of the empty shotgun lying next to her down onto the accelerator. "Now?"

"Not yet. We don't want the truck to veer off at the last second." His heart caught in his throat as the entrance loomed ahead of them. "Wait for it... Now!"

He made sure she was out the door first, then it was

his turn. He held Milo tight, gritted his teeth, and then leapt from the vehicle.

Bert twisted in midair, trying to land on his back while also managing to catch a fleeting glimpse of the now driverless truck as it sped into the loading dock.

Then it was gone from view as he slammed into the ground, the wind knocked out of him. Milo let out a yip but he held tight as he rolled with the momentum. Thankfully, the ground was as soft and muddy as he'd expected, providing ample cushion as he continued doing his damnedest to protect his dog with his own body.

He was nearly buried in sludgy dirt by the time he finally came to a halt – lying there breathing hard, yet refusing to let go of the struggling dog.

Not yet. Not until...

There came the echoing *crunch* of metal as the truck slammed into something deep inside the dock, but that was only part of what he was waiting for.

Barely a moment later, the ground beneath him jostled from the thunderous approach of several tons of angry pig. Squeals and snorts filled the air as he put his hand around the dog's muzzle, hoping to keep him quiet as the boars raced past them – still dead set on the truck and the easy meal it had been towing.

Another second or two passed and ... that was it! They were all inside.

Now came the point where he had to deviate from their plan.

Bert got up, finding himself bruised but otherwise okay – a small miracle unto itself. Milo looked a bit dazed from the ordeal, but he too seemed fine.

He turned and spied Lin across the way clambering to her feet. He waved once, then gestured for her to run.

"Go!" he hissed. "I'm right behind you."

Bert wasn't sure whether she heard him over the sounds of grunting, squealing, and splintering wood coming from inside, but she finally turned and began to limp away into the darkness.

That's one. Now for... He turned toward his dog. "Go on, boy, go with Mommy. Keep her safe."

Milo looked at him, then in the direction of the loading dock – letting out a low growl in the process.

"No! I said git!" Bert told him, louder this time. He gave the old dog a light smack on the rump, which finally seemed to get through to him.

A moment later Milo took off, racing in the direction Lin had disappeared.

Praying neither of them decided to do anything stupid, like he was about to, he turned toward the open bay.

Inside, he could hear the pigs gorging themselves. From the sound of things, they were going at it ... whole hog.

Now to make sure they stayed put until this place blew sky high. Bert had no idea how long he had, but since Martin and Charlene were supposed to set things up to leave themselves enough time to vacate, he assumed there were still at least a few minutes left.

Racing to the opening of the loading dock, he peered inside. Sure enough, the pigs were digging into the trailer's contents with great aplomb. The long chase had no doubt worked them into a frenzy of hunger.

Off to the left, past the monsters, he spied the bank of generators as well as the massive propane tanks that fed them. There was something leading from one of the tanks, past where the pigs fed, and out the other door. It took a moment, but Bert recognized it as the sheets from the house, the ones Martin had insisted on bringing.

That meant things were set on their end and it wouldn't be long.

Across the way, on the other side of the open bay doors, he spied what he'd been looking for – the chain hoist used to open the doors and keep them from closing.

He crossed the space quickly and quietly, thankfully unseen by the ravenous hogs. Then Bert grabbed the chain and gave it a pull. There came a slight pause and then he felt the locking mechanism disengage. Bert let go and stepped back outside. The door wouldn't hold them for long, but it hopefully wouldn't need to.

Rather than come crashing down, though, there came a squeal of rusty metal as the door began to inch downward, far slower than Bert had anticipated.

It wasn't the only squeal he heard, though, as he looked up to find one of the pigs had turned its head at the sound.

The boar locked eyes with him, leaving no doubt it had noticed his presence.

It let out an angry grunt, spun, and bolted toward him, moving terrifyingly quick for a beast its size.

The door continued to roll downward, but Bert saw there was no chance of it locking shut in time to stop the monster's progress.

In trying to ensure that none of them escaped, he'd instead done the exact opposite.

He could only stare in silent horror as over half-a-ton of death barreled his way on four legs.

Guess I should've followed the plan after all.

52

It was only now, listening to the carnage coming from the loading bay, that Martin began to second guess his course of action. Despite being several rooms away, it sounded like those fucking hogs were right next to them, nearly causing him to piss himself.

Holy shit. The son of a bitch actually did it.

It wasn't that he'd expected Bert to fail, just that he hadn't really considered the actual odds of success before then.

Up until that point his plan had been just that, a plan. Now, however, it had abruptly become a stark reality. And that reality reminded him way too much of being back in Nashville with Big Daddy.

When confronted with the idea that another pimp had it out for him, Martin hadn't been worried at first. It wasn't until he was tied to that chair while Big Daddy debated between using a rusty knife and a blowtorch on him that it had truly struck home just how much trouble he'd been in.

Back then he'd caved. Hell, he'd cracked like an egg.

The truth was, he couldn't get his ass out of Nashville fast enough. The thought of sticking it out and fighting back hadn't even crossed his mind – not until at least a hundred miles later when his bravado had finally returned.

Now, hearing what was going on just a couple of rooms away, he was starting to get that same sense that it was time to once again vacate the premises.

He turned and looked behind them. They'd purposely left an easy-to-follow path back to the main entrance – leaving the doors open and the way clear once it was time for them to make a run for it.

All he had to do was follow it a little earlier than planned. Hell, Charlene probably wouldn't even argue if he just told her to drop everything and run. And if she didn't listen, well, that would be her problem to…

"Now?"

"Huh?" he asked, pulled from the fugue state he'd been rapidly falling into.

"I was just asking if we should light the sheets now," Charlene said. "It sure sounds like there's enough pigs in there."

Martin blinked a few times, finally remembering the lighter still in his hand – the one they'd found in Old Man McNeil's truck before splitting up.

"What do you think, Koolaid? That's gotta be all of them, right?"

Her use of his street name, what he considered his *real name*, pulled him fully back from the ledge.

Lene's right. You ain't some pussy bitch. You're Koolaid. You're the dude who knocks down walls and delivers the flavor. Oh yeah!

He looked down and focused on the end of the gasoline soaked knot of sheets, finally remembering their purpose. More importantly, he remembered how he'd felt back in the barn, standing beside his uncle as they'd gunned down that boar.

It had been like facing Big Daddy all over again but with a completely different outcome.

Well, now there was a whole mess of Big Daddies a few rooms over, an entire goddamned convoy of those fuckers. If he could do this, he told himself, if he could end every last one of those motherfuckers and see this through, then there was literally no reason he couldn't do anything he set his mind to.

Sure, the plan was still for them to run like hell but first he had a job to do.

"What say we light this motherfucking pig of a pimp up," he said, flipping open the lighter and igniting it.

"Huh?"

"Nothing, baby," he replied offhandedly. "Just preparing myself for the fireworks to come. You ready?"

"Always, Koolaid."

"That's what I like to hear." He threw her a wink and then lowered the lighter to the improvised fuse. "Oh yeah!"

Bert scrambled away as the boar came at him. It had apparently decided he was an easier meal than fighting its friends over the bloody offal in the back of the wrecked trailer.

Come on, fall faster!

Sadly, the loading dock door was apparently not in a cooperative mood this day. It slid down way too slowly, the rusty hinges of the chain hoist squealing the entire way, albeit not nearly as loud as the pigs inside.

It was the one that would soon be outside that worried him more, though.

The door finally started sliding faster just as the boar stepped to the threshold of the bay. It hit the beast's back, giving Bert hope as he scrambled to pull the gun off his shoulder.

No good.

The boar pushed its way through, seeming to not care that the bottom of the door had sheared fur and skin off its back as it finally closed – trapping the majority of the pigs inside, all save one.

Sadly, this was a case where one was far too many.

There was no time to properly line up a shot, not when this thing was nearly close enough to spit on, so Bert fired from the hip.

As luck would have it, that turned out to be the smart move.

A shard of red hot metal sliced his cheek open as the barrel of the weapon exploded, the blowback nearly enough to knock him on his ass.

The fuck?!

Despite the shock, confusion, and pain, a part of him realized instantly what had happened. The barrel must've gotten plugged with mud when he'd leapt from the truck and he hadn't thought to check it first.

It was a stupid oversight on his part, unforgivable in nearly any other situation. Hell, he was damned lucky he hadn't blown his own fingers off in the process.

Unfortunately, it would likely still end up being a fatal mistake nonetheless.

Ahead of him, the boar let out an angry squeal that sounded much closer in pitch to a scream. Then it lowered its head and began rubbing the side of its face in the muck and dirt.

Or maybe not.

It lifted its head long enough for Bert to see the misfire hadn't been a total loss. Shrapnel had peppered the monster pig's face, puncturing its left eye and cracking the end of one tusk. A small river of blood dripped from its wounds and, judging from the sounds it was making, it must've been in agony.

Bert was no fool, though. Nasty as the beast's injuries looked, they were far from fatal. And now he was left unarmed, with no way of fighting back.

Knowing he likely had no more than a few seconds before the beast redirected its rage toward him, he did the only sensible thing – he turned and ran.

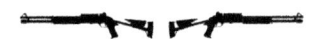

"Move your ass!" Martin cried, racing through the facility with Charlene hot on his tail.

"I-I'm trying, Koolaid."

He looked over his shoulder and found her falling behind. Tempting as it was to keep going, he slowed down and grabbed hold of her wrist. "Then try harder. Pretend the floor is a John's dick and he just told you to ride like the wind."

Martin didn't wait for her to try and make sense of that, he simply dragged her with him as best he could – all while trying to juggle the mental gymnastics of calculating how much time they had left.

The *fuse* had proven surprisingly resilient to being lit. He'd expected to no more than touch it with the open flame before having to leap back to keep his eyebrows from being singed off, but no such luck.

Instead, he'd had to work the end of the sheet with the lighter before it caught. Either the gas they'd siphoned was old or all those drive-in movies had fucking lied about how combustible gas tanks could be.

Whatever the case, once it got going the fire finally began to move down the line of gasoline soaked linens as planned.

That's when their race for freedom had begun.

In truth, he would've preferred another half dozen or so sheets added to the line – enough to give them a bit more headway to get clear of the building. Still, he was fairly certain they had enough time. By his best guess, they'd make it outside by the skin of their teeth before everything blew.

That was a little too close for comfort but the initial explosion would be on the far side of the facility – with any luck blowing the bay and every pig inside to hell and back. It would then hopefully take a bit of time for the fire to spread to the rest of the building, thus giving them plenty of time to get clear.

Or so Martin hoped.

If the explosion was bigger than he assumed or if the walls caught sooner than...

He pushed all of that from his mind as he realized they were almost there.

Just two more rooms and they'd be clear.

Stay focused! If something's going to turn to shit, this is when it'll happen.

Though he didn't give voice to his fears, a part of him was hoping he hadn't just jinxed them with his thoughts.

But then they were through, racing out the front door to the lot beyond.

Holy shit, we made it. Yeah! Fuck you, Big Daddy! "Or should I say Pig Daddy?"

"What was that, Koolaid?" Charlene gasped, sounding seriously winded from the effort.

"Nothing, baby. Just enjoying the sweet scent of victory. And in case you're wondering, I expect it to smell a lot like bacon."

He finally stopped about fifty feet from the door. "Brace yourself ... right ... about ... now!"

Nothing happened.

"Now," he repeated.

He said it three more times, growing more ticked off by the moment. Had he truly timed it that badly?

Another minute or two passed but still there was no explosion.

"Um, Koolaid, shouldn't it be...?"

"Any second now, Lene," he interrupted. "Just be patient."

Martin silently counted to ten. Then he did it again, slower this time. Still nothing.

He knew those tanks still had plenty of fuel in them. Those old gennies wouldn't be running if there was nothing but fumes left.

No. That wasn't the cause.

Martin did another quick rundown of the length of the fuse compared to where they'd lit it, trying to think of whether he'd missed anything. But there was nothing that came to mind. They'd double and triple checked it.

Of course, there was one big wild card to take into account – several tons of angry pig.

They'd tried to accommodate that in their placement of the fuse but trying to predict the motives of monster boars was about the least exact science he could imagine.

Whatever the cause, by this point there was no denying it. Something had gone wrong.

The question now was whether there was anything to be done about it.

Those pigs wouldn't stay in that loading dock for long,

not the way those fuckers could eat. Once they decided they'd had enough, they'd bust free and run amok again.

If so, that would be the end of this town and anyone left in it.

He turned away from the base, toward the darkness of the surrounding woods. There, freedom – an escape from all of this – beckoned. All they needed to do was pick a direction, start running, and hope their luck held out.

That wasn't all the darkness held, though.

In the gloom, the trees almost seemed to take on the semblance of Big Daddy's fat, stupid face. Martin wasn't surprised to find the fucker grinning at the idea that he was getting ready to run once again.

The older pimp was like a monkey on his back, one that seemed to have no interest in ever climbing down.

Not unless he did something about it.

"Lene, you still got that peashooter Bert gave you?" he asked. That was the only gun they'd brought with them. All the rest had gone with the other team.

"Right here, Koolaid."

"Hand it over."

She did so without question. "Good girl. Now I need you to do one more favor for me."

"Anything, Koolaid."

"Plant your ass here and don't even think about following."

Rather than wait to see what she had to say, Martin turned his back on her and headed once more toward the army base.

He didn't know what awaited him inside, but it had to be better than the specters that threatened to continue haunting him otherwise.

53

Bert tried to keep his wits about him as he fled from the monstrous boar. Needless to say, that was easier said than done.

Nonetheless, he did his best to be mindful of two things: the direction Lin had fled, while making sure to avoid it, and keeping track of how close the beast's angry snorts sounded.

Up ahead, the form of the chain-link fence surrounding the facility took shape in the darkness. *Great. Just what I need.*

True, several spots were clearly in disrepair thanks to the long years, but it definitely added a bit of unwanted challenge toward any hope of escaping this...

There came a grunt from right behind him, close enough that he was certain he felt the beast's rancid breath on the back of his neck.

Ignoring the fence, Bert dove toward the left, the beast's blindside, as the enormous pig charged past him.

Thank goodness for the sopping wet ground. It served two purposes in this case – cushioning Bert's landing, while also ensuring the hog slid in the muck rather than easily correct its course.

It gave him enough time to get back up and start running again.

Sadly, he knew this was one game of tag he couldn't win. Without a weapon or means of escape, he was a dead man walking.

It was simply a matter of time at this point.

Speaking of time, where the hell is that goddamned explosion? Surely it had been long enough. If Martin didn't light this place up soon, there was little chance that door would hold the rest of the beasts. Once they were back outside again, that was it. All of them would be truly and thoroughly fucked.

I am so fucked.

Martin had hoped he'd find the cause of the fuse's failure relatively close to where he'd first lit it – perhaps a break in the line they hadn't noticed.

There was no such luck.

He quickly saw that once lit, the sheets had ignited exactly as intended. He followed the still burning remnants, keeping one hand over his mouth thanks to the acrid smoke that now hung in the air.

With every step he felt his resolve wavering, as every footfall brought him ever closer to the ruckus going on ahead. For God's sake, it truly sounded like those fucking pigs were going absolutely apeshit.

Soon enough there was only one more room between him and the loading bay.

Despite wanting to do nothing more than turn and run, the specter of Big Daddy kept Martin going. Even so, he knew what moving forward meant. This close to the loading dock, there was little hope of escape. Even if he'd found the source of the problem in this room, which he hadn't, the chances of him making it back to the exit before things blew were slim to none.

It was a shame. He'd really been looking forward to sampling Lily's wares again. But oh well. Maybe some other enterprising pimp would wander into her life and put her talents to use. *A woman like that is truly wasted working retail.* Albeit he doubted there was anyone else in this corner of the state with either his vision or talent.

"That's right. I'm Koolaid, the only man who brings the flavor," he told himself, steeling his nerves as he stepped to the door of the loading dock.

The smell of propane lingered in the air, but it was just barely noticeable compared to the overpowering stench of death.

It was like the entire bay had become a slaughterhouse. He saw where Scooter's truck had crashed, spilling the contents of the trailer. Thanks to those pigs, the corpses inside had been mangled beyond recognition.

It obviously still hadn't been enough to sate their hunger as they were in the process of turning on one another – bellowing angrily as they fought over the remaining meat and intestines.

That's when he saw it – the break in the line.

One of the pigs had been gored in the side, no doubt as they'd battled over the spoils from the trailer. The creature had collapsed close enough to the fuse so that its blood had soaked through the fabric. He saw clear as day where the fire had fizzled out.

Fuck!

Beyond it, the tangle of sheets was dotted with blood, but otherwise in good condition – its far end still stuffed into the open feeder leading to the massive propane tanks beyond.

The problem was reaching it and then having enough time to reignite the fabric.

There was at least four, no five, of the monster pigs still alive inside the bay. At the moment, all of them seemed preoccupied with gorging themselves but he knew it was foolish to count on that lasting – especially since he didn't see any way to light the damned sheets without every single one of those godforsaken things noticing he was there.

The back of the bay was full of discarded equipment scattered among the rows of incinerators. He could maybe use some of that to cover the distance, but once he was there he'd be exposed for all to…

Wait, the incinerators!

If he could get one of them going again, eventually the flames inside would ignite the propane fumes seeping into the room. If so, he wouldn't need to worry about the fuse. Best yet, it might give him a fighting chance to escape.

He had no idea if any of them still worked, but it seemed possible. Hell, everything else in this place had been built to last – his tax dollars hard at work – so it was at least worth a shot. Speaking of which…

He doublechecked the revolver, confirming it was fully loaded. As ridiculously inadequate as it probably was, he felt better knowing he had at least some protection on him. Although, with any luck he wouldn't need it.

He just needed to be quick enough to get to those incinerators and quiet enough to light one without being seen.

After that, he could finally get the hell out of there, knowing this time there'd be no looking back.

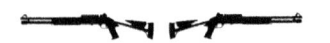

"Come on, blow up, damn you!"

Bert had doubled back to the base with the angry pig hot on his heels. If he couldn't shake this monster, then he was going to do his damnedest to make sure it wouldn't be able to threaten Lin or anyone else ever again.

Even if it cost him his life.

By this point, though, he was starting to fear something had gone very wrong inside.

That's assuming it was ever rigged to begin with.

As Bert continued trying to outmaneuver the massive boar – a feat only made possible because it was half blind, doubt began to worm its way into his gut.

What if after turning on the lights Martin had simply decided the risk wasn't worth it? There'd been no sign of the Dodge after all. They could've simply taken off, leaving him, Lin, and the rest of the town high and dry?

Had he been naïve in assuming his nephew would see this through? If so, he'd thrown his life away on nothing more than a lie.

No! He didn't want to believe that but it was hard to remain optimistic as a half-ton of enraged hog once again charged him.

It was a mistake to let doubt cloud his focus.

He realized that a moment too late as he once more attempted to dodge the feral beast. This time, however, it was apparently his turn to be betrayed by the wet ground. Bert's foot slipped, causing him to stumble.

He still managed to sidestep the angry hog but not by nearly enough.

The pig swung its massive head even as it rushed past him.

It was a glancing blow by the monster, probably the

only thing that saved his life, but Bert was sent flying nonetheless.

He landed hard, the crack of bone audible as crippling pain lanced through his chest. Bert had been unfortunate enough to be kicked by a mule several years back. The blow had cracked one of his ribs. This felt kinda like that had, only worse.

He knew in an instant what that meant. Two, maybe three of his ribs were busted. With such an injury any shot he might've had at surviving this was now gone.

Even as the pig circled back around, he tried to get back up but fell to his knees instead, coughing up blood as his body refused to heed his commands.

The boar stopped moving and regarded him for a moment, almost as if it understood this was the end – that its prey was done for.

It snorted, lowered its head, and turned to face him – its back to the still intact army complex as it stepped forward.

Bert tried to shuffle away but managed only a few feet before the pain became too great.

All he could do now was wait there defeated as his death approached ever closer.

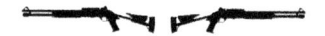

It was the space of only ten feet to the nearest pile of debris – a discarded engine block from the look of things – but it was the longest ten feet of Martin's life.

He was absolutely convinced he wasn't going to make it until he managed to slide behind it mercifully unseen. This was it. There was no turning back now.

Hell, it was a minor miracle he'd made it this far.

Worked up as they were, these pigs were still wild

animals with a vastly superior sense of smell and hearing. Fortunately, the bay absolutely reeked of blood and the boars themselves were making enough racket to wake the dead.

Talk about the least comforting thought one could possibly have at a time like that.

Still, he couldn't very well stay there forever. Martin made sure the coast was clear, then he stepped out and moved to the next bit of cover, a pile of rusted metal tubing – old ductwork from the look of it.

He slipped behind it, his heart pounding in his chest.

Almost there. Another twenty or thirty feet. The controls for the nearest of the incinerators was on this side, facing him. He'd still be partially exposed, but at least he'd have a chance to...

However, just then he realized he had no idea what to do next. Sure, he'd been familiar with these sort of machines thanks to his old man's job, but that was a long way from being certified to operate one. Would the blasted thing simply start up, or was there a goddamned pilot light that needed to be lit first? He had no idea.

Fucking fuck!

He forced himself to take a deep breath.

It was too late to back out now. Besides, he was Koolaid. He'd figure it out.

Or so he desperately hoped.

Sadly, it was the exact wrong moment to be distracted by such thoughts. As he stepped from cover again, his foot caught on a piece of the ductwork – shifting the rest just enough so that the topmost piece tumbled off.

It hit the floor with a hollow *clang* – not particularly loud compared to the commotion the pigs were making, but damning all the same.

Martin turned to see one of the boars look up from its

awful meal – a pile of organs that had spilled over the side of the wrecked trailer.

It let out an ear-piercing squeal and charged, seeming to accelerate far faster than any creature that size should be able to.

Goddamn it all!

He dove out of the way in the moment before the pig barreled through the pile of ductwork, scattering it like bowling pins. All around the bay, the rest of the beasts looked up from what they'd been doing. One by one their focus turned his way.

Martin knew in an instant that both he and his plan were doomed. There was no way he'd be able to get either the incinerators going or the fuse relit. Not now.

In fact, far as he could tell, there was only one way to see this through. There was thankfully no time for thought on the matter. He simply acted.

"Fuck you, Big Daddy," Martin cried, raising the gun and pointing it toward the row of propane tanks. "You ain't got nothing on the Koolaid man."

He squeezed the trigger just as he saw another of those monsters closing in from the corner of his eye.

Shit!

Martin fired the weapon even as he lunged out of the way, nearly catching a tusk to the gut for his troubles.

Sadly, the bullet flew wide, striking nothing but wall.

How the fuck did I miss that?

There was no chance to line up another shot. The first pig had turned around and was already charging at him again.

He scrambled away until his backside was up against the incinerator he'd originally been trying to reach. "Oh yeah? Well, fuck you too!"

Martin fired four times point blank at the boar. He

wasn't sure how many hit the mark, but it was enough to finally drop the beast.

Sadly, that left him with only one bullet and little hope as the rest of the pigs began to close in. His back was to the proverbial wall as the incinerator blocked any hope for a clear shot at the tanks.

With the remaining pigs mere moments from tearing him apart, he realized there was another use for that final bullet – one he hadn't considered before, but that suddenly seemed a much better fate than allowing himself to be devoured alive by these monsters.

He lifted the gun and put the barrel to his forehead with one last, "Oh yeah!"

54

"You get away from my Koolaid!"

Martin looked up from where he'd been less than a second away from blowing his own brains out.

Amazingly enough, the pigs likewise turned at the shrill sound of Charlene's voice. It was just the distraction he needed.

I'll be damned.

To his right, where he needed to be in order to get a clear shot at those tanks, stood another of those monsters. No way was that happening. But to his left there was an open path leading toward the rear of the bay. There, more piles of discarded equipment lay. It wasn't much, but it was more cover than he had right at that moment, maybe even enough for him to circle back and finish this.

Martin turned and ran, heading toward the back of the loading dock.

In doing so, his movement once again caught the pigs' attention. Several of them turned back to watch him sprint away. For several long seconds the remnants of the herd just stood there, as if debating between which of the two humans to kill and devour first.

Though Martin hadn't been consciously meaning to, by dividing the giant boars' attention he ended up giving them both a fighting chance. At the very least, the monsters' momentary inaction gave Charlene the opportunity to step further into the bay – along with the object she'd brought with her.

Martin reached the relative safety provided by a heavy pile of rusted machine parts in time to watch Charlene fling the metal gas can high into the air.

They'd emptied the majority of its contents on the fabric that made up their failed fuse attempt, leaving the rest behind as they'd run for safety. He realized she must've picked it up on the way back in.

There couldn't be much left in it, but what little there was sprayed out, splashing the pigs as it arced through the air before landing with a heavy *clang*.

One of the hogs turned at the sound, spearing the metal container with its tusk and resulting in it getting stuck. The beast lifted its head to shake the can free, dousing its face with the last of the flammable liquid.

It was the space of a second for Martin to realize the opportunity they'd been given. He reached into his pocket and pulled out Scooter's old Zippo lighter one final time.

I could kiss you right now, Lene.

He stepped out from behind his cover even as Charlene screamed for him to run. Rather than heed her, though, he flipped open the lighter and casually flicked the wheel until the wick caught fire.

"Smoke if you got 'em, motherfuckers," he cried, tossing it at the pig with the can still impaled upon its tusk.

He held his breath as it tumbled through the air.

Paydirt, bitches!

The lighter struck home, hitting the pig's dripping snout and igniting the hair upon its face.

"Fuck yeah! That's how you do it, Big Daddy!"

The stricken boar let out a terrible scream as it began to buck frantically, slamming its head into the pig nearest it. A moment later, the thick fur covering the second beast's side likewise caught fire.

It wasn't much, just a couple patches of burning fur, but it was enough to send all the rest of the pigs into a blind panic.

High pitched squeals and grunts filled the air as they went absolutely nuts, trying to get away from the flames but instead spreading them to one another.

As horrific yet wonderful a sight as it was to see, Martin realized it wouldn't be enough. Painful as the fire almost certainly was, it was likely superficial damage at best to these abominations.

"Are you all right?" Charlene cried, running up and flinging her arms around him.

"I am now, baby," he said, giving her a quick hug but making sure to keep his eyes on the pigs as they continued running wild – goring piles of debris, the incinerators, and even the walls.

"I'm sorry I didn't listen to you, Koolaid," she blurted out, "but I got worried after a few minutes and decided to..."

"It's cool, Lene. You did good," he told her, watching as one of the panicked boars rammed into the roller door, causing a reverberating clang to echo through the bay.

Goddamn it!

The door held for the moment, but he had a feeling they wouldn't get lucky a second time. He needed to end this now. There would be no more chances. He knew that, which meant, despite the reprieve he'd been given, his course was still set in stone.

"Really, Koolaid?"

"Yeah, really. I mean it too," he said, steering her back toward the doorway she'd entered from. "But now I need you to do one more thing for me, and no arguing this time."

"What is it?"

He glanced back, making sure he now had a clear shot at those tanks. "Go. Get out of here. Live your life, find a man and settle down, that sort of shit."

"What do you mean?"

"What I mean, is someone needs to finish this." He held up the gun. "And there's only one way for your Koolaid man to do that. Now go on. Get going."

"No."

"What did you say?"

"I – I said no, Koolaid."

"Listen..."

"No! You listen this time. There ain't no other man out there for me but you. I've had the best and ... I just don't want the rest. I, I ain't leaving. Do what you gotta, but I'm here with you until the end."

"You can't be..."

"I mean it," she snapped with surprising forcefulness. "Now come on. Let's save your aunt, uncle, and everyone else in this stupid town. Make them all remember the name Koolaid."

Martin stared at her for a moment but no more, hearing another clang as the boars continued to run amok. By then the air had filled with the scent of burnt hair and bacon.

"You sure?"

She nodded. "A Koolaid man needs his flavor."

After another second or two he finally nodded. "Then let's fucking do this shit already. Can I get an *oh yeah*?"

"Oh yeah!" Charlene wrapped her arms around his waist as he turned and took aim. "I ... I love you, Koolaid."

"I know you do, baby. As far as bitches go, you'll always be my number one."

With that, he pulled the trigger.

Bert inched slowly back, not wanting to take his eyes off the monstrous pig stalking him. It was all he could manage with his ribs busted and pain flaring like lightning up and down his left side.

He was done for. The boar, interestingly enough, seemed almost to understand this, closing in with deliberate slowness as if the damned thing were enjoying his final moments.

"Come on," he snapped, blood and spittle flying from his mouth. "I'm right here, you bastard. Finish it alread..."

The rest of what he had to say was lost forever as the base exploded behind the mammoth beast. Bert was knocked onto his back, his ears ringing from the deafening sound of the blast as a fireball rose high into the sky.

The shockwave from the explosion pinned him down into the mud in the moment before a tidal wave of rubble erupted out in every direction.

T-they did it! They actually did it!

Bert knew he was a goner. He was simply too close to survive the devastating blast, but in that moment he was okay with it. So long as the others were safe.

However, even as his shirt began to smolder from the

heat, he realized the pig's enormous bulk was actually shielding him from the worst of it.

Bert couldn't believe it. By stalking him slowly, seeming to savor the kill to come, the monstrous beast was inadvertently saving his life instead.

Not that it was happy in the slightest with that fact.

The creature lifted its head and roared in agony as it's backside ignited from the flames still pouring from the destroyed base.

Bert saw his opportunity. It was terrifyingly slim and likely the only one he was going to get, but it was a chance.

Go, he prodded himself. *You can do this. Deal with the pain later. Just run!*

Realizing he'd miraculously been given a second chance, Bert wrapped one arm around his midsection then used the other to push himself to his feet. He screamed from the effort, not that he could hear much beyond the ringing in his ears.

Gritting his teeth, he took a stumbling step, then one more, knowing that at any moment he'd likely be crushed to death by the rubble falling all around him.

Miraculously enough, though, he remained untouched as he slowly lurched away from the burning building – feeling the heat licking at his backside.

He made it maybe ten yards, fighting for every agonizingly slow step he took, when he felt something else other than the heat – a dull thud from the mud beneath his feet.

Then he felt it again.

No! It has to be dead. It has to...

There was no denying it, however. The beast's footfalls were growing steadier, more insistent. He knew what it meant.

This is gonna really hurt.

Boar War

With the last of his strength, Bert leapt to the side. Though the soft mud cushioned his landing, it wasn't enough. Every nerve in his body screamed at once, the pain nearly overpowering. That was it and he knew it. He wouldn't be able to get back up again, not before...

In that same instant, the pig, it's body still aflame, barreled past him. It roared in pain and anger, the sound just barely audible to Bert's injured ears.

It stopped and turned, looking first one way, then another. Bert was confused as to what it was doing until he saw it's ruined face. In the light of the fire still burning behind him, he realized the beast had been fully blinded from its injuries.

Flames had eaten away its fur, melting its remaining eye from the socket.

Yet still the brute refused to give up. It lowered its head and began to snuffle along the ground, no doubt trying to find his scent.

Bert realized it was only a matter of time. He had nothing else left in him. There would be no escape from this one as the boar finally turned in his direction.

Come on then, you son of a bitch!

It took a single step toward him when its body suddenly lit up, almost as if a spotlight had been shined on it.

What the fuck?

The light wasn't coming from the fire, though. It was far too bright. So then what was causing...?

Once more he felt a rumble coming from the ground beneath him, as another muffled roar filled the air – one he recognized in a heartbeat.

It wasn't a spotlight shining on the pig. It was headlights!

In the next moment, his beloved Dodge Challenger

came screaming out of the darkness only to plow into the monster's side.

The crunch of metal combined with an unearthly roar of pain as the Dodge's hood crumpled like an accordion. There was little doubt the car was totaled by the collision, but that was oddly okay right then. It had done its job. The pig's broken body lay on its side, where it shuddered once or twice before mercifully falling still.

"W-who?"

He expected to find Martin or perhaps Lin behind the wheel. But then the driver's side door opened and a slight figure stepped out instead – approaching the dead pig in the flickering beam of the car's remaining headlamp.

"M-Mikey?" Bert gasped.

"That's for my ma and pa, you son of a bitch," the boy said before turning Bert's way, tears streaming down his face. "H-he gave me the keys, told me to drive away, but I couldn't leave. I just couldn't."

That was all Mikey McNeil was able to say before he fell to his knees sobbing.

Bert collapsed next to him a moment later, grabbing hold of the boy and hugging him as tightly as he could in the flickering light of the flames still coming from the ruined base.

EPILOGUE
PRESENT DAY

"Those poor people," Danni Kent said, closing the file and laying it on the hotel room bed, alongside all the others her teammate and friend had brought her.

She glanced up at the older man's wiry frame as he stood leaning against the dresser while she'd read through the pages.

Mitchell Harkness was the team's medic and damned good at his job, but he'd also been Derek's confidant – his friend and sounding board, at least before the incident in the Bahamas that had changed everything.

"They didn't deserve any of that," Mitchell replied with a sigh. "Sadly, not the first time we've run into monsters of man's own making."

Danni gritted her teeth. It had been nearly a year since her encounter with the so-called *Jersey Devil*, yet the wounds still felt fresh.

Though she didn't know the Coopers, heck she wasn't even sure if they were even still alive, she empathized with them all the same. She knew what it was to have one's world completely upended by the unknown.

"What happened? After, I mean," she replied, noting there was no follow-up in the report.

Mitchell shrugged. "From what I understand, the explosion at the base didn't go unnoticed. The Army quarantined the whole town soon thereafter, not that there was much left of it. As for those pigs, they scoured the woods for any stragglers the fire may have missed. Not sure if they ever found any, but if they did I'm guessing they were promptly disposed of with extreme prejudice."

"I meant the people."

"I was getting to that. While the Army guys were doing their thing, the suits from the Ford Administration stepped in to handle the rest. Now, this was long before even the notion of a cryptid containment unit was a thing but it's not like this was the government's first ever coverup, if you catch my drift."

"What a surprise."

Mitchell nodded. "Anyway, they bought out those who were willing to accept an offer, of which there were no small number. The rest they strongarmed into moving on. The sheriff and that deputy ... Hendricks, they both tried to make a stink about things, but it all quieted down soon enough. I don't know what deals were offered or threats made but that was mostly the end of it. After that, everything was bulldozed over and both towns quietly disappeared from the map."

"That's terrible."

"No, that's just Uncle Sam cleaning up his messes." Mitchell blew out a breath.

"Won't lie. Kinda makes me wonder how many other Cooper's Bluffs are out there, buried so deep in the archives that they'll never see the light of day."

"Speaking of the archives," Danni said, gesturing toward the multiple case files Mitch had brought with him, "isn't being in possession of these technically a federal crime?"

"They haven't been missed if that's what you're asking. The originals are all exactly where they're supposed to be. These are just copies."

"Illegal copies."

"Illegal is such a dirty word," Mitchell remarked. "Derek liked to think of it as light reading for those rare moments of downtime."

"Pretty sure the U.S. Forest Service would disagree."

"Maybe, but they're not here right now are they? And since we're technically both on extended leave of absence while they continue to pretend we don't exist, I'm not going to lose sleep over it."

"Why are you giving these to me now?" Danni asked after another minute.

"I figured you might be interested in that one since a few of the folks involved come from your family tree."

"Oh?"

"Aldrick and Ellie Kent. And yes, I checked. Both of them cousins from your father's side. Heck, it's almost like cryptid hunting runs in the family."

"Except that they both died, Mitch."

"I never claimed they were any good at it."

Danni shook her head before turning serious again. "Why really?"

Mitchell sighed. "Because Derek would've wanted you to have them."

"I'm not this team's leader. Hell, I don't even know if there is a team anymore. We're just ... low rent reality stars right now."

"True, but you've got top billing on the show. That's

good enough for me, and I think we both know Derek would agree."

"But..."

"I was only half-joking with that light reading crack earlier. In truth, he didn't talk about it much, but I suspect he smuggled these copies out as a reminder."

Danni raised an eyebrow. "For why we do this?"

"Exactly. See? You get it. By the way, I'm pretty sure Norah knew he had them, if that helps you sleep better."

Danni shrugged. Norah had been their team's former liaison in DC. Sadly, she too had fallen victim to that debacle down in the Caribbean.

"He kept these to remind himself why we do this," Mitchell reiterated. "And why we need to *continue* doing it."

"Even though we've been officially ordered to stand down?"

Mitchell grinned at that, just as she expected. "What's the worst they can do to us? Besides, I'm sure thirty years in Leavenworth will pass just like that." He snapped his fingers.

"Says you, old man. Some of us are still trying to finish college." Danni glanced again at the file before steering the conversation back that way. "What about the Coopers?"

"What about them?"

"I mean what happened to them?"

"Funny you should ask that. From what I understand, they eventually settled down in Linda's old stomping grounds up in High Moon, Pennsylvania. She passed on a few years back, but I think Bert's still kicking."

"High Moon," Danni repeated. "Why does that name sound familiar?"

"Probably because we were right next door not too

long ago. Remember that episode we did on the Mongrel Man of Morganberg?"

She nodded. "I remember you ruining Derek's monologue because you tripped over a branch."

"It was a rock, thank you very much."

"So why is it funny that I ask about it?"

"Because it's not so coincidentally the perfect segue to the other reason I'm here. We need to convince our producers to send us back there for a follow-up episode. We're talking the sooner the better."

Danni inclined her head, curious about this new development. "What for? The Mongrel Man is just a local legend, a crank."

"Maybe not. That whole area has been heating up lately on the weirdness scale. And it all seems to center on three towns: Morganberg to the east, Crescentwood to the west, with High Moon stuck smack dab in the middle. We've got reports of unexplained sightings, missing persons, and general weirdness. Nothing that the networks would ever talk about, but there's a couple of subreddits that have been going absolutely mental over it."

"Aren't they usually pretty mental?"

"Yes, but now it's even more so. And then there's the mystery of what happened at Ventureland."

"Ventureland?"

"It's an old abandoned amusement park in the region. Been closed for years. The land's been bought and sold about a dozen times over but nobody's ever made much progress redeveloping it. That sort of thing."

"So?"

"So," Mitchell continued, "there was a huge energy bloom there just a few days back. One of our spy satellites managed to pick up on it."

"And you know this how?"

"Let's just say when you're in charge of the pharmaceuticals for a formerly active field team, you tend to make lots of friends in the business."

Danni held up a hand. "I don't want to know."

"Plausible deniability for the win."

"Anyway, the point of this?"

"The point is, one of the agencies sent in some guys to investigate but they didn't find anything. The whole place was clean."

"Okay and...?"

"As in too clean. It had been snowing like a motherfucker the night before. But while the parking lot and surrounding woods were literally covered with powder, the park itself was miraculously clear. It wasn't even like it had been plowed. More like it hadn't snowed there at all."

She shrugged, so far unimpressed.

"Not enough for you? How about this? They found fresh burns all over the Ferris wheel that were conducive with arc welding, even near the very top."

Danni actually laughed at that one. "Oh no, a burglar with a blowtorch and a climbing fetish. Let's send in the cryptid hunters."

Mitchell chuckled too. "I figured you might say that. That's why I brought these."

He pulled another file from his jacket, handing it over. Inside were a set of enhanced satellite photos, one of which was familiar to her. Though obviously of vastly different locations, they both showed a similar heat bloom in the middle.

"This," Mitchell said, pointing to the first, "is what they captured over Ventureland. And this..." He indicated the second photo.

"Is from the incident in the Caribbean," Danni finished.

"Yep. Taken at the same time that ... *thing* sitting on the bottom blew sky high."

"You're not suggesting an alien ship paid a visit to some broken down amusement park in PA are you?"

"Your words not mine," Mitchell said. "But no. What I am suggesting, though, is that something mighty fucking weird happened out there – weird enough to throw off the same kind of energy."

Danni didn't need to hear any more. What had happened down in the Bahamas had been both terrifying and unbelievable, but also slightly wonderful. They'd experienced the impossible – a breach between worlds, allowing her to be briefly reunited with the brother she'd thought lost forever. If the same thing had happened again...

"I'll call Stant in the morning and convince him we need to head back to Pennsylvania. He won't like it, but I don't think he'll fight me on it. It's not like that Ohio Grassman episode can't wait."

Mitchell nodded. "What are you going to tell him?"

"I don't know. I'll make something up about werewolves. Talk to Julie. See if she's..."

"Already done. She's on board. All I need to do is call and make sure we have some guns waiting for us."

Danni cocked her head. "That whole guy with the pharmaceuticals thing again?"

"You know it."

"Good. Oh, and Mitch ... thanks."

"For what?"

"For bringing this to me." She gestured at the case files. "All of it."

Danni couldn't help the strange feelings welling up inside her. There was a sense of foreboding, true, at once again preparing to face the unknown – and this time without the official blessing of the US government. However, she was excited too, both to be getting back out there, as well as investigating an incident that might give them some closure regarding Derek's fate – or at least more answers than they currently had.

Either way, she knew he would approve.

Danni picked up the Cooper's Bluff case file once again. She planned on going through all the others Mitchell had brought, but this one had truly served to remind her of why her team did what they did.

It was all about the people – saving those they could, but also making sure those they couldn't help weren't forgotten.

Speaking of which, since they were going to be in the area anyway, it probably wouldn't hurt to look up Bert Cooper and make sure he was doing okay.

It was the least she could do for the poor man whose life was irrevocably upended one hot summer in nineteen-seventy-four. Hopefully, he was happy and doing well.

Danni had no idea what else was waiting for them in High Moon. Though she didn't believe in werewolves, she knew that weirdness abounded in their world, and from the sound of things this town was a potential hotspot.

And where there was weirdness, there were people in need of help.

This was exactly the sort of thing the Crypto-Hunter team excelled at dealing with – even if giant pigs probably weren't part of the equation.

Hopefully anyway.

THE END

The Crypto-Hunter team will return in
BENT OVER (The Hybrid of High Moon – 5)

If you enjoyed this book, want to stay up to date on new releases, and would like to receive freebies from all of my main series, then please consider joining my newsletter at: https://rickgualtieri.com/newsletter/.

ABOUT THE AUTHOR

Rick Gualtieri lives alone in central New Jersey with only his wife, three kids, and countless pets to both keep him company and constantly plot against him. When he's not busy monkey-clicking words, he can typically be found jealously guarding his collection of vintage Transformers from all who would seek to defile them.

Defilers beware!

Also by Rick Gualtieri
TALES OF THE CRYPTO-HUNTER
Bigfoot Hunters
Devil Hunters
Kraken Hunters

THE HYBRID OF HIGH MOON
Get Bent!
Hell Bent
Bent Outta Shape
Bent On Destruction
Bent, Not Broken

THE TOME OF BILL UNIVERSE
THE TOME OF BILL
Bill the Vampire
Scary Dead Things
The Mourning Woods

Holier Than Thou
Sunset Strip
Goddamned Freaky Monsters
Half A Prayer
The Wicked Dead
Shining Fury
The Last Coven

BILL OF THE DEAD
Strange Days
Everyday Horrors
Carnage À Trois
The Liching Hour

Printed in Great Britain
by Amazon